QUAKE

QUAKE

JACK DOUGLAS

PINNACLE BOOKS
Kensington Publishing Corp.
www.kensingtonbooks.com

PINNACLE BOOKS are published by

Kensington Publishing Corp.
119 West 40th Street
New York, NY 10018

All Kensington titles, imprints, and distributed lines are available at special quantity discounts for bulk purchases for sales promotions, premiums, fund-raising, educational, or institutional use.

Special book excerpts or customized printings can also be created to fit specific needs. For details, write or phone the office of the Kensington special sales manager: Kensington Publishing Corp., 119 West 40th Street, New York, NY 10018, attn: Special Sales Department; phone 1-800-221-2647.

First printing: August 2014

ISBN-13: 978-0-7860-3465-9
ISBN-10: 0-7860-3465-3

10 9 8 7 6 5 4 3 2 1

Printed in the United States of America

First electronic edition: August 2014

ISBN-13: 978-0-7860-3466-6
ISBN-10: 0-7860-3466-1

PART ONE
Epicenter

1

Outside the United States Federal Courthouse at 500 Pearl Street in lower Manhattan, Assistant U.S. Attorney Nick Dykstra wove his way through the throng of protestors, hundreds of them hefting signs and chanting "Alivi must leave" at the top of their lungs.

Catchy, Nick thought. *But far from the best I've heard outside 500 Pearl.*

Nick kept his head down. Not that he thought he'd be recognized; the Honorable Justice Kaye Gaydos had rightly banned cameras from the courtroom for the duration of the case, leaving the public with little more than 1980s-style courtroom illustrations to gawk at when they tuned in to CNN after work to catch their highlights of the day's trial testimony. And the courtroom sketches—created by artists hanging on to an all-but-obsolete trade—hardly did Nick justice. At least in his opinion.

Besides, it was the defense attorneys who were the glory seekers; *they* had everything to gain and nothing to lose by grandstanding. Career prosecutors like Nick didn't give a damn what the general public thought of them, so long as their higher-ups caught the full show. Particularly the president of the United States; or *future* presidents to be more precise. No matter what happened at this trial, Nick thought it was highly unlikely that he would be appointed as a U.S. attorney or federal judge within the next two years. And by January 2017, when the next U.S. president took office, this trial would be long forgotten by everyone but its participants.

Unless I nail Alivi with the death penalty, Nick mused as he shoved his way through the crowd. *That* would keep the trial *and* the defendant in the minds of the American public for years to come. Years of appeals by Alivi and his lawyers would keep Nick's name in the transcripts and the New York tabloids, if not the national TV news.

As Nick approached the makeshift gate, the protestors morphed into journalists, and for a moment Nick wondered which were worse. The protestors at least had a legitimate gripe, even if Nick didn't agree with them. Hell, they were New Yorkers, and Feroz Saeed Alivi was one of the last men to be captured and charged for his role in the death and destruction that took place just a few city blocks away on September 11, 2001. And here he was, Feroz Saeed Alivi on American soil. Here he was, in New York City. In *downtown Manhattan* for Christ's sake, just a five-minute subway ride from Ground Zero. About to receive a fair trial with all the rights and privileges afforded your average American citizen.

The protestors had wanted Alivi to be tried as an enemy combatant in private at Gitmo. Osama bin Laden and the rest of the self-proclaimed jihadists who attacked the United States twelve years ago had been in the spotlight long enough; these protestors wanted them thrust back into the shadows, where they belonged. This trial, they claimed, was opening freshly healed wounds and giving Alivi the world stage yet again. In the realm of radical Islam, Alivi was being heralded as a genuine hero and a martyr to the cause.

I'll make damn sure *he's a martyr*, Nick thought as he approached the U.S. marshals guarding the gate. There were four of them and they were armed with assault rifles. Just in case someone somehow made it past the line of NYPD officers dressed in full riot gear, which Nick thought highly unlikely, if not impossible. Then again, the Boston Marathon bombing had managed to put New York on edge again, even if its impact on the nation as a whole was relatively minor and short-lived.

Nick Dykstra dipped into his suit jacket and fished out his attorney ID, flashed it to the marshals who parted the gates and allowed him through. *That's* when Nick was finally recognized, at least by members of the press. *The press.* The once noble profession was noble no more, in Nick's opinion. Over the past two decades the twenty-four-hour cable news networks had gleefully reduced the profession of Edward R. Murrow to an around-the-clock reality show that better served as a punch line for late-night talk show hosts than as a serious source for information on current national and global affairs. So Nick wasn't the least bit surprised when reporters started barking questions at him as though they were at a mock press conference being held in a high school gymnasium rather than standing in front of a federal courthouse during one of the most important trials of the new century.

"Counselor, what do you say to the hundreds, maybe thousands, of New Yorkers out here today demanding that the defendant be sent back to Guantanamo Bay for a military tribunal?"

Nick turned toward the closest camera and said, "No comment," then thought, *What the hell*, and spun on his heels to face the music.

Nick raised his voice as much as he could so that he could be heard over the hecklers. "Actually, I say the jury has already been selected and sworn, and that, like it or not, opening statements in this trial begin this morning. I understand the protesters' gripe and certainly sympathize with them, but at this stage in the game I'm afraid it's a moot point."

"But do you think this is the proper forum?"

Nick strained his voice again. "I can think of no better place to achieve justice for the American public than in a United States federal courthouse, particularly here in New York City where the damage Alivi did was felt so deeply."

"Are you promising New Yorkers here that you'll win a conviction?"

"I'm promising that I will damn well try."

Nick had turned and started through the gate toward the concrete steps when he heard one last question he felt compelled to answer.

"How confident are you that Alivi will receive the death penalty?"

"Confident enough," Nick shouted back over his shoulder, "that I've already picked out the suit I'm going to wear to his execution."

There's your sound bite, he thought as he hurried up the steps toward the heavy double glass doors. He turned once more to take a look at the scene. A mob of New Yorkers gathered in front of 500 Pearl for a good (albeit misguided) cause. He glanced up. The sun had already risen high over the skyscrapers and it was promising to be another perfect autumn day.

If only they knew, he thought. If only they knew that Assistant U.S. Attorney Nick Dykstra had as much riding on this trial as anyone. And that the stakes for Nick had absolutely nothing to do with his career as a federal prosecutor. If only they knew that among the nearly three thousand victims at the World Trade Center on that hellish day twelve years ago was Sara Baines-Dykstra, Nick's late wife and the mother of his only child, his beautiful seventeen-year-old-daughter Lauren—the only light left in Nick's life.

Nick had been downright ecstatic when the U.S. attorney general announced that Feroz Saeed Alivi would be tried on American soil, following his capture fourteen months ago by authorities in Yemen. Even more so when his boss, U.S. Attorney of the Southern District of New York Preet Bharara, called Nick into his office and told him that Nick would serve as lead counsel if the case ever made it to trial.

Because for AUSA Nick Dykstra, this defendant wasn't just another criminal. He wasn't just another terrorist. For Nick Dykstra, the case of *The United States of America versus Feroz Saeed Alivi* wasn't just another trial. For Nick, this was personal. And Nick had months ago vowed that he would *personally* send Feroz Saeed Alivi to his death, in order to avenge his wife, Sara, and to finally gain a scintilla of closure for himself, for his beloved daughter, Lauren, for his city, and for the rest of the nation.

2

The courtroom was packed but under control. Dozens of voices competed for vocal superiority, but not one exceeded the decibel level appropriate for a federal courtroom. State courthouses in New York City all but invited chaos; judges shouted, court officers dozed, lawyers often arrived at court disheveled and unshaven, reeking of alcohol, dressed in suits they'd probably slept in. But federal courthouses commanded respect. Even with no judge sitting at the bench, lawyers refrained from shuffling newspapers; journalists chatted as softly as though they were in a church; and the public spectators sat quietly with their hands in their laps, feeling lucky simply to have gotten a seat to the show.

By the time Assistant U.S. Attorney Nick Dykstra walked through the tall, mahogany double doors, most of the stage was already set. The wood was meticulously polished, the marble almost sparkling. The fine maroon carpet appeared as though it hadn't been treaded upon by a single pair of shoes, let alone the dozens of spectators who had entered the courtroom before him.

Nick's second seat, AUSA Wendy Lin, stood at the

prosecutor's table sorting through the massive file, much of which remained classified. Two prosecutorial assistants, one male and one female, sat just behind her, alternating between anxiously tapping their feet and biting their nails.

Nick walked slowly up the aisle of the public gallery, the briefcase in his hand largely for show. Inside were some handwritten notes, which he'd neither need nor use in his opening statement to the jury.

The moment Nick stepped past the rail he was accosted by Kermit Jansing, lead counsel for the defense. Jansing was a smarmy character who looked as though he just stepped out of a Grisham novel. At five and a half feet, his eyes always seemed to lock on Nick's throat, which never ceased to send a shiver up Nick's spine. Meanwhile, Nick could almost check his reflection in Jansing's shiny scalp.

"Good morning, counselor," Jansing said loud enough for the press in the front two rows of the gallery to hear. He stuck out a sweaty palm and Nick grudgingly took it in his own.

"Kermit," Nick said, unable to mask his distaste. "Nice suit."

Jansing took a step back to allow Nick to take in the entire package. The suit, which was a charcoal three-piece with thin pinstripes, would have better befit a wiseguy on his way to getting made than an officer of the court about to deliver an opening statement in defense of one of the world's most notorious terrorists. But Nick let the little guy have his moment. The suit probably cost Jansing a couple grand, or two hours' work on behalf of one of his many white collar clients on Wall Street, depending on how you looked at it.

Jansing turned back toward the defense table, where a young female associate sat waiting. She was at least four inches taller than Jansing, beautiful, with long, shimmering blond hair and a pants suit two sizes too tight. Nick guessed she was probably just out of law school. Given Jansing's track record, she wouldn't last the month before the *eww* factor kicked in and she ran for the hills, a victim of one of Jansing's impromptu attempts at a neck massage.

"Morning, Wendy," Nick said to AUSA Lin as he set his briefcase down on the table. "Wedding day jitters?"

She forced a smile at the inside joke. Her fiancé, Brett, hadn't thought it so funny when following the U.S. attorney's office softball game, she admitted (after three too many drinks) that she was more excited and better prepared for Alivi's trial than she was for her own nuptials one month later.

"I was listening to the news on the way into the city this morning," she said. "The NTAS issued an elevated alert for the metropolitan area."

Homeland Security's National Terrorism Advisory System (NTAS) had replaced the color-coded Homeland Security Advisory System a couple of years back, and while definitely an improvement, it still managed to rattle citizens even when there was no credible or imminent threat. New Yorkers, Washingtonians, and now Bostonians were particularly frazzled by such announcements. And this one was no doubt precipitated by the mere fact that Feroz Saeed Alivi's trial was beginning in earnest today. The elevated threat level gave ammunition to critics who warned that Alivi's trial in a civilian court would jeopardize the lives of millions of Americans. No doubt the advisory had also served to further fuel the protests Nick had passed through outside the courthouse.

"I don't think there's anything to worry about, Wendy," Nick said. "The most significant threat to our national security is about to be escorted into this courtroom in shackles by six armed U.S. marshals."

No sooner than Nick said it than the side door from the lockup area opened onto the courtroom. In the center of the half-dozen marshals staggered a dark, bearded man of six feet and maybe a hundred and fifty pounds soaking wet. Either Alivi had gone on a hunger strike, or the Metropolitan Correctional Center had severely cut back on the portion sizes of prisoners' meals. The religious robe Alivi wore could have fit both him and his lead defense counsel at the same time.

"There's your boogeyman," Nick said to Wendy. "Still worried?"

As though Alivi heard him, the terrorist turned his head and leveled his gaze on the federal prosecutor across the aisle. Nick held his stare, his eyes narrowing, neck reddening in unadulterated hatred.

Looking forward to seeing those eyes while they stick the needle in your arm, you vicious little bastard, Nick thought.

Then he cleared his throat, looked away, and took a seat next to Wendy. Having seen Alivi again up close, Nick couldn't help but think of his wife Sara's final moments on the eighty-fourth floor of the South Tower. For the past twelve years, they'd flash uninvited in his mind like summer lightning. He'd hear her voice as he had through the phone that morning while he sat in his office. His pulse would race and he'd become short of breath and he'd begin to sweat as though he was once again rushing across town in a futile effort to save Sara.

Just as suddenly he'd snap out of it.

"Please rise," Justice Gaydos's clerk intoned from in front of the bench.

Nick and Wendy stood as one as the courtroom fell silent.

"The United States District Court for the Southern District of New York is now in session. The Honorable Justice Kaye Katrina Gaydos presiding."

Regal in both posture and black flowing robe, Justice Gaydos blew into the courtroom like a hard wind, her face completely devoid of emotion.

"Be seated," she said as she climbed to the bench.

Nick made the mistake of again glancing across the aisle. Once more he caught the malevolent gaze of the bearded defendant, Feroz Saeed Alivi, and once more he froze as visions of the Twin Towers crumbling before him came unbidden into his mind.

"Nick, we can't—" Sara's voice cut in and out. "We're too high up. We can't evacuate. Oh, God, Nick, the office is filling with black smoke. There's a fire. . . ."

Nick could never remember what he said in reply to her. He could only remember how he felt. As though someone had reached inside his chest and with all their strength squeezed his racing heart.

"I love you, Nick. I love you. I . . . have to go now. P-please, please tell Lauren I love her, and that I'll always be with her. . . ."

Sara had trailed off, her voice replaced by some monstrous sound Nick now knew to be the bending—the shrieking—of immense beams of steel in unthinkable temperatures and under an unfathomable weight.

And then, nothing.

Justice Gaydos asked the clerk to call the first case.

The clerk rose and said, *"The United States of America versus Feroz Saeed Alivi."*

Justice Gaydos said, "Attorneys, please make your appearances."

Nick steadied his legs and rose to his feet, summoning all the power he could muster to strengthen his voice.

"For the United States government," he boomed, "Assistant U.S. Attorney Nicholas Michael Dykstra."

3

"Ladies and gentlemen," Nick said as he paced the length of the jury box, "you will be burdened with an extraordinary responsibility in the days and weeks to come. As you well know, the man sitting with his attorneys at the far table is no ordinary defendant. He stands before this court charged in connection with one of the most heinous and cowardly acts in human history. The defendant in this case is charged with mass murder; mass murder and *conspiracy* to murder thousands of American citizens, right here, on our front doorstep. In *our* city. The defendant stands before this court to face responsibility for his role in the September 11, 2001, attacks on our nation. And it will be your awesome responsibility at the conclusion of this trial to bring justice to this man for the nearly three thousand souls lost at the World Trade Center here in New York City, at the Pentagon in our nation's capital, and in a field near Shanksville, Pennsylvania, where a group of courageous American passengers, not so unlike yourselves, perished in a horrific plane crash while attempting to overcome their armed hijackers in order to save not only their own lives but the lives of countless others below."

Within minutes of beginning his opening statement, Nick had settled into a rhythm. He had practiced this opening in front of a mirror in his home on the Upper West Side more times than he could possibly remember. Because he knew he'd need to keep his emotions under control. He wanted to speak to this jury with passion and zeal, but not with the all-consuming grief of a widower who had lost his wife and the mother of his only child. He needed to speak to this jury first as a representative for his country, and second as a New Yorker. The jury needed to know that what was at stake for him was at stake for each of them, and all American citizens and their allies around the world.

As the first hour passed, Nick went on to describe in vivid detail the physical and circumstantial evidence against Feroz Saeed Alivi—recorded messages, intercepted letters and e-mails, photographs, and lengthy confessions. He reminded these twelve men and women what they needed no reminder of—the horror and devastation caused by the attacks twelve years ago on a beautiful September morning, much like this one. He spoke of the aftermath, of the toll on survivors, and this he could describe all too well, because it seemed as though he could recall every moment of his own pain and suffering, every word uttered by his then five-year-old daughter, Lauren, who was trying so hard to understand why she would never again see her mother, and why anyone in the world would have wanted to take her mother away from them.

Nick talked about the years of training and planning that went into the September 11 attacks. The acts the defendant engaged in were cold-blooded and premeditated, the plans worked and *re*worked to cause maximum pain and suffering to the United States of America and her citizens. Nick touched briefly on the subsequent wars in Iraq and Afghanistan and assured the seven men and five women of the jury that while their Al-Qaeda enemies were decimated and on the run, the threat they posed to New York and all American cities remained very real.

In the second hour, Nick spoke of the witnesses who would present testimony against the defendant in the days and weeks to follow. Investigators from the Federal Bureau of Investigation, the Central Intelligence Agency, and yes, even a few of New York's Finest would take the stand.

Throughout his opening, despite what the legal pundits had repeatedly said, Nick never once allowed himself to feel as though all of this was unnecessary, and that any third-year law student could try and convict a defendant like Feroz Saeed Alivi. Nick understood the importance of this trial to human history, and its psychological impact not only on himself and Lauren, but on everyone who had been touched by the events of September 11, 2001. And yes, Nick had an agenda that went well past a conviction on all counts contained in the book-length indictment. Nick wanted—no, he *needed*—for Feroz Saeed Alivi to die at the hands of the United States government. Nick was under no illusion; for the first time in his career, he wanted blood. He wanted to witness firsthand Feroz Saeed Alivi's ultimate demise by lethal injection.

Throughout his adult life, Nick had struggled with his feelings about the death penalty. Given the opportunity, he could passionately argue either side. But in the past twelve months, since Alivi's capture in Yemen and Nick's appointment as lead counsel, Nick had read and heard and observed evidence that left no doubt in his mind that capital punishment was right and just under certain circumstances. And this case certainly qualified. Not only because of the carnage Alivi and his cohorts inflicted on this country more than a decade ago, but because he was unrepentant, and because he continued, even after his capture, to make threats against American citizens and their allies and interests around the globe. And yes, because some of those threats had been directed specifically at Nick himself, in his capacity as a federal prosecutor. And because those threats hadn't been limited to him, but included the only person he had left on this earth. Threats that had included his seventeen-year-old daughter, Lauren.

For the past year, Nick had lived in a constant state of terror. It had started with anonymous letters in his home mailbox and was followed by e-mails from self-proclaimed jihadists. After a few weeks, Nick's office phone began ringing. Weeks later, his home phone. After Nick had his number changed, his cell phone was compromised. And then his daughter's. That's when Nick got angry. Livid. That's when Nick first demanded a face-to-face meeting with Feroz Saeed Alivi.

"Not going to happen," Kermit Jansing told him one day over the phone.

In a barely controlled rage, Nick shouted, "You tell your client to lay the hell off my family, or I'll . . ."

"Or you'll what?"

Nick finally realized how helpless he was. Alivi, though behind bars, was provided more protection than any other inmate in the history of the United States. Alivi couldn't communicate with the outside world except through his lawyers. So he couldn't be pulling the strings; he couldn't be threatening Nick and his daughter through his associates in the United States and abroad. Or could he? Was Kermit Jansing—wittingly or unwittingly—carrying coded messages on behalf of his client? There was no way to know. The attorney-client privilege rigidly protected all communications exchanged between the two men. For a while Nick began to wonder whether bringing Feroz Saeed Alivi to trial in New York City had been the right call by the U.S. attorney general after all.

But no, as time went on, Nick refused to be intimidated. When his boss, U.S. Attorney Preet Bharara offered to replace Nick on the case, Nick flew into a frenzy. This was *his* case, *his* conviction. And he wouldn't be frightened off.

During the summer months, as the threats became greater

and more specific, Nick finally accepted protection from the FBI and New York Police Department. "Don't watch me," he told the special agent in charge of his family's safety, "watch Lauren. Make sure she's protected at all times, day and night."

If anything happens to Lauren, he'd thought grimly, *I won't be able to go on.*

But nothing happened. Alivi's people, it turned out, were all bark and bluster. And now the long run-up to the trial was finally over. Here he was, standing in a lavish courtroom at 500 Pearl, delivering his opening remarks to the jury that would ultimately convict this world-infamous terrorist who had played a major role in the attacks that had torn apart Nick's family.

As the morning wore on, AUSA Nick Dykstra grew more confident and more relaxed. He hadn't just settled into his rhythm; he was in a zone. The twelve men and women sitting before him were captivated. At various points in his opening, one or more jurors even had tears in her eyes.

"And so," Nick said, "at the conclusion of this case, I'll return to this rail, and having fulfilled each and every promise I made to you this morning during my opening, I will ask you to once and for all consign this madman to the dustbin of history. After you have seen all the evidence and heard all the testimony, I will return to you in my summation and ask—"

The softest rumble seemed to emanate from the walls. The sound echoed throughout the gallery, rose until it ricocheted off the sides of the vaulted ceiling. The chandeliers overhead shook briefly, their jingle like a wind chime before a storm.

During the vibration, Nick turned to look at Wendy, whose eyes had gone wide with fright. When nothing more happened, her face slowly returned to normal and he looked back at the juy, expressionless.

Nick was at a pivotal point in his opening and he was afraid to lose his rhythm so he began his last sentence from the top.

"After you have seen all the evidence and heard all the testimony, I will return to you in my summation and ask you to go into your deliberations with—"

The floor beneath Nick's feet shifted ever so slightly. It felt as though a pair of mice had skittered under the soles of his shoes.

After a momentary hesitation, he continued. "After you have seen all the evidence and heard all the testimony, I will return to you in my summation and ask you to go into your deliberations with *one* image at the forefront of your minds—"

Then it happened.

This time there was no mistaking it.

Abruptly, the entire courtroom began to shake.

4

While Assistant U.S. Attorney Nick Dykstra delivered his opening statement in the trial against Feroz Saeed Alivi, Nick's teenage daughter, Lauren, walked the grounds of Columbia University's campus at 116th and Broadway. A freshly minted senior at York Prep, a private preparatory school near Lincoln Center, Lauren—like most high school seniors, she'd been assured by her guidance counselor—was torn between going away to college and staying near home. Of course, she wanted the "full college experience" that most teens dreamed of, and with her grades and SAT scores, she had her choice of Ivy League schools. In addition to Columbia, she'd already applied and been accepted to Yale, Harvard, Brown, Smith, Princeton, and Stanford, as well as a half-dozen safety schools. All other things being equal (yeah, when does *that* ever happen?) Lauren would have accepted Stanford's offer of a nearly full ride in a hummingbird's heartbeat. Attending a top tier college less than an hour's drive from San Francisco would have made her life complete. *Almost.*

But Lauren had someone else to consider. Sure, she wasn't

the only high school senior with a single parent. Her friend Madison just had her mom. So did Eileen and Kerry and Justin and Connor. None of their mothers had remarried. Well, Justin's mom had, but that lasted all of a month. But all their moms *did* have active social lives. And Madison's mom had younger kids who would remain in the nest for at least the next three years. Eileen's mom had her boyfriend, James, not the greatest conversationalist, but still he was something. Kerry and Connor both came from large families, so their mothers were never alone. And Justin's mom, well, let's just say that Justin's mom was never alone either.

Lauren's dad, on the other hand, had no one but Lauren. He didn't *have* to be alone, of course. He was a great-looking guy (a real *stud*, according to Justin's mom), and he was *always* the smartest guy in the room. He could be funny when he wanted to be, but he also went through several bouts of melancholy each year. Well, ever since Lauren's mom died, and since Lauren had only been five at the time, that was the only Nick Dykstra she'd ever known.

He'd certainly never blamed Lauren for his being alone, but Lauren couldn't help but feel as though she'd been a major cause. Yes, her dad threw himself into his work like few fathers ever do, but all of his spare time was spent with or *on* Lauren. That was why she often justified—at least in her mind—going away to Stanford. Maybe while she was on the West Coast, her dad would go out more (or at least *some*) and eventually meet somebody. In that case, her going away to Stanford would be a *good* thing for him, right?

But no. Deep down she knew that her dad would just spend more days at the office, more nights reading case law and drafting motions and briefs for other attorneys at home in his study. He'd just take on more trial work; trials kept him busy 24/7.

Hardest of all was that Lauren knew her dad *wanted* her to stay near home. His enthusiasm for the schools she applied to was directly correlated with their geographic proximity to their home on the Upper West Side. Mentioning Columbia, for instance, got him all misty eyed. Cornell, too. At least until he MapQuested Cornell and realized Ithaca was four and a half hours away. Then he was all like, "Well, Columbia's certainly the better school." Princeton would get him smiling again ("What's that, about an hour from here?"), but talk of Brown and Smith would cause him to fall silent.

It was difficult for any parent to argue against Harvard or Yale. So that was when Lauren's dad became a bit passive-aggressive. "Harvard's fantastic; I don't think *everyone* there is stuck up, do you?" And "Yale's great, honey, and New Haven isn't *too* dangerous these days, is it?"

Then there was Stanford. "I grew up on the Left Coast, sweetheart; it's not all it's cracked up to be. Speaking of 'cracked up,' did I ever tell you about the time I got caught in that earthquake in San Francisco? Luckily, we went through drills all the time. You always have to be prepared for the Big One when you live in the Bay area. Always."

All right, so maybe he was slightly more subtle. But that was what Lauren heard when he spoke. And she knew he wasn't worried about his daughter being swallowed up by the earth at Stanford; or being robbed and shot at and stabbed in New Haven, Connecticut, all in the same night. Lauren knew that was all pretense.

But she never called him on it. Because she loved him. And she knew he loved her, and that was why he didn't want her to leave. She was his best friend, his *only* friend. She was his star at full dark; she was the air he breathed. She was his world. She was his everything.

He could have thrown his hands in the air and given up after Lauren's mother died. But he didn't. Instead, he did as a father what he always did as a lawyer when the chips were down. He stepped up his game.

He comforted Lauren. In the dead of night when she woke

up and cried for her mother, he was there. He'd sit up with her until dawn, if that was what it took. Even if he had to be in court early the next morning.

He tried to make her less afraid. In the months following 9/11, when nearly everyone was too fearful to fly, he took her on trips to the Caribbean and the Hawaiian Islands. In the city, he made sure they took the subway whenever they could, because Lauren had heard on the news that New York's subway system could be the terrorists' next target. And he wanted to assure her that their city was safe.

He took her to 26 Federal Plaza to meet the assistant director in charge of the FBI's New York field office. He introduced her to special agents assigned to the newly formed joint terrorist task force. He brought her to One Police Plaza, where she met the New York City police commissioner. "These are the people who are going to protect us," her father told her. "I want you to know their faces. I want you to see them, not the bad guys, when you fall asleep at night."

She'd always known her dad was one of the good guys. But it wasn't until after her mother died that she fully comprehended what her dad did for a living. He brought her to his office, introduced her to the U.S. attorney for the Southern District of New York. He escorted her around the federal courthouse and introduced her to the federal judges.

A few days before the first anniversary of her mother's death, he took her to Gracie Mansion to meet the mayor of New York City, whom *TIME* magazine had named the Person of the Year for 2001.

This is *our* city, her father told her. Not theirs. Not the terrorists.

Now she'd just spent an hour with a lovely woman named Caroline Reignier, the director of admissions for Columbia University. And she knew that she was that much closer to making her decision. Going away to Stanford didn't just mean leaving her father; it meant leaving her city. *Their* city. She wasn't sure she was ready to do that just yet. She wasn't sure that she'd ever be ready. Despite the inarguable allure of San Francisco, it still wasn't New York City.

As they walked along the paved paths toward Butler Library, Caroline Reignier pointed out some of the more jaw-dropping architecture. Lauren was impressed. All right, *beyond* impressed. Although the university was located in the heart of a major city, its spacious lawns and plazas gave it a warm, almost rural feel.

"As I'm sure you know," Caroline said, "we're one of the nation's oldest universities. This campus is actually our third location."

"Oh?" Lauren said, then immediately regretted it. That was something she should have known. That tidbit was probably in every piece of literature the university had sent her over the past three years. Lauren could certainly rattle off trivial facts about Stanford, if she were asked. But this was the first time she felt deep down as though Columbia University could become home for the next four years.

"Yes," Caroline said. If she was surprised by Lauren's ignorance of the university's history, she didn't let on. "Our first campus was founded in 1754, as King's College. It was actually situated close to where the World Trade Center had stood."

Lauren involuntarily glanced at Caroline, who appeared to be biting down hard on her lip. Caroline had made a mistake, too, a *faux pas* that could well have proved costly to her. Surely, Caroline Reignier had read and reread Lauren's admissions essay, which had centered on the challenge of growing up without her mother, whom she had lost in the September 11 attacks.

"I'm sorry," Caroline said, halting in the middle of the path. "I didn't mean to . . ."

"No," Lauren assured her. "It's all right."

Now Lauren felt bad for the woman. Caroline's cheeks were glowing red, a blush made all the more noticeable by the woman's jet black hair and fair skin.

"The current campus," Caroline said in an attempt to recover, "was actually built on the site of the Bloomingdale Insane Asylum."

"Interesting," Lauren said as they continued to walk.

"We've had some very accomplished students pass through our halls since then. Isaac Asimov, the prolific science fiction writer. The author of *The Catcher in the Rye*, J. D. Salinger. The actor James Cagney. And, well . . ."

"Well, what?"

"Well, Joan Rivers."

"Oh."

"I don't know why I mentioned her," Caroline said.

"That's all right."

"We've had three U.S. presidents," Caroline continued, "nine justices of the U.S. Supreme Court, three of whom served as chief justice." She paused. "Your father is an assistant district attorney here in New York, isn't he?"

"In the Southern District, yes."

"That's wonderful. And are you interested in going into law?"

"I haven't decided yet."

"We have an excellent law school, of course. Franklin Delano Roosevelt attended Columbia Law. Theodore Roosevelt, too."

Approaching Butler Library, Lauren's eyes widened. While flipping through the brochures Columbia had sent her, she'd dismissed the building as pretentious, but now its grandeur moved her much in the way other New York City landmarks often did. The neoclassical columns brought to mind the state courthouse downtown at 60 Centre Street, a façade often used in crime movies and on television despite the fact that it was a civil, not a criminal, court. The criminal courthouse stood just a block away at 100 Centre. But 100 Centre was a flat, shapeless building with an exterior that wasn't nearly as dramatic.

Lauren looked up and read some of the names chiseled into the stone above the columns: Homer, Plato and Aristotle, Cicero and Horace, Dante, Shakespeare, Milton, Voltaire, and Goethe.

Okay, so maybe the building's a bit pretentious.

As they walked up the concrete steps to the library, a young man (obviously a student here) emerged through the heavy front door. He had thick, dark brown hair with matching eyes that looked crystal clear through black wire-rimmed glasses. He wore a striped button-down shirt, untucked, with navy straight-legged jeans, and black shoes that Lauren immediately guessed were Kenneth Coles.

"Lauren," Caroline said, "I'd like you to meet Raymond Knowles. He's a sophomore here at Columbia. Ray, this is Lauren Dykstra."

They shook hands; his touch was warm and inviting.

Caroline said, "I'm going to leave you two for now. Ray's going to show you the library and any other building you'd like to see while you're on campus. I'll be back at my office if you need anything or have any questions. Please don't hesitate to drop by. Or if something comes to you after you've left, feel free to drop me an e-mail or give me a call. It was truly a pleasure meeting you, Lauren."

"Likewise."

Once Caroline started down the stairs, Lauren and Ray entered the library and started up the marble staircase. A portrait of Dwight D. Eisenhower hung to her right.

"Butler is the largest of Columbia's libraries," Ray said. His voice was soft but contained a definite edge. He motioned to the painting. "Ike, of course, once served as the university's president."

Should have known that, Lauren thought. But she quickly pushed her guilt aside when the library proper came into view.

Lauren absolutely *loved* libraries—and here there was a lot to love. Her gaze instantly shot toward the upper floors, to the catwalks and iron rails and labyrinthine stacks of books housed over their heads. Each floor above appeared exactly the same as its neighbor below so that it was like looking into a vertical hall of mirrors. After a few moments, she felt dizzy.

Lauren finally lowered her head, stole a glance at Ray, then stared ahead. Below was one great open space where students worked at tables, some individually in cube-type spaces, others in groups of chairs.

"Let's start upstairs," Ray said.

The smell of the library was as classical as its architecture. Lauren felt as though she'd been transported back in time. Everything—the paneled walls, the parquet floor, the thick bookcases, the countless tables and chairs—were made of the same exquisite old wood. It gave off the charming effect of being surrounded by all things academia. Lauren felt a flutter in her stomach.

On the second floor, they walked along the rail, Lauren now looking down at the students below. Everyone seemed so committed, so consumed, so *mature*. She loved it.

"Favorite author?" Ray said as they stepped down a narrow aisle between shelves.

Oh, my God, I should have an answer to this question ready to roll off my tongue.

The aisle smelled a bit musty and, as she stared at the bindings, she frowned. Medieval French history; that wasn't going to help her any in naming a favorite author. Silly as it was, she suddenly felt claustrophobic. Ray had her all but cornered. A wooden cart on wheels stood dead ahead as though to block her pass if she tried to make a run for it.

Gustave Flaubert, or will I come off as a literary snob? Talk about pretentious. But then, I can't exactly say J. K. Rowling either. Someone in between. Someone he won't be expecting. Not a canned answer like Mark Twain or Charles Dickens.

As she thought, a pair of thick books jumped off the top shelf and landed on the floor in front of her with a *thunk* that she felt in her belly. She hopped back a step as dust came billowing up from between the books' yellowed pages.

A moment later, she tried to peek through the stacks to see who was lurking in the next aisle over. She was hoping to receive an apology for what *had* to be an accident. But before she could steal a glimpse, a single book struck her on the top of her head.

"*Ow,*" she said, rubbing her scalp and staring down at the large old volume. Now she wondered whether it was an accident at all, or perhaps the students at Columbia weren't quite as mature as she'd previously thought. She peered through the stacks again. "That *hurt,*" she hissed.

Ray held up a finger to silence her. "Hear that?"

"Hear what?"

But then she heard it, too. A low rumble, as though they were trapped inside the belly of a great beast and it was hungry.

"We'd better get back downstairs," Ray said.

But as soon as the words left his tongue, he and Lauren were knocked into one another as the shelves on both their left and right poured more books down upon them. Together they fell to the floor, watching in terror as the tall bookcases themselves began to shudder, threatening any second to crush Ray and Lauren under their weight.

"What's happening?" Lauren cried, though she didn't get, nor had she been expecting a response, at least not from Ray. But as if to answer her question, a series of images popped instantly into her mind.

Her mother.

The towers.

The second airplane.

The blaze and billowing black smoke rising to blot out the sky.

No, she thought. *It can't be. We can't be under attack again.*

Her father's words rung in her ears. "We're safe, honey. This is *our* city. We have nothing to be afraid of."

She thought, *Then why the hell were FBI agents and undercover cops following me around all summer? Huh, Dad?*

5

Nick froze. He stood before the jury box as still as stone, just as he had a dozen years ago when he finally reached the outer perimeter raised by the NYPD around the World Trade Center. Even as jurors jumped from their seats and leapt the rail, Nick stood stationary. In his mind a montage of violent images roared across the stage. Images of the South Tower as it began to crumble from the top down, followed thirty minutes later by the North. The mammoth clouds of dust and debris that immediately billowed toward the sky, blotting out the sun, simultaneously breaking off at the feet of the towers and racing down the streets like a living force.

He'd frozen then, too, his feet becoming part of the ground, as hundreds of spectators started toward him, trying to escape the carnage. Then he'd been thrown from his stupor by the stampede, and nearly trampled a few moments later.

Now he came out of the daze himself, as the camera in his mind turned to Lauren's crying at her mother's funeral. Lauren at five. Lauren at nine, as she tried to comprehend. At thirteen, as she began asking questions about the mother she was losing all over again in her head. "I can't remember her,

Dad. It's like a photo from an old newspaper; she just keeps fading and fading."

As the floor shook, Nick spread his feet farther apart to maintain his balance. He needed to get the hell out of the courthouse—because Lauren couldn't lose another parent.

Swiftly, Nick turned, his eyes searching for Feroz Saeed Alivi like a heat-seeking missile. In the chaos he couldn't see him. Was Alivi behind this? Had the bastard made good on his threats? Were the poems he wrote in prison a coded call to a sleeper cell here in the city to unleash hell on the first day of his trial?

In his ears Nick heard random shrieks.

"It's a bomb!"

"We're under attack!"

"A plane hit the courthouse!"

Nick turned and saw the courtroom spectators battling each other with stiff arms and sharp elbows as they tried to squeeze through the tall mahogany double doors all at once. The court officers clawed at the edges of the human heap, but were outnumbered and helpless to control the crowd.

Nick spun, searching for another exit. The jurors were following the judge's clerk into chambers. He envisaged the chambers and immediately knew his jury was doomed; in the judge's chambers there was nothing to duck under and there was no way out.

He swung his head back in the direction of the defense table. No sign of Alivi, but Kermit Jansing was following a pair of U.S. marshals into the lockup. As a prosecutor Nick had never been back there, but he was sure there was no easy way out. The worst of the worst stepped through those doors almost daily; none, to his knowledge, had ever escaped.

The shaking continued. Windows suddenly shattered and the walls around him began to crack and crumble. A few feet away a chandelier crashed to the floor, and Nick's mind turned again to the threats Alivi had made before his trial.

Could they have struck again? he thought.

Right now it didn't matter. Regardless of the cause, Nick needed to make it out of the courthouse alive, for his daughter.

The tremor continually worsened and finally took Nick to the floor. As he rose, he spotted the judge's black robe swooshing toward him.

"*Your Honor*," he cried, "*this way!*"

He grabbed her arm and led her straight toward the throng trying to get through the tall mahogany double doors.

"We're going to be *trapped*," the judge shouted, trying to pull away from him.

Nick tightened his grip on her wrist to the point where he could feel bone. "It's the only way out," he said. "You have to trust me."

It was a surreal moment; Nick had spent his entire adult life trying to persuade federal judges to trust him. Never before, though, was so much riding on one judge's faith in him.

In front of them, the dense pile looked like crazed players in a lawless rugby match. Nick saw no openings, at least not at first. Then his gaze lifted. The doors to the courtroom were at least fourteen feet high. Above the top of the throng he could see the white marble wall in the hallway.

Nick quickened his pace to gather steam, dragging the judge along with him. As they neared the human obstruction, he turned his head and shouted "*Up*" into Justice Gaydos's left ear.

Nick's right foot found a calf and he climbed, his left foot landing on a man's lower back milliseconds later. From there, his momentum took him up a spine, onto a pair of shoulders. When his foot touched someone's head, he immediately leapt over the top of the pile.

In flight he lost hold of the judge's arm and hit the marble floor hard and tumbled. As the walls shook on either side of him, Nick pushed himself up and appraised his body for injuries. Pain on the entire left side of his body. A cut in the middle of his forehead had opened and blood streamed down his face and spilled onto the white marble.

He spun and found the judge on her hands and knees, the floor lifting and falling beneath her, trying to toss her off like a mechanical bull. He helped her up as more bodies spilled out of her courtroom and into the hallway.

Though his ears were ringing, he heard the judge shout, "I'm fine. Just run."

Thinking only of Lauren, Nick started down the hallway, bouncing off the walls like a ping-pong ball, each smash giving him a jolt of pain instantly dimmed by adrenaline.

Above his head he heard a creaking sound and looked up to see flakes of ceiling raining down on him, bouncing off his head and shoulders like hail.

He kept moving. Ran past the elevators. Accelerated as he approached the red metal door at the end of the hall. Crashed into the crash bar and barreled into the stairwell.

The stairwell was pitch black and moving like a special effect in one of Lauren's Harry Potter movies. He gripped the green rail as tightly as he could and started down the cement steps, taking two or three at a time, hoping against hope that one of his legs wouldn't give out.

On the second landing he paused. He listened hard and heard the screams of men and women emanating from each of the first three floors. What he didn't hear was the guttural groaning of the courthouse structure. At least for the time being, the building wasn't in immediate danger of falling.

The violent shaking finally stopped. Maybe the worst was over.

If there had been bombs inside the building, it was possible that all of them had already gone off.

It was also possible that the bombs were set on a timer and that more explosives were scheduled to detonate in a few minutes in order to create maximum chaos and wipe out as many of the city's first responders as possible.

Maybe Nick was safer remaining in the stairwell until help arrived.

But then Nick heard the familiar sound of steel beams bending. If the upper floors collapsed, Nick would be trapped under the rubble and likely killed.

Lauren can't lose another parent.

He grabbed hold of the handrail and hurried down the stairs as quickly as he could.

When he reached the door to the first floor, he slammed into the crash bar but the door didn't budge. It wasn't locked, Nick was sure of that. Locked doors in public buildings created fire hazards. He pressed his face against the glass of the narrow vertical window that looked out onto the lobby. A pillar had toppled over, lodging itself against the metal door, trapping him inside.

Cursing under his breath, Nick pushed at the crash bar again. His feet slid backwards as though he were moonwalking. He needed to gain some leverage, but the stairs were too far back. So he retreated to the first step and got himself into a three-point stance. Like a linebacker waiting for the center to snap the ball he remained motionless, trying to decide exactly which part of the door to strike. Then he took off in a sprint and slammed his left shoulder into the crash bar as hard as he could.

Immediately, he went down in searing pain. Grimacing, he scanned the side of the door; it had opened only an inch or so. But it *had* opened.

Nick just needed to put more strength into it.

Yeah, right, he thought. He'd given that try everything he had.

Suddenly the stairwell began to shake again, this time even more violently than the last. The off-white walls started to splinter. If another bomb had gone off, it had been the largest blast thus far. Nick needed to get the hell out of the court-house, and fast.

He got to his feet and steadied himself as best he could. He went up the first five steps, hoping to gain more momentum. Ceiling flaked down in front of him, like a sudden winter. He took a deep breath, and then raced down the stairs, leaping the last two and continuing toward the door with his left shoulder down.

Screaming, he slammed into the crash bar again.

This time the door moved significantly. Not enough to let him through, but enough to give him hope.

He didn't waste any time. Just began pushing and shoving, taking a few steps back and ramming the door again and again.

Another few inches.

Then another.

He was breathing hard, his heart pounding, sweat and blood mixing and streaming into his eyes, blinding and burning him, but he kept at it.

Another running start, another strike to his upper body, and this time he went down fearing he'd dislocated his shoulder.

He wiped the blood and the sweat from his eyes and stared hard at the door. That last shot had done the job. It'd be tight, but he thought he might just fit through the narrow opening.

While the stairwell shook, Nick pushed the pain aside and slid his right arm through first, followed by his right leg, then his right shoulder. He tucked his stomach in as much as he could and squeezed through the opening. The edge of the metal door caught on the flesh on his forehead, cutting him further. The violent shaking threatened to crush his ribs.

As wide tears of blood slid down his face, Nick continued to squeeze and push. From the other side of the door he imagined it looked like the stairwell was giving birth.

Finally he fell forward into the lobby, his momentum carrying him several yards and landing him flat on his stomach just as the latest tremor faded.

He glanced up. The opulent ground floor looked like a war zone.

Pillars had fallen, court officers had been killed, their bodies lying sprawled among mammoth puzzle pieces of ceiling in pools of their own blood.

Nick pushed himself to his feet and staggered from one body to the next, trying to find a survivor.

But there were no survivors to be found. Not here.

He gave a fleeting thought to the cell phone he had checked as he entered the courthouse this morning. He glanced toward the room where the phones were held but it was sealed off by the fallen pillar.

Finally, he looked toward the heavy glass doors. Outside, the world was a swirl of dust and debris. All of Pearl Street was occupied by a massive force eerily resembling the clouds that had chased hundreds down the streets of lower Manhattan on the morning of September 11.

Slowly, he moved toward the doors.

Slowly, he pushed through the crash bar of the door on the far right.

Slowly, he stepped into the brown and gray city, and he knew right away that Manhattan was once again under attack.

Not, this time, by men.

But by nature.

Mother Earth herself had declared war on the island of Manhattan.

6

The earth settled. Nick Dykstra stood on the concrete steps he'd stood on only hours before. Only this time as he looked out at the scene in front of him he saw not a mob of protestors and journalists but a panorama of death and destruction. Bodies lay bloodied in piles under rubble along Pearl Street. Squinting against the storm of dust, he spotted some movement, but most of the block remained motionless. The street itself had opened along its center, creating a horrific gash that had swallowed dozens of protestors. Car alarms and building alarms screeched like a murder of dying crows, while police and fire and ambulance sirens sounded helplessly in the distance.

Nick took the first step down and leaned over to examine one of the fallen U.S. marshals who had led him through the gate that morning. The marshal's face was horrifically bruised and bloodied, his body surrounded by glass that had shattered and showered him from the upper floor windows of 500 Pearl. Nick knelt and placed his right thumb in his mouth and bit down until he could no longer bear the pain, then he reached for the marshal's neck and felt for a pulse. As Nick suspected, the marshal was already dead. His assault rifle was nowhere to be seen.

As he rose to his feet, Nick felt the concrete tremble beneath his feet and a fresh wave of fear and nausea washed over him. Gazing up, he saw the windows of the buildings across the street shedding more glass, watched the roofs shake back and forth and begin to crumble. Above the alarms and sirens he heard screams of terror rise from the shadows.

Unlike the tremors before, this one shot up in intensity in seconds and knocked Nick down the cracked concrete stairs. At the bottom of the steps he rolled to a stop and buried his head beneath his arms.

As he waited out the tremor, Nick tried to remember everything he'd been taught about surviving earthquakes while growing up in California. He'd already covered his head and face with his arms to protect himself from the shards of flying glass from blown-out windows. If it weren't for Lauren, he'd have been safer staying inside the courthouse and standing in a doorway or ducking under a sturdy desk or into a closet. But he had no idea where the epicenter was, and he had to do whatever it took to get to his daughter as quickly as possible. He had to know she was safe. And more important, *she* needed to know that *he* was.

Now that he was outside, Nick needed to move as far out into the open as possible to remain clear of falling material. No easy feat on a New York City block crowded with skyscrapers. And there was a tremendous fissure in the center of the street. If he got too close to the middle, he'd be sucked in and swallowed like the dozens of other people who'd been outside the courthouse when the first tremor hit.

As the ground shook beneath him, Nick chanced a glance up at the street. He'd be safer in a car, of course, but only if he kept the car glued to one spot, and he had no intention of staying downtown. Not while Lauren was helpless somewhere on the Upper West Side.

The tremor suddenly stopped.

Nick tried to discern how long each quake had lasted. No more than a minute or two apiece, he was sure.

All right, he thought, *what else was I told as a kid?*

Earthquakes were psychologically devastating. It was crucial to remain calm and composed. Panic led individuals to take unnecessary and dangerous actions. Panic during an earthquake got people killed.

Nick waited a few extra moments before rising to his feet. He didn't know whether these tremors were aftershocks or the real thing. Hell, for all Nick knew these tremors could merely be a preface to the Big One.

He looked at his hands and saw that they were covered in dried blood. He wiped them as best he could against his suit jacket and then felt along his forehead. When he stared down at his hands again they were colored with fresh blood. He was bleeding and already feeling light-headed. He needed to stop the flow before he lost too much blood and passed out.

Nick quickly undid the knot in his tie and yanked it out from under his shirt collar. The tie was red; it was one of his favorites. His wife, Sara, had given it to him for his birthday back in 2000. It was one of the last presents he'd ever received from her.

He placed the tie across his forehead and pulled it tight before tying it off at the back of his head. That would at least staunch the blood flow, he thought, and keep the blood from streaming into his eyes.

He was sweating and wanted to remove his suit jacket. But he had no idea what hell lay before him; the jacket might come in handy later so he decided to hold on to it. He dusted himself as best he could. As he did he felt around in his pockets. He carried no handkerchief and knew that his search was in vain, but he needed something to cover his nose and mouth, to keep out what dust and debris that he could. Finally, he turned up his collar and pulled it up over his face as far as possible.

Visibility was next to nothing so he listened intently for sounds. He could hear cries for help, but they were either far away or muffled by the rubble.

Limping, he moved in the direction of the closest sound he heard. As badly as he needed to get to Lauren, if there were survivors here he had a duty to stay and help them.

As he moved, gravel crunched under his feet. At several points the crunching ceased and he knew he was traversing over poster-board signs protesting the U.S. attorney general's decision to try Feroz Saeed Alivi in a civilian court in the United States.

He looked down. Beneath his tired feet was a mammoth sign with big, bright and bold red letters: NOT ON AMERICAN SOIL.

The terrorist's face again flashed in his mind and Nick again wondered whether Alivi had been killed in the quake or somehow, in the utter chaos of the courthouse, managed to escape.

Nick suddenly sensed movement to his left and swung his head in that direction. The dust cloud made it impossible for Nick to see anything; it was as though he were standing in the middle of the Mojave Desert during a sandstorm. He shielded his eyes with his right arm and staggered toward the faint sound of moving rubble.

After a few moments, he heard a groan emanate from the rubble a few feet in front of him and he immediately dropped to his knees. Blindly, he reached forward and when his hand hit something solid, he began digging, slowly at first, then faster as the groans became louder and clearer. His pulse raced. The rubble scraped his hands and he grimaced but kept digging and digging. Until, finally, he felt flesh. Felt the fingers of another survivor close around his hand and squeeze tightly.

7

Nick tugged gently upward on the bloodied arm and the groans became louder. He set his foot against a pile of rubble for leverage and then pulled harder. He heard a cry of pain and immediately stopped but didn't let go. A voice emanated from the rubble. . . .

"Pull harder! Please. It's gonna hurt like hell and I'm gonna scream. But you have to keep pulling. You have to get me the hell out of here."

Nick dug a little deeper, then gripped the arm with both hands and pulled. Finally, the shape of a body started to materialize through the cloud of dust.

Nick could make out that it was the body of a man but nothing else.

The man leaned on Nick for support and hacked violently until he finally doubled over. He needed oxygen, but there was nothing Nick could do about that just now.

The man pushed himself away from Nick and attempted to stand on his own. His face was covered with a thick layer of brown dust. Blood spotted him from head to toe.

It wasn't a protestor. The man was wearing a suit very

similar to Nick's. It may have been navy at the start of the day but now there was no way to tell. The suit was shredded beyond recognition.

The man slowly opened his eyes and Nick thought he recognized him.

The man looked back at Nick and recognition washed over his face as well.

"Francisco," the man said. "Special Agent Francisco Mendoza, Federal Bureau of Investigation." He held out his hand.

"Frank?" Nick said.

Mendoza nodded. "AUSA Dykstra, right? I was told by your office to be here this morning. That you were going to call me as your first witness."

Nick sighed. "Hate to be the one to break it to you, Frank, but you're a day early."

Mendoza stared at him for several seconds before his mouth finally cracked into a mirthless grin. "You goddamn lawyers," he said.

Nick allowed himself some deep breaths but the air was stale and dirty and he coughed. "I was going to phone you during the first recess," he rasped. "Have you come down to the office this evening to go over your testimony."

Mendoza seemed to have tuned him out; the cop was turning his head a hundred and eighty degrees each way, taking in the destruction.

"You injured?" Nick said.

Mendoza chuckled. "Does it matter?"

Nick pursed his lips, and turned to gaze up the road. The intersection was blocked by rubble and an overturned bus. "I guess not."

Mendoza patted himself down, finally reached into his pants pocket and pulled out a BlackBerry. Nick watched as Mendoza dusted it off with the tail of his shirt, then punched the ON button. The cracked screen came to life and Nick felt a momentary rush of optimism.

Mendoza pulled up his contacts and hit a button and then put the phone to his ear. After a moment, he shook his head. "Nothing," he said. "You got yours?"

Nick glanced back at the courthouse. "They take your phone at the door." He swallowed hard and turned the corners of his lips up at the irony. "Safety concerns."

"You the only one to make it out of the courthouse?"

Nick shrugged. "Maybe. But that doesn't mean there aren't survivors."

Mendoza started toward the courthouse steps. "Let's go take a look, then."

8

Nick's strained voice echoed through the lobby of 500 Pearl Street. The voice sounded entirely alien to him and he hesitated before calling out a second time. "*Hello . . . can anybody hear me?*"

Mendoza was kneeling next to a fallen court officer. He checked for a pulse, then crossed himself the way Nick's grandmother had every time she'd gotten into a car. Mendoza stood, turned to Nick, and shook his head. "Can we get upstairs?"

Nick glanced in the direction of the door he'd squeezed through just twenty minutes earlier. More of the ceiling above the doorframe had collapsed and helped the pillar seal the door shut. "There's another stairwell in the rear of the building," Nick said. "Just past the elevators. We can try that one."

"Careful," Mendoza said, as they crept toward the back of the lobby. "Listen for anything. Not just calls for help but for complaints from the structure. If more of the ceiling decides to fall, we might be crushed. And even if we're not crushed, there's a good chance we'll be trapped."

Nick and Mendoza stepped around the corpse of another

uniformed court officer and stepped over a fallen light fixture to reach the red metal door that opened into the rear stairwell. The door itself was clear of obstruction and opened easily. But when Nick stepped inside he stopped short, his breath caught in his throat.

"What is it?" Mendoza said quietly.

Rather than answer, Nick simply stepped aside to reveal the lifeless body of Helen Healy, a court stenographer who'd worked at least half of Nick's trials over the past two years. Before that, Helen had worked in the state criminal court at 100 Centre for thirty-plus years.

Now her skull was dented, her neck bent at a grotesque angle. The heel of her left foot rested on the second step, while most of her body lay on the first floor landing. Clearly, she'd been heading up the stairs when the first tremor hit.

Nick had seen plenty of bodies in his career as a federal prosecutor. Just last year he'd prosecuted a key figure in the Tagliarini crime family, and the three soldiers who had turned against the defendant described murders so heinous Nick wasn't able to eat or sleep the night after they testified. There were plenty of photographs of previously unsolved homicide victims to corroborate the testimony. But this was somehow different, so different that Nick had to be steadied when his knees suddenly turned to rubber and he thought he might faint.

"You okay?" Mendoza said.

Nick replied with a nod of the head and stepped over Helen's body. As he climbed the steps, one at a time, pain shot up his left leg. He paused for a moment when he reached the second landing and pulled up the left leg of his suit pants to the knee. He shuddered when he saw the bruise, but was grateful that he could still walk. His adrenaline had masked the pain up until this point, but now he began feeling it every-where. In the shoulders he'd repeatedly thrown into the crash bar to escape the front stairwell. In the left arm he'd landed on when he leapt over the human heap trying to flee Justice Gaydos's courtroom. His forehead throbbed where the skin had split open and he touched his fingers to the tie he'd placed around his head. His scraped fingers burned from digging at the rubble to rescue Mendoza. The base of his neck ached like hell, as it typically did during periods of great stress.

Mendoza stepped around him and started toward the next landing. Nick followed, his gaze inadvertently falling back down to Helen Healy's ruined body on the lower level. Something lurched in his stomach and he dry heaved.

This time Mendoza didn't say anything, just placed a gentle hand on Nick's shoulder and waited for him to stand up straight.

Mendoza pushed through the door on the second floor and together they entered the marble hallway. The darkness momentarily surprised Nick because the emergency lights in this stairwell had apparently been operating on auxiliary power. The dark stairwell he'd been in just an hour or so earlier now felt as though it was weeks behind him.

"Stay here," Mendoza said. "If there's a hole in the floor or the ceiling comes down, no reason both of us should get killed."

"Frank . . ." Nick started.

Mendoza placed a firm hand on Nick's chest. "No, I'm serious, Nick. If something happens, I want you alive and well to try to save me."

Nick nodded in the darkness.

Mendoza moved slowly forward, Nick listening to the agent's footfalls on cracked tile. Suddenly, those footfalls ceased and Nick experienced a spark of panic.

"You all right, Frank?"

"I'm fine," Mendoza called back. "But we've reached

the end of the line here. The ceiling's collapsed. There's no way through."

"Hear anything over there?" Nick said when he felt Mendoza at his side again.

"Not a peep."

Nick pushed open the metal door and stepped back into the stairwell, thankful for the splash of light.

"What now?" Mendoza said.

Nick started slowly down the steps, bracing his left leg against the pain.

"I need to get uptown," Nick said.

"Uptown?"

"My daughter's there."

"If she's uptown, she's probably fine."

Nick shook his head. "We don't know where the epicenter is. Could be beneath this courthouse, but it's doubtful. May be somewhere in midtown, may be somewhere uptown."

"Could be under Hoboken, New Jersey," Mendoza said.

"Could be."

"How you planning on getting uptown, Nick? I didn't even see a way off this street."

Nick stepped over Helen Healy's body a final time and pushed through the door into the lobby.

"There's got to be a way," Nick said.

"And if there isn't?"

"There's got to be."

Mendoza stopped as they neared the glass doors leading back outside. "Where uptown?" he said.

"North end of the Upper West Side," Nick said, turning back to face him. "Columbia University. She's a high school senior. She's visiting the campus today."

Mendoza nodded. "My wife, Jana, she works as a nurse at St. Luke's-Roosevelt on West Fifty-ninth Street."

"You saying you want to come with me?"

Mendoza shrugged. "Sure. I got nothing better to do."

Nick turned and pushed through the door.

"You know," Mendoza said, "even if we do make it up there, my wife and your daughter are not going to be happy that we risked our lives to make sure they survived."

Nick held the door for him, and said, "This isn't just about me making sure that Lauren's safe. My daughter lost her mother in the World Trade Center twelve years ago. She needs to know that I made it out of this courthouse alive."

9

Nick Dykstra and Francisco Mendoza walked down the cracked concrete steps of the federal courthouse and turned north toward Centre Street. As they did, Nick glanced over his shoulder. To the south was Park Row, home of the Metropolitan Correctional Center (MCC), the federal detention facility housing pretrial and holdover inmates. Some of Nick's most recent convictions were still there, awaiting transfer to a medium-security federal correctional institution like Otisville in upstate New York (if they were lucky), or to a high-security U.S. penitentiary such as Lewisburg in Pennsylvania (if they were not).

He wondered how the MCC had held up during the quake. The Federal Bureau of Prisons could anticipate any number of scenarios, but a magnitude six or seven earthquake striking New York City was something only Hollywood could have imagined.

Mendoza looked back, too. "You thinking what I'm thinking?"

Nick nodded. The MCC served as a temporary home to over 800 inmates awaiting trial or transfer. Murderers, rapists, Mafia bosses, drug kingpins, weapons traffickers—and terrorists. Feroz Saeed Alivi was currently housed there, as was Sulaiman Abu Gaith, the son-in-law of Osama bin Laden, and Abu Hamza al-Masri, aka Mostafa Kamel Mostafa, the Egyptian cleric who masterminded the 1998 kidnapping of westerners in Yemen and established a bona fide terrorist training camp in Oregon in 1999.

"On the bright side," Mendoza said, "the earthquake may have saved the federal government millions in trial costs and prison expenditures."

Nick said nothing. His thoughts had already turned from the vicious criminals currently behind bars in New York City to the hundreds of thousands who were running loose. Images of the LA riots popped into his mind. Looting and mass hysteria might have already begun in some parts of the city, for all he knew. He thought of Lauren and stepped up his pace.

To his right, the pentagonal structure of 60 Centre Street had collapsed completely. From Nick's vantage point, nothing resembling the state courthouse could be seen. Meanwhile, across the street, the building housing the United States Court of Appeals for the Second Circuit had fallen over, blocking their path to Foley Square.

Mendoza stopped, and said, "How do you plan on getting past that, counselor?"

Nick studied the rubble, searching out handholds and footholds. He opened his mouth to speak but found he had no voice left. He was parched, his mouth filled with dust, his throat on fire. He could barely breathe.

If only he could see more than a few feet in front of him, Nick thought maybe they could backtrack down Pearl Street and cut across Cardinal Hayes Place. That would put them on the other side of the court of the appeals, from where they could either reach Centre Street or search for the Chambers Street subway station.

Nick turned and began his retreat, directing Mendoza with

his hands. "This way," he muttered but he couldn't know if Mendoza heard him.

Nick considered what moving in this direction meant. They'd have to cross directly in front of the Metropolitan Correctional Center. But they had no choice. Whatever the risk, whatever the cost, he needed to reach Lauren.

As they neared Cardinal Hayes Place, Nick could faintly hear shouting. Only then, as he listened, did he realize there was a ringing in his ears. Whether it was from the fire alarms that went off in the courthouse

They had gone off, hadn't they?

or the constant wailing sirens emanating from all around him now, he didn't know. He stretched his jaw in a yawn and tried to clear his ears but the ringing continued.

The voices beneath the ringing grew louder—and angrier—and Nick steeled himself for a confrontation. He felt some small comfort that Mendoza was right on his heels, but as the blurred scene became clearer he could see at least a half dozen bright orange figures standing in a semicircle at the mouth of Cardinal Hayes Place.

Nick flashed on one of the first cases he worked on at the U.S. attorney's office. It was thirteen defendants imprisoned and awaiting trial for plotting to bomb the United Nations, Hudson River tunnels, and other New York City landmarks. At the head of the list of co-conspirators was Sheik Omar Abdel Rahman, the blind Egyptian cleric, whose prosecution grew out of the investigation into the 1993 World Trade Center bombing.

Behind bars at the MCC, one of the sheik's co-defendants had the audacity to complain about the wait for a pair of prescription reading glasses to replace the ones he lost during his arrest by the FBI. Another complained that he had to work five hours a day swabbing floors or face twenty-three hours a day in solitary confinement. But the most surreal complaint came from a defendant named Ibrahim, who during an interview with a *New York Times* reporter, said that he despised the orange color of his jumpsuit.

Again Nick thought of Feroz Saeed Alivi, wondered whether the madman was dead or alive, and had to tamp down the fury rising uninvited in his chest.

The half circle of inmates tightened around what looked like a large metal box, and soon Nick was able to make out a seventh figure, a skinny man with dark skin and a white T-shirt saturated with blood.

"Please," the man cried, "just leave me the hell alone."

One of the inmates stepped forward. "Hand over that fucking cart, Apu, and you can go wherever the hell you please. But if you think you're leaving with our food and drinks, then you're just another dead man standing outside the MCC."

"Please," the man cried again in what sounded like an Indian accent, "I will give you a drink—*one*, that is all I can spare. Then you must let me go. I don't want any trouble."

"Look around, motherfucker. Ain't nothing but trouble still standing down here. Ain't no gods, ain't no guards. And there sure as hell ain't no law."

Nick squinted through the dense fog of dust and saw the Sabrett hot dog logo centered on the metal cart. Mendoza's voice suddenly emanated loudly and clearly from behind him.

"Better be sure of that," Mendoza said, stepping forward.

The half circle of inmates loosened and Nick looked over at Mendoza and spotted the Glock 22 at the end of his right arm.

Bad idea, Nick thought. There were at least six of them. They could rush Mendoza and get the gun. Sure, he might take out two or even three, but ultimately these guys would be able to wrestle the weapon away from him.

Nick moved to a spot between Mendoza and the inmates and placed his arms in front of his chest, palms out.

"No need for this," he said, eyeing each of the inmates,

hoping not to recognize any as defendants he recently prosecuted. "Do you hear those sirens, gentlemen? They're coming closer. The police will be down here to restore order within ten minutes. Right now, you have your freedom. If you want a chance at keeping it, I recommend you follow Park Row east until you hit Kimlau Square. Once you're there, continue walking down East Broadway until you get to the Manhattan Bridge. Turn right onto the bridge, cross the FDR and the East River, and you're in Brooklyn. Find yourselves a change of clothes and vanish. It's your only chance."

"Who are you?" one of the inmates said as he inched closer. "Why do you want to help us escape?"

"I don't," Nick said. "I just want to get uptown and find my daughter. And watching you six get yourselves shot and killed over some dirty water dogs and an iced tea isn't going to get me there any faster."

10

The aluminum can of Nestlé iced tea was empty but Nick kept it upturned and to his lips to ensure he got every last drop. Then he dropped the can on the ground and flattened it under his foot.

He turned to Mendoza, who had just polished off a can of Sprite. "Ready, Frank?"

"As ready as I'll ever be, I suppose."

The Sabrett hot dog vendor had given each of them a beverage in gratitude, but he'd had no food that wasn't covered in the thick dust that hung everywhere around them. Nick felt a grumble in his stomach but ignored it. The sun was hanging high in the sky and there was no breeze, but the dense brown fog kept them from feeling the worst of the heat as they crossed the plaza toward Chambers Street station.

As they skirted the edge of the municipal building on Centre Street, Nick realized he no longer heard the sirens. The sirens had been replaced by an eerie silence and he was almost thankful for the incessant ringing in his ears. He couldn't help but wonder what the silence meant. Whether the ambulances and fire and police vehicles had headed uptown or simply given up for the time being trying get through to lower Manhattan.

When they reached Centre Street, they stopped and watched thick black smoke billowing into the sky just a few blocks away.

"That's coming from City Hall," Nick said.

A few minutes later, they stood directly in front of the municipal building, which had stood up fairly well to the tremors. The same couldn't be said for Chambers Street. Chambers Street was ripped apart as far as the eye could see. Bodies lay scattered, vehicles crushed under rubble.

In the distance Nick could see a pair of people scrambling along the edge of the crevasse in the direction of Church Street. He turned toward the entrance to the Chambers Street subway station and took a few steps toward it before turning around.

Mendoza stood frozen, gazing at the stairwell leading underground. "I'm not so sure this is a good idea," he said.

"We have no choice, Frank. I'd like nothing more than to take a nice, leisurely stroll north along the Hudson River all the way uptown. But look around. Every street is blocked by fallen buildings."

When Mendoza spoke again there was a sharp edge to his voice. "And what do you expect us to find down there, counselor? For all we know the subway system is flooded. Below us there may be trains cracked up and on fire. If another quake hits, the street may cave in and bury us alive."

"If you don't want to come with me," Nick said, "I understand. But this is a chance I have to take." He pointed into the darkness. "If this tunnel's clear, we can take it all the way to West 59th to St. Luke's-Roosevelt. You can find your wife and I can continue all the way to 116th Street to find my daughter. Quickest way from point A to point B is a straight line. That's pretty much what's waiting for us down there."

"That may not be all that's waiting for us down there,"

Mendoza said. "Roaches? Rats? Crazy people looking to a take a brick to someone's skull? A gas leak waiting to ignite and turn the tunnel into an inferno."

Mendoza's last words caught in Nick's mind like a pushpin. But it wasn't a gas leak that suddenly terrified him. The Indian Point Energy Center, a nuclear power plant station, stood on the east bank of the Hudson River, just thirty-eight miles north of New York City. In the decades since it opened, particularly in the years since 9/11, there had been much highly publicized debate over whether to allow the plant to remain open. On the one hand, the positive economic impact the plant had on counties like Westchester, Orange, Rockland, Putnam, and Dutchess, were undeniable. Closing the plant would cost thousands of jobs, cost New York State hundreds of millions of dollars.

On the other hand were the safety concerns. The Indian Point plant had experienced a number of accidents and mishaps since its inception. The plant was once on the federal list of the nation's worst nuclear power plants. In 2000, a small radioactive leak from a steam tube closed Indian Point for eleven months. New York's version of the Environmental Protection Agency had repeatedly declared that Indian Point's spent fuel pools were exposed and unsecured and vulnerable to a terrorist attack. And given New York's varied seismic past, the plant's susceptibility to earthquakes was studied. The company that owned the plant stated that Indian Point was built to withstand a magnitude 6.1 quake. But the tragedy resulting from Japan's Fukushima nuclear power plant was still fresh in everyone's memory.

Right now Nick recalled it as vividly as if it were playing out on a television directly in front of him.

"Whoever or whatever is down there," Nick finally said, "those are bridges I'll have to cross when I get to them."

"You're not going to do your daughter a whole hell of a lot of good if you're dead, counselor."

"I'm not doing anyone much good standing around here waiting for something to happen either. Look, this isn't something I'm going to be talked out of. With or without you, Frank, I'm heading into the tunnels."

Mendoza shook his head even as a smile cracked his lips. "You goddamn lawyers," he said. Mendoza stepped past Nick and started slowly down the steps into the station. From the pitch blackness, he called out, "Well, counselor? What the hell are you waiting for?"

Nick took a long, deep breath of dust-ridden air, and then tried to hack it out of his lungs, just as he had as he finally moved away from the World Trade Center twelve years ago.

Finally, he stood up straight, took one last look around at the destruction aboveground, and took his first step down, into the darkness.

PART TWO
9.0

11

Assistant U.S. Attorney Nick Dykstra and Special Agent Francisco Mendoza of the FBI completely lost track of time during their trek north through the subway tunnel from Chambers Street to Canal. At the point where the J line merged with the R, they could finally see a train stopped cold dead ahead. Nick figured they'd walked no more than half a mile, but it was a half mile along an underground train track littered with fallen pipes and beams of steel, lousy with rats and other vermin. And though neither man knew the intricacies of the New York City subway system, both men had decided to stay well clear of the third rail.

The train up ahead was dark and, as they came closer, Nick could see that its cars were at an odd angle, indicating that the train had gone off the rails. Despite the searing pain in Nick's left leg, he hurried his step and heard Mendoza's footfalls quicken behind him.

"Looks like it just barely made it into Canal Street station," Nick said. "At least the first half of the train did."

Nick garnered some momentum and leapt onto the backside of the last car, grabbing hold of the thick chain to pull himself up. Painfully, he lifted his left leg over the chain, followed by his right. Cupping his fingers around his eyes, he put his face to the rear Plexiglas window and peered inside.

There was what looked like the body of an elderly homeless man lying lengthwise across the floor, his head propped up against a subway pole in the center of the car. Nick immediately went to work on the door and it unlatched and glided open surprisingly easily. As soon as the door slid open, an awful stench smacked Nick squarely in the face. But it wasn't the stench of the dead; it was the peculiarly pungent odor of a vagrant who hadn't gained access to a shower in months.

The dead don't smell yet, he thought. *It's only been a few hours at most.*

He instinctively glanced at his watch but it was useless. Even if it weren't too dark to read the watch, the old Rolex he'd inherited from his father six years ago wouldn't have done him any good. At some point during the quake, the protective glass had cracked, dust had gotten inside, and the large and small hands were forever frozen in place.

Breathing through his mouth, Nick stepped into the car. He walked slowly, balancing himself with the overhead bar on the right so as not to slide to the left, giving into gravity and the train's odd angle. As he stepped past the old man, he looked down for signs of life, but the man's chest didn't appear to be moving and there was no sound emanating from the vagrant's nose and mouth, not so much as a quiet snore.

Once he cleared the body, he focused on the car ahead. The train wouldn't have been crowded at the time the first tremor struck, but if the cars were relatively empty, Nick was sure there would be survivors. And if there *were* survivors—

Something suddenly gripped Nick's left ankle and he yelped in pain as it twisted and he lost his balance and fell to the floor. Startled, he looked back and stared into the vagrant's wild bloodshot eyes as the man attempted to drag himself forward, using Nick's left leg as a rope.

"Gonna kill you for this, mothafucka," the old man muttered

as he tucked one hand into his filthy overcoat and withdrew a blade.

Nick didn't hesitate. He kicked out with his right foot and connected with the man's face. The knife clattered as it struck the floor. The grip on Nick's left leg loosened and the vagrant suddenly seemed to be vanishing backwards into the darkness like the victim in a supernatural horror movie. The old man screamed as he was swept backwards by an unseen force.

"You all right, counselor?"

Mendoza's voice emanated from the blackness and then his face appeared in shadow.

"I'm fine, thanks," Nick said, scrambling to his feet.

"Good." Mendoza stepped past him toward the next car. "Let's get the hell off this train as quickly as possible."

They walked forward purposefully, pausing only to slide each door open so that they could exit one car and enter the next.

Finally, roughly midway through the train, they saw a glimmer of light.

"That's got to be the station," Mendoza said.

As soon as they could read the words CANAL STREET on one of the pillars, Mendoza turned toward a set of doors, placed his fingers between them and spread the doors apart using both arms.

Nick wiped the sweat dripping from beneath the necktie tied around his head and took the short leap from the toppled subway car to the platform. Mendoza followed.

Once they were clear of the car, Nick saw that the train had been stopped in its tracks by fallen debris. The front car was smashed in and it seemed clear that the conductor had attempted an emergency stop just a fraction of a second too late. But the lack of bodies was telling: The people aboard this train had ultimately escaped.

The subway platform was fairly clear of debris, but there were abandoned handbags and briefcases scattered from the train all the way past the turnstiles, even on the steps leading up to the surface. Nick and Mendoza stepped over and around the dropped items and headed up the stairs toward the light.

On the way up the steps Nick sniffed the air; it smelled sulfuric, like a box of burned matches. He slowed as he approached the top, his mind escorting him back twelve years to the day Sara died at the World Trade Center.

"Nick, we can't—

"We're too high up. We can't evacuate.

"Oh, God, Nick, the office is filling with black smoke. There's a fire. . . ."

The odor grew stronger as Nick breached the surface and his watering eyes immediately caught on a flickering brightness all around him, an illumination that transformed the city dusk into a ferocious hellscape.

"Christ," Mendoza mumbled over Nick's shoulder as he, too, reached the top. "All of Chinatown's on fire."

12

From the intersection of Broadway and Canal Street looking east, it appeared to Nick as though every building was ablaze. The collective heat coming off the burning structures was so intense that it nearly drove him and Mendoza back down into the subway station.

As Mendoza again crossed himself, Nick watched people materialize in the middle of Canal Street, fleeing in their direction, then past them toward Tribeca.

"Excuse me," Nick yelled as the survivors ran past him. "*Please stop.* Just for a second."

Aside from Mendoza and the old vagrant on the train, these were the first survivors Nick had encountered and he was desperate to speak with one to ask for news, but everyone was too panicked to stop and talk. As frustrating as it was, Nick couldn't blame them. But finally, a young woman appeared heading toward them, moving slowly because of the toddler she held in her arms.

Nick darted forward to meet her in the middle of the intersection, fearing she'd turn right or left onto Broadway.

"*Miss*," he cried out. The young woman was Asian, most

likely Chinese, and for a moment Nick worried that there would be a language barrier. But the young woman stopped right in front of him, and Nick held out his arms to take the toddler. He held the young boy to his chest and placed a light kiss on the child's forehead.

"My name's Nick," he said to the woman.

Panting, the young woman opened her lips but no words escaped until she finally bent over, gripping her knees, coughing like a victim of advanced emphysema.

"My name is Maylin," she finally croaked. "You're holding my son, Bo."

"Maylin, have you spoken to anyone?" Nick said urgently. "Have you heard any news? Any news at all about what happened?"

"Just speculation," she said. "A man from my building . . . I lost him back there in the smoke. I think he went into another building looking for his ex-wife. . . . He said—"

An explosion sounded from two or three blocks in the distance, and he and Maylin looked up just in time to see a fireball blast through the smoke and light up the sky over Chinatown.

Nick turned back to Maylin. "The man from your building," Nick said, "what did he tell you?"

"He said it was an earthquake. He said that just moments before the first quake hit, an emergency broadcast came over the television. They said something about seismic activity occurring somewhere here in the city."

"Where?" Nick said breathlessly. "Did he say where it started?"

"They said something about a fault line running under Third Avenue, I think. That's all he heard. That's all he told me."

Third Avenue, Nick thought. Third Avenue ran north and south on the east side of the city. He pictured a map of Manhattan. After Third came Lexington and Park and Madison, then Fifth Avenue. Moving west from Fifth Avenue was Central Park, but Central Park only ran from 59th to 110th Street. Columbia University was farther north at 116th Street, adjacent to Harlem.

All right, he thought. If the epicenter of the quake was on the east side there was a good chance Lauren was safe. Even if the epicenter was on the *Upper* East Side, she still had a chance. But if the epicenter *was* on the Upper East Side and the earthquake did as much damage as it had all the way south to City Hall, what was the chance Columbia University had been spared?

"Thank you," Nick said, handing Maylin her child. "Thank you so much." He paused, looked around for Mendoza and found the agent resting against the gate closing off the subway. He turned back to Maylin and asked, "Where are you heading?"

"The Holland Tunnel," she said. "I don't know what we'll find when we get there, but I want to get Bo off the island as fast as I possibly can."

Nick placed a hand on the child's head, looked into Maylin's frightened eyes, and said, "Good luck. And again, thank you. Thank you so much for stopping to speak to me."

Maylin nodded, tucked her son in as close to her chest as she could, and hurried past him.

"Frank," Nick said, "let's get moving. We can head west along Canal to Sixth Ave and walk north from there."

Mendoza gave a tired nod.

As they started, Nick stole one last glance at Chinatown as the neighborhood burned. He and Lauren had come down to Chinatown fairly often, especially during Lauren's Chinese food phase that began roughly when she hit twelve. But they hadn't just visited Chinatown for the food. They'd visited the art galleries, browsed the antique stores and curio shops, and celebrated at festivals such as the Chinese New Year.

Everything I told her has been a lie, Nick thought. *All those reassurances that we were safe, that no one could touch us, that nothing could take us away from each other—it was all fantasy. Every word was pure bullshit. What would she say if she saw this? How could I make her feel safe after she watched Chinatown burn to the ground?*

The thought caused him to search the skies for news choppers, but there were none in sight. With zero visibility, he shouldn't have been surprised. Yet somehow Nick would have felt better had the media vultures been circling. Nothing could have felt more normal than the twenty-four-hour news networks exploiting another New York City tragedy. Especially one so close to the twelve-year anniversary of 9/11.

But the world's busiest air corridor was empty.

13

Lauren Dykstra's eyes fluttered open and all she saw was blackness. She swallowed a scream and immediately tried to control her breathing. But maybe it was too late; she sounded and felt like she was hyperventilating.

Dad? she thought and almost shouted.

But no, she wasn't at home, was she? The last thing she remembered was walking the aisles of Butler Library with that cute guy in the black-framed glasses. Ray something or other.

She remembered now that a book had struck her. Struck her in the head. And not just one but two or three. Then . . .

Oh, my God, no. Was it a terrorist attack?

Warm tears immediately welled in her eyes, spilling over and down the sides of her head and dripping onto her ears as she lay flat on her back, a monstrous bookcase pinning her down just above the knees. Should she scream for help? What if it had been a bomb and there were terrorists roaming the aisles with assault rifles, ready to shred to pieces any survivors?

"You're safe, honey," her father had repeatedly told her. *"This is our city. Not theirs. Not the terrorists'."*

A rush of anger flooded her gut. She shouldn't have been here at Columbia today. She should've been at school or at home riffling through her Stanford brochures and filling out private student loan applications. She'd made her decision, hadn't she? She knew Stanford was where she wanted to spend the next four years. But Dad . . .

She felt her face glow red with rage. Her dad wanted her here in the city. Here with him because he was lonely. He'd spent the past dozen years trying to convince her that New York City was safe when it wasn't. The Big Apple was a target. The World Trade Center had been a target in 1993, and it sure as hell had been a target in 2001. This city had taken her mother. Swallowed her whole, and yet Dad couldn't understand why Lauren would want to leave New York, leave the entire East Coast. And now look at her, wounded and helpless on Columbia's campus. Oh, God, as much as she loved books she didn't want to die in a library, at least not for another sixty or seventy years.

She listened intently for voices. Heard only the thumping of her own heart. Her ribs hurt and she was having difficulty breathing.

Oh, shit. What if I'm bleeding internally?

She tried to move and when she did a searing pain shot up both legs. This time it was futile to try to prevent her scream. She let out a terrified cry that echoed in the bookcases all around her. Tears now fell freely and she felt as desperate and as lonely as she had felt when she was five, when she learned her mother was never coming home again because people had intentionally flown airplanes into the tall buildings where her mom worked.

Lauren listened, wondering whether her scream was heard by anyone. Was anyone in Butler Library even alive? She had no way of knowing. She had no way of knowing how long she'd been unconscious. And she had no way of knowing whether help was on its way or whether someone would eventually find her and whether it would be too late when they did. If she'd suffered internal injuries she might not have much time.

She screamed again, this time intentionally, this time at the top of her lungs.

No one can hear me, she thought. *Everyone in the library was killed. And I'm going to die, too. Because no one will find me. No one even knows to look for me, except maybe the director of admissions. Oh, what was her name? Caroline, it was Caroline. Caroline Reignier. Yeah, Caroline knows where I am.*

But then, maybe Caroline was dead. If so, Lauren had no hope. She was going to die here in Butler Library. Of internal bleeding or dehydration or asphyxiation. She tried to control her breathing, but it was impossible.

She thought: *I'm going into shock.*

She thought: *If I do go into shock, I'm dead; there will be no coming back.*

She thought: *Calm down. You need to calm yourself down.*

She thought: *How the hell can I calm down? I'm fucking buried alive.*

She woke again hours later. Opened her eyes and saw nothing but blackness. Still. She listened for outside sounds but heard as little as she could see. Which was nothing at all. Only the increasingly ragged sound of her breathing was audible. A grim thought crossed her mind: *Breathing won't be a problem much longer.*

What if she died?

She pictured her dad at her mom's funeral twelve years ago. How he had broken down and cried during the service. As soon as she'd seen that, she'd fallen apart, too. Daddy was so strong, so courageous; if *he* was crying it just might be the end of the world, after all.

She suddenly felt guilty over her earlier thoughts. No one had heard them—they were just in her head. But, still. How could she have turned on him like that?

I was scared.

Nothing in the universe could justify those thoughts. Her dad had sacrificed *everything* for Lauren. He never went out, never got drinks, never dated. Never got laid. All right, that was none of her business. But it was true. He'd given himself *fully* to his only daughter over the past twelve years. Other dads watched football on Sunday, not the first season of *Girls* on DVD. They went out with the guys one or two nights a week. Instead, her father took her on daddy-daughter dinner dates. And always let *her* pick the restaurant. Even if she insisted on going to the same restaurant in Chinatown for eleven months straight, like she did back when she was a kid.

He's safe, isn't he?

Of course, he was. Whatever happened, it happened here on the Upper West Side, not downtown by the courthouses. And that's where Dad was, making opening statements in the high-profile trial against—

That terrorist, could he be behind this?

If so, her dad wasn't safe at all. She shivered. She didn't know what she would do if she lost him. It was too horrible an idea to even contemplate.

How could I have even considered leaving him for the next four years?

The debate that had gone on in her head for the better part of the past year was a farce. Why didn't she see this until now? It took a bookcase falling on top of her and crushing her legs and trapping her for her to figure this all out?

She felt ashamed.

Guilty.

What must my dad think of me for wanting so badly to leave?

Her father must have thought she was a selfish, ungrateful

brat. My God, what had she put him through these past twelve months? He'd lost his wife, and for the past year he thought he was losing his only daughter? What kind of a person was she to put him through all that?

He's got to be safe. He's just got to be.

If he was, she hoped he wasn't worrying. She could just imagine his reaction if he heard there had been a terrorist bombing at Columbia University this morning. And what did that tell her about her situation?

If he could have been here he would have by now.

How deeply was she buried? Had the entire building collapsed the way the Twin Towers had? Was the bookcase providing her with a pocket of air? If so, how much of that air could possibly remain? How long did she have? Was she under so much rubble that she'd be a skeleton by the time she was found?

They were pulling bodies out of Ground Zero even months after 9/11. The sifting just ended in 2010, and they're still *finding human remains.*

How could she have blamed her father for this predicament she was in? Ludicrous. It wasn't his fault. It wasn't Lauren's either. She was here at Columbia University for a completely legitimate and useful purpose. To tour the campus. To consider whether she wanted to call it home for the next four years. Because she hadn't yet made up her mind about Stanford.

Hadn't she though? Hadn't she made up her mind in Butler Library before the sky came falling down?

She had.

She'd decided.

She'd chosen Columbia University.

She'd chosen to stay close to Dad.

She'd chosen to stay close to home.

14

In the lockup adjacent to Justice Gaydos's courtroom at 500 Pearl Street, U.S. Marshal Darren Shaw regained consciousness and lifted himself off the gray concrete floor. A fog of dust hung in the air like poison gas. Shaw rubbed at his eyes, summoned as much saliva as he could (barely a drop), and spat on the ground. His body was weak, his throat raw. He twisted his head to look around but saw nothing but rubble. Where were his fellow marshals? And just as important, where was his prisoner, Feroz Saeed Alivi?

He could practically hear his wife, Tamron, in his ear. "Don't you worry about that goddamn terrorist. You get yourself the hell out of that courthouse and get yourself home. Your three children need their daddy, and I need my husband."

Darren Shaw still had no clue as to what had happened. But even assuming the worst—a natural disaster that devastated the entire island of Manhattan—he didn't think its effects would be felt as far as his family home across the Hudson River in Jersey City.

First time in my adult life I'm glad we moved to New

Jersey near Tamron's mother instead of Battery Park like I'd wanted.

Shaw took two small steps forward, testing first his right leg, then his left. Sore, but nothing broken. Nothing dislocated, as far as he could tell. He flexed his arms, wriggled his fingers and toes.

Everything still there, he mused, though looking around he was certain that not everyone was so lucky.

Maybe the prisoner Feroz Saeed Alivi was dead. Maybe. But without a body, Shaw had no choice but to start looking. Not just to save his job, but because he loved his country. Shaw wasn't going to let his nation experience another 9/11 because he had allowed his prisoner to escape in the chaos.

The path back to the courtroom was blocked, so there was only one way for Shaw to go—deeper into the lockup. From what he could see, the power had been knocked out. Which meant the electronic doors were useless at confining anyone. Not that Shaw or his colleagues had had time to secure Alivi. Just as he and the others entered the lockup, the ceiling started falling. The last he'd seen the prisoner, Alivi was heading in the direction Shaw was heading in now.

Darren Shaw wasn't necessarily afraid of the dark, but this was ridiculous. He couldn't see two feet ahead of him. He walked with his arms out in front of him, like a blind man without a dog or a cane.

"Daddy, I don't like the dark. Can you put on my light-night?"

"Night-light, honey."

"That's what I said! Light-night."

That was his youngest, Denise. Denise was two going on twenty-two. That's how it was when a girl had two older sisters. Denise was growing up faster than any of them. Which wasn't so much of a concern for Shaw now. But in ten or fifteen years? He knew he'd be singing a different tune if

Denise grew up before her time. All children should have a chance to be kids. No need to grow up fast; nothing waiting for them that won't be there when they're old enough to appreciate it.

Shaw felt to his right, searching for the metal door that opened into the private stairwell used just by the marshals to bring prisoners up to the courtrooms. Cell, wall, cell, wall, do—

No door, just open air and Shaw stumbled through the doorframe and nearly tumbled down the stairs. He turned back, felt around but the door wasn't open; it just wasn't there. The door had come off in the—

In the what? Shaw thought. The explosion? The earthquake?

Does it matter?

No, whatever happened, Shaw's duty remained the same.

He reached out in search of the railing. When his fingers finally found it, he grasped it like a lifeline and took the first step down. Wishing the whole while that he could reach out to Tamron, let her know he was all right. She'd be worried. His oldest daughter, Isis, she'd be nervous, too. She was only twelve but already felt she had the weight of the world on her shoulders. Growing up as she was in this post-9/11 world, he shouldn't have been surprised. He and Tamron had tried to shield her as much as possible in the first few years of her life, but once she started school, it became more and more difficult. Now, she was on the Internet for hours on end each day. She went to sites like WebMD and worried herself senseless about cancer and exotic diseases like SARS. Her counselor at school even had a name for that—cyberchondria. But she wasn't just a hypochondriac; she was terrified of just about everything. Terrorism, crime, poverty—that's right, she was even worried about the global economy. And she didn't like what her daddy did for a living at all. "What if some of your prisoner's friends decide to help him escape? What if they bring guns? What if they set up one of those IEDs along the road like in Iraq?"

"This isn't Iraq, sweetheart," he'd told her more than once. But it did little good. Even when he succeeded in comforting her, her fears blew right back through the window the moment he left for work.

Shaw found the landing and took several deep breaths.

Halfway there, he thought.

And then what?

Well, that depended entirely on what he found down there, didn't it?

He started down the next flight of stairs same as he did the first. Thinking of his middle child, Tiana. She was the quiet one. Seven years old and hardly ever made a peep. Oh, Tiana was smart, he knew that. She made straight A's in school and excelled at standardized tests. She just didn't say much. Shaw often called her an *observer*. She watched everything and everyone and though she didn't offer an analysis afterward, Shaw could tell she was constantly analyzing, reading the situation, adapting. . . .

When he reached the bottom of the stairs, Shaw heard a movement deep in the shadows. He fought the urge to call out. Instead, he stood stock-still and listened. He heard what sounded like heavy breathing. Heavy breathing followed by a whimper.

Cautiously, Shaw approached the sound. He kept low, one arm out of front of him to guide him through the darkness. Suddenly, he heard:

"Who's there?"

Shaw jumped slightly at the sound but quickly recognized the strained voice of his colleague, Marshal Randall Trocano.

"Randy?" Shaw said.

"Darren, is that you?"

Shaw hurried over to the voice, which seemed to be emanating from the floor. In the pitch blackness, he could finally make out the shape of Randy Trocano.

"You hurt?" Shaw said.

But Randy didn't have to say a word. Shaw's hands were already on the marshal's chest and already covered with a dark liquid that smelled like blood.

"Oh, man, Randy, what happened?" Shaw felt around for Randy's skull. "Something fall on your head? We've got to stop the bleeding."

Randy placed his hands over Darren Shaw's and guided them downward. Placed them squarely on Randy's chest. Shaw instantly felt the hole.

"Oh, no, man." Shaw tried to remove the urgency from his voice; his panicking wouldn't help his friend. "It's all right. You're going to be all right."

"No." Randy's voice sounded thick and wet. "It was . . . It was Alivi. . . ."

As Randy's words trailed off, Shaw lifted his head and peered into the darkness. Randy's wound was fresh, which meant that he had been wounded not too long ago.

Which meant Feroz Saeed Alivi could still be in the room.

In the room with a weapon. Ready to do to Shaw what he'd already done to Randy.

15

As they walked north along Sixth Avenue, what little remaining sun there was gradually dipped behind crumbling skyscrapers and collapsed buildings until it was finally full dark. Nick and Mendoza knew it had been roughly seven hours since the first tremor but, otherwise, their timeline was a complete blur. They encountered a number of survivors as they headed uptown. A young Korean artist who'd narrowly escaped from her loft in SoHo. A bankruptcy lawyer begging each passerby for a look at his or her phone, convinced that service had returned on at least one cellular network. "Please," he'd said, "I just need to contact my mom, let her know I'm all right."

Nick and Mendoza exchanged information with everyone they met. Most people were anxious for news about lower Manhattan. Nick was cautious in what he said; he kept the conversations general. He didn't know which of these people might have had a brother arguing a motion before Judge Hobbs at 60 Centre Street, which might have had an aunt who worked as a court officer in the criminal courts building down the street at 100 Centre.

No one they met had received news from a credible source outside Manhattan. It was all secondhand information and much of it was terrifying. The Brooklyn Bridge collapsed, a couple told them. Gridlock at the Lincoln Tunnel had forced people to abandon their cars and move forward on foot, only to find that the egress on the New Jersey side had caved in, forcing them back to Manhattan. The Holland Tunnel, an NYU student assured them, was much worse. The tunnel was packed with pedestrians when the last tremor hit, and its structure cracked and it flooded with water from the Hudson River killing everyone inside.

"Hear anything about Indian Point?" Nick had asked every person who'd stopped to talk to them. Some didn't know what he was referring to; others shrugged it off as though a leak at the nuclear plant was the least of their worries.

The owner of a small shoe store was passing out small bottled waters as survivors walked by. He was an Eastern European man (Romanian, Nick thought), with a thick accent and kind eyes. "I have heard that no hospitals on the island are functioning," he said. "They have all collapsed. Yankee Stadium in the Bronx has been turned into an open-air infirmary, but from what I understand it is already full."

Nick watched Mendoza's face drop at the news about the hospitals. But the agent quickly recovered once they walked away from the shoemaker.

"He doesn't know any more than anyone else," Mendoza said. "He's listening to rumors, just like us."

Nick agreed; he had purposefully refrained from asking anyone about Columbia University for exactly that reason.

What truly bothered Nick was that the farther north they walked, there was no less devastation. Buildings had toppled, cars had been crushed. Streets were torn to shreds and the dead lay all around. Looting had clearly been rampant. Every bodega they passed, the windows had been shattered, the shelves and coolers emptied and trashed.

"Where are all the cops?" Nick said at one point.

Mendoza shrugged. "They probably have no way to communicate with each other. They're probably helping or fending for themselves just like everyone else. Don't need to put on a uniform to do that."

"We're approaching West Fourth Street," Nick said a few minutes later.

"When's the last time you were in the Village?" Mendoza replied.

Nick thought about it. Early in his career, he'd spent a lot of time in Greenwich Village. He'd loved the restaurants and dive bars in the area, especially those on West Fourth between Sixth and Seventh Avenue. That was when the West Village still had character. Before *Friends*. Before the area turned mainstream and became expensive. The East Village, too, was presently trendy but no longer cheap. Hell, even the Meat-packing District was now considered a hot spot.

Nick saw a number of flashlight beams turn on suddenly in the area of Washington Square Park. These days, Washington Square Park was overrun with NYU students. You could still pick up a dime bag if you so desired, but you also risked getting caught in a verbal headlock with a freshman film student.

Several of the beams of light turned in their direction and began an approach. Nick squinted, held his hands in front of his eyes to block out some of the light. These young men didn't look like NYU film students. They wore big, bulky North Face winter jackets despite the warm autumn temperatures. Their jeans sagged almost to their knees. Two of the five wore hoods and kept their heads down so that Nick couldn't see their faces. The young men swaggered toward them the way many of the men he prosecuted swaggered toward the defense table during their initial arraignment. As the cases wore on, however, most of the defendants eventually lost that swagger, and Nick typically took that as a sign that they were finally resigning themselves to their fate. That was the point when Nick could call the defendant's lawyer and get serious about plea bargaining.

The young man in the lead shined his beam first in Mendoza's face, then Nick's. "Wallets, watches, money clips, phones, whatever you got on you. Turn out your pockets, now."

Nick stuffed his hand into right pants pocket. They could have his thin money clip, they could have his wallet. Hell, they could have his father's broken Rolex. None of it was going to help Nick locate his daughter.

But from his periphery, Nick could see that Mendoza hadn't moved. Nick thought of the Glock in Mendoza's jacket and sighed inwardly, wondering whether these young men were armed, too. Their swagger said yes, but young men with gang experience were often superb at bluffing.

"What kind of shit is this, huh?" Mendoza said to the leader. "What the fuck do you guys think you're doing? The city is burning. People are dying all around us. And you're out here robbing? What kind of person does that make you?"

"It's gonna make me a rich motherfucker, old man, that's what it's gonna make me."

The others laughed with him.

Then he turned serious again. "So, you two Wall Street chumps better start digging in your pockets and coughing up the cash before you're just another statistic of this apocalypse, you feel me?"

Mendoza stared into the leader's eyes. "Do I look Wall Street to you?" he said in a low, gravelly voice. "Because I'm not Wall Street, you piece of shit. I grew up on the South Side of the Bronx. I was putting caps in punk asses like you since you were in diapers. So I'm going to give you five seconds to back the fuck off or I'm going to kill two of you and let the other three run off. Do *you* feel *me?*"

The leader turned to his crew with a wide smile. "You hear this suit? Thinks he's a fucking outlaw and shi—"

Mendoza reached into his jacket and pulled out his Glock and smashed the leader in the nose with its butt before he could turn back around. The teenager's nose cracked under the blow and bright red blood spewed from both nostrils as though a dam had broken. He immediately dropped to his knees and pitched forward.

Mendoza turned the gun on the others. "Which one of you badasses is next, huh? Which one of you really wants what we've got in our pockets? Wants it so bad that he's willing to die for it?"

16

Jasper Howard, maintenance supervisor for the Indian Point Energy Center, a name that conveniently left out the word "nuclear," covered one ear against the blare of sirens meant to warn people up to ten miles away while holding a two-way radio up to his other.

"Say again, Control. Open which gate?" Jasper shook his head while he waited for a reply.

Oh, boy. It finally happened. He glanced up at a long section of the perimeter chain-link, razor-topped fence that had been twisted to the dirt during the quake.

And today of all days.

Less than four hours ago, the power facility's management had welcomed an inspection team from the U.S. Nuclear Regulatory Committee. Constructed in the mid-1970s to service New York City and surrounding communities, Indian Point's reactors had reached the end of their original operating licenses. Opposition to the plant's continued operation ran high, including from the governor of New York himself. Safety violations in the previous decades were numerous, after all, and in fact the installation was once bestowed the dubious distinction of "America's Worst Nuclear Power Plant" by a national magazine. Furthermore, New York City needed another potential terrorist target like it needed a hole in its collective head. But with profits to be generated and a power-hungry metropolis to feed at the same time as public sentiment turned against CO_2-generating fossil fuels, the facility's owners had filed for a controversial license extension that would permit it to operate for the next twenty years.

Today's NRC team had come with an eye toward granting that extension, protestors be damned, provided The Point could pass a newer, more rigorous inspection.

"—said Gate Five damn it, now!"

Jasper shook himself from his reverie. The nagging fear he'd endured throughout his seventeen-year career at the plant—*earthquake*!—had finally reared its dreadful, shaky head. How many times had he fielded the same basic question from loved ones, friends, even strangers? He flashed on the day seventeen years ago when he told his parents he'd gotten a job as a maintenance worker at Indian Point. The opportunity had come to him following a long stretch of unemployment, and he'd jumped at the chance, crossing his fingers that the pot he'd smoked five months before wouldn't be revealed in some fancy new drug screening, or that any one of an assortment of youthful lapses of judgment wouldn't make themselves known to the background checkers. But a few weeks after he'd applied, the call came. A bored-sounding HR person informed him that he was being offered the position and if he still wanted it he'd need to come to the office headquarters in White Plains for processing. He'd told no one about any of it until he actually started working the job, out of fear of jinxing his luck or being told he was wasting his time even to bother, or that a call would come any day to say, "We're sorry, Mr. Howard, but an item in your background screen . . ."

And after all that, when he'd finally told his parents, they responded with, *Jasper, that's . . . It's great, but is it safe? What if there's an earthquake?*

And so began a conversation he would have in one form or another every few months with somebody or another for the next seventeen years. Jasper: *It's New York, there aren't a lot of earthquakes here, but they build to code for up to a 6.1 anyway. . . .* Them: *But they do happen, right?* Jasper: *The last significant one was in 1884.* Them: *Oh, well, then we're due for another!*

If that wasn't enough, after only a few years on the job he began to encounter a new, more bitter flavor of The Conversation, one that to him seemed pretty much the same, but with a trendier buzzword: *Terrorism.* Them: *Don't you worry about working at a terrorist target?* Jasper: *Sure, it's a concern, but we're prepared. There's a National Guard station a mile from us. Other security measures I can't tell you about.* Them: *They tried to fly one of the 9/11 planes into Indian Point.* Jasper: *It flew nearby but at no time did it actually approach. We're just one of many possible targets. . . .*

But truth be told, in the dark of night, in his private thoughts, there were things that most people didn't know and would rather not know that gave him pause. Things like the fact that an East Coast earthquake affects a wider area more intensely than does one of equal magnitude in the west. He certainly wasn't a scientist, but knew it had something to do with how the fault lines connected with one another and how deep they ran. Not to mention, this wasn't the West with its vast expanses of open desert. Los Angeles County had, what—eight million people? The Point serviced more than twenty-two million souls less than an hour's drive away. These were the kinds of tidbits Jasper did his best to keep out of The Conversation.

But they were on his mind now. The Point, with its redundant systems and elaborate safety nets, had access to a better flow of information than did the average New Yorker. They had satellite phone links, even ham radio if those failed. So they knew within a few (terrifying, to be sure) seconds that this was an earthquake, and not a terror attack. He hadn't heard a Richter number yet. He knew that 5.0 was the largest recorded earthquake in history for the New York region. What was this—a 5.0? 5.5? The shaking had been petrifying, throwing him to the ground. Higher than the plant's rating of 6.1? From what little he'd been able to get out of the reactor techs so far, the damage was containable; they'd shut down the reactors according to protocol and managed to extinguish a number of spot fires. But what had this latest aftershock done? Would there be more?

Looking down to the Hudson River, the view looked pretty much the same to Jasper. But there were a few trees toppled on the far bank, and . . . what was that? He squinted through a haze of light smoke. An eighteen-wheel tractor trailer that had nearly slid into the water. And on the grounds of The Point, while there were no deaths yet that he knew of, there had been more than a few broken bones and gashes requiring stitches. Most of the buildings were still standing, but they were definitely compromised. Procedures called for a strict facility lockdown to prevent breaches of access pending evaluation.

And now they wanted him to *open* a gate? But orders were orders, and as soon as he pressed Talk on his radio to say the words, "Copy that, opening five," he thought he understood. He trotted to the perimeter fence, past two of his workers already on scene at the tangle of toppled razor wire, and when he saw the black SUV driving up to Gate 5, he was sure he understood.

The NRC people wanted out. Or at least some of them did. With the tinted windows he couldn't see how many people were inside, not that it was any of his official business. Though he had a nice title, in reality he wasn't much more than a glorified groundskeeper. He was the facilities guy. He was the guy in charge of fixing anything that wasn't related to the actual power-generation equipment like the reactors. The eggheads handled that stuff while he dealt with routine things like maintaining the vehicle fleet, tree trimming, fixing water pipes in the kitchens, repairing broken windows, and scheduling everybody to get all that done. After this, he'd be assigning overtime shifts for months.

Jasper punched a keypad on the gate post and frowned when the backlit buttons remained dark. Of course, power was out but they had backup generators. If those were also down . . . well, he didn't know exactly what that meant but in all his years here he'd never seen it happen before so it couldn't be good. He searched through his hefty ring of keys and found the one that opened a lockbox on the gate so that it could be opened manually. One of his guys came over to help him push it aside, and they forced it open while the SUV idled. No sooner did it open the width of the SUV, then the government vehicle shot through the opening, tires spitting gravel as they departed.

"Leaving so soon?" Jasper joked to his employee. But the man wasn't laughing as he slipped through the gate on foot.

"Hey, where are you going?"

"Sorry, Jasper. I hope it's okay, but . . . I gotta go, man." He spun on a heel and ran.

Jasper let go of the gate and breathed a heavy sigh. Could he blame him? Could an hourly worker be expected to risk his life? He wondered how many others had jumped ship while he was working. He looked around the grounds and saw a few men—mostly his, which wasn't all that unusual. Most of the scientists and engineers would be inside the reactor control buildings.

Just how bad were things? The sirens still blared, alerting nearby residents that they should evacuate. But that was just a precaution. *Right?* A mandatory goodwill action to placate the NRC and not-in-my-backyard neighbors alike. If he was in danger here at the plant, reactor management would tell him. *Right?* He knew that the shutdown procedure was complex and sometimes failed in drills, that the plant had suffered incidents and accidents related to it in the past. Had it not gone smoothly now?

He switched radio channels and keyed the transmitter. "Reactor Two, this is Perimeter, requesting status, copy?" He repeated himself two more times before a gruff male voice answered.

"What is it, Jasper?"

"Give it to me straight. This earthquake. How bad was it?"

A lengthy pause while Jasper heard the sound of breaking glass in the distance, followed by radio static. Then the reply.

"Good news is we got through on the sat-phone half an hour ago and Caltech is saying we had a *seven-point-one* shaker, only six miles deep in the Ramapo fault not ten miles from here."

"So we're near the epicenter?"

"We damn near *are* the epicenter. We fared pretty well if you ask me. Still got four walls around us down here. I heard the city's in pretty awful shape."

Jasper swallowed hard. "And the bad news?"

"The spent fuel pools are heating up because the cooling units were damaged. Short version: If the water boils away, the fuel rods are exposed to air and can set on fire. Besides that, there are some cracks in the pool structures—we're not sure how extensive those are yet."

"Jesus." Jasper closed his eyes as he pictured the concrete containment structures closer to the river's edge that held the highly radioactive cooling water after it passed through the reactors. The monumental gravity of the situation took hold for him. If this ultra-toxic wastewater was to be released into the Hudson, or into the air, or both . . . He didn't even want to think about it.

"The situation is holding for now, Jasper. Don't repeat any

of this to anyone. But just between you and me, I'm not sure we can handle another aftershock."

Jasper thought about his wife, his parents, his grown kids, one of whom lived in the city.

"Sam, be straight with me. Should I get out of here?" He knew Sam was a reactor tech—an engineer, basically, with a degree in physics, though not one of the superstar geeks who designed this place. Still, he knew what was happening with the radioactivity, and he was over there in close proximity to it. Except he was also wearing all kinds of protective gear. He'd seen him once or twice in there and could picture him now, in one of those funny blue suits with the face shield and the gloves, behind the yard-thick lead walls.

Sam lowered his voice, even though Jasper could hear chaos emanating from his end—some shouting, maybe an argument—a weird klaxon alarm, different from the evac sirens. "I would if I were you, Jasper. We're only still here because we can stop a meltdown, save millions of people's lives. But if we do melt down, unless you're more than a hundred miles away, it's not going to matter. And from what little news reports I've had a chance to hear, driving a hundred miles away right now may not even be an option."

17

Nick and Mendoza continued up Sixth Avenue, past Washington Square Park and New York University on their right, Sheridan Square and the Jefferson Market Courthouse on their left. Mendoza had several times suggested turning west, at Bleeker Street, at Waverly Place, and again at Greenwich Avenue. But each time Nick replied, "Let's keep going. We can cross over to the west side once we get farther north."

Now they were approaching Fourteenth Street, the next logical place to turn left. Only Nick wasn't ready. He wasn't ready to see that the devastation had reached the west side. Wasn't ready to find a collapsed Port Authority Building, a flattened Chelsea Hotel. Continuing along Sixth Avenue, also known as the Avenue of the Americas, shielded him from such sights, and he was tempted to suggest they follow it all the way past Bryant Park and the New York Public Library, to Forty-second Street before finally hooking a left and walking through the Theater District and past Times Square to Eighth Avenue.

When they finally reached Fourteenth Street, all of Nick's deliberations didn't matter. At the intersection of Fourteenth and Sixth Avenue, they found a hulking crater that reminded Nick of the one he and Sara climbed during their honeymoon in Honolulu. Diamond Head was its name. Only Diamond Head wasn't situated in the dead center of a major metropolis. And Diamond Head had been formed some 200,000 years ago. This crater at Fourteenth and Sixth had only been here since around lunchtime today.

"Christ," Mendoza said, crossing himself again. "How the hell do you think something like that happens? It looks like a goddamn asteroid hit the city."

For a moment, Nick considered the possibility. But no, there were multiple tremors, which would have meant multiple asteroids striking New York City all at once. And NASA was tracking these so-called Near-Earth Objects anyway, right? What hit today was a quake. A magnitude 7.1 if the postal worker (and amateur geologist) they'd spoken to was correct. This crater had to have formed as a result of an explosion beneath the surface of the street.

Nick glanced around the intersection. The full moon was providing just enough light for him to see that whatever had caused the crater had also blown the tops off several buildings to the east and west. Whatever it was had also shredded Fourteenth Street in the direction of Seventh Avenue.

"We can't get past this," Mendoza said. "What do we do? Backtrack?"

Nick shook his head. "I'd prefer not to, if we can avoid it. After all the walking we've done, moving south even for a street or two would probably break my spirit beyond repair." He pointed to the right. "There. We can get around it. Turn up Fifth Avenue and cross over to the west side at the next major hub, which would be Twenty-third Street."

Mendoza said nothing, for which Nick was grateful. They were about to go out of their way solely because Nick had refused to turn west earlier for no apparent logical or rational reason.

"Let's do it, then," Mendoza finally said.

They walked one long city block, then turned north onto Fifth Avenue. Nick removed the tie from his forehead and stuffed it into his jacket pocket. He was grateful that he'd held on to the suit jacket. Even though he was sweating from exertion, he felt a chill throughout his entire body, and his arms were experiencing the worst of it.

As they crossed the next intersection, Nick caught Mendoza staring at the street sign on the opposite corner. *East* Fifteenth Street, it read. It didn't mean anything, of course. Had they made a quick left they'd have been back on *West* Fifteenth Street. But Nick imagined that the word was having as much of a psychological impact on Mendoza as the thought of backtracking had had on Nick ten minutes earlier.

They walked silently. Past Sixteenth and Seventeenth and Eighteenth and Nineteenth Streets. The farther they got uptown, the more survivors they saw. Mobs of them, in fact. Not because there was less devastation, Nick knew, but because there had simply been more people north of Houston Street than south of Houston when the tremors hit.

Nick struggled to keep up as Mendoza hurried his steps past Twentieth Street and Twenty-first Street. Nick's left leg screamed out in pain, but there was nothing he could do it for it just then. He favored his right, but it didn't seem to be doing a hell of a lot of good.

The Flatiron Building came into view. Nick instantly thought of its architect, Daniel Burnham. He and Lauren had both recently read Erik Larson's *The Devil in the White City*, a nonfiction narrative about 1893's Chicago World's Fair, of which Daniel Burnham had been the chief architect. While Burnham oversaw the design and construction and maintenance of the World's Columbian Exposition, a doctor named Henry Howard Holmes was engaged in the murder and mutilation of at least two dozen victims, many of them young women, just a few short blocks away.

When it was completed in 1902, the Flatiron Building was the tallest in the world.

Twelve years ago the Twin Towers held that honor, Nick thought as a lump rose in his throat. *At least they did until those religious fundamentalists flew airplanes into them.*

The building at 175 Fifth Avenue had earned the name Flatiron because of its odd triangular shape, but some had referred to the building as Burnham's folly, because experts predicted that the winds along Twenty-third Street would knock the unusual structure over; it was just a matter of time. A century and some later, Burnham's Flatiron Building was still standing. It even appeared to have withstood the quake.

"Do you feel that?" Mendoza said.

Nick turned. "I don't feel anything."

Mendoza stared down at his feet. "I think the trains are running again. Which line is directly below us? The N and R or the 4, 5, and 6?"

Nick tried to picture one of the ubiquitous subway maps that could be found underground. He saw a green line and a yellow line splitting at Fourteenth Street, Union Square. The green line—the 4, 5, and 6—continued north along Lexington all the way to the Upper East Side and into the Bronx with a stop at Yankee Stadium. The yellow line—the N and R—curved west along Broadway and therefore would run under the Flatiron at Twenty-third Street and Fifth Avenue.

Nick said, "It would be the N and—"

Before he could finish his sentence he felt the sensation that Mendoza was referring to, only it was much stronger. So much stronger that it nearly knocked him to the blacktop.

Screams suddenly filled the air all around them.

The earth began to shake and all Nick could think was: *No, please. No. No, not again.*

18

Nick dropped back, pulling Mendoza along with him. He pointed up at the Flatiron Building as windows burst on nearly every floor. The building itself swayed like a small tree in the wind, and Nick thought it was just a matter of time before it toppled.

As he and Mendoza broke into a run, Nick searched for cover but no place looked safe. All of those drills he'd been forced to go through as a child in California were useless right now. There were no desks to duck under, no thick door-frames to stand between. All they could do was run down the middle of the street and hope to avoid the falling debris.

Mendoza stumbled and fell to the pavement. Nick stopped short, barely maintaining his balance as the street bucked beneath his feet. He ran back to Mendoza and helped him up. As he did, he watched over Mendoza's shoulder as the Flat-iron Building tipped like the leaning tower of Pisa. Only this tower was tipping over in their direction and it wasn't going to stand much longer.

Nick tried to get Mendoza to run with him, but the agent

pushed him and shouted, "I *can't*. I twisted my ankle. You keep going. I'll do my best to follow!"

Nick gazed up at the Flatiron Building and tried to gauge its distance from them. It was difficult to tell but he felt certain they were still in the building's shadow. So he lowered his head, grabbed Mendoza around the waist, and grunting, lifted the larger man onto his shoulder with all his strength.

Nick's knees threatened to collapse beneath him as he turned and began at a much slower pace down the street, away from the Flatiron. Behind him he could hear those horrible sounds—that shrieking of steel, the crumbling of concrete— and he knew they might not survive the next sixty seconds.

Back at the Federal Courthouse at 500 Pearl, the defense lawyer Kermit Jansing finally crawled free of the rubble he'd been digging through for hours. He had no clue as to where he was in the building, or even if the building still stood. The last thing he remembered was running into the lockup with two federal marshals, his assistant Courtney trailing just behind him. From the lockup they'd rushed down a set of concrete stairs and pushed through a door on what may have been the first floor. That was all he could recall; after that, nothing but blackness. His only comfort now was that he was no longer pinned under immense pieces of wood and steel and concrete, and gazing up, he could even see a sliver of the night sky.

I made it, he thought.

With a great deal of pain in seemingly every part of his body, he attempted to lift himself off the ground, but cried out the moment he tried to put weight on his right leg. He looked down, gently wiped off some of the thick dust that covered him head to toe, and grimaced at the sight of his knee. The shape was grotesque; clearly his kneecap had been dislocated.

With another yelp, he exhaled and prepared to fall to the ground.

But he suddenly felt a pair of strong arms around his waist, and heard a gentle voice in his ear. "It's all right, counselor," the voice said. "I'm just going to set you down a few yards away where it's safer."

As the man lifted him off the ground and carried him over to a spot clear of debris, Jansing tried to get a look at his face. It was far too dark, but in the sliver of starlight he could tell that the man was dressed in a bloodied white short-sleeve shirt and dark pants. Jansing could make out patches on the man's arms and knew instantly that he was a court officer.

"Thank you," Jansing mumbled. "Thank you, thank you."

The court officer set Jansing down. Jansing blinked several times, wiped dust from his eyes, but it only caused them to burn more.

"Here, counselor," the court officer said, lowering Jansing's hands and placing what felt like a wet towel over the lawyer's eyes.

"What's happened?" Jansing rasped, surprised at the weakness in his own usually powerful, booming courtroom voice.

"Earthquake, we think," the court officer said.

We? Jansing quickly removed the towel from his eyes and blinked rapidly searching for other survivors. When his eyes finally began cooperating, he stared at a shape not far off on top of a pile of rubble.

"Courtney?" he said.

The court officer pulled a small Maglite from his pocket. He twisted the front of the flashlight and a narrow beam appeared. He shone it in the direction in which Jansing had been looking.

"Dear God." Jansing could make out her long, flowing blond hair, her porcelain skin. He tried to move toward her but the court officer gently held him back.

"I'm sorry, counselor. We did all we could but your assistant didn't make it."

Jansing immediately felt tears well in his eyes and a powerful pang of grief in his chest.

The poor girl, he thought. *She was only a kid. So enthusiastic about the law, so excited to become a lawyer.*

Jansing hung his head. When would this nightmare finally be over?

Just as he thought it, an intense rumbling sound emanated from below.

When the Flatiron Building finally toppled, Nick and Mendoza were clear of its shadow. As the ground shook, Nick finally collapsed in the street. With Mendoza lying next to him he braced himself as a cold wind of dust and debris washed over them like angry surf.

Nick held his breath as long as he could, but when he finally inhaled he knew no matter what happened in the next twenty-four hours, his lungs would never recover from what he breathed in during this crisis.

After a minute the ground calmed again.

We have to keep moving, he thought. Waiting for the dust to settle, so to speak, was impossible. They would be there for weeks, maybe months or more. Against the cold wind, he lifted himself up. Leaning over, he placed Mendoza's arm around his shoulder and lifted the agent to his feet.

"Leave me here," Mendoza wheezed.

"The hell I will."

"Nick, you've got no choice."

"There's always a choice."

Nick tightened his grip on Mendoza's forearm and held it over his shoulder.

Together they trudged west toward Sixth Avenue, then past it to Seventh, where they turned right and continued true north.

19

After excruciatingly slow progress, navigating debris heaps and dodging potholes, on Seventh Avenue, Nick and Mendoza reached a snarl of toppled infrastructure two blocks north. A power pole, a lamppost, a telephone booth (Nick wondered if maybe this quake would be the end of phone booths in the city once and for all), and a bus stop bench were among the objects Nick recognized in the pileup. As he was plotting a way around the obstacles, he noticed a bicycle wheel, still spinning, protruding from the mess.

"Hold on." Nick removed Mendoza's arm from around his shoulder and eased the agent away, taking care that Mendoza had his balance on his good ankle before letting him go. "Maybe we can use this."

Nick went to the bike, which was pinned between the phone booth and the bus bench. He squatted to look deeper into the destruction and that's when he saw the body.

"Christ!" Nick recoiled, knocking his head into a toppled telephone pole still festooned with flyers for nightclubs that no longer had an audience, if they still existed at all.

The city's gone, he thought. *This town will never be the same.*

The bike's rider was still on the bike, helmet on his perfectly intact head; even his glasses were still in place. But his body was crushed beyond all hope of repair, nothing more than a bloody pressing of intestines and gore. A messenger bag lay pinned beneath the bicycle. Nick guessed that this man was—used to be—one of Manhattan's omnipresent bike messengers who couriered documents all over town.

This town will never be the same, he thought again.

He blocked out his inner voice and walked back over to Mendoza.

"Maybe if we ride the bike it'll be easier going. I can pedal. Think you can balance on the handlebars?"

Mendoza wiped his brow before returning Nick's gaze. Then he looked back toward the crumpled Flatiron, then to his grime-caked shoes. "Just take it, Nick. Take it and go to your daughter."

"I was kidding, Frank. You can ride and I'll push. This way you can keep your weight off that ankle."

Mendoza shook his head. "The bike will slow us down even more. You need to keep moving, Nick. I'm not going hold you back any longer."

"I can't just leave you here. I won't."

Mendoza appeared to be lost in thought.

"Frank, what is it?"

Mendoza finally held Nick's stare. "I can't allow you to continue helping me like this, Nick. You're a good guy who needs to get to his little girl. I can't . . ." He sputtered to a halt, watching what must have amounted to thousands of reams of paper fluttering by on ground level and in the air. "I can't let you do this."

Nick threw up his hands and glanced north on Seventh Avenue. "Spit it out, Frank. We're on a mission, remember?"

Nick began to wonder if the stress had become too great for the agent.

Just then the ground vibrated with another temblor, smaller than the last but still strong enough to make Mendoza cry out in pain as the ground shifted beneath his turned ankle.

Once the tremors faded, Mendoza coughed once before speaking and said, "Look, Nick, there's something I've got to get off my chest. In case one or both of us doesn't make it through this."

"Okay. Make it quick."

Mendoza reached out and gripped Nick's shoulder. "You remember the Boneta case?"

Nick frowned and imparted a sarcastic inflection to his response. "No, it must have slipped my mind. Why don't you refresh my memory. Of course, I remember it; it turned into the biggest debacle of my career. What gives?"

Nick's memories of the case were painful enough to pierce even his sense of urgency to reach his daughter. For a few whirlwind seconds Nick forgot about the ruins of Seventh Avenue and the city full of hurt through which they'd trod in order to reach their loved ones, and he remembered. . . .

Luis Boneta. A Puerto Rican murder defendant Nick had prosecuted seven years earlier. Boneta was a Class-A scumbag who had been committing atrocities in four of the city's five boroughs for nearly a decade. Murders, rapes, violent robberies. Sometimes he acted alone; other times he directed a loosely organized network of mercenary-like thugs. Some of the investigators on the case claimed he had a fetish for sadism, because it seemed like he inflicted more and graver injuries than were necessary to commit his crimes. One time he'd even put on a mask and raped the wife of a small-time drug dealer who'd been late paying him, while his associates held the dealer down, filmed it, and posted the footage to a popular online video sharing service. It was viewed millions of times in the short duration it remained live before being removed.

These and other twisted exploits eventually made Boneta a high-profile target for not only the NYPD, but the FBI. Boneta was an agile chameleon, though, with many aliases, disguises, evasion techniques, and well thought-out contingency plans, and for a time it seemed he would make a mockery of any law enforcement entity that crossed his path. But his slipup came, as they often do, for the most mundane of reasons.

FBI agents were alerted to a Manhattan residential address from a grade school application for one of Boneta's daughters. Turned out his ex-wife had used the address to try to get her child into a better school district. She'd been under surveillance for a long time running and agents were privy to her attempt to enroll her daughter into a highly regarded school by providing an address within that district rather than that of her own Brooklyn duplex. A warrant was issued for the address and federal agents raided it several days later at four a.m. on a Monday to find Luis Boneta sound asleep in a four-poster bed next to a coked-up male whore. Both men were arrested; the prostitute was ultimately released in exchange for additional information on Boneta.

Nick was assigned the case for the U.S. government. His preparation and performance in the courtroom was second-to-none (except perhaps his opening statement for Alivi which he didn't get to finish), and Boneta was convicted and later handed a twenty-five year sentence.

Flash forward a year and a half and Boneta was back in court after his attorney—Kermit Jansing, in fact—had filed a motion for a new trial based on the allegation that Boneta's confession had been coerced.

Nick had put up a valiant fight and the court of public opinion remained firmly on his side, but in the end the "blatant misconduct of one or more bureau agents" noted by the Court of Appeals proved insurmountable, and Boneta was released. It disgusted Nick to no end that all of his hard work—the bleary-eyed string of one-hundred-hour work weeks he'd put into nailing that subhuman monster—had come to naught. And worst of all, to add insult to grievous injury, not even a full year had elapsed before Boneta killed again. And this time it hit home, and hit home hard. The victim was an innocent bystander, and an old friend of Nick's—a law school colleague who'd been caught in the cross-fire of one of Boneta's brazen newsstand drive-bys—wrong place, wrong time, wrong, wrong, wrong.

Mendoza's voice pulled him back to the present. "So then you remember why his conviction was overturned?"

"The Court of Appeals threw out his confession. Some asshole—apparently outside the view of the interrogating officers—worked him over for forty minutes before he gave his statement."

Mendoza swallowed, said in a low voice, "That asshole was me, Nick. I was the agent who went into that interrogation room. I never had the balls to tell you. I . . ."

The sound of indeterminate cries for help echoed across the wreckage of the neighborhood during the silence that followed.

Finally, Nick spoke, voice tense. "*Why* are you telling me this *now*?"

Mendoza shook his head, stammered a few syllables of something unintelligible.

"*Why*, Frank?"

"I told you, I just . . . In case we don't make it . . . It's something I've always meant to tell you."

Nick flashed on all the times he'd cursed aloud whoever the hell it was who had worked Boneta over. He'd even called in a few favors with some of the specialists he was on good terms with at the bureau to try to find out who'd been responsible, but the feds refused to give up one of their own, even informally.

Nick felt his temper rising along with the plume of black smoke that issued from what used to be the Flatiron. He reached out with both hands and grabbed Mendoza by what was left of the agent's lapels.

"For the last seven years you couldn't find the time to tell me? Just too busy, I guess?" He gently shoved his former colleague backwards and the man teetered on his bad ankle.

Mendoza held up his hands in a gesture of surrender but remained silent.

Nick shook his own head violently, as if clearing a thought he didn't wish to act on.

"We'll talk about this later, Frank. But this . . ." He waved an arm at the grim rubble scape. "This doesn't change anything tonight."

"I know that."

Nick appraised Mendoza's condition, lingering on his wobbly ankle. He didn't want his anger clouding his judgment in the hours that followed, and being near Mendoza would ensure that he remained furious.

"You're not far from the hospital," Nick said. "Maybe you're right. Maybe this is where we part ways."

Nick bent down and extracted the bike from the dead messenger. He righted it, wiped the blood from the seat with his shirttail and hopped on. He swerved at first over an uneven mound of displaced roadbed, and then settled into an uneasy rhythm north, toward Columbia, toward the only person on this earth he trusted not to lie to him, even though he had lied to her (*this city is safe*), toward Lauren.

20

The voice was faint but Lauren Dykstra was sure she wasn't imagining things. It was Ray's voice, the last voice she'd heard before the world came tumbling down on top of her. Ray's voice. And he was calling her name.

"I'm *here*," Lauren called back. But her voice was weak and thin and she doubted he could hear her. "I'm *here! Please help me!*"

She listened for a reply but none came.

Maybe Ray went to get help, she thought. The bookcase was too large and heavy for any one man to move by himself, and Ray Knowles wasn't exactly bursting through his shirt with rippling muscles. He was soft, bookish, and she liked that about him. His greatest strength was probably his mind; he'd figure out what to do to rescue her.

Lauren loved smart men. Smart men like her father. But her father wasn't just smart, he was tough, too. He used to tell her about his days on California's beaches, surfing, playing football with friends, even boxing. To this day he kept his body in tremendous shape, even though no one special got to see it.

"Why do you bother?" she asked him one day when she found him on the floor of his bedroom strenuously doing push-ups.

"What do you mean?"

"Why do you bother keeping your body in such great shape?"

"Well," he said, "I'd like to live a long, healthy life, if that's what you mean."

"You *know* that's not what I'm talking about. You don't have to build muscle to stay healthy. You can do cardio and—"

"Lauren, honey, what's this all about?"

She knew her tone had become angry. "I just don't understand why you want to be ripped, yet you refuse to go out on dates."

"I do this for myself, Lauren, not for anyone else."

She took a step back from the doorway, debating whether she should shut her mouth or come right out and say it: "*Are you planning on never having sex again for as long as you live?*"

She'd decided to shut her mouth.

And days later what her father said started to make sense to her. Who should he have been trying to impress? What a burden it was, keeping away from sweets, burning as many calories as possible every day so that she could fit into her size zero jeans. She began to wish she didn't care so much about what guys thought of the way she looked. But it was impossible in today's society, right? Just look around Times Square with its billboards covered with super-skinny supermodels. Everything in New York City seemed to scream sex, sex, sex.

Of course, she didn't expect California to be any different. If anything, from what she knew of the Golden State, especially LA, it would be worse.

Lauren found herself drifting off again. She bit down hard on her tongue to wake herself up. If she fell asleep (lost consciousness), it could be permanent. Or she could miss Ray calling out to her again.

Ray.

Ray of sunshine.

What she wouldn't give to see either right now.

In the intensive care unit at St. Luke's-Roosevelt Medical Center, Jana Mendoza hurried from patient to patient, watching monitors, checking and rechecking vitals, while trying to comfort and reassure not only her staff but the few frightened family members who had been visiting their loved ones when the first tremor struck. The hospital was hot and sticky. The generator was functioning as it was supposed to, but it only provided power to essential, lifesaving systems. There was no air-conditioning. Most of the lights were off to help conserve generator power and now that it was full dark, it was near impossible for Jana to read her watch when manually calculating her patients' heart rates. Worst of all, there seemed to be no end in sight, and not a single doctor, not a single nurse or administrator, could tell her definitively how long the generator's power would last.

Jana stood in the doorframe of Mr. Radcliffe's room and watched orderlies running up and down the halls, delivering meds and IV bags, as fast as their legs could carry them. She was impressed with how her unit was performing under such grueling conditions, but she feared that in the end, it would all be for nothing. If help didn't arrive before the generator gave out, every patient in the intensive care unit would expire. Machines, after all, were the only things keeping her patients alive.

By now, Jana was mostly used to the stench but every so often she'd be subjected to a fresh blast—a foul wave of excrement, urine, and rotting flesh. Her eyes watered and she wiped away the tears, along with the pouring sweat, and tried to clear her mind, if only for a moment.

Once she did, her husband, Francisco, took front and center stage in her head. He'd been downtown when the first tremors struck, and though she'd received no conclusive news about the damage to lower Manhattan, she'd heard plenty of rumors that the courthouses had been reduced to rubble.

"*Please*, Jana, you've got to let me *leave*. I *need* to get home to my *son*."

Jana turned, trying futilely to keep the angry expression off of her face. It had been like this for hours, Camille running up to her in a fresh state of panic, begging, pleading, threatening that she be allowed to leave the hospital for her home in Jamaica, Queens.

Jana must have said it a dozen times, but she said it once more. "Camille, you *need* to understand. I can't *allow* you to leave and even if I could, I wouldn't because we're short-staffed and the needs of the patients of this hospital have to come before our own needs. And you've heard it from every person who's walked into this hospital—there's *nowhere* to go. The devastation in this area is complete. You're safer in here than you would be anywhere else."

And it was true. St. Luke's-Roosevelt was still standing. Other hospitals, she'd heard over and over, had collapsed.

"But you don't *understand*," Camille cried. "My son is *alone*. I don't *know* where his father is, and his grandparents live all the way up in Yonkers. I've got to get to him before something happens to—"

Jana pointed a finger at her, something she couldn't remember ever doing before to a member of her staff. "Camille, don't you *dare* tell me what I do and don't understand. Every doctor, nurse, and orderly on this floor is in the same exact predicament as us. Your son is sixteen years old and he's probably safer in Queens than he would be in any other borough, especially Manhattan. You need to settle yourself down—"

"You don't fucking *understand*, Jana. You don't *have* kids. You don't *care* about anyone the way parents care for their children."

At that, Jana slapped her in the face. Not hard, but enough to freeze everyone in the hallway. Enough to shut Camille up, maybe even calm her some.

"I'm sorry," Jana said, "but you need to *stop*. Do *not* presume to know *who* I love or *how much* I love them. I have a husband out there who means the world to me. And if he's dead . . ."

Jana couldn't continue. Something had caught in her throat and for a moment she thought she might choke on it.

"If he's dead . . ." she finally started again, tears streaming down her face, mixing with the puddles of sweat. "If he's dead . . ."

Dr. Kelly Lambert stepped between her and Camille and laid a gentle hand on each of their chests. "It's okay, ladies," Dr. Lambert said. "Everything's going to be all right."

Dr. Lambert's tone, usually strong and confident, was this time anything but, and it made Jana sink into a despair she was completely unfamiliar with. She looked into the doctor's face and saw nothing to reassure her. Suddenly she felt sure that Francisco was dead. And that help wouldn't arrive before the generator gave out.

Before long, she thought, every patient on this floor would be dead. And for the rest of them, there may never be a way out.

Despite all her efforts, Lauren did finally doze off. And while she was unconscious, she dreamed of her mother. Except for her image, Lauren's mother felt like a stranger. A stranger who still somehow seemed filled with love and kindness and understanding. In the dream, her mom sang, but

Lauren didn't know the song. She spoke, but Lauren couldn't make out the words.

Once in a while, over the next couple hours, Lauren would breach the surface of consciousness and find herself still enveloped in blackness. She'd then fall immediately back to sleep as though dragged under by a stone.

Each time after that first, Lauren knew she was dreaming. But she couldn't control what she said or what she did. It was like watching a movie starring herself, but a movie she knew she'd never acted in.

When she opened her eyes again, she couldn't move. Not just her legs; now she couldn't wriggle her toes. Couldn't move her arms or control her hands. Couldn't so much as turn her neck. She was paralyzed and her fear took on new meaning.

I'm still dreaming, she thought.

And she was. Yet it was of little comfort. Because when she did finally wake she knew she'd still be pinned under the bookcase. She'd be able to wriggle her toes, move her arms, and control her neck, but a hell of a lot of good it would do her, so long as she was buried alive.

Her father wasn't coming.

Ray had no doubt given up, thinking she was dead.

Caroline, the admissions director, had been killed. By one of the blasts or shots from a terrorist's gun. It didn't matter which. Lauren was simply sure she was gone.

Life had come down to these final dark hours of paralysis and fever dreams. Lauren would never again see the sky. She'd never again be held in her father's arms. She'd never know romantic love, never experience sex in an actual bed. All those hours she spent studying, all those nights she'd been consumed in her schoolwork, they'd all be for nothing. Because nothing came after this; of that she was sure.

When she breached the surface of consciousness again, the most awful pain was her thirst. Her head was dizzy with hunger, her stomach now rumbling louder than the slowing beat of her heart.

"Don't be frightened," her father's voice said. *"I'm on my way. Just hang in there as long as you possibly can. You're going to be fine. You're going to live a long and happy life. Years from now this will be nothing but a bad memory."*

"Dad," Lauren whispered aloud.

Then she fell quiet.

21

Marshal Darren Shaw had remained with his friend and colleague Randy Trocano until Randy's final breath. After covering Randy's face with a handkerchief he'd found in Randy's pocket, Shaw had pushed himself off the floor, ready to proceed, ready to locate his prisoner, Feroz Saeed Alivi. But before Shaw could manage two steps, another tremor had struck, this one more ferocious than any of its brothers.

The ceiling had come down in large, concrete chunks, and Shaw had had no choice but to cover himself using Randy's body. He knew now, as he dug through the fresh rubble, that the late Randy Trocano had saved his life. If Shaw made it out of this courthouse alive, he'd have to write a report. And he'd already decided to alter a few facts, one of which being that Randy Trocano was alive when that last tremor struck. Randy had thrown Shaw to the ground, Shaw would write, and then covered his body with his own. As far as the world was concerned, Randy Trocano had died saving Shaw's life.

Shaw reached inside the tunnel he was slowly creating and dug out another large piece of rubble. He crawled deeper into the hole and paused, suddenly sure he'd heard voices.

He was about to call out but then caught himself. What if he called out and the rest of the rubble was removed by someone on the other side, and then Shaw crawled forward, directly into Alivi's knife?

He had to be careful.

Quietly, Shaw continued digging and moving forward. The voices became louder, clearer, but he still couldn't make out what was being said. Both voices were male, of that he was fairly certain. But not knowing *who* was on the other side kept Shaw silent.

Within a few minutes, Shaw thought a final push would get him through. He took a deep breath, mouthed a silent prayer, and went for it.

When he finally emerged Shaw saw only a small man with a miniature Maglite sitting in a corner, sweating, trembling, clearly in terrible pain. Shaw recognized the man immediately; it was Alivi's defense lawyer, Kermit Jansing.

Jansing eyed Shaw as Shaw stood, dusting himself off.

"Counselor?" Shaw said. "Who were you just speaking to?"

"No one," Jansing said. "I was speaking to no one."

Shaw narrowed his eyes. "I *heard* you. Just a few moments ago."

"To m-myself," Jansing said. "I was talking to myself. Trying to keep myself sane in all this madness."

Shaw scanned the area with his eyes and finally pointed to a spot on the far side of the room. "The light," Shaw said, "shine it there."

Slowly, Jansing turned the Maglite in the direction Shaw was pointing. There, slumped against the far wall, was the body of a court officer Shaw knew only as Chuck.

"What happened to him?" Shaw said.

"I don't know," Jansing said rapidly. "How should I know, he was like that when I found him."

Shaw didn't need to approach the body to see that the

blood on Chuck's body was fresh. As fresh as the blood had been on Randy Trocano's.

Shaw's fingers instinctively clenched into fists, his eyes darting from one corner of the room to the next, searching for a spot where Alivi could be hiding.

Behind him, Shaw heard movement and spun just in time to see a pile of rubble open like the maw of a giant beast.

Before Shaw could react, Feroz Saeed Alivi was on him, stabbing him in the gut with what looked to Shaw like a jagged shard of glass.

Kermit Jansing watched in horror as his client attacked one of the U.S. marshals who had escorted him into the court-room some twelve hours earlier. He'd wanted to warn the marshal, wanted to scream the moment the marshal material-ized from the hole. But he was scared, so goddamned scared. Alivi, who had killed the court officer who'd helped Jansing out of the rubble, had moments before threatened his life.

"Make a sound," Alivi had whispered in his ear as they listened to digging from the other side, "and I will stick you like a pig."

Now Jansing looked on as Feroz Saeed Alivi shed his re-ligious robe and began undressing the dead marshal, first removing his jacket, then pulling off his slacks.

Jansing eyed the shard of glass still stuck in the marshal's stomach.

Could I snatch it while Alivi's dressing? he wondered.

No, Jansing was hurt; he could barely move at all, let alone win a footrace. Jansing knew then that he would be entirely at his client's mercy in a few moments.

"We are on the same side, you realize," Jansing tried as the terrorist zipped up his fly. "I stood up for you. I've been working long days and nights this past year in order to save your life."

Alivi looked at him and smiled; Jansing thought it was one of the ugliest things he'd ever seen.

"You are an American," Alivi said.

"*No!*" Jansing cried.

"No?"

"No, I mean . . . I was born here, yes. But I reject America's policy abroad. I reject our interference in the Middle East. I reject our foreign—"

Alivi shook his head. "This, none of you seem to understand. That it is not only your foreign policy that makes your nation so despised. And it is not just Muslims, not just Arabs, who hold you in such contempt. People all around the world are *sick* and *tired* of living under an American economic occupation. Your politicians, they talk of globalization. But what they *mean* is Americanization. Your country will not rest until the entire globe reflects your values."

"I agree c-completely. One hundred percent. Everything you say is true. But I'm not *part* of all that. I've nothing to do with any of it. I represent criminals, for Christ's sake. People who shun the U.S. government. Not the sheep who—"

"*Silence!*" Alivi, now dressed in the U.S. marshal's suit save for the bloodied shirt, took a step toward Jansing. "You are not part of this America, you say? Look at you, Kermit. Look in the mirror and tell me you are not American. How much money did you pay for that suit? How much for those shoes? For those cufflinks? How much, Kermit, did you pay for that house in Morris Plains, New Jersey? Or for the Jaguar you drive to and from the city each day?"

How the hell does he know what I drive? Where I live?

"Oh, yes," Alivi said as though reading the lawyer's mind. "I know everything about you, Kermit Jansing. And I know everything about the attorney who is prosecuting me as well. I know everything about the judge."

Jansing nodded.

"I will let you in on some news, Kermit Jansing. We do

not hate America only for what it does. We hate America for what it *is*."

Alivi bent over and retrieved the shard of glass from the marshal's belly. He raised the shard to his neck and for a moment, Jansing's hope soared; he thought Alivi was going to cut his own throat. Instead, the terrorist put the shard to his beard and began hacking away at it.

When he was done, he looked down at Jansing again, wearing that same insidious smile. "Where was I?" he said.

"You said you don't hate America only for what it does, but for what it *is*."

"Precisely, counselor." He pointed to Jansing's right hand. "Tell me, how much did you pay for that ring on your pinky finger?"

For the first time Jansing wondered whether he could possibly buy his own life from his client. He started to name the price, but was cut off.

"We hate America for what it is," Alivi hissed. "And you, Kermit Jansing, you are the living embodiment of this country."

Alivi took several steps forward, leaned over, and planted the shard of glass in the center of Jansing's chest.

PART THREE
Aftershock

22

Nick Dykstra pedaled the Stradalli Fixxx slowly up the destroyed blacktop of Seventh Avenue. Having long ago befriended the bike messenger who usually delivered his last-minute motions and briefs to defense counsel around the city, he knew he was riding an $800 bike. But what truly disrupted his thoughts was trying to figure out the last time he'd ridden a bicycle on an actual street.

Sure, he'd ridden—if *ridden* was even the right word—stationary bikes at his twenty-four-hour local gym, but that didn't count. And although Nick didn't believe in having a car in the city, he'd never once ridden a bicycle to or from work; it was simply too far. He took subways and, when the circumstances absolutely called for it, taxis.

He hadn't ridden a bicycle as a law student either, not that he recalled. But wait, hadn't he ever ridden with Sara, either before or after they were married? She'd talked about riding bikes once in a while, said it was one of her favorite things about growing up in South Jersey: riding bikes along the boardwalk during the off-season, from Labor Day through Memorial Day. But Nick couldn't recall them ever riding together, and that bothered him, because he knew it was something she'd asked him to do.

So many things with Sara had been left undone. They'd talked often about traveling to Tokyo, about taking a cruise to Alaska, about spending a Christmas in Paris. They'd spoken endlessly about writing a novel together; a novel having nothing at all to do with the law, but something more along the lines of *The Lord of the Rings*, a complete fantasy set in another world. They'd discussed how things would change in their relationship (at least the things that would change for the better) once their daughter, Lauren, went off to college. (And this was when Lauren was only a toddler.) They'd have more alone time together, be able to resume their movie nights, go out to dinner, drink cocktails, and make love until the sun came up.

Surprisingly, Nick hadn't given much thought to what Sara would say about Lauren's choice of colleges. Of course, they had no idea Lauren would be as brilliant a student as she was. Sure, they'd said she would grow up to be a genius—maybe cure cancer, invent the flying car, become the first female president of the United States—but they couldn't have known their daughter would actually have her pick of Ivy League schools like Yale and Harvard and Stanford and Princeton.

Sara and I had always used the words "go away" to college, he thought, and wondered why this had never crossed his mind earlier. Maybe because he didn't want it to. Maybe because then he'd have to admit that if Lauren's mother were still alive, he'd be all for his daughter going off to Stanford, if that was where she wanted to go.

Nick steered around a body lying in the street and took a deep breath. He pictured Lauren on her tricycle during an upstate vacation. Pictured her with training wheels and later without. Always when they were away. For all he told Lauren about how safe she was in New York City, he'd never wanted her to go jogging or rollerblading or bike riding alone around Central Park. Always in the forefront of his mind was that Central Park Jogger case.

Christ, he thought, *I've been holding her back. I've been clinging to her. She wants to go to Stanford and I'm pushing her to stay here in the city.*

Of course, he was. Lauren was all he had. He'd told himself all these years since Sara's death that that was how things had to be. That his wife was taken from him on September 11, 2001, so he'd dedicate himself wholly to his daughter and to his work, both of which were important after all. But did he *really* have to be alone? Or was he just scared?

Nick pedaled past the spot where there had been a small police substation, then pressed his brakes and brought the bike to a halt. In front of him stood Times Square.

Or what used to be Times Square.

23

"Jasper, where are you going?"

Jasper Howard had just reached his car in the staff parking lot when he heard the voice: male, booming, pissed-off. He'd heard the man bellow at his employees from time to time over the years, but never had much occasion to work with him. He knew he was the reactor operations manager.

Shit. What does the scientist in charge of the techs who run the reactors want with me?

Jasper clenched his jaw and turned to face Stephen Jeffries. *Someone must have ratted my ass out. Sam? Nah, but maybe Jeffries overheard him talking on the radio?* Even in the face of the compromised containment structures, Jasper felt a wave of embarrassment at being caught running away. He thought fast.

"Hi, Stephen. Glad to see you're okay. I was just heading out to see if I can make it to a hardware store. Machine shop's leveled after the last aftershock. I might also try to pick up some emergency medical supplies while I'm at it. I know there are some guys hurt here, and there could be more."

Jeffries shot him a no-nonsense stare and spoke in a rapid-fire delivery. "You got some big brass ones, volunteering to drive around right now. I doubt you'll be able to get medical supplies, though. Radio reports I've heard have it that the city's been damn near leveled and all of the hospitals are short on everything. Even if we were up and running, most people can't even use our power because the utility lines are all down."

Jasper started to acknowledge Jeffries's information but the reactor manager continued, waving him down. "But listen, this is urgent. I'm real glad I caught you before you left. We need a ladder—taller the better. The built-ins we need are all twisted to hell. My guys can't get down to the SFPs. Can you help me?"

Jasper visualized the spent fuel pools and the system of catwalks and iron rungs fixed to various walls and structures that provided access. Then he pictured one of his maintenance sheds, roof askew but still standing and probably accessible; more important, with an extension ladder inside.

Jasper eyed his car. Seemed like Jeffries had bought his lie, or maybe he just didn't give a crap one way or the other. But that only made him feel guilty for some reason. He could tell him where the ladder was and be on his way. But then a new direction of thinking took hold. Maybe he should just stick around. This could be his chance to shine. He recalled the time about ten years ago when he was still just a maintenance worker and the maintenance supervisor had fallen suddenly ill. Jasper had stayed on extra shifts, volunteering to pick up the slack wherever possible, and it had worked. A few months later when the supervisor retired early for health reasons, Jasper had been promoted as his replacement.

If he helped Jeffries out now during his time of need, when others—no doubt at least a few of Jeffries's own— were fleeing in fear, Jasper Howard could save the day, even be a bit of a hero of sorts. Maybe get promoted. Besides, both Jeffries and Sam had a point. It wasn't exactly safe to be driving around out there right now, and if he could only get a few miles away that wouldn't help if this place melted down. He noticed the wind was strong and blowing toward the city, ready to carry a radiation plume to millions of New Yorkers. . . .

"Jasper? You okay? We need that ladder, *stat*."

Jasper thought about asking him how close they were to melting down but decided he'd rather not know. What the hell. Live a little. Ride out a nuclear meltdown, maybe end up some kind of a hero, get your fifteen minutes of fame.

Got anything better to do with yourself?

The truth was that he did not. He had a wife but as good fortune would have it she was in Kansas visiting relatives. He'd been invited but made the excuse that they needed him at the plant and he couldn't take off (*how's that for karma?*). He had a daughter in Omaha, also suitably far away. He did have a son in the city but he was his own family man now and wouldn't be waiting around for dear old dad to help him out, if that was even possible. In fact, Jasper reasoned with himself, the best way to help him just might be for him to help Jeffries and do his part to contain that spent fuel.

"I think I can get to one. You want to come with me or should I bring it to you?"

"Is it on the way to Reactor Two?"

"No, east perimeter."

"I've got to get back in there. Just bring the ladder to the Reactor Two entrance."

Twenty-five minutes later, Jasper reached the door to Reactor 2, carrying the extension ladder with one of his employees who had earlier worked on the perimeter fence. As soon as they approached the door, however, the worker dropped his end of the ladder and took off at a jog in the opposite direction. He was still there, helping, but he obviously had his limits. Jasper eyed the security camera over the door and just as he was wondering if it still functioned, Jeffries appeared in the doorway with one of the reactor security detail. Jasper noticed that this man had a service pistol at the ready—not drawn, but one hand over it in the holster, catch undone. That kind of state of readiness wasn't usual for the plant.

"Thanks, Jasper. This way, please." Jasper noticed that Jeffries now wore what he knew to be a dosimeter on a lanyard around his neck—a credit card-sized electronic device with a color LCD screen that measured radioactivity levels.

Jeffries motioned for the security detail to assist with the ladder and he did so, apparently satisfied that no security threat presented itself. The two men carried the ladder into a hallway, Jeffries walking a few steps ahead of them, talking into his radio as he went. Just as Jasper read a sign on the wall (ALL INJURIES ARE PREVENTABLE!) he heard a new distress signal start up, blasting from speakers placed every few feet along the ceiling. He wasn't sure as to its meaning, but whatever it represented, somebody sure as heck wanted people to hear it on this floor, Jasper thought, hefting the ladder to negotiate a corner turn.

They came to a concrete stairwell, the tubular metal railing hanging askew from the wall. Jeffries trotted down the steps while waving his hand for Jasper and the security detail to hurry up with the ladder. They reached a landing. The stairs continued down but a metal door set into one of the landing walls opened. A technician Jasper didn't recognize, wearing a white lab coat, nodded at Jeffries and jerked his head, indicating they should follow him through the door.

Jasper noted that the tech was not wearing protective gear and it made him feel better about his own lack of radiation protection.

We must not be close enough to the waste to need protection. Better not be. I'm not going near that stuff.

They wrangled the ladder through the door. Jeffries slammed it behind them and the shrieking alarm faded. The tech pulled a blue rubber suit from a hook on the wall and started pulling it on. As he did, he looked both the security detail and Jasper in the eye, in turn, and then eyeballed the other suits hanging on adjacent hooks.

"Each of you, put one on, please."

24

Francisco Mendoza limped west along Thirty-fourth Street toward St. Luke's-Roosevelt Medical Center. After Nick had taken off on the bicycle, Mendoza realized how good it had been to have company in this situation. Now he stumbled alone through the obstacle course the city had become with his Glock held in one hand. He couldn't run on his bad ankle and had no one to watch his back. He wanted his weapon at the ready until he reached the hospital.

Jana.

He prayed she was all right. He tried his BlackBerry again, just in case, but no luck. He plodded on, avoiding any signs of people in order to stay on track. It surprised him how easy it was to lose his bearings (even in an area of the city he knew well) with most of the structures in shambles. Once he passed a parking garage with odd noises emanating from within, arguing, perhaps, but mostly there was only a little-changing expanse of ruin, almost to the point of monotony. The bleak uniformity of his once vibrant surroundings lulled him into a near daydream state. He thought about many things as he dragged himself toward the hospital. At first he considered whether his wife's place of work would still be standing, or if it would prove to be like so many of the other buildings he passed—seemingly destroyed by an invisible wrecking ball. But this line of speculation proved too worrisome and so he soon pondered other parts of his life. His old FBI days, some of the cases he had, how trivial some of it now seemed by comparison.

Nick. He was a good guy and would have made a good friend. Mendoza reflected on whether he'd made a mistake telling him about the Boneta case. *No. He had to know,* Mendoza thought as he sidestepped over a fallen billboard, trampling across the face of some young Calvin Klein model. He regretted his mistake, but what's done is done and the only thing he could do now was to try to make amends. Thinking about the old case took his mind off his ankle and he found himself subconsciously inching his way faster toward the hospital as the details of the Boneta case welled up in his brain once again.

That bastard Boneta, he'd terrorized most of New York City, but he'd concentrated his efforts on Mendoza's old neighborhood in the South Bronx. Growing up, Mendoza had hated watching his family and friends in constant fear for their lives. His mama cooking, worrying that a stray bullet would come through their window and strike Francisco or his kid sister. As he grew older, Mendoza realized that, as run-down as it was, it wasn't the physical neighborhood that was inherently dangerous, it was the warring gangs that made it that way. It was domestic terrorism, pure and simple. And Mendoza had decided long before he finished high school that he'd wanted to be in law enforcement, wanted to dedicate his life to cleaning up hoods like the one he'd grown up in.

Boneta reminded Mendoza so much of the bastards he and his friends and family had grown up fearing that Mendoza had wanted off the FBI-NYPD Joint Terror Task Force so he could take the lead against Boneta and his minions. But his boss, Craig Carson, wasn't having any of it. So Mendoza continued his counterterrorism work and watched the Boneta case unfold from afar.

When Boneta was finally arrested, Mendoza was ecstatic. Finally, the bastard was going to get what he deserved. The night Boneta was being interrogated, Mendoza hung around. He watched Beltran and Lefkowitz switch off, listened to them discussing tactics. When Beltran finally broke away from his partner, Mendoza had grabbed him and pulled him over to the water cooler.

"What's going down?" Mendoza had asked his old friend.

Beltran shrugged. "He's clamming up. Gonna ask for a lawyer any second now. He's been playing us these past few hours."

"But you got enough on him for a conviction, right?"

Beltran shrugged again. "Maybe yes, maybe no. The AUSA wants murder and racketeering, and I don't know that we have that. If we don't get a confession out of this son of a bitch, the prosecutor may drop the case."

"Who's the assistant U.S. attorney on the case?"

"Dykstra. Nick Dykstra. Downstairs they call him 'Conviction Nick' because he doesn't take anything to trial he might not win."

"So, this Dykstra, he'll let him walk?"

"He's pissed that we pulled Boneta in early. But we had no choice. Our CI told us Boneta was about to blow the country, head down to Caracas or some fucking place."

"And you told this to Dykstra? What the hell did he say?"

"Dykstra said if our confidential informant is right and Boneta takes off for Venezuela, then he's not our problem anymore."

"Christ." Mendoza shook his head. "But Boneta, he hasn't lawyered up yet, right?"

"Nah," Beltran said. "But it's just a matter of time, Frank. We even found a lawyer's business card in his wallet."

"Who's the lawyer?"

"Some fucking Muppet."

"Muppet?" Mendoza thought about it. "You mean, Kermit Jansing?"

"That's the one. You know him."

"Hell, yeah, I know him. He reps a lot of the Islamist radicals we take in."

"He any good?"

Mendoza frowned. "He's the best." He watched as the door to the interrogation room opened again. Lefkowitz walked out shaking his head.

"There it is," Beltran said. "Must have asked for counsel."

Mendoza said, "I didn't just hear you say that. Go take Lefkowitz out for a cup of coffee, all right?"

"Why, what are you going to do?"

"I'm gonna have a little talk with Boneta before his Muppet lawyer shows up."

The rest is history, Mendoza now thought. But telling Nick Dykstra didn't quite lift the weight off his chest as he'd expected. *That's okay. I've got bigger fish to fry tonight.*

MEDICAL CENTER. The two words jogged his consciousness back into action. He almost didn't even recognize the building and was glad he'd snapped out of it before he trudged into God knows what in his retrospective stupor. The rest of the sign atop the fractured—yet somehow still standing—building was gone. As he looked to the ground beneath the sign, he spotted a litter of alphabet letters strewn about like some giant baby had dumped them on the floor, letters which only hours earlier had spelt "St. Luke's-Roosevelt."

Jana.

He'd made it. And there was hope. The structure was still upright—a fact that he did not take for granted. But as Mendoza approached the hospital, his initial rush of elation was quickly replaced by a deep sense of dread. There were no people going in or out, and in the turnabout that fronted the main walk-in entrance, an ambulance lay overturned, lights still flashing, smashed into two other cars. A section of the overhanging roof lay crumpled atop the vehicular wreckage. Tipping his head skyward, he could see that many of the windows in the upper levels were dark.

But none of this mattered. Jana was inside this place. He winced as he forced his bum ankle to propel him much faster than it should. He had almost reached the double glass entrance doors when they blew open in front of him, a massive African American woman shouting as she crashed through onto the street, eyes wide as if she had seen terrible things.

"They can't help nobody in there. Can't help nobodeeeeeeeeee . . ." She screamed off into the night, a trail of bloody slime defacing the ground in her wake.

Mendoza slipped through the first of two sets of double doors just before they swung shut to avoid having to touch the handles. He bypassed a trickle of what he hoped was only water falling from the ceiling and then had to pull open the second set of doors. He stepped into a lobby that looked more like a scene from a military field hospital than a major urban healthcare center.

Dozens of people lay about the room in various states of infirmity. A few had set up small camplike enclaves and talked softly among themselves, playing cards or reading, but most were periodically yelling for help or arguing with other patients that they were here first. Some of these people, Mendoza thought, looking around, appeared not to even be seeking medical aid but merely the shelter of a building still standing. But there were also those who were gravely injured, including one elderly man bundled in soiled sheets in a wheelchair pushed into a corner. Mendoza went to him and put two fingers over his carotid. He was dead.

Mendoza looked up, expecting to find a hospital worker on whom to target his outrage, but there were none in sight. He walked deeper into the hellish reality, approaching the intake window where he caught a glimpse of a harried woman in an admin uniform trying to appease far too many patients at once.

"... *been waiting seven hours!*"

"*We were here first!*"

"*Doctor Sykestra said I need my painkillers right now!*"

But even worse to Mendoza than the general pandemonium was the smell of the place. There was still some of the antiseptic tang common to most hospitals, but it was nearly overridden by the unbridled stench of too many ill, unwashed people in a confined space at once. It made him nauseous to think of his wife being inside this horridly unsafe place, exposed to all of the germs that must be running rampant though here. A major metropolitan hospital wasn't the greatest place to be, even in the best of times; this was just insanity.

A minor scuffle broke out when a white-coated doctor, respirator mask over his face, latex gloves on, breezed through a swinging door out into the lobby. He glanced at a clipboard and called out a name, but he was forced to backpedal in the face of the approaching throng.

"People, *please*," he called. "We can't help you if you don't remain calm. We're doing the best we can. Please . . ."

Mendoza saw an opening through the door the MD had just come out of and took it, slipping behind his back into the intake office where the admin worked. The young woman shook her head at him immediately upon his entry. "Sir!" she began, already pointing out into the lobby. He continued to approach. Her eyes grew wide in fear, centered on his midsection, and he realized that his Glock was still in his hand. He quickly tucked it in his waistband and apologized.

Jesus. He was lucky he hadn't gotten himself killed already. If there had been a cop in here . . .

Suddenly the woman scrambled for something just out of sight, under a counter. Mendoza stepped forward quickly and saw her slapping at a small hidden area, but he knew what she was doing. It saddened him to think that he had frightened her enough to hit a panic button—an alarm signal that would summon security or police. But from the way she repetitively batted the thing, her face growing more and more panicked, he guessed that it wasn't working.

He held up both hands, palms out. "It's okay, it's okay! I'm law enforcement." The nurse appeared to relax just a little but was still plenty scared.

"My name is Frank Mendoza. I'm looking for my wife, Jana."

The woman let her hand slide from the button, throwing her head back in exasperation as she exhaled heavily and jerked a thumb upward. "Jana's on floor four." She held up four fingers, accustomed to over-instructing people in the chaotic environment, before adding, "She'll be real glad to see you. Elevator's out, take the stairs—out this way to the left, down that hall, first right."

"Thanks, and sorry." Mendoza pulled his shirt over the Glock and took off at a wobbly trot.

25

Standing amid the wreckage of Times Square, Nick Dykstra recalled a bleak Tom Cruise film called *Vanilla Sky*. He remembered seeing it the day it opened on his birthday in December 2001. It was the first evening he'd spent away from Lauren since Sara had died. He'd been antsy throughout the entire movie, anxious to get back home to his daughter. His "date" was his sixty-year-old secretary, a woman he'd worked with since he'd started as a young lawyer for the U.S. Attorney's Office. She'd insisted he take two hours for himself on his special day, and though reluctant at first, he'd finally caved.

But it was the movie itself he thought of now. The scene where Tom Cruise ran through a completely empty Times Square. Nick couldn't remember now whether the scene was meant to be real life or just a dream (probably the latter), but what had made Nick shiver at the time was seeing another part of New York City suddenly completely devoid of people.

Of course, the movie was filmed prior to September 11.

And Nick later learned that the scene was made without using movie magic. They'd actually cleared Times Square to capture the eerie scene. It was probably the only time in history that Times Square was entirely empty of life and utterly silent.

Until now.

Nick and Sara had been here in Times Square on New Year's Eve when the ball dropped ringing in the new millennium. They'd frequently come to Broadway plays, and it was a tradition he'd carried on with Lauren after Sara's death. Times Square was perhaps the most recognizable, the most vibrant spot in the United States of America, if not the world.

And now it had fallen.

In the moonlight, Nick could see bodies everywhere. Eaten by blacktop, crushed by electronic billboards. Bodies as far as the eye could see. Yet no life whatsoever.

He stepped off the bicycle and let it fall to the ground with a *clank*. He could no longer hold back his tears. He wept for his city.

Not since that terrible day twelve years ago had Nick felt so alone. He thought of Francisco Mendoza and cursed himself for splitting them up.

I should have gone to St. Luke's-Roosevelt with him. What was I thinking?

Nick had allowed his rage over a seven-year-old case to dictate his next move. The Boneta case, he'd always said, was his Achilles' heel. Bring it up during any conversation or argument, and Nick would find himself so lost in thought that he couldn't continue. He'd stood up and left meetings at the mere mention of the case. When it was referenced over the phone by a defense attorney, Nick would hang up.

And it all culminated with Mendoza's confession.

Still, Nick missed his friend. He wondered whether

Mendoza had made it to the hospital and whether he found his wife, Jana, alive when he got there. He was so used to living in a world where you could get into an argument with someone one minute and call his or her cell the very next. But that wasn't the world Nick was living in any longer.

He may never live in that world again.

26

Jasper Howard stared slack jawed at the radiation suit hanging from the wall.

"You want *me* to put one on? What for? I'm just dropping off a ladder." The technician looked back and forth between Jasper and the security man.

Stephen Jeffries intervened. "We need to get this ladder down into the containment building—part of the radiologically controlled area of the plant—so that our guys can access it. The catwalk system was compromised in the quake; we can't get down there."

The security man pulled down a suit and began climbing into it. Jasper watched as he removed his sidearm and holster before zipping up the suit, and then fastened the holster on a belt outside the suit. He practiced drawing the weapon with the gloves on a couple of times in rapid fashion. Satisfied, he started to zip up the hood with its integrated face shield, but the tech held up a finger in his direction.

"Hold on, before you zip up, you'll want to take two of these." He passed the security specialist a blister pack containing a pair of brown capsules. "Potassium iodide. Just a precaution. It'll block your thyroid from being able to uptake anything else, including radiation."

Jasper shot Jeffries a look of incredulity. "What's going on here? Why are you sending an armed security officer down to the containment area on a ladder? And why do you need me to go?"

Suddenly Jeffries's radio burst forth with a shrill noise—a braying, high-pitched alarm, followed quickly by an intermittent male voice. ". . . ing don't know where they went . . . thing is offline. . . ."

Jeffries silenced his radio and addressed Jasper. "We're having trouble communicating with some of our techs who are already down at the spent fuel pools, and like I said earlier, we can't physically get to them, nor apparently they to us. Mr. White, here—"

"Call me Alex," the technician said, eliciting a frown from Jeffries.

"*Alex* is the only one of our SFP techs still up here. So I need for you two"—he waved a hand at Jasper and the security specialist—"to escort him down there and make sure that he gets access to where he needs to go. I would do it myself but I need to monitor the control station up here, and not only that, I've already hit my max allowable dose," he finished, holding up the dosimeter that hung from his neck. Then, in response to the worried look on Jasper's face, he added, "Two thousand millirems of radiation is our self-imposed maximum allowable dose per *year*. The NRC limit is more than twice as high as that, but we like to have a safety margin. I slightly exceeded my two thousand millirem cap in the previous week preparing for the NRC inspection."

"Two thousand's not bad," Mr. White interjected as he removed his lab coat and grabbed a hazmat suit off the wall rack. "You get about three hundred millirems per year just from the being outside, anywhere. I need your help, guys. Just get me down there, I'll do my job for a few minutes, and back up we go. Next time we can get to a happy hour in the city, drinks are on me." He looped a dosimeter around his own neck and then passed one each to Jasper and the security man. While Jasper was looking at his device (he noted it read "10" on the screen), White pressed a pill pack into Jasper's hand, squeezing it. "Take these, Mr. Howard."

"Call me Jasper," he said, popping the pills into his mouth. *What the hell. Take a pill, drop down the rabbit hole.*

At that moment a flashing red light activated on the ceiling of the small room, accompanied by a low buzzing. "Temperature alarm. I have to get down to the control rod station," Alex said, donning his helmet.

Jasper awkwardly wriggled into his suit, accepting assistance from Jeffries, who pulled the headgear into place for him.

"—radio link," Jasper was surprised to hear White say from inside his helmet. "Operations channel's gone to hell." Apparently this was directed at the security man, who nodded in reply and said, "Understood."

"Jasper? You hear me?" Alex said. Jasper heard him as if he were inside his head. "There's a two-way UHF radio inside your helmet with a voice-activated microphone. Talk to me."

Jasper eyed the technician through his face mask. "I hear you."

"Great. Mr. Peterson?" Alex looked at the security specialist and Jasper realized that it was the first time he'd heard the man's name. Not that he supposed it mattered. How many times had he done something like set up a ladder on a jobsite with some guy who didn't even speak English?

"I copy you both," the security man said.

Jeffries, still unsuited, grinned at the three of them as he spoke into his handheld radio. "Control to Response Team Three, I copy. Do you read?"

Jasper wondered if that designation meant there were two

other response teams, and if so, what had happened to them, but he merely uttered, "Yes."

"Let's move out." Alex White led the way to the door, clearly experienced at walking in the bulky suit. Mr. Peterson and Jasper hefted the ladder and then moved with it slowly out onto the stairwell landing. Behind them, Jeffries closed the door to the little room and ascended the stairs while the rubber-suited trio continued downward. By the time Jasper and Peterson had settled into a working gait with the heavy ladder, they came to a wire mesh door with a sign reading:

LEVEL A PROTECTION REQUIRED
BEYOND THIS POINT

It was a scary warning referring to the highest level of hazardous materials shielding, but for some reason it comforted Jasper to know that even if he were visiting this area of the plant without the earthquake, the hazmat suit would still have to be worn. White used a key on the gate and held it open while Jasper and the security guy got the ladder through. "Don't worry, these are Level A suits," White directed at Jasper. Were his thoughts that readable?

"Good to know," Jasper replied, pulling the ladder back from the wall as the security man turned a half a flight of stairs below him.

"Containment building," White announced. He stopped walking as soon as Jasper reached Peterson's level. They set the ladder down on the polished concrete floor and stared at another closed door, this one larger than the last two. When Alex had manually keyed it open, Jasper took in the new view.

Although in his years of service to the plant Jasper had seen the outside of this building countless times, never before had he witnessed the sheer enormity of the facility's interior. Words like *massive* and *cavernous* seemed inadequate to convey its vastness. They stood at the top of a roughly square-shaped building, at the bottom of which sprawled a bright blue body of water, lit from below by underwater lights, which might have looked like a swimming pool but for the odd matrix of cerulean latticework at the pool's bottom. By contrast, the rest of the space in the air above the pool was illuminated only by a scattering of utility lights on tripod stands, the overhead rack lights apparently having succumbed to the earthquake.

None of the three men spoke for a few seconds as they took in the situation. None of them needed to, for the problem they faced stretched out before them in the form of a dangling catwalk. Jasper shivered involuntarily as he comprehended what they needed to do. Then White spoke, giving a voice to his trepidation.

"As you can see, this bridge used to connect to the other side of the pool, where the stair-ladder is that allows access to the pool's operating deck, twenty feet below us. The pool itself is twenty-three feet deep below that. I need to get down there to see what I can do about the spent fuel rods, some of which seem to have been jammed in place in their control rod columns—see, each one of those little squares down there in the pool houses a fuel rod assembly—and some of them are close to . . . Never mind, the upshot is I need to get down there," he finished, directing his gaze to the catwalk. The end nearest them was still connected, but the suspended walkway dangled down over the pool where it had been torn from its structural support on the other side in the earthquake.

Jasper guessed there was probably twenty-five feet of open space from the edge of the hanging catwalk to the far edge of the pool. "My ladder's twenty-eight feet, fully extended," he said. While he and White were appraising the gap, mentally calculating if twenty-eight feet was enough, eyeing the mangled end of the little bridge they'd have to put themselves out on in order to mount the ladder, Peterson had produced a flashlight from his belt and was shining its beam down around the pool's operations deck.

Their helmet earpieces crackled with the sound of Jeffries's voice. "Control to Response Team Three: what's your status?"

White responded. "On site at the pool catwalk. Deploying ladder now."

"Good. Get it done. Out."

White looked at Jasper and the security man, then out to the edge of the catwalk. "I'll go first; you follow me with the ladder. Nice and slow." He walked out onto the catwalk, motioning for the ladder-carriers to follow. To Jasper it looked as though the first half of the catwalk was reasonably stable, but beyond that he had no idea. He looked Peterson in the eyes. "You want to go first, or me?"

"You go first."

Jasper immediately regretted offering the choice. He'd been bringing up the rear up to this point, and he should have left it alone. But at the same time it felt silly to stand around arguing about who would take which end of the ladder. The security guy probably didn't like having to work outside of his normal area either, Jasper supposed.

"Let's go, guys," White transmitted from a few feet out on the precarious bridge. Peterson lifted his end of the ladder and waited for Jasper, who was looking out to the jumble of twisted metal at the far end of the catwalk. He lifted his end of the ladder and turned out onto the catwalk, making sure the end of the ladder fit between the waist-high metal railings on either side. Peterson followed with his end. Jasper wished they had more light as they carefully stepped out along the compromised metal span.

White stooped on the walk about a dozen feet in front of Jasper to pick up a length of cabling that had fallen there. He coiled it up and sidearmed it like a Frisbee where it landed on the far side of the pool's deck, the same place he himself needed to get to. Jasper felt the catwalk sway with White's throwing motion. The reactor tech continued out along the walk. Jasper and Peterson slowed their pace a bit, but then resumed their own progress.

White halted when he reached the snarl of metal where the walk had parted ways with the other side, holding a hand out behind him. He was maybe three feet from the edge of the catwalk. "Set the ladder down, and walk slowly out to me please," he instructed. "Let's look at this."

They eased the ladder to the floor of the walk and both made their way out to the end. Jasper was relieved to see Peterson's flashlight come on. He wished the radiation suits had headlamps in them. Weren't they supposed to have headlamps? He wanted to ask White, but didn't want to appear stupid or distract him at the moment. The unlikely trio huddled at the end of the destroyed walkway, a few feet back from where it bent sharply downward, and gauged the distance to the other side.

"Gotta be at least twenty feet, maybe more," Peterson said. They briefly discussed how they should bring the ladder to this point, extend it, and then raise it straight up and push it over, letting it drop to the other side. In agreement, Jasper and Peterson went back to retrieve the ladder. They got it into position at the end of the walk, White holding Peterson's light for extra illumination. It wasn't easy but Jasper and Peterson managed to get the ladder fully extended, sticking straight up. They gave it a shove and it fell through the air in a slow arc, dropping onto the safety railing on the other side with a resounding clang.

"Hold it down!" Jasper said, knowing their end of the ladder would bounce when it hit on the other side. The three of them pounced on it, keeping it in place. Jasper looked out along the ladder and saw that it had hooked nicely over the rail. *So glad I ordered the model with the hooks. And to think*

Finance gave me a hassle over that "superfluous expense." White put both hands on the ladder and shook it hard.

"That should do," he said. Then he stood up and turned to Jasper and the security guy. "Just hold it in place for me. As soon as I get over there, it shouldn't take me more than ten minutes to do what I have to. I'll need you to hold this thing in place so I can get back." He handed Peterson his light.

Jasper and Peterson nodded while Alex got into a crawling position on the ladder. After one last little bounce to test its stability, he crawled out past the edge of the catwalk. Peterson shone his light beam a little in front of him.

Their earpieces buzzed again with Jeffries's voice. "Control, Team Three: status?"

Suddenly they heard a shriek of metal and felt a jolt. Jasper's end of the ladder went airborne for a second before coming to rest again.

"Catwalk's falling from this end!" Peterson shouted.

And then it actually went, buckling at its remaining attachment point. Reflexively, Jasper clutched at one of the metal rungs and the next thing he knew he was freefalling through the air. The bottom of the ladder slammed into the wall on the far side of the pool, Jasper—and Peterson a couple of rungs below him—hanging on for dear life.

Jasper saw a bluish blur pass before his field of vision. He looked down in time to see a human form splash noiselessly into the spent fuel pool twenty feet below.

"Alex?" he screamed. "Mr. Peterson?"

"What's happening?" This from Jeffries.

"I'm right below you," Peterson said. "Climb up, hurry!"

The ladder was still hooked to the railing above, but now hung vertically along the concrete wall. Jasper looked only at the handholds in front of him, his feet naturally falling into place from years of ladder experience. Soon he was throwing a leg over the metal safety railing and dropping over onto the other side. He immediately turned around and held a hand out for Peterson, helping the security man over the rail.

Then he looked down into the spent fuel pool. Alex White's blue form floated lifelessly over the array of turquoise rectangles.

27

The hospital lights began to flicker just as Mendoza reached the stairs. He took them two at a time, using the railing to compensate for his weak ankle. Four little flights of stairs were not going to keep him from seeing Jana as soon as possible. But as he rounded the second floor landing and started up to three, the lights blinked out and stayed out. It was pitch-black in the stairwell.

He halted his upward progress, cursing the fact that he didn't have a flashlight on him, not even a little penlight. *Getting sloppy in my old age.* He smiled to himself and shook his head in the dark as he recalled all the optional gear he used to carry when he'd first started at the bureau and been very active in the field. Tactical flashlights, multi-tools, folding knives, a lock-pick set—little mini-backup versions of each attached to his keychain. What he wouldn't give now for even the stuff he used to carry on his keychain.

He took inventory of what he did have while he waited to see if the lights would come back on. His wallet: cashless. Also a mistake, he realized. He'd grown so accustomed to buying everything with a plastic card or electronic transaction that he rarely carried cash anymore. But paper money was no doubt king in the apocalyptic here and now. He knew there would be a few adventurous storekeepers here and there who kept their doors open in the dark, lighting lanterns and putting handwritten signs in the window proclaiming, OPEN, CASH ONLY. Some would be gougers, charging twenty dollars for a bottle of water or a single AA battery, while others would simply be opportunists—out to make an honest buck while providing a needed service at the same time. But none of them would be accepting MasterCard or American Express.

He had his keys, too, but the only attachment to them he carried these days was a computer flash drive. *Great. I'm ready to transfer documents for people,* he thought bitterly.

But he did have his trusty Glock, and with a spare clip to boot. If he could only have one thing, he supposed the Glock would be it. He'd gotten that right, at least. He'd get through this.

Mendoza decided that the lights weren't coming back on so he started inching his way up the stairs, right hand making exploratory sweeping motions out in front of him, the left clutching the railing. He registered *three* to himself as he reached the third floor landing and then made the turn up the final flight to the fourth floor. He heard screaming from one of the floors—the fourth? Had the lights gone out throughout the entire hospital? He thought about how difficult it would be to find Jana in that situation, but then told himself that this was a hospital, they must have emergency lighting, even beyond the main generators. He sure hoped so, anyway, as he pushed open the door to Four.

The hall was lit mostly by lengths of LED strip lights along the floor, like the kind they had in airliner aisles, and the occasional ceiling fixture such as a red EXIT sign or small utility light of some kind, a smoke detector. Some of the patients' rooms did seem to have auxiliary lighting, though, as an occasional cone of light flooded into the hallway through an open door. To Mendoza, the lighting was more than adequate after spending the last few minutes in absolute darkness, although he realized that for the people who worked here—including his wife—it would be a most unwelcome development.

He passed a patient's room and heard a doctor say, "You'll have to do without that for the time being but you'll be okay." The doctor told the patient he had to go now, and the patient hollered obscenities in protest. Up ahead, Mendoza saw a reception area of some sort and picked up his pace toward it. He saw several people clustered in front of a long desk, huddled in conference. Mendoza approached the group, but before he got to them, a bulky male orderly cut him off and asked him if he required assistance. He told the man he was looking for his wife, Jana, and the orderly relaxed.

"Jana's fine, she's been working nonstop since the quake. I don't know what we'd do without her," the orderly said, beckoning Mendoza to follow him a short distance down the hall. They reached an open area with a row of unoccupied surgical beds, and Mendoza spotted Jana talking to a female nurse. He heard her say, "I'll go. I can do it. You stay here and triage north wing. There's no attending physician."

Mendoza uttered a quick thanks to the orderly and walked toward her.

"Jana!"

Both women turned to look at him.

"Frank!"

"I'm here, baby. I'm here!"

The couple locked in an embrace. The nurse Jana had been talking to observed the reunion momentarily and then left the area. For a long time the two only held one another, not speaking. Then Frank gave her a recounting of the courthouse collapse, his rescue by Nick, and their split on Seventh Avenue.

"I'm just so glad you're here," Jana said. "I was so worried about you. I wanted to go look for you but . . . But people were dying here, Frank. So many . . ." She broke down, sobbing into Mendoza's shoulder.

"It's all right," he said, trying to comfort her, but he knew it was a stupid thing to say. What was all right about this? Other than the fact that they were together again—nothing.

She raised her head, regaining some of her composure. "I'm glad you got here when you did. I was getting ready to leave, to go to another hospital to get supplies."

Mendoza's eyes bugged out. "*What?* Who's making you do that?" He looked around, as if he could spot the person and confront him right now.

"Nobody's *making* me do it. I *volunteered* to do it. I *want* to do it." She pulled him even closer. "Frank, we have nothing to work with here. The quake damaged our infrastructure and more than quadrupled our patient influx at the same time. We've had a few doctors go AWOL to be with their own families, and a few that were killed in the quake. One slipped and fell on a ruptured Sharps container." She winced with the memory. "Anyway, if I can make it to another hospital I can explain our situation, get some supplies—maybe even some doctors—to bring back here. We are *desperate*." As if in confirmation of this fact, they heard someone shout, "Get somebody in here, *stat*. . . . Find a way, damn it, she's *flat-lining*."

Mendoza took a deep breath. "From what I've seen so far, Jana, it's not going to be much better anywhere else around here." Then he perked up.

"What is it?" she asked. "I know that look. You've got an idea."

Mendoza nodded. "Nick was heading to Columbia University, to find his daughter. There's a hospital there, right?"

Jana's face brightened. "Yes, a research hospital."

"And it's a little farther away, so it might have fared better in the quake."

"Okay. Let's go."

"You weren't really considering going out there alone, were you?"

"Well, I don't know. I haven't been outside yet—how bad is it?"

Mendoza slowly shook his head. "You'll see. C'mon."

The married couple headed for the stairs.

"Oh, wait a minute, hon. Can you get a flashlight up here somewhere? Stairs are pitch-black."

Jana smiled and reached into a pocket of her scrubs. She produced a slender penlight, pointed it at Mendoza and flicked it on.

"You *are* the light of my life," Mendoza said, taking his wife's hand. "C'mon, let's get to Columbia."

28

Whap!

She was woken by what sounded like the slap of a hammer.

Whap!

The sound reverberated inside the bookcase.

Whap!

Lauren felt it in her stomach.

Whap!

She counted. One Mississippi, two Mississippi, three Mississippi.

Whap!

The *whaps* were coming roughly every three seconds.

Whap!

She counted again; she'd need to time her scream impeccably.

Whap!

"*Help me,*" she cried. And waited.

Silence. Whoever was out there pounding away had heard her.

"*Help,*" she cried again. And listened.

A voice so muffled it could have been sounding from underwater touched her ears. Whose was it? Who cared? She needed to get out from under here. She felt woozy and was sure she wouldn't last much longer.

Another sound—a scratching sound—emanated from somewhere near her knees. Her fingers balled up into fists and she clenched her jaw. The sound was steady, but whoever it was didn't seem to be making much progress. Whatever they were trying to do.

"*Please, help,*" she shouted.

The sound ceased. Then she heard the clatter of a tool dropping on top of her bookcase and she startled. Then whoever it was went to work on the spot down by her knees again.

Finally, after several grueling minutes that felt like hours, a sliver of *light*.

"*Lauren?*"

She recognized the voice but her mind was slow in registering whose face it belonged to.

"*Ray?*" she cried.

"Lauren, are you all right?"

"I-I can't move, Ray. One of the shelves is pinning my legs down. They might be broken, I don't know."

"All right. Listen, I can't get this bookcase off you. . . ."

Lauren felt her heart sink.

"But I was able to shoehorn it just enough to let in some air. And my voice."

"What's happening out there?" Lauren cried, trying helplessly to keep the anguish out of her voice.

Ray hesitated. "I think it was an earthquake."

"Is everyone all right?"

Again there were a few moments of silence before she heard Ray's voice. "The library's a disaster zone, Lauren. Everyone who was on the first floor was crushed."

She pictured the scene she'd walked in on hours earlier and

suddenly the blackness she'd been staring into all day started turning white.

No, you can't pass out now! Help is here.

"Crushed?" she said. "What do you mean? How?"

"The ceiling has caved in. The bookcases and the floors above us saved you and me. But no one else was so lucky."

Tears trickled down the sides of her face. Her cheeks, in fact. But how? Her tears had been falling freely into her ears for as long as she could remember after coming to.

"Ray?"

"There's something else, Lauren. I don't want you to be scared. Because we're going to get out of here, you and me."

"What is it, Ray?" But she thought she knew.

"Our floor, it's sort of on a diagonal. Pointing downward. We're . . . Well, we're sliding. We've been sliding for a long while. But we're moving very, very slowly. We should be fine, so long as someone finds us in the next few hours."

"How long have we been here?"

"I don't know exactly. But it's dark outside. And it's been that way for a while."

Lauren swallowed hard. "Can't you get help?"

A sigh. "My left leg is broken in at least two places," he said. "There's no way for me to get downstairs without killing myself, and possibly toppling this entire floor."

Now that he said it, Lauren realized that the intense pain had been evident in his voice. That was why she hadn't recognized whose voice it was when she first heard it. The edge had vanished completely, replaced by sheer horror. Ray sounded now like a frightened little boy.

"Don't *leave* me," Lauren suddenly shouted, unsure why.

"I'm not going anywhere. But I've been fading in and out from the pain. If I'm silent, Lauren, it won't be because I left you here, I promise."

Of course, Lauren had been struggling with consciousness all day as well. She worried now that it may be a head injury.

That she may be suffering a brain bleed. She thought of that lovely British actress who'd been married to Liam Neeson. What was her name? She couldn't remember. All she remembered was that she'd died after a skiing accident. She'd been fine at first. Up and walking and talking and joking around. Then she was just . . . gone. *Talk and Die Syndrome*, she'd heard it called. Or something like that.

Goddamn WebMD.

She chuckled despite herself. While most parents were blocking porn sites, her dad had tried to block WebMD. Just now, she wished he'd succeeded.

Definitely not *going into pre-med*, she thought.

"Ray?"

"Yeah?"

"Please, talk to me?"

She heard him laugh out loud, the sound echoing throughout the rubble.

"What is so funny?" she said.

"Nothing, really. I was just about to ask you the same thing. Ask you to tell me a story or . . . Or something."

She smiled. "Let's agree to keep each other company, then. Okay?"

"Okay."

He coughed loud and long and Lauren realized she might have been spared the worst of the dust that had no doubt risen out of the rubble. She remembered watching over and over again on television the clouds of dust and debris that raced down the streets of lower Manhattan after the towers collapsed. When she first saw her father that evening, he'd been covered in the beige fog, from head to toe. As difficult as it must have been for him, her dad didn't even let her hug him until he'd had a long shower. Even then, he'd been hacking for weeks afterward.

"What do you want to talk about?" Ray said, his voice lilting.

"I don't know. Why don't we learn a little about each other? Let's ask each other questions. You first."

"All right," Ray said. "We'll pick up where we left off before everything went to hell. Who's your favorite author?"

Lauren sighed. *Goddamnit. He had to remember* that?

"Given our current predicament," she said, "let's avoid the subject of books, shall we?"

"All right," he said with a chuckle that quickly morphed into another coughing jag. "What's your favorite movie?"

"*The Shining*," she said without hesitation. "What's yours?

"*Braveheart*, I think."

She frowned in the darkness. "You think?"

"Well . . . Mel Gibson, you know?"

Lauren smiled. "I get it. What's your favorite TV show?"

"Oh, wait until next year, Lauren. Your TV-watching days are over if you come to Columbia. But what's yours?"

"Can it be a past show?"

"Of course."

"Then it's *The Wire*. My dad got me hooked. He says it's the best show ever made for television."

"Is he a cop?"

"He's a prosecutor."

"Really? An assistant DA?"

"An assistant U.S. attorney in the Southern District."

"A *federal* prosecutor." Ray whistled, but it sounded weak and dry. "Impressive. Is he working on the Feroz Saeed Alivi case at all?"

"My dad's the lead attorney. He gave his opening statement this morning." She paused. "At least I hope he did."

Ray's voice turned somber again. "I'm sure he's fine all the way downtown, Lauren."

Lauren wanted to quickly change the subject, so she asked

the first question to pop into her head. "How about your dad? What does he do?"

"He's a dentist," he said solemnly. "He has a practice in Clifton, New Jersey. At least he did the last time I saw him."

"How long ago was that?"

"Three and half years. My parents split when I was in middle school."

"I'm sorry."

"Don't be. My father was a bastard. He'd get plastered every night and then come home and raise hell. He hit my mom more than once. If I never see him again it'll be too soon."

Lauren nodded in the darkness, thinking of how lucky she was to have her father.

"Lauren?" Ray said.

Natasha, she thought. *Natasha Richardson.* That was that beautiful actress's name. The one who was married to Liam Neeson. The one whose life ended far too soon, all because of some dumb skiing accident. *Natasha Richardson.*

"Lauren?" Ray said again.

Lauren gathered her thoughts and replied, "Yes?"

"Thought I lost you there for a few seconds."

"I'm all right," Lauren said. "What is it?"

"Nothing, really. I was just going to ask you about your mom."

Lauren had been five years old the day the towers came tumbling down. It had been a bright and shiny Tuesday morning, a day that she'd argued was too nice to spend in school.

"Summer was too hot," she'd complained to her mom that morning before her mom left for work. "Vacation stunk because it was too hot and sticky. Too *yoom* . . . What's that word, Mommy?"

"Humid."

"Right, too *humid*. We should have off all of September instead."

"Well, you don't, sweetheart. Now finish your cereal."

"Let's take the day off, Mommy. You, me, and Daddy. Let's all take the day off and, I don't know . . . maybe go shopping?"

"Shopping?" Her dad stepped into the room with his usual wide morning smile. "We just did all your back-to-school shopping, dear. What else could you possibly need?"

"I could want only one scooter."

Dad ruffled the hair on her head. "There are so many things wrong with that sentence—not the least of which is that I said 'no scooters until you're six'—that I'll pretend I never heard it."

After breakfast, her mom got her dressed. Lauren remembered her being so rushed.

"I've got to get downtown early this morning. The client hasn't even been prepped for her deposition yet."

"Maybe your client will see what a nice day it is and decide not to show up either," Lauren said helpfully.

"Doubtful, sweetheart. My client stands to make a lot of money from this lawsuit. I think she'll be there with bells on."

"With *bells* on?"

"It's an idiom."

"What's an *idiom?*"

"An expression."

Lauren still wasn't sure, but she picked up on the stress in her mom's voice and decided to leave it at that. She turned to her father.

"How about you, Daddy? Want to take the day off with me?"

"*Me?* Play hooky? As Paulie Walnuts says on *The Sopranos*, 'Fughedabowdit.'"

Lauren scrunched up her features. "*Play hooky?*"

"It's an idiom, dear."

"An *express-shun*."

"That's right." He leaned over and kissed her on her head. "You're so smart. You get that from your mommy."

"What do I get from you, Daddy?"

"So far," her mom chimed in, "the way you throw a football."

Her dad snarled, showing his teeth. "Low blow, Sara. A very low blow."

Lauren's mom hurried up the stairs for "finishing touches."

While she was gone, Lauren said, "*Finishing touches*?"

Her dad was propped against the wall, reading the *New York Times*. "It's an idiom."

"An *express-shun*."

"Right, dear."

"But *what does it mean?* These idioms have to *mean* something, don't they?"

Her dad looked at her over his paper. "*Finishing touches* are last-minute adjustments. Maybe your mom's upstairs adding blush to her cheeks or running a brush through her hair. I don't know. Men don't usually add finishing touches unless they're painting a house or building a model airplane, I guess."

"Because men don't care what they look like?"

"I don't think that's true, exactly. But maybe women care a little more."

"That's sexist," her mom said as she came hustling down the stairs.

Lauren didn't notice any finishing touches. Except when her mom passed her, Lauren smelled the expensive perfume she and Daddy had bought her for her birthday.

"What's *sexist?*"

"What your father said."

"No, I mean, what's *sexist* mean?"

Her parents exchanged glances, then simultaneously looked back at Lauren and said, "It's an idiom."

An express-shun, Lauren thought. But she didn't think Mom and Dad were telling her the truth about this one.

Her mom turned to her dad. "You sure you're all right dropping Lauren off at school this morning?"

"I'm more than all right with it."

"Thanks, honey." She kissed him on his cheek, leaving behind a red lip print. Her father licked his right thumb and rubbed it off as soon as her mom turned away.

Then her mom stepped over to Lauren and got down on her haunches. "Have a wonderful day at school, sweetheart." She kissed Lauren on her forehead. "Remember how much I love you. Don't take crap from any of the boys. And don't take any wooden nickels."

"'Don't take any wooden nickels'?" Lauren said.

"It's an idiom," Mommy said, smiling.

"An *express-shun*."

"Right, sweetheart."

"But, Mom, what does it *mean?*"

"It's just something my grandfather used to tell me any time I left his and my grandmother's house. It's something you say when someone leaves. You're telling them to be careful, to be safe. Like 'Have a good trip and don't take any wooden nickels.'"

Her mom rose off her haunches and turned for the door. Lauren followed. When her mom opened the door and started down the concrete steps, Lauren held the door open and watched her go. She was heading down to the subway station. The subway would take her all the way to the World Trade Center.

Lauren felt a pang in her stomach. She had the strongest urge to race down those stairs and chase after her, to ask her mom if she could make it a "take your daughter to work" day.

Instead, she stood there. Waited until her mom was almost out of earshot, then yelled at the top of her lungs, "*Mom!*"

Her mother stopped halfway down the block and turned back to her daughter. "What is it, sweetie? I'm running very, very late. I have to go now."

"I know," Lauren called back. "Just . . . just don't take any wooden nickels, okay?"

"Okay."

"You promise?"

"I promise." Her mom smiled. "I won't take *any* wooden nickels today."

Lauren smiled back and said, "Thanks, Mommy," and waved as her mother turned and started down the block again.

It was the last Lauren ever saw of her. Nearly three thousand people in New York City would take wooden nickels that day.

29

Feroz Saeed Alivi switched off the flashlight he'd plucked from his dead attorney's fingers. "You will provide the light that leads my way to freedom after all, infidel," he had muttered to himself before low-crawling into a twisty tunnel of ruins which eventually led to the windblown opening where he now crouched.

Even after dispatching the Americans once charged with his fate, he was under no illusion that his escape was a foregone conclusion. He had no idea what the death toll was, or what things were like outside the courthouse. Nevertheless, Alivi took a certain satisfaction in the thought that the very building meant to facilitate the end of his life now served as his impromptu hideout, shielding him from his hunters, sheltering him from not only law enforcement and the military's special teams, but the common rabble he knew would seek to capture him for the bounty on his head, if not for a misguided sense of justice or revenge. By way of motivation, he pictured some fat, pink American posing with a rifle in his hands, Alivi's bullet-ridden body under one of his booted feet with a smartphone camera held high in one hand. For he knew that he would be hunted until he was either recaptured or his body found, identity confirmed with DNA, after which the disposition of his corpse would be argued over until he was buried at sea or some other injudicious infidel construct designed to stifle his martyrdom.

Peering up into the night sky (it always amazed him how few stars could be seen from New York; in his homeland, the night sky was a sparkling tapestry provided by Allah to light his people's way), Alivi listened carefully while he slowly swiveled his head left, right, then back left again. There was no sign of it yet, but he knew full well that rescue crews would be combing through the rubble at first light, special forces teams mobilizing, converging, striking. He wished he could remain in the ruins for longer. Unlike everyone else, Alivi found the close confines of his rubble-strewn lair somewhat comforting, probably because they reminded him of times long past in the mountains of Kyrgyzstan when he'd live in caves for weeks on end. Those times were a simple yet fulfilling existence full of prayer, sleep, organic meals, meditation, and strategic thinking—thinking that had eventually led him here—a simple farmer's son, halfway around the planet, one of the most notorious people on Earth. He'd even graced the cover of major Western magazines in the weeks leading up to his trial, a controversial firebrand who demanded—nay, who deserved—recognition.

But he was well aware that his current situation was no mountain retreat, not even a defensible battleground deep in his homeland where the infidels must journey to fight him and his own army on his own terms. He was as deep in enemy territory as he could get, literally in the belly of the beast. And he was alone.

Or was he?

Although Alivi himself had been locked up for some time,

he knew that his organization would have descended upon New York in advance. In fact, coded messages passed through his attorney, very limited as they were, told him as much. Not that they had had the capabilities of extracting him from the maw of the infidel beast—far from it—but with the eyes of the world on the trial at Ground Zero, they would not wish to miss an opportunity to spread their message.

But now the earthquake had changed everything. His deployed sleeper cell—depending on how they had weathered the quake—would be shifting their focus from multimedia propaganda machine to paramilitary extraction unit. If he could reach any of his people here in the city, Alivi might have a prolonged chance at avoiding detection. As it was, he was a stranger in a strange land. Even wearing a suit with his beard chopped (forgive me, Allah, peace be with you) he knew all too well that he would not go unnoticed for long.

But where to find his fellow jihadists? He had no method of communication. He could probably scavenge a mobile phone from one of the corpses, which would not be traceable to him, but even the man who had once effectively communicated for an entire year using nothing but carrier pigeons was aware that the cellular networks would be nowhere close to functional yet. And even if they were, to call any of the numbers he had committed to memory would no doubt run the risk of triggering a flag in some computer algorithm running on the MacBook Air of some analyst in Virginia.

But although he did not have an address for a safe house, he recalled one of his strategizing sessions, years ago, where he and a band of his close confidants—some of whom were now sleeper cell leaders—had discussed how to regroup following a strike. And this was certainly the equivalent of a strike, Alivi thought, taking in the tortured quake scape spreading out from the decimated courthouse, myriad spot fires dancing in the dark like spirited harem girls.

He allowed the fires to warm his memory, until he was sitting cross-legged on luxurious Afghan rugs spread out on the floor of a cave, smoking from a hookah while he and his associates had opined on the Quran. He intoned the words from what he knew to be verses 56:58–70, taking comfort in their familiar voice:

"And have you seen the water that you drink? Is it you who brought it down from the clouds, or is it We who bring it down? If We willed, We could make it bitter, so why are you not grateful?"

The relationship between water and Islam was one that represented purity and renewal. The ablution rituals required it. It ran in the afterlife through rivers on whose banks basked endless virgins. . . .

Alivi summoned the rest of the conversation stored deep in the convolutions of his brain matter.

"If nothing else, we can always make it a point to reconvene along the nearest body of water," one of his lieutenants had said.

"Fresh water," another had clarified, "not ocean or swamp. It must be pure. But lakes, and especially—"

"*Rivers*," another had said excitedly.

"A river would be most excellent, if available."

Alivi forced himself back to the present. *A river . . . New York City . . .*

Once again he flashed back to one of his countless "war room" gatherings, where this time a printed map of NYC was spread out on the floor of a desert mud hut. He visualized it now, cross-checking what he saw with his recent knowledge and experience.

The Hudson River.

Certainly, if his sleeper cell colleagues carried out their old plan, the Hudson was where he would find them. It was a huge river, but if nothing else, Alivi reasoned as he directed his gaze to the west, it would make a decent travel corridor.

And he was thirsty. So thirsty.

Alivi slithered down from his perch onto the scarred ground. For a while he alternately ran at a crouch and then crawled through jumbled patchworks of scattered debris, but before long he had reached the uneven perimeter of the courthouse's field of ruins.

Careful.

He wished he had a compass. He needed to strike out in a westerly direction to hit the bank of the Hudson. He could not afford to meander in the wrong direction.

And then he heard it—what he thought was a female cry for help. Weak, barely audible. Like a wolf drawn to a trapped animal, Alivi approached the source of the suffering. He stayed low, crawling between chunks of concrete, until he reached a sizable fracture in the earth itself.

A small chasm had opened and filled partially with wreckage. Six feet deep in this pit lay a young woman, still clad in the uniform of the infidel—a charcoal pantsuit—now shredded and dust-caked. Her face was streaked with dried blood, hair that was once blond now a mottled tapestry of dust, soot, and blood. He saw her eyes alight with hope at the sight of him. She tried to reach out an arm, but was tightly caged in a twisted matrix of rebar and concrete.

He eased his way down into the crevice until he was even with her.

"Thank God you're here," she nearly whispered. "Water . . ."

A thought flashed reflexively through Alivi's skull, something about thanking the wrong God, but he kept his focus, knowing that was what Allah now demanded.

He stretched an arm through the snarled lattice of rebar and felt along the woman's suit. So many pockets.

"What . . . ?" she seemed not to have the energy to complete the question or possibly the protest. Alivi continued frisking her until he felt a solid bulge along the side of her midsection. He slipped a hand inside her jacket and felt a cell phone in the inside pocket. He dug his leading foot deeper into the dirt so as not to lose his balance and impale himself on the rebar next to the woman, and then slid the phone out of the pocket, across her breast, and out of her jacket.

He powered the device on, watching the victim's eyes track his every movement. As expected, once it came alive the phone's screen indicated it had no carrier signal. But he did not wish to make a call. He recognized the smartphone as one that featured GPS, which he knew to run directly off a satellite network, separate from that of the cellular carriers. He opened a map application and was pleased to see a marker pinpointed on the screen indicating his current location. He zoomed out the map, patiently fumbling with the tiny buttons until he succeeded. And there it was, a big blue line, just northwest of here.

The Hudson.

He took the phone to the top of the pit where he oriented himself, turning with it and watching the map rotate around his position marker. He looked up and picked out a landmark in a northwesterly direction. He balked at the distance, all the open space. He knew that as bad as the quake was, that there would be many people still about in this city of millions, and soon more would be arriving from outside.

But he had been prepared to die years ago when he had embarked on the first of many holy missions. It was almost as if he had resigned himself to a suicide that had failed to work, and so every day he lived thereafter was but a miracle bestowed upon him by none other than Allah Himself. This earthquake, it was yet another confirmation that he'd been chosen to carry out the will of Allah. Death didn't scare him—failing to deliver after being given this new lease on life did. He had to contact his people.

Pocketing the phone, Alivi lined up his landmark and ran.

30

"Control to Response Team Three, I repeat: What's your status?" Jeffries's voice was loud and rife with concern.

Jasper Howard looked at Peterson, who was rubbing his right shoulder where it had hit when the ladder slammed into the wall. Jasper's left knee had suffered a similar fate, and he was dismayed to notice he was favoring it, leaning on his right even as he gripped the railing with both hands while he peered down at Alex White's floating body.

Peterson responded first. "Mr. White fell from the ladder into SFP number two."

"What? Is he alive? The readings down there are—" He cut himself off. "Mr. White! Can you hear me?"

At the mention of "readings," Jasper went to consult his dosimeter, but it no longer hung from his neck.

"He's unresponsive, floating on his back, not moving," Peterson said, shining his flashlight beam on the blue hazmat suit floating in the pool.

"I'll need you two to carry out Mr. White's activities in his place," Jeffries said.

"What!" Jasper said. "We have to get him out of there."

"The buoyancy his suit provides will keep him afloat as long as he didn't tear it on the way down. He might get out later."

Jasper made a spitting noise in spite of himself. "What are you talking about, he *might get out later*? He's not floating on a raft at Waikiki Beach! He fell two stories into a contaminated waste pool. And who knows what he hit on the way down."

Jeffries sounded calm. "Take it easy, Mr. Howard. I'm only trying to point out that it's possible he's unconscious."

Jasper was quick to respond. "Is there even a way to get out from down there? In case he is?" Peterson let the conversation play out while his flashlight beam roved first over White's body, then slowly traced the perimeter of the pool's waterline.

"There is an access ladder that our divers use for periodic maintenance inspections." This was from Jeffries. "But listen, we're getting off track here. I'm afraid that there's very little we can do for Mr. White at this time, and meanwhile, there are certain actions we can take that may ensure the safety of not only ourselves, but millions of people."

To Jasper, who had always gone to great lengths to all but guarantee the safety of his workers—the guys who entered crawl spaces and climbed rooftops and used power tools—abandoning an injured or even dead worker was unthinkable.

Jasper quickly considered the situation from Jeffries's end before speaking. "But we need him, right? For the fuel rod controls? And whatever else might go wrong down here? So if there's a chance he's still alive, shouldn't we find out?"

"If it doesn't take too long," Jeffries conceded.

"So where's this ladder?" Jasper asked, afraid to ask how long was "too long." He doubted the question had a simple answer anyway, but no doubt would begin with "It depends . . ." He was getting sick of it, and wished he was back on his normal job where he was in control and understood anything that might come up.

"Let me check the schematic for pool two. . . ." They heard him tapping a computer keyboard before continuing. "Okay. Iron rungs, fixed into the pool wall on your side, to your left if you're still at the catwalk's former connection point. And if they weren't damaged in the quake. Can you see them?"

Jasper leaned over the rail and looked down along the concrete wall. Peterson shone his light. "Yeah, the rungs are still there," he said.

Jeffries said, "Is his body even close enough to the bottom of the rungs that if one of you went down there, you might be able to get ahold of him, at least close enough to see if he's breathing?"

Peterson nodded silently while Jasper said, "Yes, right now, anyway. Looks like he's slowly drifting out toward the center, though."

"So let's do this if we're going to. Which one of you is going down the ladder?"

"My knee's messed up," Jasper admitted.

Jasper and Peterson eyed one another through their faceplates. Peterson spoke first.

"You've got to do it. I must maintain watch."

"Watch? Watch for what?" Jasper asked, looking around at the seemingly deserted facility.

A lengthy silence followed. Jasper broke it.

"Will one of you say something? I said my knee's messed up. Why can't Peterson go?"

"My shoulder's been dislocated from hitting the wall on the ladder," Peterson said.

"Oh, so you're a medical doctor now?" Jasper retorted. "You already know it's been *dislocated*?" Jasper was used to ribbing his maintenance guys when they made some excuse to get out of a job, or occasionally for a workman's compensation claim.

But Peterson's response was matter-of-fact. "Medical doctors told me I dislocated it once before playing high school football. Believe me, it's not hard to recognize. Anterior dislocation. Hurts like a bitch." He gingerly flexed his shoulder.

"Well, I think I tore my ACL when I hit the wall," Jasper said.

"Really, so you're a medical doctor, too?"

"Well, I used to play hockey, and—"

"Ladies, please," Jeffries cut in. "We've got one hell of a job to do. Now tell me. Do either of you have any rips in your suit?"

That shut them both up. Silence followed while both men self-examined the integrity of their hazmat suits, especially the areas over their injuries.

"Not that I can tell," Peterson said.

"Ditto," Jasper added.

"Inspect each other's suits on the back and places you can't see yourself," Jeffries instructed. Jasper and Peterson walked around each other in turn, looking at the suits.

"Your suit's intact," Peterson said.

"Yours, too," Jasper confirmed.

"Good. Now Jasper, you're the one who wanted to check Mr. White. Mr. Peterson needs to maintain watch. So you go ahead and descend the ladder, please. Try not to come into contact with the water, but if you do, as long as your suit is intact you should be fine."

"*Should be* fine. Great." Jasper walked along the rail until he reached the access ladder, with the nuclear technician's body floating beneath it. He eyed the rungs. They looked sturdy, but after the earthquake it was possible that some of them were "loosey-goosey," as he liked to say. But there was a man floating down there who could still be alive. Jasper didn't know what kind of stress Jeffries was under to ask them to just leave White behind, but he couldn't bring himself to do it. So he threw a leg over the rail, bounced on the first rung a couple of times while still holding on to the railing. It was solid. He hoped the ones below were, too.

Peterson shone the beam for him while he slowly and methodically descended toward the radioactive pool. When he reached the bottom, he knew right away that he wasn't going to be able to retrieve Alex White if he was alive. A little too far away. But he did have a clear view of his face. He asked Peterson to turn off the flashlight because it was reflecting off White's faceplate.

Peterson killed the light and Jasper got a look at Alex's face.

Not breathing.

Worse, Jasper could now see that the man's eyes were open.

He watched for a full minute more, just to be sure. The radiation suit was too bulky to be able to see the chest rising, if he was breathing. But his face was perfectly still, eyes unblinkingly open. He looked for evidence of what had killed him, but didn't see anything obvious—no suit ruptures, no water in the suit that he could tell. He wasn't glowing green or anything like that. Then a new notion overtook him: Could this water be so highly radioactive that it killed him right through the suit? The thought made Jasper want to jump back up the rungs and he forced himself to calm down. He should have asked Peterson for his dosimeter to bring down here.

Whatever you do, don't fall into this damned pool. And note to self: After you get back up, stop volunteering for stupid shit.

"He's dead. His eyes are open. I don't see anything wrong with his suit."

"It's possible that he hit his head on one of the rungs when he fell," Jeffries speculated.

Jasper took a last look at Alex White and wondered how long he'd be floating in this godforsaken pool. If the place had a full-on meltdown and they all died, possibly indefinitely? The spent fuel pool would eventually be sealed beneath lead containment domes for a century before anyone would even think about entering again, complete with a preserved corpse (or perhaps a skeleton?) in a sealed hazmat suit floating through the next hundred years in a radioactive sarcophagus like a toxic pirate guarding a noxious treasure in the afterlife.

Then he shook aside the grim imagining and got his bearings on the rungs, remembering to favor his left leg before he started. Jeffries talked while he climbed.

"So back to my original course of action. I'm going to need both of you to get over to the fuel rod controls that Mr. White was trying to access. I'll have to talk you through the procedure. . . ."

Jeffries continued transmitting, but Jasper tuned out the rest of what he was saying while he ascended, for along with his next thought, it was all he could do to concentrate on having a safe climb.

If Jeffries said his guys can't reach the control area, and now my ladder bridge is on this side of the pool . . . How the hell am I going to get out of here?

31

Nick Dykstra walked slowly through the carnage at Times Square. Exhaustion threatened to bring him to his knees, while thoughts of Lauren, alive and safe and in his arms, pushed him forward. There were too many obstacles in the square to continue on the bike, so he'd left it behind. Instead, he moved around the fallen like an automaton, trying like all hell to avoid gazing downward into the victims' frozen faces.

So much history here in Times Square, he thought. The area had served as the heart of New York City's theater district since the late nineteenth century. The square got its name from the twenty-five-story *New York Times* Tower not long after the turn of the century. Within a couple decades, the square was lit glowing neon. Billboards advertising new Broadway plays were soon joined by the *New York Times'* bright newswire. Then the sex shows began popping up, replacing the plays at many of the area's grand old theaters. From the 1930s all the way through the 1990s, Times Square had been considered an area in steep decline. Then Broadway came back to life. The city began rooting out places that advertised with the letters XXX, and those places were soon thereafter purchased or leased by the large corporations that epitomized the Western world.

Times Square represented everything Feroz Saeed Alivi hated about the United States of America.

And now, tragically, ironically, Times Square was no more. It had fallen much like the Twin Towers. Not brought down by the hands of men, but by the arbitrary hand of Mother Nature.

As Nick traipsed along Seventh Avenue, he looked left down Forty-second and saw the toppled forty-five-story Westin Hotel. At Forty-fourth, he looked right and tried to determine whether the Belasco Theater had been left standing. The structure was over a hundred years old.

MTV Studios was demolished by the quake. As was the J. P. Stevens Tower. The Celanese Building. The McGraw-Hill Building. All of them, reduced to rubble.

Nick wondered whether Lauren's favorite midtown eatery, Sardi's, was still standing. Whether its walls were still lined with the caricatures of Broadway stars such as Fred Astaire, Lauren Bacall, Humphrey Bogart, and Kermit the Frog.

Kermit.

Nick wondered whether Jansing had survived the quake. More important, what had become of Kermit Jansing's client?

Because of the fallen buildings, Nick found himself turning slightly left onto Broadway. Past Forty-eighth Street. Past Forty-ninth. When he reached Fiftieth Street, he was forced to come to a complete halt.

The Deloitte building was leveled.

He looked left. West along Fiftieth Street had fared no better.

To his right, a jackknifed tractor trailer blocked any chance of heading east.

He couldn't turn back.

He wouldn't.

He needed to keep moving forward.

Less than halfway up the long city block between Fiftieth and Fifty-first on Broadway was a Metro station. It ran along the 1 line, which began all the way at the bottom of Manhattan at South Ferry and ran north with stops at Bowling Green, Rector Street, Chambers Street, Franklin Street, Canal Street, Houston Street, Christopher Street, Fourteenth Street, and Penn Station. It traveled below Times Square, the area Nick had just left, and then curved westerly beneath Broadway, to Fifty-ninth Street, Columbus Circle, where Mendoza was headed to find his wife.

The line then ran parallel to Central Park, past Lincoln Center, along the Upper West Side, past LaGuardia Airport, to 116th Street and beyond.

But Nick needed to go only as far as 116th Street. That was where he'd find Columbia University. That was where he'd find his daughter, Lauren.

He began edging along the fallen Deloitte building toward the Fiftieth Street station. He needed to go belowground again. This time he'd be heading under the city's surface alone, without Frank Mendoza and his Glock.

He thought of their earlier venture into the subway system. The rats. The stench. The fallen pipes and beams of steel. The third rail.

He thought of the trapped train. Of the homeless man he was sure was dead—until the man opened his wild yellowed eyes and grasped his leg, causing him to tumble to the floor. He thought of the vagrant's knife, his reflexive kick to the man's face, and of course, Frank Mendoza's timely rescue.

Nick reached the entrance and hesitated, resting his hand on the green railing. He took several deep breaths, flashing on the fires alighting Chinatown, the falling Flatiron Building, the utter lifelessness of Times Square.

Then he thought of Lauren.

Of the days and weeks and months after she lost her mother.

He thought of her being alone in the world until he couldn't stand the thought any longer.

Silently, he moved around the rail and stepped forward, downward, once again into the darkness.

PART FOUR
Blind Thrust

32

A dead man lay at the bottom of the concrete steps in the Fiftieth Street station. A dead police officer. An African-American man dressed in full NYPD blue.

Assistant U.S. Attorney Nick Dykstra knelt next to the body and ran his hands down the dead man's shirt front and short sleeves. He felt the officer's badge, his embroideries. He reached down to the man's waist and was relieved at the feel of the thick leather belt all officers wore. Attached to that belt was a large flashlight. Nick removed the flashlight and twisted it on. Felt a heavy wave of relief as the light temporarily blinded him.

Quickly, he aimed the light on the officer's face. The dead man had been young, in his mid to late twenties at most. A deep indentation at the man's hairline seemed to indicate blunt force trauma, and when Nick shone the light in the surrounding area he immediately discovered the culprit: a football-sized chunk of concrete lying bloodied a few feet from the officer's head.

Nick heard a noise emanate from deep inside the subway tunnel and swiftly spun the flashlight around but spotted nothing. He then shined the light on the ceiling above him, hoping to find the spot the chunk of concrete had fallen from. But nothing. It could have come from anywhere. Meaning it may not have fallen and struck the officer at all. It looked heavy yet small enough to carry singlehandedly. It was possible some crazed vagrant or junkie had come up on the officer from behind, and struck him dead with the chunk of concrete.

If so, whoever that was might be still be around.

Nick aimed the beam of light on the dead man's belt again. His service weapon remained in his holster. Nick quickly reached for the holster and popped it open, then slowly removed the gun. A SIG nine millimeter. Nick was familiar with guns because of his job as a federal prosecutor. But his knowledge was entirely academic. He'd never shot one. Had never had the desire to shoot at anyone or anything.

Except maybe at Feroz Saeed Alivi when the bastard threatened my daughter.

Nick released the clip, checked that it was full. Made sure there was a live round in the chamber before double-checking that the safety was on.

He thought about snatching the cop's holster, but it looked like too much trouble and he needed to move on. He stuffed the gun into his waistband at the small of his back and stood up, shining the light one last time on the dead officer's face.

So young. Almost as young as Lauren.

He shined the light on the officer's badge and made a mental note of the badge number. This young man was someone's son. If Nick made it through this alive, he'd have information on at least one of the dead. One of New York's Finest.

Nick turned and crossed the subway platform, thinking about the days following September 11, 2001, when there were posters and pictures hanging on every telephone pole and lamppost, in every shop window, on every bar and restaurant door.

The *missing.*

The word itself implied such hope. And in the early days it was possible to find a loved one who could have otherwise been lost in the attack. Hospitals were filled with nameless faces, people who had survived in and around the World Trade Center. Many were in drug-induced comas and couldn't speak. Others suffered amnesia. Some had loved ones they simply couldn't get in touch with for days because of fallen cell towers. Still some seized the opportunity to vanish intentionally.

As he lowered himself from the subway platform onto the rails, Nick remembered the cold process of identifying bodies pulled from the rubble. He wasn't a religious man and couldn't quite understand why it was so important to some that their loved ones' bodies be found. Yet he, too, stood at the fences overlooking Ground Zero. He, too, sat by the phone, waiting for the call to learn that his wife, Sara Baines-Dykstra, had been found and identified.

She never was.

She never would be.

It had upset Lauren, of course. She didn't talk about it any longer, but Nick could sense what she was thinking when she'd suddenly fall quiet during a news report on funerals and memorial services for the fallen.

Nick heard the clicking of tiny feet on the rails and shined his light downward. Watched as a pack of rats scattered and scurried into holes he couldn't see.

He stopped.

Listened.

In the distance he heard the same sound he made as he crunched gravel under his feet. The sound—the *footfalls*—were coming from the direction in which he was headed.

Instinctively, he shut off the flashlight, switched it to his left hand, and removed the SIG from his rear waistband with his right.

He kept the muzzle pointed downward, but bent his elbow, ready to aim at whoever was moving toward him.

It was difficult for him to judge distance by the sound, but whoever it was couldn't have been more than fifty yards away now.

Had he seen the light?

Nick stood stock-still but clicked the safety off.

As soon as he did the footfalls stopped.

All Nick could hear now was the sound of his own breathing.

Then suddenly the sound of feet on gravel filled the stale air again.

And this time they were coming at him in a run.

33

It took two hours for Feroz Saeed Alivi to run, crawl, walk, and jump his way to the bank of the Hudson River, a taxing journey of less than a mile. The first thing impressed upon him had been the sheer devastation of the quake. Even in darkness—real darkness, not the usual nightscape of city lights—the degree to which the metropolis had been destroyed was apparent. Those buildings still standing showed significant signs of wear, and most of them were dark. It was especially surreal for Alivi, whose recent time in New York until today had been limited to the sterile corridors of various detention centers lit by 24/7 fluorescent lights.

He felt like a phoenix rising from the ashes to be born anew. Looking out over the water from the cover of a fallen tree in a riverfront park, he surveyed his surroundings. The Hudson. It was a hugely substantial river that Alivi judged to be three-quarters of a mile across. He knew that to his left, it led to the Atlantic, which in turn led to Europe, which was connected directly to the Holy Land. This river, ugly and brown as it was, represented nothing less than freedom.

And to the right . . . he knew only that it led deep into the homeland of the infidels.

He focused on the details of what he could see from his present location. The far side of the bank was too far away to make out significant features in the dark. On his side of the bank from where he squatted in the grassy park, he could see a small marina to his left, possibly deserted but he did notice a few dim lights aboard some of the boats. There was a ferry terminal to his right with the highest concentration of human activity he'd seen since his escape from the courthouse. The ferries were full of people, although none of the boats seemed to be moving or even preparing to depart. It looked as though they were being used as stationary shelters, probably for the newly homeless. They were some of the largest structures still standing.

The wind was blowing from upriver and Alivi caught the smell of food from the ferryboats. The scent exacerbated his hunger and he briefly entertained the idea of boarding a ferry to mingle with the disaster refugees in order to procure a meal, but of course it wasn't worth the risk. His discipline easily overcame the urge and he stayed put, contenting himself with scooping water from the river and splashing it into his mouth. Like a prey animal on the bank of a watering hole, Alivi scanned the urban waterway while he drank for anything that might pose a threat. But also like a predator, he watched for what he might be able to use to his advantage.

After he drank, Alivi retreated to his tree and observed the river. He was about to make his way to the small marina in order to better evaluate his chances of stealing a boat when a light on the water caught his eye. Not on the bank of the river, he determined, but actually out on the water. A boat. Small boat, but not very small like a dinghy; listening carefully, he could hear its motor rumbling in the distance. It wasn't the first watercraft passing by he'd seen. The river was an excellent transportation corridor and those fortunate enough to have access to a vessel were making use of it, even at this late hour.

But it was the light from this craft that really made it stand out. In contrast to the standard navigation lights common to all vessels, this one was very large, and very bright. Flashing. At first he feared it was the searchlight from a law enforcement craft looking for him. He withdrew deeper into the ground beneath his tree, pulling some leafy branches over his prostrate form that he'd carefully culled for this very purpose. But as he continued to watch, he could tell that this was no searchlight. He shrugged aside his foliage cover and stood up beneath the tree to get a better look.

The boat traveled toward the Atlantic. On its deck was mounted what Alivi recognized as a signal light, and he ballooned with hope.

A device not in widespread use since the 1930s, a nautical signal light was essentially a spotlight on a stand fitted with shutters that could be opened and closed to produce visual Morse code. Long having been interested in nondigital means of communication, Alivi had experimented with using many types of historic communication modes. He'd utilized Morse before. Even semaphore flags, smoke signals, human and animal messengers. Anything that was not electronic and therefore difficult or impossible to trace, record, and decipher. As he stared across the river at the blinking light, he concentrated on the number and length of flashes. It was definitely Morse, he decided. As soon as he identified repetition, Alivi uttered each letter aloud:

H . . . O . . . U . . . R . . . I
Praise Allah, peace be with Him!

Although Morse code was rooted in the English language, Alivi had long used it to communicate phonetically in Arabic. The word houri in the Arabic language, which Alivi knew in true form as حورية, referred to an alluring woman from the Koranic paradise.

Houri! I must go to you.

His people were aboard that vessel.

It was a brazen act, exposing themselves in this way. A lot of people knew Morse code, particularly those in search and rescue or special operations roles. But then again, Alivi reflected, smiling at the passing boat, even if someone was interpreting it, the letters would mean nothing to them. He made a mental note to find out who was responsible for this ingenious decision and reward them well.

But then Alivi panicked momentarily as he wondered how he would reach the boat. It was much too far out to get to by swimming and he had no idea where it was headed. And then he remembered what he had in his pocket. He took out the flashlight courtesy of his dead attorney and switched it on. He pointed it at the boat and then transmitted code of his own, using his hand like the shutters on the nautical signal lamp to pass over the light's lens.

H . . . U . . . R . . . R.

Again, this was a phonetic Arabic word that would make no sense to anyone trying to interpret the message. But those aboard the vessel would understand it perfectly.

Free.

In response, the boat's signal light went dark, but its course changed abruptly.

34

Jasper Howard was about to ask Jeffries how he was supposed to get out of the containment structure when a new alarm made itself audible over the cacophony of existing ones. Jasper had no idea what it meant, but he saw the security man, Peterson, immediately look down into the spent fuel pool, now guarded by Alex White's dead body.

"Control to Response Team Three," Jeffries's voice came over their helmet radios. "I need you to get down to the control rod station now, please. Take the first right on the walkway behind you."

"What's that new alarm?" Jasper queried. Peterson was already moving behind him onto the walkway that led to the needed control station.

"Water level dropped below a critical warning level," Jeffries said matter-of-factly.

"What's that mean?" Jasper asked.

"The water in the pool over the spent fuel rods is what keeps the radiation those rods still have from escaping into the air. The rods are so hot that without actively cooling the water—with chillers—the water heats to a boil. Because our cooling systems have been down since we lost power—and most backup power—in the quake, the water is heating to the point that it started evaporating off. I don't want to speculate, but it may be the temperature of the pool that killed Mr. White. Sensors tell me it's just below boiling."

"What happens if all the water evaporates?" Jasper asked, even though he wasn't sure he wanted to hear the answer.

While Jeffries spoke, Jasper watched Peterson scout ahead down the walkway with his flashlight.

"If the spent fuel rod assemblies become exposed to air, they'll catch fire. In a worst case scenario the fire can spread from one assembly to another—each one of the three thousand-some-odd rectangular openings down there in the pool contains one rod assembly—and in turn each assembly contains about fifty rods of uranium and other radioactive materials."

Jasper didn't bother trying to do the math. "That's a lot of rods."

"Over 150,000. Anyway, it's called 'propagating zirconium cladding,' where the fire spreads from one spent fuel assembly to the next."

"And once they're all on fire?"

He heard Jeffries sigh, resigning himself to the fact that if he wanted to motivate Jasper, he would need to spell out for him the consequences of failing to act.

"This spent fuel pool stores about twenty times the amount of spent fuel as was contained by the Fukushima plant in the Japan quake of 2011. If the rods are allowed to burn directly into the atmosphere, they release that radioactivity into the air which, if the wind favors it, could blow right into the city. It would be like a Chernobyl on steroids—New York City could be rendered uninhabitable for decades," he finished, leaving the communication channel eerily silent while Jasper processed the significance of what he had just heard.

Looking into the pool below, he could now discern that its surface was bubbling—not a roiling boil like a pot on a stove, but more like the soft, popping fizz of a hot tub. He wondered if Alex had been boiled alive. What if his suit radio had shorted out when he hit the water and he had been screaming while he boiled but they just hadn't heard it? This was all getting too much for him. He wanted to run. But to what? Even if he found a way out, he'd rather stay here and see for himself what was happening, know firsthand his own fate and that of millions of New Yorkers.

"Control station is this way, Mr. Howard."

Peterson was about forty feet away from the edge of the pool, about to turn a corner. Jasper turned and followed. Jeffries spoke while they trotted through a maze of metal pipework past turbines, arrays of gauges, valve wheels, and instrument panels.

"Mr. Peterson is leading you to a stair ladder that leads down to the SFP operation deck. There's a control panel there that will hopefully allow us to lower the control rods. The rods were displaced in the quake and are situated higher in their columns than they should be."

"But lowering the rods won't cool the water," Jasper pointed out.

"Correct, Mr. Howard. But it'll buy us some time to work on the cooling problem, which has some real complexity."

Jasper sighed and descended a metal stairway behind Peterson. They emerged on a concrete deck fronting the spent fuel pool six feet above the water level. Jasper found it disconcerting to be so close to the deadly water, remaining a good five feet back from the edge even though there was a stout safety railing. To their right he could see White's body rafting out toward the center of the pool.

Jasper was grateful when Jeffries's voice distracted him from the perturbing sight. "Now tell me, you should be able to see the control rod station, yes?"

Whatever instrument console it was that sat a few feet from him appeared totally foreign to Jasper. It occupied a small alcove that jutted out over the pool, the railing tracing its outline. Jasper stared dumbfounded at the machinery. It wasn't overly massive, consisting of a gray, L-shaped metal console about chest high and four feet wide. Its vertical face contained round buttons that were red, white, or green. A few switches. A couple of oddball components he didn't recognize at all. A nest of wires ran from the back of the machine over the railing and down into the pool. Jasper looked over at Peterson to see if maybe he could take the lead on this, but as usual the security man's attention was focused outwardly on their immediate surroundings. He played his flashlight beam around the walls of the containment structure, spotlighting a ladder here, or tracing the outline of some fallen equipment there. His right hand rested on his holstered pistol.

"Mr. Howard?" Jeffries prompted.

"Uh, yeah, I see a gray machine set out over the water. Is that it?"

"That's it. Okay, Jasper, have you seen those movies where something happened to the pilot of an airliner and someone from air traffic control has to talk to a passenger to tell them how to land the plane?"

Jasper couldn't help but wonder what Jeffries would say if he replied that no, he'd never seen one of those, but he bit his tongue. "Sure."

"We're going to have to do something like that here. Please walk up to the control station, and don't touch anything until I tell you. Okay?"

Jasper walked up to the machine. "Okay, I'm in front of it." There was no chair or stool, but Jasper found the controls to be at a comfortable height, designed to be operated while standing.

"I'm looking at a digital representation of the same control station on my computer. When you do something on the real machine, I'll be able to see in real time what it was and how it affected things in the pool."

"Okay."

"The control columns—the little squares at the bottom of the pool—are divided into four main quadrants based on how old the spent fuel rods are that they contain. The older they are, the safer they are. Quadrant One, far corner to your right, is the youngest—some of those spent rods came out of the reactor only last week. Quad Two, to the left, is next youngest, with the safest one being the one you're standing over, Quad Four. Some of those have been in there for years."

"Well, that's a relief."

Jeffries snorted into his mic but had no specific reply to this.

"What happens when you run out of room for more rods?"

"That's more of a long-term operational problem. Let's not go there, shall we? We've got enough on our plate at the moment."

"Sorry."

"So this machine you're in front of controls automated handling systems that can move the rods."

"I was hoping for a giant claw grabber like those arcade games where you pick up a stuffed—"

Jeffries cut him off. "Some of the older systems are more like that, but this one is state of the art and all you have to do is press the right buttons and the rods will move on their own. Before the earthquake, anyway," Jeffries qualified, before adding, "we'll start with Quadrant One. If you look on the instrument panel in front of you, you'll see that there are white lines dividing the panel into four sections. . . ."

Jeffries paused while he waited for Jasper to acknowledge this. "Okay, I see that. Lemme guess, one for each quadrant?"

"Good man. So right now we're only going to deal with the upper right one. Go ahead and press the red button in the upper right quadrant."

Jasper followed the instruction.

"Now press the white button. . . ." After carrying out several control operations such as this, Jeffries gave an uncharacteristically long pause.

"What is it?" Jasper asked.

"It isn't working. Too many of these rods were broken or displaced in the quake. They can't be manipulated by the handling system the way they were intended to."

Jasper lifted his hands from the controls to rub his temples through his suit.

"Let's move onto Quad Three."

Again Jeffries told him which buttons to press and again the outcome was the same. "We're still unable to move the rods." They tried the other two quadrants with the same lack of results.

"Now what?" Jasper asked. He stared over the edge of the now useless machine into the pool of bubbling water, watching it evaporate along with his hopes of survival.

35

Ray Knowles had fallen quiet.

Lauren Dykstra didn't know how much time had passed but it had to have been an hour now, at least.

"*Ray?*" she called out as she had several times before. But just as before there came no answer.

He's dead.

No. She couldn't think that way. He was in horrible pain; he'd broken his leg. He'd just passed out. He'd be fine once they were found.

If they were ever found.

She thought her eyes would well with tears again, but she discovered she was all cried out. It had happened when she was a child, too. One day, a few months after her mother died, she went to her room and stared at a family photograph that usually set off the waterworks. But this time nothing happened. The strange thing was she had *wanted* to cry. She'd been crying for weeks and it never once failed to make her feel just a little better. But this time as she lay on her bed she felt entirely empty of emotion. She felt . . . dead.

She didn't feel empty for long. After a while she became

mad at herself. Her mother had died just a few months ago, and here she was, unable to shed another single tear. What kind of a kid was she?

She'd put the picture away in her drawer and decided she'd try again after a nap.

She'd dreamed a completely meaningless thing—and this, too, bothered her; why wasn't she dreaming of her mother as she had in the days following her death?—then awoke and hurried to the dresser and removed the photo from the drawer again.

She stared at it and . . .

And nothing.

Lauren had felt that she had to keep this senseless lack of feeling a secret. She'd been seeing a therapist ever since mid-September, and the therapist had assured her time and time again that it was *perfectly normal* to cry. "I'd wonder what was wrong with you if you *didn't cry*," her therapist had said.

And now she couldn't. There *was* something wrong with her after all.

Under the bookcase Lauren opened her eyes wide. She needed to remain awake. If Ray woke up . . .

Not if, *when.*

. . . he'd call for her and if she didn't answer he'd get frightened, as frightened as she was right now.

So she *was* feeling something. She was scared. Fear had eaten away at her other feelings until there was nothing left but to be afraid.

She couldn't cry. Earlier, when she thought about all she would miss out on in life, she'd sobbed like she had when she was five.

I'll never . . . she thought again.

I'll never graduate high school and go on to college.

I'll never fall in love.

I'll never have a career.

I'll never get married.

I'll never have children.

Sure, those were the biggies, but what had truly bothered her before were the small things.

I'll never vote.

I'll never drive.

I'll never order a drink at a bar.

I'll never sing along to my favorite song on the radio.

I'll never go on another date.

I'll never see another movie.

I'll never . . .

She would never see her father again.

She closed her eyes and pictured him in his suit and tie, delivering opening remarks to a jury. She pictured him asking her to dance at her wedding. She pictured him as he looked on the morning of September 11, on the day her mother died. Or at least as she remembered him looking. Those bright eyes, that wide smile.

She pictured him crying at her mother's funeral.

And that finally helped her to cry again.

36

"We should cut through here."

The fear in his wife's eyes did not escape Frank Mendoza. Since leaving St. Luke's-Roosevelt Medical Center, Frank and Jana had picked their way through obstruction after obstruction, the going tortuously slow. Fallen buildings and downed power lines were everywhere. Roving bands of thugs had started to appear, too, the gangs realizing that those who were uninjured in the quake had an opportunity to make forays into enemy territory or to take their chances with looting and robbing. Anything goes. Even walking was not safe and Mendoza, whose ankle was hurting the hell out of him, was beginning to think that they might be better off back at the hospital. But stretched out before them now was an immense expanse of wide open space, seemingly free of toppled building materials. That potential freedom of movement came with a price, however, for the grassy, treed area was dark, shadowy, murky in the absence of all streetlights.

Central Park.

Nearly a thousand acres of Manhattan land initially set aside in the 1850s with the goal of providing much needed open space for the denizens of America's most populous city, the famed urban park stretched into the night before them.

"Through the park?" Jana asked, peering down the walkway that led into the sprawling garden setting.

"I think so. There might be some fallen trees and statues, crumbled little footbridges, maybe, but it sure beats the collapsed skyscraper obstacle course, right?"

Jana flicked on her flashlight and pointed the beam into the park. It illuminated the gravel path before them that led into a grassy area, but not much detail beyond that.

"I don't know, Frank. Central Park at night?"

Mendoza shrugged. "We've been here at night before."

Mendoza saw Jana frown just before she lowered her light. "Being here at sunset for the summer concert series is not the same as being here late at night with all the lights out due to the power outage from a killer earthquake, Frank."

He sighed heavily. "I still think it's better than trying to walk through what's out there," he said, jerking a thumb behind them. "At least we'd be able to actually walk without having to climb over some pile of junk every few feet. And we know there are hooligans walking around out there," he finished.

"I guess it would be faster going, and I do need to reach that hospital. If I'm gone too long, they'll start to think I just deserted them. But it scares me who might be in there."

He wordlessly held up his Glock in response.

"Let's go." Jana held her flashlight in one hand, aiming it ahead of them as they walked side by side into the park.

When they reached the grass, Mendoza covered her beam with a hand. "Let's turn it off for now. It'll attract attention if there is anyone in here. Our eyes will adjust if we give it a couple of minutes." The couple stood there, listening while they waited for their night vision to acclimate. So far it was spookily quiet. "A normal night here is louder than this," Jana said.

"I have a feeling it's going to be a while before we see another one of those. Let's go."

They walked out onto the open grass.

"Which part of the park is this?" Jana asked. The park had numerous sections, some secluded and meditative, others open and geared toward large-scale entertainment. Both of them had been to Central Park many times but after entering through an unfamiliar walkway in the darkness, it took Mendoza a moment to get his bearings.

"I think this is the Sheep Meadow," he said, looking around at several acres of lush grass with a perimeter of thick trees. So named for the flock of animals that had inhabited the meadow until the Depression era, the zone had been used off and on throughout the modern decades as a concert grounds, especially in the 1960s and '70s, and in recent times had become a popular place for picnic outings. Mendoza was pleased to note that it was the least changed area of the city he'd seen thus far, being just a flat expanse of grass. He knew that the iconic Tavern on the Green restaurant was nearby, and he mentally oriented himself based on that.

"I'm pretty sure if we go this way, we'll be heading north through the park the long ways. That way we can travel in here as long as possible before we're on the streets again." He pointed across the flat meadow. Jana nodded her agreement and they set out at a brisk walk. They might have been power-walkers out for some exercise in the cool air if not for the surrounding devastation.

"I wonder what our place looks like," Jana contemplated when they had reached the midpoint of the grassy field.

"Been trying not to think about that, but seriously, even if it's a total loss I'm happy." He grabbed her and pulled her toward him.

"Me, too," she said, and the two lovers kissed despite the exigency of their situation. "Let's go see if we can help some people," Jana said, and they jogged the rest of the way across the Sheep Meadow. At its northern end, they emerged onto a footpath that wound through a lightly wooded area. They came to a small lake and were disheartened to see the wooden bridge that spanned it floating in the lake itself.

"Gotta go around," Mendoza said, looking right, then left to try to guess which direction offered the most expedient route. "This way," he said, opting for left, and they soon found themselves on another walking path devoid of people.

"Central Park all to ourselves—who would've thought?" Jana exclaimed. "Reminds me of our first date!" Mendoza flashed on the day years ago when he'd rowed her across the lake in one of the wooden rowboats for rent, a bottle of wine and some cheese and crackers in a basket. They'd paddled to a secluded cove shrouded in foliage, and despite the crowds in the park, for a brief moment they had felt as though the grounds belonged to them.

But now Jana was reaching for his right hand and he had to switch his Glock to the left in order to accommodate her. How long would it take for things to return to normal? Would they ever be able to return to normal? He forced himself to focus on the present as they came to a serene garden spot.

Wrought-iron benches were lined up along a manicured hedge row, a few of them overturned. They passed between rows of stalked flowers and saw flickering light ahead. The Mendozas ducked behind a topiary animal as they heard a human voice. Apparently, it was some kind of singing. They looked at one another in surprise as they recognized the words.

"'Strawberry fields forever!'"

Horribly off key but still recognizable, the tune made instant sense to Mendoza. Strawberry Fields. Yes, it was the well-known song by the Beatles, but it was also the name of this area of the park, Mendoza realized, looking around at the carefully sculpted foliage and tranquil garden spaces. This was the place where John Lennon himself used to visit, and in fact he was gunned down at his residence not far from here. This section of the park had been named in his honor.

"'Strawberry fields forever.'" Apparently that was the only part of the song the man knew, for he repeated it ad nauseam in what appeared to be a drunken stupor. They could also smell the man from a distance. As far as they could tell he was alone. He was caked in filth as though he had not bathed in months, his clothing almost indiscernible from the grime that covered it. He had rags of some sort tied around his head in a Rambo-style bandana. In one hand he twirled a lighted fire stick with a certain level of skill and dexterity that belied the man's overall condition, and Mendoza supposed he was, or at least had been at one time, a street performer. Jana started to retch from his potent reek and they increased their radius from him, backing up so as to be able to monitor him. Mendoza couldn't help but notice that the bottle of alcohol he held was not some cheap wino special, but a rather fresh looking bottle of Moët White Star. *Probably snagged it from Tavern on the Green somehow or maybe found it in a picnic basket abandoned when the quake hit.*

The oblivious performer either didn't notice the Mendozas were there or didn't care, because they transited through the garden without any kind of interaction with him. Soon they were running across a tile mosaic featuring the word *IMAGINE*, and Mendoza tried to dream of a day when the City of New York would once more be returned to a state of normalcy. *Imagine there's no earthquake. . . .*

Finally, they reached the other side of the lake. They passed by another lawn area, this one occupied by a couple of knots of people conversing in muted tones. The Mendozas speed-walked by without stopping. Besides trading hearsay on what buildings were still standing and which areas were hit the hardest, what could anyone do for them and what could they do in return? Their objective to resupply Jana's hospital was a worthy enough goal and it gave them a sufficient sense of purpose to keep moving forward.

They had been trekking in silence for some time and were making their way around a large reservoir when they first heard the sound. A kind of howling.

"Drunks?" Jana wondered. They heard it again, more sustained this time, and more than one voice.

Her husband shrugged. "Maybe. Weird, though. Whatever it is, let's see if we can avoid it." They picked up their pace on the walkway that skirted the reservoir. When they reached a tennis court, a lengthwise crack marring the clay, they heard the noises again, behind them. An ethereal moaning. They started around the court and then heard the same vocalization coming from somewhere ahead of them as well.

Jana clutched Mendoza's shoulder. "Frank, what *is* that! It can't be people, so many of them acting like that?"

Mendoza was about to try to cheer his wife up with some humor about the nightlife of Central Park when he saw eyes glowing ahead of them.

Animal eyes.

Jana shone her light on the glowing orbs and revealed the head of a dog, with three more close behind it. As they watched, two of them engaged in a game of tug-of-war with some sort of food product they'd scavenged off the ground, probably somebody's left-behind lunch.

"Look at all these dogs," Mendoza said.

"More behind us," Jana pointed out with her light.

"Let's keep walking, regular pace, not too fast. Just walk on by them; don't look them in the eyes."

They edged past the rowdy dogs and hiked north through the park. Within a few minutes, however, it was clear that the animals seemed to be pacing them on the other side of the foliage that bordered the walkway they took—sniffing, rooting at the ground, yelping. What's more, their numbers increased as they went, with more dogs falling into the roughly organized line. Occasionally, one would dart across the pathway a few yards in front of them and disappear into the greenery.

No two of the dogs seemed to be alike, either. There were mongrels, poodles and terriers alongside Rottweilers, whippets and pit bulls. It was as if every dog in the city that had been displaced by the earthquake had joined forces and taken up residence in Central Park. As they crested a small footbridge, with Mendoza reminding his wife not to break into a run, Jana shone her light off to their right and gasped in disbelief. Her flashlight could reveal no end to the line of foraging canines. The ones closest to them seemed to casually pace the humans, while others wrestled with one another, and still more at the limit of Jana's light simply sat on their haunches, watching the lead dogs. Or watching them? A few of them wore collars, their ID tags glinting in the light beam, while others were obviously permanent strays. Many of them howled or barked.

A Labrador bolted out in front of them, nearly at the foot of the little bridge and spun in place, baring its teeth. Jana shrieked and Mendoza raised his arms and shouted at the beast. The challenge surprised the dog and it retreated to the company of its companions.

"Now. C'mon!" Mendoza took Jana by the hand and led her down off the bridge to the walkway leading north. Even though they kept their pace to a walk, the dogs seemed to increase their pace, with those in the lead passing them as more trotted up from behind. They randomly nipped at each other as they went, while a group of three engaged in a vicious fight maybe a hundred feet away.

And then a Doberman pinscher turned onto the path in front of them and charged in their direction.

"Frank!"

Mendoza raised his Glock. He pointed it at the approaching animal. "Stop! Hey!" he tried to shout the beast down to no avail. It kept coming. He fired twice, not confident he'd be able to hit the fast-moving, slender target in the darkness before it was upon them. His first shot did nothing, but the second struck the dog in the chest. It crumpled to the ground without so much as a yelp.

Four more dogs trotted onto the path and ran towards the couple in loose formation—two in front, two behind. "Frank, do something!" Jana shone her light at the approaching pack members. Mendoza raised his weapon again. He shot at the largest attacker, what he thought might be a mastiff. From the sudden lopsided gait the beast took on he knew he'd hit his mark. Its companions passed it by and flanked the Mendozas. Still other dogs ran behind them onto the same path. They were encircled.

"Frank!"

He could barely hear his wife over the barking marauders. Taking aim, he fired a round into the head of a pit bull, followed by two more in quick succession for a sizable mutt baring its teeth.

"Time to leave the park," he shouted to his wife. Another dog lunged at his ankle and he kicked it in the head while shooting two rounds into a leaping Rottweiler. Jana picked up a rock and hurled it at another animal that went whining off into the night.

They had an opening in the pack in front of them. Through it Mendoza spied a break in the tree line, a building with a few lights on beyond.

"Street," he pointed. "Run for it!"

Jana was breaking into a sprint before he even finished his sentence. At first, he backpedaled while firing off three more rounds. Then seeing at least ten more of the brutes running their way from deeper inside the park, he turned and broke into a panicky dash. He didn't have enough bullets for all of them. Jana reached the edge of the park first, where there stood an iron gate. She ran through it onto the buckled sidewalk. Mendoza heard barking close behind him. He turned and pulled the trigger twice, but the gun only discharged one time.

Jana lobbed another rock at the approaching pack and Mendoza pulled the gate shut as he passed through it. He doubted it would hold them for long if they were determined to find a way past, but hoped that the concrete wasteland outside the verdant park setting would prove unappealing for the dogs.

"This way." He led Jana on the street to Central Park North. At Frederick Douglas Circle, where a bronze statue of that area's namesake lay toppled and broken on the concrete, Mendoza realized he could no longer hear the dogs. Jana grabbed his arm, pulling him to a stop. She put her hands on her knees like a distance runner taking a breather. Mendoza stared into the park, looked down Central Park West from whence they'd come, but the herd of free-ranging canines seemed not to have ventured outside the park.

They'd been lucky. But as he removed his empty Glock clip and let it drop to the ground, he knew that luck had come at a price.

He was down to only one more clip.

37

Feroz Saeed Alivi stood on the deck of the Sea Ray sport cruiser, now safely back in the middle of the river after venturing to shore just long enough for him to board. He was surrounded by three of his men, while a fourth piloted the boat at a leisurely pace upriver. They had already held a brief reunion celebration that was full of hugs and prayer and praises for Allah, after which Alivi had regaled the men with the tale of his heroic escape from the crumbled courthouse. He thanked them for following through with their years-old plan to meet up on a river, and then talk turned to the inevitable.

"It is time we capitalize on the incredible gift Allah has bestowed upon us," Alivi began. His associates nodded earnestly and their leader continued. "This earthquake is heaven sent. We must not squander the opportunity it presents. I see that only four of you are here. How many others in your sleeper cell are on land? Please update me on what has been planned so far."

The three sleeper cell members not driving the boat exchanged awkward glances. One of them—a fit twenty-something sporting a close-cropped beard and shaved head—addressed Alivi.

"Sir, our ranks were decimated in the earthquake, as well as our safe house and our two cars. The four of us—and this boat—since it was on the river already when the earthquake struck, are all that is left."

Alivi looked around the boat—up to the driver, at some fishing rods in holders on the deck, and back to his soldiers. "This boat is yours—it is not recently stolen?"

The three sleeper cell agents shook their heads. "It's ours," the one who'd been talking said. Then he appeared to blush and added, "We thought it would be a good alternative mode of transportation."

"We didn't buy it simply to go fishing and cavorting about on the river," another added, sensing his colleague's concern at what their supreme leader might think of them spending their time in such a hedonistic, Western manner.

Alivi shot them a serious but forgiving look. "Speak no further of the matter. You have done very well and will be rewarded, not only in the afterlife, but as soon as we have won this new battle in our jihad. I will personally see to it that all . . . four of you"—he paused to point out the boat's pilot, who banked their craft right to follow the gentle curve of the river—"will be recognized." The three men beamed with pride, one actually wiping away a tear.

Alivi sat on one of the leather bench seats and took a bite from one of the rice cakes offered to him upon boarding. "Let us discuss our next steps. While we have had the favors of Allah with us to this point, we need to act decisively. What plans do you have?"

The man with the shaved head spoke up again. "There is a nuclear power plant about twenty miles up this river." He raised his eyebrows at the end of the sentence, allowing his words to sink in before continuing. "We are prepared to mount a two-pronged attack on this facility in order to ensure that they experience overwhelming safety and technical issues."

"If they haven't already," Alivi said.

"What little reports we have heard about the plant so far— mostly over this boat's marine VHF radio—are not favorable for the plant's continued operation. We will provide the tipping point to a total nuclear meltdown."

At this a rare smile took shape on Alivi's face. "You said two-pronged attack?"

"Indeed. Two of us will make a landing a quarter of a mile from the facility and attempt to infiltrate it by land."

"And the other prong?" Alivi prompted.

The spokesman for the terror cell grinned. "The other pair will take the boat to the nuclear plant's water intake pipe, a location we have already saved into the boat's GPS, about 600 meters from the riverbank where the plant sits. We will don SCUBA gear and attempt to swim into the plant through the intake pipe, power to which will have been shut off during the reactor shutdown procedures."

A look of concern crossed Alivi's face, but it was not for the safety of his soldiers. "And you have the equipment to facilitate such a mission?" He looked around the boat and settled his gaze on the fishing gear. One of the other two extremists beckoned Alivi toward the boat's cabin. He opened its door and ducked into the small space, quickly returning with a large duffel bag.

"We were able to salvage some items when the earthquake struck," he said, unzipping the bag and laying it open at Alivi's feet. "Not everything we would have liked, but enough to be effective if we are careful." The duffel was full of assault rifles, handguns, ammo boxes, fixed blade fighting knives, a pipe cutter, and even a few hand grenades. A second man beckoned for Alivi to peer into the cabin. As he did, he pointed to four silver cylinders with attached hoses lying on the forward berth.

"SCUBA gear," he said proudly. "We have two full air tanks each. With Allah's blessing that will be sufficient to penetrate the intake pipe far enough to surface deep inside the energy center's containment building."

Alivi's eyes took on a feral gleam of intensity as the moon-lit river reflected in them. "I see you have put serious study into this plan. I am most pleased. Nuclear destruction could annihilate the infidels' most prized city. Where they used to cry over a couple of buildings, now they will weep for a lost metropolis."

"Allah willing," the bald-headed one said. They all repeated him.

Then the sleeper cell leader directed a question to Alivi. "Do you wish to join the land assault team?"

Alivi looked at the bag of weapons, then back to the man. "We will actually conduct a three-pronged attack."

The trio of followers tittered with excitement. "Three? Tell us!"

His face set into a mask of grim seriousness, Alivi responded. "In addition to the double-pronged nuclear strike, we must personally attack those directly responsible for prosecuting me, and by extension our organization and very way of life. I myself will lead that attack."

Alivi's men appeared excited but also confused. The shaved head leader voiced their concern. "You will lead it right now? Tonight?"

Alivi nodded. "Tell me what intel we have on those who led my prosecution."

The shaved head man nodded at one of the other two to respond.

"Sir, so far we are unable to confirm the whereabouts of the attorney who prosecuted you, Nick Dykstra, nor can we confirm that he is still alive. Same for the judge. Your defense attorney has already been taken care of, as have two marshals." Two of the men laughed in approval at the reference to

Alivi's murderous escape from the courthouse rubble. The sleeper cell leader continued. "However, we did glean one piece of highly reliable intel just before the ground began to shake."

"Go on," Alivi said.

"The daughter of Mr. Dykstra—Lauren Dykstra—was on a campus tour of Columbia University as the earthquake started. If she was not killed, she may well still be trapped there or be sheltering in place at that location."

"We heard radio reports that Columbia had significant damage," another of the men added.

Alivi said, "This university. Where is it in relation to our current location?"

The bald man answered. "It is between here and the nuclear plant, on the right-hand side."

"It can be reached from the river?"

"Easily."

"Then it is settled." Alivi reached down into the bag and removed one of the automatic rifles along with a pistol, knife, and a single grenade. He began strapping the war implements to his body.

"But, sir, all four of us are required to execute our specific missions as we outlined them to you. We cannot—"

Alivi interrupted. "As I said, I will carry out this part of the offensive on my own. You will execute your mission as planned."

"Sir?"

Alivi finished fastening the knife sheath to his belt and looked at the bald cell leader. "I said that *I will carry out this part of the offensive on my own.* Do you have trouble hearing?"

"No, sir, it's just that . . ." He paused, unsure of what to say to the face of his organization's highest chief, a man that before this day he had met only once. His two associates looked at him askew, eyes wordlessly urging him to be cautious.

"It is just that what?" Alivi challenged.

The bald man took a deep breath before replying. "It's just that I thought the attacks on your persecutors could wait until later. You have already eliminated some of them yourself, for one thing, and for another, those who remain could well be dead already."

"I would like to confirm that for myself," Alivi said.

"Sir, may I speak plainly?" the cell leader asked.

"If Allah wills it, peace be upon Him."

The bald extremist nodded. "Sir, we have an unprecedented opportunity in the form of a direct nuclear strike on American soil—at *ground zero*. It strikes me as silly that on this day of greatness you would choose to divide our limited resources by putting a personal matter first."

Alivi's eyes narrowed, and his carotid bulged in his neck as he raised his voice to reply. "What *personal matter* do you refer to?"

The bald leader shrunk back a little, but took another full breath and voiced his reply. "Killing the daughter of your prosecutor. It is a mission of petty revenge. Not that it is entirely unworthy, mind you, but at this time I feel that it is in our best interests to focus our remaining resources on—"

Alivi's right hand struck with lightning fast ferocity, and the sleeper cell leader felt the tip of Alivi's knife press into his throat as he said the word *on*. He did not utter anything else, but stood there looking Alivi in the eye as the barest trickle of blood fell from his neck.

The wound was only superficial, but the message was clear.

"The four of you will carry out your two-pronged assault. I will be the third prong. Have I made my point?"

The bald man responded by issuing a command to his colleagues, and within seconds the Sea Ray's speed increased as its prow sliced its way up the Hudson.

38

"I need the two of you to find a way over to the cooling apparatus," Stephen Jeffries said into his radio transmitter.

Jasper was somewhat alarmed to hear Peterson respond with, "What about just bringing in new water instead of fixing the cooling system?" Until now the security man had seemed unconcerned with anything except whatever the heck it was he was "watching" for all the time. All of a sudden he doesn't like Jeffries's proposed technical solution?

"The pumping station for the intake pipe is a total loss. The intake is inoperable."

"I know that, Mr. Jeffries, but isn't there some alternate method of supplying river water—or any water—to the plant? An emergency cooling system?"

The silence over the radio link said it all. "I take that as a no," Peterson snapped.

Jasper watched him standing there, for once not shining his light around. Was he worried about their safety—about being able to get out of here—and that was making him irritable? Why wasn't he just going along with what Jeffries asked?

"Mr. Peterson, please let me worry about determining our

course of corrective action. That's why I'm up here with the diagnostic systems and the computers, remember? The fact is that my initial response team tried to fix the intake pumps already, but they told me it was hopeless and shortly after that I lost all contact with them. That's why I need you and Mr. Howard to make your way to the cooling system so we can fix it. You know the physical layout down there extremely well, so I'm hoping you can lead Jasper to it, and then stand guard while he operates according to my instructions."

Jasper spoke up. "Or we could locate the team, right? So that *they* could fix the cooling system?" It made him a little edgy to second guess Jeffries, but Peterson was a security specialist who didn't have much more technical experience than he did, and he was making suggestions. Sure, he spent more time down here—a lot more—but he wasn't an engineer or a scientist.

If Jeffries was put off by the question it wasn't evident in his voice. "If you could locate them, and then if at least one of them is alive and in suitable condition to work, and then again if they're able to get to the cooling apparatus from wherever you find them . . . sure. But there's got to be a good reason we haven't heard any sign of them, and I remind you that time is of the essence."

Jasper pictured the water in the spent fuel pool evaporating away while Jeffries went on. "If I can get you two to the cooling station, then I believe we have a decent shot at fixing the problem without locating the initial response team first."

At the mention of the previous team, Jasper grew concerned. "Did one of your earlier teams try to fix the cooling system before?" He thought of Sam, who'd told him he ought to leave. Sam worked in the reactor. He wondered if he was one of the technicians trapped in there now, or if he had gotten out at some point once either his job was done or he could no longer be of help.

"I don't believe so. They were concentrating on the

reactor itself, in the heart of the containment building—and they did a great job there according to my telemetry and instrumentation. So none of them were—or should have been, to my knowledge—in the fuel handling area of the containment structure—that's where you two are now—when the catwalk separated. I think they've been sealed inside the reactor, where the lead walls are too thick to permit radio communication. Usually we use a hardwired intercom system in there, but that went down right after the quake."

"So let's get on with it," Jasper said, looking at Peterson. This was met with radio silence.

"Mr. Jeffries?"

"Sorry, I thought I heard someone come up the stairs—was hoping one of the early response team members finally found a way up here, but there's no one here. Probably just loose infrastructure rattling around in the walls."

"Which way do we go?" Jasper asked. He wanted to get back outside.

"Take the walkway leading away from the pool straight back as far as it goes, to the far wall."

Away from the pool sounded good to Jasper. He started walking without waiting for Peterson, who was now back to playing his beam around the pool area.

"When you get to the far wall . . ." Jeffries trailed off.

"When we get there . . . what?" Jasper prodded, watching Peterson's light shine off of a row of metal pipes from behind.

"There are two different areas of cooling apparatus and I'm trying to think which place is best to start out with. . . ."

Great, he doesn't know what he's doing, Jasper thought as he stepped over a fallen fluorescent light fixture. But then he cautioned himself to go easy on the man. Operating this place after the huge earthquake and aftershocks they'd just had couldn't be easy. His employees either dead, deserted or missing . . . He was doing the best he could.

"When you get to the wall, take the walkway to your right."

"All right, but no guarantees that'll be possible," Peterson warned. "I see lots of damage up ahead," he said as he passed Jasper on the walkway, aiming his light beam up into a jumble of ruined metalwork.

"Let me know how it looks when you get there," Jeffries said.

They walked on in silence for a couple of minutes until Jasper saw Peterson's light stop bobbing around as he stood in place. When he caught up to him, he saw Peterson checking his dosimeter.

"You getting an elevated reading?" Jasper asked.

"Elevated reading of what?" Jeffries replied. Jasper saw Peterson let go of the dosimeter and turn to look back at him. "He was asking me about my dosimeter reading."

"Mine fell into the pool when I went down to look at Mr. White."

"How's your reading, Mr. Peterson?"

"Higher, but it's okay for now." Jasper wondered why Jeffries didn't press him for a number, but figured he knew what it was when they'd started out. Jasper decided he was glad he no longer had the dosimeter, kind of like a smoker who refused to get screened for cancer. If he was getting it, he was getting it. He didn't need to know. Even if he did know he was receiving too much radiation, what could anybody do about it right now? He wasn't even positive he could physically escape this building if he wanted to. He felt a rising wave of panic induced by these thoughts and he willed himself to push them aside. Just focus on the next little step. *Get to the wall. Get to the wall . . .*

They kept moving down the walkway until Jasper saw that Peterson had stopped moving. He caught up to him to find what looked like a gigantic fan lying sideways across the path. On either side of them was a thick forest of pipes. Jasper judged the obstacle in their way to be about head high. Peterson's voice cut through his helmet speaker.

"Turbine's knocked over on the cross-through."

"Can you get around it?" Jeffries asked.

"Gotta climb a little, but, yeah. This way, Mr. Howard. Put one foot here, one hand here, and follow my path exactly. Don't let your suit get snagged on anything."

"Copy that." Jasper was grateful for the warning. In his current state of mind there was no telling what he might not notice. He walked up to the toppled turbine and climbed it slowly and deliberately, copying Peterson's movements after he saw that they worked. When his feet hit the walkway again, on the other side of the ruined machinery, he was pleased to see a concrete wall only about fifty feet in front of them.

"Now approaching the west containment wall," Peterson told Jeffries. He walked a few feet farther and then added, "It looks passable in either direction, at least as far as I can see with this flashlight," he said, shining the beam to their left. Jasper noticed that it was very dim here. He saw only a single utility light at least two stories above them.

Jeffries said, "Take the right fork, please, and continue about three hundred feet."

Jasper made the right turn onto an elevated walkway with a railing on the right side, smooth concrete wall on the left. Looking over the side, he saw a solid floor with painted lines and arrows, and various heavy equipment including a forklift and a scissor lift.

Then he heard Peterson saying, "This is it," and saw him halt his forward progress ahead. The security man pointed to some kind of machinery console before walking off ahead a bit, exploring with his light.

"Mr. Howard, do you see the cooling station? Should be a gray metal chassis, with—"

"I see it," Jasper said, balking at the daunting array of controls. In addition to the standard-looking switches and buttons, there were also assorted plumbing fixtures like valve wheels, PVC piping with attached temperature gauges, and even some equipment that Jasper was surprised to recognize: a generator, an air compressor. But he had no idea what their role was connected to the rest of the stuff. "It looks a lot more complicated than the control rod thing."

"It is."

"Great, so talk me through it."

"Okay, so next to the leftmost switchgear panel—that's the thing with the four dial gauges on it, and three LCD screens below that?"

"I see it."

"Next to that, there should be a . . . hold on, let me bring up my diagnostic. . . ." Jasper heard him humming a flat tune while he tapped at a keyboard before continuing. "Yeah, there should be a second switchgear panel that controls the primary cooling loop. If you look out over the rail you can see it— the loop—down on the floor. Kind of looks like the spokes of a wheel?"

Jasper squinted into the darkness. "Peterson, I need some light."

The security man walked back over—quickly—Jasper was relieved to notice, and shined his beam to where Jasper pointed.

"Yes, I see it, looks like a big octopus, with a huge metal thing in the middle that looks like it could be an engine, and then one blue metal thing on the end of each spoke."

"That's it. All right, so next I need you to—"

Suddenly, Jasper heard a noise so loud in his earpiece that it caused him to momentarily hunch over from the pain. He saw Peterson's flashlight bounce off the walkway next to him. He must have heard it, too. Then he heard a muffled shout, and another loud *pop* that distorted his headphones. He saw Peterson's hand scrambling for the flashlight, too late, as it rolled off the edge of the walkway down to the work floor below, leaving them in near darkness.

"Mr. Jeffries?" Peterson yelled. "Jeffries, can you hear me?"

Then a response came, but it wasn't from Jeffries. A male voice, but younger sounding than the reactor operations manager's.

With a strong Arabic accent.

"He can't hear anybody anymore. Do precisely as we say and you will live."

39

Nick raised the gun, his finger resting on the trigger. Should he fire blind? *Could* he?

As the footfalls neared, he dodged to his left and rolled across the tracks. In the darkness he heard the figure trip and fall, releasing a painful grunt.

Nick scrambled to his feet and twisted the flashlight on. Aimed the beam at the sounds.

"*Don't shoot*," the man cried, shielding his eyes with a bloodied arm.

Nick said nothing as he studied the man's face.

"Please," the man said. "I have children. Two girls and a boy."

But the man appeared to be much older than a father of school-aged kids would usually be. Late fifties, early sixties, at least. It was possible, but the improbability of it set Nick on edge.

"Why the hell did you charge at me?" Nick yelled.

"I couldn't *see*. I just wanted to get past you, I swear."

Nick kept the weapon leveled at the man's chest, the flashlight aimed at his face.

"Where are you heading?" Nick said.

"Heading? Who the hell knows? I'm just trying to ride this shitstorm out like everyone else. I'm just trying to keep myself alive."

The man looked as though he'd been dressed well when he left for work (or wherever) that morning.

"What's your name?" Nick said.

"Charles. Charles Leighton. I'm a broker downtown. I left the office at eleven this morning because I had a dentist appointment on the Upper West Side. Fucking root canal." He smirked. "Not something I was looking forward to. Just before the first tremor I thought how could this day get any worse?"

Nick lowered the gun but kept the flashlight trained on him.

The man squinted, tilted his head as though trying to make out Nick's face in the shadows.

"You look familiar," the man finally said. "Hey, do I know you?"

"Not likely," Nick grumbled. The adrenaline was wearing off and the exhaustion was setting back in.

The man took a step forward. "You were on the news this morning. Yeah, you were on the news, I saw you. You were prosecuting that scum who attacked us on nine-eleven. You had that great line about already having your suit picked out for the bastard's execution."

"That's me," Nick said quietly. "Assistant U.S. Attorney Dykstra. You can call me Nick."

The man folded his arms across his chest and stepped forward. "My friends call me Chuck." He motioned to the tunnel. "Hey, where are you heading to, Nick?"

"Hundred Sixteenth Street. Columbia University. My daughter Lauren's there, visiting the campus."

"Have you heard anything about a potential rescue operation, Nick?"

"Nothing," Nick said. "As far as I know, there's been no contact at all with anyone not on the island."

"Christ," Chuck said. "I haven't eaten a thing all day. I'm starving. I nursed a bottle of Poland Spring, but that's long gone now, too."

"Wish I could help you," Nick said, turning his back. "But I've got to keep moving."

"Nick, there's nothing up that way, believe me. The train I was on crashed and there's no way past it."

"Which stop?"

"The train went off its rails somewhere between Columbus Circle and Lincoln Center."

Nick bowed his head. "Then I'll surface at Columbus Circle. A friend of mine was heading there to find his wife. She's a nurse at St. Luke's-Roosevelt."

"I heard that place is nothing more than a smoldering pile of rubble."

"Heard it from whom?"

"A couple of survivors on the train. Two young ladies and a young man. College students visiting from Italy, I think. The young man was injured; they couldn't move him. So they went to the surface for help. When they came back, they said the hospital was leveled. Didn't matter much by then. By the time they got back their friend was dead."

The words *college students* bounced off the walls of Nick's fogged mind.

Nick said, "I'll take a trail along Central Park, then. Good wishes, Chuck."

"Hey, man. Don't . . . ya know, don't leave me."

Nick turned back and looked at the man's face. His eyes were wide, his lower lip trembling. "You can come with me if you'd like."

"I just told you, Nick. There's nothing up that way. I just came from there. What you and I need to do, pal, is . . . We need to find food. Something to drink, ya know?"

When Nick spoke again he did more forcefully. "My way is north. I'm going to Columbia to find my daughter."

"All right." Chuck threw his hands in the air, exasperated. "All right. Do what you must, counselor. But . . . You've got to . . . I mean, please. Please, give me the flashlight." He held out his hand and took another step forward.

Nick stepped back. "Easy, Chuck. The flashlight's mine."

"The hell it is, Nick. Come on now, hand it over."

"It's *mine*, Chuck, and I'm taking it to find my daughter."

"It not *yours*, Nick. It's the nigger cop's."

"What did you just say?"

"The dead cop up on the platform. It's his fucking gun, not yours. Now hand it over."

"You were coming from the north end of the tunnel. How do you know about the cop?"

Chuck gave an uneasy smile. In the beam of the flashlight he began to look like a rabid dog. "Look, none of that matters, all right? I mean, we're here in the subway, you and I, during the fucking apocalypse. Just hand me the flashlight, and I'll let you go on your way."

Nick raised the gun. "I don't think you've thought this entire situation through, Chuck. Now, listen. I don't want to hurt you. But if you take one step closer to me, I'll put a bullet right between your beady eyes. Understand?"

Chuck nodded his head theatrically. "Oh, yeah, I understand, Nick. Sure, sure. But tell me, did you check the nigger cop for any other weapons?"

Before Nick could respond, Chuck extended his right arm and a thick stream of liquid shot into Nick's eyes.

He staggered backwards, blindly raising his weapon in Chuck's direction. But he tripped and fell, hitting his head against the rail. His eyes felt as though they were on fire and as he rubbed at them with his forearm, he could hear Chuck Leighton approaching.

Nick was blind.

Shoot?

Or toss the weapon and hope that Chuck doesn't get it?

But there was a third option. *Fight.*

Quickly, Nick clicked off the flashlight, got to his feet, and swung it in a wide arc in Chuck's direction. He felt a tinge of satisfaction at the sound of the heavy flashlight connecting with Chuck's head. Nick tried to follow through, but his next move was a swing and a miss.

Then he felt a hard, quick kick to his groin and dropped to his knees, pain firing up both legs. He still couldn't see and he couldn't allow Chuck to gain the advantage, so he flung the flashlight as far as he could up the north end of the tunnel.

Nick turned and raised the gun, but before he could get his finger around the trigger, he took another kick to the face. Then Chuck tackled him, pinned his arms to the ground.

Nick used the only part of his body that was free and slammed his forehead into Chuck's face.

Chuck screamed.

Nick took the opportunity to throw his attacker off of him. Then he picked up the gun, still unable to see. He listened as Chuck got to his feet.

"Sorry, Nick," the guy said, "but I'm afraid that today, it's survival of the fittest."

He heard the man charge him again, and Nick raised his weapon.

And fired. Once. Twice. Three times in rapid succession.

Nick heard Chuck Leighton's body drop onto the tracks and he took a deep breath, before plugging him again, just to be sure the bastard was dead.

40

"I said, do as we say and you will live. What is your location?" The Arabic male repeated himself over the radio link.

Jasper looked over at Peterson, who held a finger up to his faceplate in front of his lips. Jasper stifled the overwhelming urge to speak. He didn't see how long that was going to be an option since he and Peterson had no way to talk to each other except over the radio transmitters inside their face masks, the channel now shared with whomever had appropriated it. Shouldn't they ask if Jeffries was all right? Surely the intruders—or *intruder—he said "we" but so far there was only one voice*—knew that if Jeffries was speaking to someone that they were down here?

But then he saw the logic of Peterson's command. He was a security expert, after all, so this incident was firmly within his domain. If Jeffries had been . . . shot? Was that the sound he'd heard? If he'd been shot, then it was most likely a terrorist act *(that's what Peterson's been on alert for down here all this time)*, so what good could come from providing their location? On the other hand, Jasper thought as he watched Peterson slide under the rail, presumably to retrieve his flashlight, even if they did know where they were, they couldn't get to them, so what difference did it make? Furthermore, if he and Peterson couldn't solve this cooling issue, it was all going to be a moot point, and they needed to communicate in order to do that.

Screw it. He was about to disregard Peterson's silence command and give in to his overwhelming urge to make sense of this situation *right now*, when he spotted something dangling from the cooling control station. He wouldn't have recognized it in the faint light but for the fact that Peterson's beam had passed over it earlier.

A metal logbook of some type hung from the instrument console on a metal umbilical. If he was lucky (and he obviously wasn't since here he was, but Jasper told himself he'd have to mull that one over later), there'd be a writing utensil attached. He needed more light to see what the hell he was doing, though.

He looked over at Peterson clambering back onto the platform, light clenched in hand. Jasper pantomimed that he needed to see something over at the cooling station. Peterson looked as though he about snapped his neck, he turned his head so fast to look, and Jasper realized that he must have scared him into thinking there was someone over there.

He shook his head and pushed his hands down toward the floor. *Calm down, Peterson.*

Then they heard the radio wave interloper from Jeffries's end again.

"Very well. If you do not wish to cooperate, then we will just have to start pushing random buttons up here. Let me see, what does this one do . . . ?"

Jasper looked over at Peterson who waved his hand in a dismissive gesture. *Ignore that.* Made sense to Jasper. They may be terrorists, and if they were of the Islamic ilk, then they most certainly weren't afraid of all the virgins waiting in the afterlife. But then again, they didn't come all the way here to press some random buttons, many of which no longer worked, anyhow. They wanted mass destruction. They wanted a way into the containment buildings. And for that they needed assistance.

In reply, Jasper waved to gain Peterson's attention. He led him back to the cooling station where he wordlessly pointed out the hanging logbook. Peterson immediately gave him a thumbs-up sign and handed Jasper the light while he picked up the book. Flipping it open, he plucked the pen from a clip on the inside and flipped about halfway through the book until he found a sufficiently clear page. It was still a form titled "Service Log," but it contained enough white space to work with. As Peterson began to write, they heard the hostile transmission intrude into their headsets once more.

"We can hear you breathing. There are three hazmat suits missing from the rack in here. Do you think us to be stupid?"

Jasper forced himself to slow his breathing rate as he shone the light on the page while Peterson scribbled.

DON'T KNOW HOW MANY WE ARE—
ADVANTAGE!

Jasper nodded and gave him a thumbs-up, although he wanted to write, *Don't know how many they are—disadvantage!* Peterson scratched out another message.

DON'T TALK FOR NOW! THEY'RE FISHING
FOR INFO. LESS THEY KNOW THE BETTER.

Jasper nodded his agreement once more and grabbed the pen from Peterson. He handed Peterson the light back and wrote.

THINK THEY SHOT JEFFRIES?

Peterson nodded vigorously. He pointed to the pen and Jasper gave it to him. He held up his firearm before jotting:

I'D GO TRY TO NEUTRALIZE THEM AND HELP
JEFFRIES IF NOT DEAD, BUT FOR NOW
THERE'S NO WAY BACK THERE.

Jasper gave a terse nod. He sure didn't like to think about trying to get back to Jeffries's control room to join a terrorist gunfight. Nor did the notion of Peterson leaving him down here alone sit well at all. He coaxed the pen from his unlikely cohort and put it to paper again.

WHAT ABOUT FIXING THE COOLING
SYSTEM?

He saw Peterson go still while he contemplated this. Jasper added another line to his note.

DO YOU KNOW HOW TO CONTINUE WHAT
JEFFRIES WAS TELLING ME TO DO WITH
THE LOOP?

Peterson shone the light over the rail to the primary cooling loop out on the work floor he'd just come back from, then back to the switchgear panels in front of them. Jasper's heart dropped as he shook his head. Peterson indicated he wanted to write and Jasper took the light while the security man penned his longest note yet.

I DON'T KNOW THAT PROCEDURE. I KNOW
THERE'S ANOTHER COOLING STATION WITH
DIFFERENT CONTROLS THAN THIS ONE OFF
TO OUR RIGHT, NOT SURE WHAT THEY DO.
BUT LISTEN . . .

Peterson held the pen poised in the air and looked Jasper in the eyes, or at least where he would have made eye contact if not for the flashlight glare. He pointed back down to the paper and kept writing.

I THINK OUR ONLY SHOT AT THIS POINT IS
WHAT YOU SUGGESTED EARLIER.

Jasper's blood ran colder than the water temperate they needed the spent fuel pool to be lowered to. *Only shot!* But he didn't interrupt as Peterson kept writing.

WE HAVE TO GET TO THE TECHS THAT ARE
PROBABLY TRAPPED IN MAIN REACTOR #2
AND LEAD THEM BACK TO THE COOLING
SYSTEM.

He paused to look up at Jasper to see if he was following. Jasper gave a slow, ponderous nod, and Peterson continued.

EVEN IF WE FIXED THE COOL SYS WE'D
STILL HAVE TO FIND A WAY OUT, RIGHT?

This elicited a quick and decisive nod from Jasper. Peterson bent to the logbook once again.

SO WE GO TO THE REACTOR, TRY TO LOCATE
A TECH. GOT TO BE AT LEAST A FEW STILL
ALIVE. WE ESCORT THEM TO THE COOL
STATIONS SO THEY CAN DO THEIR JOB AND
THEN WE CAN WORK ON FINDING A WAY
OUTSIDE.

Peterson looked up at Jasper and threw his hands up as if to say, *that's all, folks!*

"We will find a way down to you, and when we do, you will wish that you had been inside the spent fuel pool when the water boils off of it, compared to what your fate will be at our hands." Jasper jumped at the disembodied voice in his head, so lost in concentration had he been. The actual content of the message disturbed him as well. The invisible enemy had specifically referred to the spent fuel pool water, as opposed to the reactor core, which indicated they were aware of the more accessible peril.

Peterson seemed to ignore the threat and pointed off to their left before he wrote another line.

YOU WITH ME?

Jasper didn't see as he had much of a choice. He motioned for Peterson to give him the logbook and proceeded to yank on it, separating the book from its metal cord. Peterson drew his pistol and pointed with his light beam to their left along the wall walkway. Jasper tucked their low-tech communications system under one arm and together they charged off toward the reactor.

41

There was no train. Charles Leighton had lied about that. No train had crashed between Columbus Circle and Lincoln Center, so Nick remained in the tunnel. If Leighton lied about that, then he almost certainly lied about St. Luke's-Roosevelt as well. So Francisco Mendoza's wife could be fine. She could be in Frank's arms by now, in fact. He sincerely hoped so.

But for now he was just glad that he could stay underground and continue his way north. As long as there really wasn't a crashed train down here, and as long as his trusty flashlight (and gun) held up, this was as good a place to be as any for the trek north. For every one Charles Leighton he encountered down here, there were probably fifty more roaming about topside. There were definite advantages to being aboveground, though. He could find food, for one thing. Leighton had mentioned food and the truth was that Nick was hungry—famished, even—he'd burned a lot more calories today than he was used to. But he had to keep going. Lauren was not that far away now, and she probably needed his help. Must be worried sick about him and about the prospect of being left parentless.

As he walked, he reiterated to himself all the ways he'd be a better father if he and his daughter both made it through this in one piece. He didn't care what happened to his house or his car or his belongings, didn't care if the bank with his safe deposit box full of his only valuables was disintegrated beyond all recognition; he only wanted the chance to be with his daughter again so he could start off on the right foot this time. No more would he pressure her about where to go to school, or whom she should date. He had to let her be her own woman. But he'd be there for her, always just a phone call or e-mail or text or Skype call away. That was fine. He'd give her some space, allow her to grow but make himself available, and that way he'd see what she really wanted from him. Probably just holiday visits home, for a while, and that was fine. She needed to get out there and experience life. God, how he hoped now that she would get that chance. He didn't know why it took so long for him to come to this realization, why it took a New York City earthquake (the guy from the salsa commercial interrupted his thoughts: *New York City?)* to shake him around to her way of thinking, but it had a peaceable effect on him.

He forgot about his hunger pains as he plodded on, shining his light beam far in front of him to see if there were any human threats or large obstacles up ahead, then waving the flood of light by his feet to make sure he wasn't going to trip over anything. At one point, he came across an open manhole or access port cover of some kind on the right side of the tracks, and he thanked his lucky stars that he'd been shining the light close by his feet. It was just a small space large enough for one man to drop into. He shone his beam down into it but saw no rungs leading down, just a dirt floor far, far below. He'd heard of the city beneath a city—the labyrinthine network of subterranean passages that represented a layer of humanity long since built over. He had no idea what the space was, and didn't care.

He kept going.

A long procession of rats passed along the other side of the tunnel, heading fast in the other direction, chittering and squeaking and scratching their claws along the tunnel ground. Nick wondered what they might be running from but could see or hear no potential threats. Then he saw a brown lump of blankets lying up ahead, right in front of him. He stepped around while shining his beam on the disheveled mass. A dead homeless man, curled up in what was likely his only earthly possession. Nick considered the possibility that the man could have been dead in here for quite some time, perhaps before the earthquake even happened. He thought about all the potential for cover-ups in the wake of this disaster, the missing persons cases that would be erroneously blamed on the quake, how it could impact his job as a prosecutor, if he could ever have a normal life again.

On an even more sinister level, Nick knew that some of the scum he'd prosecuted were not above using this earthquake as a cover to commit heinous crimes they otherwise wouldn't have any hope of getting away with. If a floater was to be found in the Hudson River tomorrow, after all, who would suspect foul play? There would probably be several corpses littering the banks of the river when all this was said and done. That business partner you always wanted out of the picture? Today was not the day to be the victim of a violent crime in Manhattan, Nick decided.

He kicked a beer bottle onto the tracks and then conducted another long-distance check with his flashlight, second nature now, without even thinking about it. Nothing up ahead, so he went back to his thoughts.

Feroz Saeed Alivi was exactly the type of man to take advantage of a disaster like this, he decided. What had become of him by now? He liked to think that he was either still in the custody of U.S. marshals, or else had been killed in the quake. But until he had some definitive proof, he wouldn't assume anything. He'd seen that courthouse following the quake. It was deep, deep rubble, and although overall it was devastating and the eventual death count was not something he looked forward to learning, there would no doubt be survivable pockets throughout. He himself had made it, after all. Others could, too. Including Alivi.

He shivered as he thought about the terror leader's threats against Lauren.

If he did survive and had also managed to escape . . .

Nick had to jump down onto the tracks to avoid a pile of shopping carts. He'd no idea how those found their way down here. Another distance check, all clear. Back to one foot in front of the other.

If Alivi did escape, he may come after me. He may even come after Lauren. Nick wondered if he was being . . . *arrogant? Was that the right word?* . . . by assuming that he held enough importance in the jihad-obsessed man's mind that he would focus on Nick—his prosecutor, but still only a single man—rather than use this opportunity to either flee the country or else take advantage of the quake-distracted authorities to assemble a rapid-strike terror event. Was his organization agile enough for something like that? Nick wasn't sure, but he knew one thing as he spotted a subway sign reading 116TH STREET / COLUMBIA UNIVERSITY.

He needed to get to Lauren, and get to her fast.

PART FIVE
Shadow Zone

42

The closer Jasper and Peterson came to the reactor building, the more the damage was increasingly evident. More and more fallen utility fixtures littered the walkway and the surrounding work areas. Birds' nests of loose wiring hung suspended from the ceiling. Then the walkway itself that led them away from the cooling station had ended abruptly in a snarl of unadulterated wreckage, a shocking display of force that the earthquake must have unleashed in order to rip the iron structure from the concrete wall and upend it.

Adding to their general unease, the radio channel had been silent since leaving the cooling controls. Had the terrorists left Jeffries's control room looking for a way down here and not even put on the radiation suits? If they were jihadists, maybe they wouldn't bother with the suits, sort of like the 9/11 pilots who supposedly de-emphasized the landings portion of their flight training. Perhaps they weren't aware that the suits contained radios? Jasper and Peterson had no way of knowing, but they maintained radio silence in case it was a ploy to get them to think no one was listening. Now they found themselves picking their way across a barely lit concrete floor crowded with machinery and equipment to the reactor—the container within a container where atoms were split in order to generate the heat that would boil water and spin a turbine.

Peterson pointed his light beam in front of them and Jasper followed its path with his gaze. Immediately he could see the problem. An iron staircase wound its way up and around the outside of the cylindrical concrete reactor building in a colossal spiral, but a section of it had come loose and fallen over the ground level doorway, obscuring it almost completely. In addition to the stairs, there were also numerous chunks of displaced concrete. Peterson waved an arm, indicating for Jasper to follow. They had to skirt around a downed tank of some kind in order to walk up to the blocked doorway.

Peterson handed Jasper the flashlight and he gripped the mangled stair ladder with both hands. He yanked on it several times with full strength but it did not budge. He rested a moment before moving his grip to different points of the broken structure and trying again. Still, the displaced stairwell held fast. Peterson looked at Jasper and shook his head. Then Jasper aimed the light toward the ceiling, tracing the stair ladder along its course up the reactor containment building. It was still there, but it dangled precariously in some sections and was outright missing in others, leaving gaps that would have to be climbed somehow in order to reach the top. And they couldn't see from here what its condition was as it wound up the other side of the structure. One of the missing sections was at the bottom of the stairs, beginning just above the span that blocked the reactor door.

Jasper waved to get Peterson's attention and handed him the flashlight. He opened the logbook to a fresh page and penned a message.

WHAT'S ON TOP?

He pointed up the stair ladder to the top of the reactor containment structure, then followed with another note.

NO WONDER THE TECHS COULDN'T GET OUT
THIS WAY. HOW MANY OTHER DOORS?

Jasper pointed around the side of the containment structure
and traded Peterson the logbook for the flashlight. Peterson
gripped the pen and wrote.

ON TOP IS AN ACCESS PORT TO BE ABLE TO
WORK ON THE VENTS AND STUFF UP THERE.
INSIDE, UNDERNEATH THE ROOF, IT DROPS
DOWN TO A CATWALK AND LADDER
SYSTEM—IF THAT'S STILL EVEN THERE.

He paused his pen for a moment while he tipped his head
back to look at the stair ladder's condition along the length of
the containment cylinder, then wrote again.

THIS MIGHT JUST BE CLIMBABLE BUT THERE
IS ANOTHER DOOR LIKE THIS ONE ON THE
OTHER SIDE. LET'S CHECK THAT OUT FIRST.

Jasper nodded agreeably, not at all liking the fact that
they were even entertaining the notion of climbing the
broken stair ladder. They set out to the left along the containment cylinder, toward what appeared to be the path of least
resistance. Peterson led the way with his light, Jasper close
behind. Both of their heads were on swivels, hyper-alert for
threats not only due to the damaged nuclear facility, but also
from the terrorists somewhere in the vicinity. Jasper hoped
the intruders wouldn't find a way down here that he and
Peterson had missed.

As they worked their way around the reactor containment
structure, they noticed cracks and buckling in the steel-lined
concrete, though none was large enough to be actual openings
to the inside. Jasper saw Peterson consult his dosimeter once,

but he didn't try to see the reading himself. He just kept putting one foot in front of the other, trooping toward that other door. He hoped that they would be able to get into the reactor somehow, that when they did, there would be a tech in there, and that whoever had shot Jeffries wouldn't be able to get down here.

After a few more minutes of negotiating the industrial surrounds, Peterson waved his light around in a bid to catch Jasper's attention. As soon as he could lift his gaze from the jumble of corrugated pipes he was stepping over on the floor, Jasper looked up and saw Peterson shaking his head. Jasper walked over to him and shrugged. *What's the problem?* Peterson was illuminating the side of the containment building with his light. The concrete was cracked into what looked like fallen blocks, but it was nothing they couldn't walk around to continue moving around the structure. Then Peterson took the logbook and wrote fast.

THIS WAS THE OTHER DOOR! WALL CAVED IN AROUND IT, FROM UP ABOVE IT LOOKS LIKE.

He stared up at the broken concrete wall, the steel liner ruptured in a long seam beginning about ten feet up and continuing for thirty feet or so. On either side of that seam were loose pockets of exposed concrete and jagged rips of protruding rebar. Jasper traced the damage down to the door and saw how everything that had been knocked loose from above had piled up in the doorway—probably on both sides, he figured—effectively entombing the entrance and exit in chunks of raw building materials.

Neither of them had anything else to write. This was not going to be a way in or out for anybody. But then Jasper happened on a loose length of rebar and an idea occurred to him. He picked it up and walked over to the ruined doorway, looking for a good place to bang on that might resonate well enough for the men inside to hear. He could at least let them know they were trying to get to them, sort of like the old submarine movies he'd seen where a diver would rap on the hull of a doomed sub, even though he couldn't gain entrance to the craft himself. But then it occurred to him it might be a cruel act, since the techs trapped inside would assume they were being rescued, when in fact even if Jasper and Peterson did manage to free them from the reactor, they would only be going from the proverbial frying pan to its complementary fire, for they would still have to fix the water cooling problem, and fast. And beyond that—they still had no way out of the larger handling building. Jasper forced himself to calm down and focus on one problem at a time. If the trapped men knew someone was out here, maybe they could help somehow, perhaps by clearing debris from the inside?

Jasper banged the pipe against another piece of rebar poking out from the wall. Peterson gave his approval in the form of a thumbs-up and Jasper was surprised to feel a minor swelling of pride. He came down here to work. This was his plant, too, even though he was in an area that he normally had nothing to do with. But he could still be useful here. Even so, after a couple of minutes of banging and listening, banging and listening, no indication had come that they had been heard. At first, Jasper had been concerned that they wouldn't be able to hear ambient noises well enough with the suit hoods on, but he could hear his own hammering well enough and it was not being transmitted through their headset microphones.

Jasper dropped the metal rod and turned to Peterson with a shrug. *Now what?* Peterson jotted a note on the pad and held it out for Jasper to read.

LET'S CONTINUE CIRCLING THE REACTOR.
NO MORE DOORS BUT MAYBE SOMETHING
ELSE OPENED UP?

Jasper nodded. Might as well, although he didn't hold out much hope. If something opened up, then the guys trapped inside probably would have gotten out already, right? *What the heck were they gonna do? And at any moment the terrorists could find their way in here.* Peterson's frantic light waving commanded his attention long enough to duck under some hanging cables. Then they continued on around the mostly intact wall. Jasper examined the sides high up the wall and didn't notice any further significant damage.

He had just stepped around a forklift when he stopped in place. This one was actually still upright. *Why walk when you can ride?* Although it had been a while, Jasper had operated them before and felt comfortable enough behind the controls. He took a look at their immediate path ahead, though, and realized that with all of the fallen machinery and debris it would be easier just to walk. But then a thought occurred to him.

Jasper took a seat inside the forklift and was pleased when it came to life after hitting the start button. He took a few seconds to get a feel for the controls and then put the thing into gear, rolling slowly across the debris-strewn floor. He caught up to Peterson and was going to honk the horn, but then recognized that spooking a guy with a gun in an iffy situation wasn't the brightest move, so he refrained. Peterson heard the approaching motor, though, and whirled around. He threw his hands up when he saw Jasper behind the wheel. Jasper ducked out of the machine and held up the logbook. Peterson tapped a foot while he shone the light for Jasper to write by.

MAYBE I CAN USE THIS LIFT TO KNOCK
THE STAIR PIECE AWAY FROM THE FIRST
DOORWAY!

By the glow of the flashlight Jasper saw Peterson's eyes widen behind his faceplate before he smiled and gave a vigorous thumbs-up. Jasper got back into the forklift and put it into gear again, moving slowly behind Peterson, who scouted ahead to remove obstacles for their new hope.

Fifteen minutes of careful maneuvering later, Peterson signaled that they had reached the first doorway. This also meant that they had completed their circumnavigation of the reactor containment building, leaving only two possibilities for entering: One, climbing the downed external staircase to access the rooftop infrastructure. Or two, using the lift to clear enough wreckage from the doorway that they could walk through on floor level. As Jasper backed the forklift into position, he fervently hoped for success in the latter possibility.

Peterson stood off to one side of the blocked doorway and aimed the light onto the displaced section of stairway. Jasper put the lift into forward gear and positioned it so that the lifting forks were beneath the metal. Then he raised the lift. At first nothing happened and he feared the wreckage was immovable. But then suddenly the forklift lurched as the bulky obstacle moved. He could see Peterson nodding. It was working! Peterson also grabbed on to the stairs and was able to pull them aside where they crashed to the floor with a discordant shriek.

Jasper continued his excavations with the machine, patiently backing up and moving forward into a new piece of debris. Behind the stairs were numerous chunks of concrete. Sometimes he found he could use the industrial machine as intended and lift large pieces up and then back them away and lower them back to the ground, with Peterson helping to kick them off the forks. Other times, he had to use the vehicle like a battering ram to run into a piece of concrete in order to dislodge it. In this manner he worked doggedly for half an our, and then Peterson approached the opening with his flashlight probing.

Jasper dismounted the forklift and saw Peterson crouch, duck-walking forward. He frantically signaled with his light.

Jasper joined him at the jagged aperture, taking care not to snag any part of his suit as he ducked inside.

Light!

He couldn't see much with Peterson in front of him, but in a few more seconds Peterson was standing, out of sight on the other side. Jasper was astonished to see a mammoth, open room. The cavelike space was perhaps a shade brighter than the fuel handling building they'd been working in.

After a fretful look behind to see if anyone might have observed them, Jasper stepped into the reactor building.

43

Jasper Howard had never been inside the reactor building before, but he didn't need that experience to tell him that horrific things had happened here. No matter which way he faced in the oversized containment building, he was confronted with equipment and infrastructure that was knocked over and shattered. One end of a massive ceiling-mounted crane lay on the floor about twenty-five feet in front of him.

Blood stained the concrete around it.

The center of the high-ceilinged room was occupied by another square pool similar in appearance to the one for spent fuel, with the reactor itself suspended over that—a silver-colored cylinder ringed with gold-colored tubular rods. Jasper was relieved to note that the reactor at least superficially appeared to be in one piece. Peering high above his head, he could see sections of the catwalk system that Peterson had mentioned hanging askew. He was glad they'd found a way in on ground level.

Jasper was trying to guess what some of the other equipment throughout the room was when he saw Peterson waving at him to approach the fallen crane. Jasper ran to the dangling machinery, sickened by the sight of all the blood on the floor. He saw Peterson beckoning from the other side of the crane and he didn't want to go but forced himself to walk around the drying blood puddle to where Peterson stood, pointing at the floor.

As near as Jasper could tell, no less than four men had met their demise here, apparently crushed when tons of falling metal had impacted the cement floor. He looked up and saw Peterson rubbing his temple though his suit. He looked at Jasper and shook his head. None of these guys was alive. He pointed around the perimeter of the building as if to say, let's look around. Jasper nodded. He wished they could simply shout, "Hey, anybody in here!" but their suits prevented that. Speaking of radiation, Jasper thought, he wondered what Peterson's dosimeter read in here, right next to the reactor, but he focused on keeping his nerves about him while he walked with the security man through the reactor building.

There was no one at the reactor itself in the center of the room, so they hurried past it toward the opposite wall. So much debris littered the floor here that Jasper had to walk almost side by side with Peterson in order to have sufficient light to negotiate the wreckage. He couldn't even see what most of the stuff was, it was so dim. But it was clear to Jasper that this part of the plant had not been spared the brunt of the earthquake's wrath.

They reached the curved wall of the building and began to trace its path around. They found another hazmat-suited body buried beneath a colossal chunk of dislodged wall concrete— two legs protruding. Jasper bent down to make certain the person was dead. He and Peterson worked to pull off some of the more manageable cement chunks. Then Jasper pulled on the legs and was mortified to extract them without an attached torso. He spun and knelt, suppressing the urge to vomit in his suit because removing the headgear was not an option. Peterson could see him struggling and patted him on the back.

In a couple of minutes, they got underway again. Soon they found themselves traipsing across a strange rubber matted floor and then, after that, the low walls of some sort of workstation appeared in front of them. They walked around one end of the structure and stepped into a cubicle area, filled with computers that controlled various machinery and systems on the floor. They zigzagged through the mazelike work area, following the contours of the desk dividers. It would have been almost pitch-black in here were it not for the glowing LCD screens. Most of them appeared to be functioning, Jasper thought; some had actively scrolling streams of cryptic-looking data that made him think of the movie *The Matrix*.

They made a turn around an L-shaped corner and stood bolt still when they saw two men at workstations directly across from one another—one sitting and one standing. They stared intently at their screens. Peterson raised his pistol and assumed a two-armed firing stance, rapidly switching the barrel from one man to the other. Jasper didn't know if Peterson had seen into their faceplates and did not recognize them, or if he was merely being cautious. Couldn't blame him if he was, Jasper thought. If these were terrorists, though, he further supposed, they appeared awfully calm, pecking away at computer keyboards as if they might be at home composing an e-mail to a friend. Except for the level five radiation suits. If they were talking, it wasn't on their same radio channel because Jasper couldn't hear them.

First the man on the left slowly raised his hands. The one on the right kept typing, apparently oblivious to the gun trained on him. Could they be terrorists intent on issuing commands that would cause a meltdown? Peterson inched his way to the right until he was well within the man's peripheral vision. The man on the right looked up and jumped in his chair, startled, but put his hands up. Then he turned to look back at his colleague, confirming that he, too, had surrendered.

With the men facing them, Peterson handed the flashlight back to Jasper, who shined it directly into the faceplate of the man on the left. Peterson angled his head so as to see who it was. Apparently, he recognized him, for he lowered, but did not holster his gun. Jasper shined the light into the face of the other man, and Peterson had a brief look at him, too, before turning around to Jasper and giving him the "okay" sign, thumb and index finger in a circle. Peterson holstered his firearm. Jasper walked up to the man on the right and held his arm out.

Sam!

It seemed like eons ago that he'd spoken on his yard radio to the reactor tech while standing in the parking lot. *Probably should have listened to you, Sam, when you told me to leave.* But clearly the wide grin on Sam's face said that he was awfully glad Jasper had stayed behind. He shook Jasper's hand and pointed to an ear. Jasper shook his head. They were on different radio frequencies and Jasper didn't see how he could change his; he certainly couldn't take his suit off to fiddle with the radio. He opened up the logbook and showed Sam the pen. The tech understood immediately and started to write.

DO YOU KNOW WHAT FREQUENCY YOU'RE ON?

Jasper shook his head and passed the pad to Peterson, who promptly nodded and wrote down a number. He showed it to Sam, who turned back to his computer and tapped on the keyboard to bring up an application. Then he keyed in the number Peterson had written. He turned around to face them again and mouthed the words, "Hi, Jasper! Boy, am I ever glad to see you!"

And Jasper was surprised to actually hear Sam's voice.

Sam added, "Sorry, I'm glad to see you, too." He turned to Peterson. "I've seen you around but I don't believe I know your name."

"Call me Peterson. Listen, we were maintaining radio silence because this channel has been compromised. We think Stephen Jeffries was shot by unknown intruders who could be monitoring this frequency."

Sam nodded and held up a finger. *Hold on a minute.* He turned back to his computer and tapped away for a couple of minutes. Then they heard his voice again.

"There. We're still on the same frequency, but I added a privacy tone—basically just a modified squelch control, but if both radios don't have it set exactly the same, they won't be able to hear each other."

"So the four of us can all hear and talk to each other, but the terrorists up there can't?" Peterson clarified.

Sam nodded. "Unless they happen to hit on our same privacy codes, which is statistically about as probable as this place ever getting another operating permit," he finished with a laugh, waving an arm about to indicate all the destruction on the other side of the workstation walls.

"Great, if and when we all make it out of this in one, nonradiated piece, we can look forward to finding another job," the other tech said.

Jasper wondered how they could be so jovial in the face of such tragedy—surely they'd seen their dead and mutilated coworkers over by the reactor? But then he supposed that the levity was a coping mechanism of sorts. These guys were dealing with the highest potential for danger of just about anybody.

They heard Peterson sigh into his mic. "People, let's not forget that we've still got quite a situation here." He looked over to Jasper as if for confirmation of this fact. "Mr. Howard here was in the process of fixing the spent fuel pool cooling system, under the direction of Stephen Jeffries, when Jeffries was shot by unknown intruders. With him gone, we figured our only hope was to see if any of you guys were still left in here."

"Good to know that if the cooling system worked you'd have left us here," Sam joked.

"Actually," Jasper said, "even that's not an option." He explained the broken catwalk and how his ladder had fallen.

"We better get to that cooling station," Sam admitted after hearing the account. "The reactor core is under control, shut down with no residual problems. Unfortunately, all our technicians except for us either left before things got too rough or . . ." He jerked a thumb toward the reactor and choked up a bit. Jasper clapped him on the shoulder. "We'll get through this. Let's get some work done."

Sam nodded and picked up a flashlight from his workstation. Jasper ditched the logbook. The four nuclear employees exited the cubby system and strode across the reactor housing floor until they reached the door.

"This was closed off earlier," Sam said.

"We tried for an hour, couldn't budge all the crap that was piled up. How'd you get through?" the other technician asked.

"Heavy machinery," Jasper answered, ducking through the opening. He emerged first and stood with a hand on his trusty forklift until Sam had made it through.

"Good thinking," Sam said.

Sam led the way back across the fuel handling building to the cooling station. Peterson was glad to be back on true security detail, bringing up the rear while constantly looking around with his light beam for signs of trouble. And this time he knew they were out there.

They reached the walkway along the wall and climbed up. It appeared the same as before and they walked quickly along it to the cooling equipment station. Peterson shined his light first on the switchgear consoles and then out on the floor.

"That's the primary cooling loop Jeffries had Mr. Howard working on," Peterson told the technicians.

Sam walked up to the switchboard controls while his colleague played his own flashlight over the instrumentation. After a couple of minutes of knob-turning and dial-setting, Sam told the other tech to go out on the floor to the cooling loop. He was there in short order, describing the technical settings to Sam, who would adjust the controls on the switchgear panel before asking him to do something else to the loop. After about fifteen minutes of this kind of back-and-forth, Sam told his co-worker to rejoin them on the walkway.

"Everything's optimal here," Sam told the group, "but we're not finished yet. We need to go to the other cooling system station and make some crucial adjustments there. And we've got to hurry."

"We do," the other tech agreed.

Peterson shone his beam to the right along the catwalk. "Down this way, right?"

"Correct," Sam said, already moving in that direction. After a few minutes, they came to a buckled section of walkway that was impassable, so they dropped to the work floor to skirt around it. Sam was leading the way across the floor in the direction they were traveling on the walkway when they heard him make a kind of coughing noise, followed by, "What's that?"

All of a sudden, he started backing up, flailing his arms, until he tripped over a small step in the concrete that differentiated two work areas.

"What is it?" Peterson demanded, starting to run from his place at the rear of the group. Jasper could hear his footfalls pounding the concrete though his suit.

"Something's coming out of the transfer canal!" Sam stammered.

"What's the transfer canal?" Jasper asked.

Sam's co-worker answered, speaking rapidly as they caught

up to Sam. "It's a waterway that connects the spent fuel pool to the reactor pool, so that when the fuel rods from the reactor are no good anymore, they can stay underwater while they're moved over to the spent fuel pool. It's under the floor in some parts, and exposed in others like where Sam is now."

"Two men—coming out of the canal!" Sam warned.

44

Jasper thought that maybe Sam was cracking from the stress, but as the other technician jogged left up ahead, he saw what looked to him like two Navy frogmen—deep sea divers with suits and tanks and masks on, shimmying out of the water onto the work floor on their knees, then pushing to their feet, standing there dripping for a split second while they slipped out of their dive gear.

Jasper watched in horror as one of them removed a pistol of some type from a sheath and leveled it right at Sam, while the other diver took aim with a similar weapon at Peterson, who was already firing at these new threats.

Thanks to Peterson's rapid response, the diver aiming at Sam went down clutching a knee in agony. He was still dangerous, though, firing off his gun largely at random while writhing around on the floor. The other nuclear technician dropped to the ground, flattening himself out while shining his flashlight into the eyes of the other diver. It was a poor tactic, since that diver whirled around and fired at the light source.

Jasper saw the tech's faceplate spiderweb into a maze of cracks as the bullet impacted it.

"Can't see, I can't see!" the tech shouted over the com line. Jasper wasn't sure if he meant he was literally blind from being shot or if he just couldn't see through the fractured faceplate. The tech began rolling on the floor away from the divers.

Peterson, meanwhile, was engaged in a full-out gun battle with the second diver. He was using a group of fifty-five-gallon drums as cover (God only knew what the hell was in them, Jasper thought), reaching his shooting arm only around the edge to return fire. Then they heard a grunt of pain over the radio and Jasper knew that one of them had been hit. He looked at the tech rolling across the floor and saw a fat smear of blood on the concrete in his wake. As he watched, he saw his roll slow until he lay facedown on the floor, unmoving.

It was then that Jasper realized he was just standing there out in the open—the only one who was not either taking cover or actively fighting. He was lucky to be alive, and now with the tech down, he knew the diver who had shot him would be seeking a new target.

Jasper dove headlong onto the floor to avoid the gunfire he was sure was coming. He landed beneath a large hook hanging from a suspended steel cable. He heard a splash and saw the diver Peterson had been shooting at land in the transfer canal from whence he came.

The second diver now turned his attention to the armed resistance. He dropped the pistol he'd been using—either out of ammunition or jammed from being in the water—and immediately drew another from a second sheath around his thigh and started triggering it off at Peterson.

Two of the metal drums on the top of the stack the security man hid behind were knocked over by clanging rounds, causing a brown viscous substance to drool onto Peterson's head.

Jasper could see that the terrorist shooter had learned only Peterson had a firearm, for he allowed himself to be close to Sam without looking his way while shooting only at Peterson. But when Peterson ducked back behind the remaining upright barrels, the terrorist spun and took aim on Sam.

"I'm out of ammo!" Jasper heard Peterson say.

Jasper grabbed the hanging hook and pulled it back, lining it up with the remaining opponent, who now began to advance toward Sam, who had moved to the canal to check on the man who'd fallen in.

"The guy in the canal's dead," Sam hollered.

"Sam, look out!" Jasper said as he swung the heavy hook toward the shooter. The jihadist was able to dodge it, but the act threw him off balance and at that moment Peterson took a chance. He rose from a crouch like a sprinter and charged at Alivi's man like a mad bull. When he was five feet from him, while the man was still recovering his balance, Peterson leapt.

He tackled the terrorist to the floor and they grappled, two men in different kinds of exposure protection suits each seeking to kill the other. To Jasper, it was a surreal moment but he also recognized that it was now three-on-one: himself, Peterson, and Sam versus the remaining aquatic gunman. The attacker was armed, however, while the three of them no longer were.

Jasper and Sam both moved toward the two ground fighters from different directions. Sam was closer, and he had almost reached the wrestlers when they heard a shot echo throughout the nuclear facility. The terrorist rolled out from under Peterson's body and pushed him toward the canal. He landed on his back, one leg dangling into the water, and Jasper sucked in his breath sharply as he saw the red circle in the blue suit over Peterson's belly. Gut shot. Sam flung himself atop Alivi's man, concentrating on the hand with the gun.

"I'm hit," Peterson managed, but his voice was feeble.

Jasper saw the terrorist's gun clatter to the concrete and

nearly bounce into the transfer canal. He scooped it up, spun around. Alivi's henchman slammed Sam's head into the floor and was pulling him up by the neck, preparing to do it again when Jasper shot the man in the chest with his own weapon. He heard a dull thud as the projectile impacted the neoprene wetsuit. The man dropped to his knees before collapsing forward onto his ditched scuba tanks.

At that moment an earsplitting alarm sounded, high-pitched and demanding attention.

"We've got to get to that second cooling station," Sam warned.

Jasper ran to Peterson and looked into his eyes through their faceplates. They were closed. He appeared absolutely still. He shook the security man and yelled into his microphone. "Peterson, wake up! We need you!"

"He's gone, Jasper. And we are, too, if we don't fix this cooling system. This way."

Jasper looked over at the dead terrorist on the floor, at the smoking gun in his own hand. What had he become? He'd come down here to try to help people, and now he was a . . . *a killer*? Even though it was an act of self-defense for him and others—potentially millions of others—the deed still didn't sit well with him. He had shown up to work today like any other, ready to do an honest job for fair pay. The situation in which he now found himself was so far beyond that. . . .

"Jasper! Snap out of it, buddy. We can do this. C'mon!"

"On my way." Sam was right. Standing around mourning their losses wasn't going to prevent the radioactive conflagration that was on its way if they couldn't fix that cooling water system. Jasper took one last look at Peterson and saw his flashlight lying on the floor beside his blue-suited corpse. He reached down and grabbed it, then hurried across the floor after Sam, who led the way with his own light.

Sam moved faster than Jasper was comfortable with, running across the compromised industrial workspace, relying on his flashlight to point out the innumerable tripping hazards and obstacles. But in minutes they had reached the cooling loop on the floor in front of the walkway.

"Up here!" Sam scrambled onto the walkway and ran to the left. Jasper followed suit and in another few minutes he saw Sam slow to a jog, then a walk, and then stop. Jasper caught up to him and saw another switchgear panel alongside a metal rack that housed a series of machines with LCD readouts. A thick cluster of PVC pipes ran from a suspended rack down into the floor.

"Hold this on the panel, here, will you?" Sam thrust his flashlight behind him. Jasper took it, now aiming two lights onto the switchgear station. Sam muttered to himself as he turned various knobs and flipped dense arrays of switches. Occasionally, he'd stoop to look at some numbers on an LCD, then go back to adjusting more controls. Jasper kept one eye on his light duty and the other on the dark work floor beyond, ready to trade one of his lights for the gun if necessary.

While Sam worked, Jasper thought about the terrorists. Who were they? Did the threatening voice he'd heard over Jeffries's radio belong to one of the two scuba instigators? If so, then they must have found a way down here, and not just any way but one that allowed them to transport the dive gear. He wasn't sure but doubted that this was possible. And if it wasn't possible, then it must also be true that whoever had spoken to them earlier from above was still there. And how much had Peterson and Jeffries known? Had they received a credible threat or were they simply on elevated watch status because of the disaster . . . ?

Suddenly the most frenetic-sounding of the cacophony of alarms stopped and Sam turned away from the cooling station controls.

"Fixed it?" Jasper's voice was edged with hope.

But Sam shook his head. "No, sorry. I've set the controls to where they need to be, which is what stopped the alarm—

but these controls don't know yet that there's no water for them to deliver. The fact of the matter is that we're going to need to bring chilled water to the system and it's not coming from the river through the intake."

"Can we fix the river intake?"

"No, sir. Believe me when I say that it's crushed beyond all hope and will never be operational again. Two of our men died trying to fix it earlier."

"Then what's the next best thing? There must be something we can do."

Sam threw his hands up. "Got any ideas?"

Jasper looked across the foreboding work floor, the dystopian symphony of systems alarms a fitting soundtrack for his apocalyptic thoughts. *Everyone warned me about the inevitable . . . New York City uninhabitable for decades, even centuries. . . . The water unsafe to drink . . . The water . . . water . . . Water!*

"Sam! Can we get to a working radio that can contact the city?"

45

"Is that it?" Frank Mendoza asked his wife, pointing to a large building still standing with some lights on. Neither of them had ever been to Columbia University's research hospital. With the destruction of the quake, it would take some effort to recognize in the darkness. Most of the road signs were laid flat.

"I think so," Jana said, looking at the pancaked landscape ahead. "The main campus was off to our left not long after we came out of the park, and it's a couple of miles north of that, so . . . do you think we've gone that far yet?"

Mendoza frowned. For the length of time they'd been traveling, they should have been much farther than two miles from the park. But when you were picking your way in the dark through mounds of scattered debris and monumental drifts of wreckage, normal walking speed was far from guaranteed. "I think that's about right. Let's take a look."

They walked toward the upright structure. Around them everywhere were cars abandoned in the roadway, many of them wrecked. They passed a silver tanker truck that appeared to be left behind, for it looked to be perfectly drivable.

"This is it!" Jana exclaimed as they neared the building.

"They've actually got working ambulances out front," Mendoza noted. It was a good sign. There were entrance lights, too, and as they watched, a group of people exited, none of them running or screaming. Compared to Jana's place of work, this hospital seemed like it could be almost operational.

They hurried to the entrance, where an ambulance had pulled up and a paramedic crew was unloading a patient on a stretcher. The siren and lights on another ambulance came to life and the emergency vehicle took to the streets.

"Looks promising," Jana said. They pushed through the revolving doors into the lobby and were greeted with a semblance of order, compared to St. Luke's-Roosevelt. A multitude of patients and their families and friends still jammed the lobby beyond normal capacity, but several hospital employees were present and working to maintain order. Power was on.

"Sort of looks like a hospital," Mendoza quipped.

"Instead of a war zone, right?" Jana said as she homed in on a man holding a clipboard near the front of the lobby. She held her own hospital ID badge out as she approached. She explained that she'd walked here all the way from St. Luke's-Roosevelt and needed to speak with someone about obtaining assistance. "We desperately need supplies, ambulances, doctors—whatever you can spare," she finished. The man told her to wait and retreated out of sight back into the reception desk area. Another couple who'd been waiting off to the side approached the Mendozas.

"I heard you say you came from St. Luke's," the woman said. "Is it really bad? We're looking for our son—working our way south. If he's not here we might try St. Luke's next." Mendoza was in the process of explaining to them that even if their son was there, he didn't see how they would be able to locate him with all the power problems and general chaos they were experiencing when an older man in a rumpled suit and tie emerged from the admin section with the employee Jana had just spoken with.

"You came from St. Luke's-Roosevelt?" he said, eyeing the couple.

"She works there, I'm her husband and just escorted her here for safety reasons," Mendoza clarified.

The businessman nodded and extended a hand to Jana. "I'm Greg Randall, director of managed care operations." He paused to shake Mendoza's hand before continuing. "I'm glad you were able to make your way to us. We have some outside communications, but they're spotty. It'd be great to get some firsthand reports from our community level colleagues. Come on with me up to the third floor and we'll see what we can do to help the good folks over at St. Luke's. You know I used to work there? Over two decades ago now, I'm afraid, but I met some great people there and enjoyed it immensely. I think Dr. Henderson's still there. If you please, this way."

They followed him back into the employees-only area and were pleasantly surprised to see that the elevator was working. They rode it to the third floor and followed Randall to a closed door. He knocked and then opened it without waiting for a response, sticking his head inside.

"Dr. Jackson?" he called. "Could you come out here, please?" A man in a white lab coat appeared at the doorway. Randall introduced the Mendozas and gave a brief summary of the purpose of their visit, ending with, "Do you think you could take them around to see if there's anything we could do to help the good folks over at St. Luke's-Roosevelt?"

"Happy to, let's start over by the lounge. If there's a physician on break, I'll nominate him to go." Dr. Jackson laughed. "Seriously, though, I do think we should be able to spare some resources. . . ."

He began explaining to Jana the different ways in which they might be able to help St. Luke's-Roosevelt. As they walked down the hall, Mendoza noticed a closed door with a placard reading COMMUNICATION ROOM. He asked Randall what that was.

"It's our amateur radio room. It's got ham radios for emergencies. Overall, it's been our best source of information. Unfortunately it's run by volunteers, and only one of them has been able to make it by, but he left a while ago, and none of the rest of us know how to really operate the stuff. Still, we've been pretty lucky so far just to be able to continue operating relatively normally."

"Actually, I know how to operate those types of radios," Mendoza said. "Would you mind if I had a listen? I'd really like to hear some status reports from around the city, see what's going on. Maybe listen in on the police and fire bands to see how the rescue efforts are developing. I don't think Jana needs me to follow her around in here," he finished.

Randall stopped. "Absolutely. You can update all of us. We haven't had a chance to even listen lately. Hold up, Dr. Jackson, Jana?" They interrupted their conversation about which medical supplies were most critical in order to look back at Randall and Mendoza.

Mendoza pointed at the radio room, which Randall opened. "Honey, I'm going to be in here while you're getting things together. I want to see if I can hear some news. As soon as you're ready to go, just come and get me, okay?"

Jana gave him a kiss and left with Dr. Jackson and Mr. Randall. Mendoza entered the communications room. It wasn't much larger than a broom closet, he guessed, judging by the narrow confines, but it did have a window out of which snaked an antenna cable. Like Randall had said, there was no one in the room. He looked at the shelves on the wall and saw a couple of radio units, their backlit displays indicating that they had power. Mendoza took a seat in a swivel chair facing one of the units, which he recognized as a shortwave radio set that would have a longer range than higher frequency walkie-talkie and police units, which depended on external infrastructure like antenna towers to increase transmitting range. He'd already seen firsthand what it was like within a few miles. He wanted to get a feel for the scope of the earthquake's effects.

He adjusted the volume on the unit while turning the dial to make sure it was working. Mostly static, but then the dial caught on a frequency with some clear chatter. They were speaking French, though, and Mendoza figured they were probably French-Canadians north of the border, so he continued scanning the dial. He heard one report from a ranger station upstate, saying that a forest fire had started as a result of a downed power line. There was nothing Mendoza could do to help with that and it was far away, so he went on with his tour of the dial. He was about to give up on shortwave and see what was happening on the AM broadcast band when an LED on the receiver lit up green and a strong signal came through. It carried a male voice fraught with worry along with a cacophony of sirens in the background.

". . . Indian Point . . . I repeat . . . Attention, truck drivers and transportation companies: My name is Jasper Howard. I am a maintenance supervisor at the Indian Point nuclear power facility twenty-five miles north of New York City. We are in imminent danger of having a radioactive fire here in spent fuel pool number two. We need large amounts of cold water right now in order to prevent this from happening. If you can hear me, please acknowledge."

Jasper started repeating his message but Mendoza picked up the microphone, wondering if it was live. He keyed the transmitter and broke into Jasper's transmission.

"Acknowledge your transmission, Indian Point. This is Columbia Research Hospital, do you read me?" He repeated his own message and then heard the airwave go silent. At first, he thought his transmission was being received on the other end only as garbled static, the distance too long, or the interference too great, but then Jasper's voice emanated from the speaker once more.

"I read you, Columbia! I read you! Can you hear me, copy?"

"Yes, I hear you. My name is Frank Mendoza."

"Frank, real glad we were able to reach you. Listen, we're in a tough situation here. We need lots of cold water, as soon as possible. Stat, like you'd say in a hospital right?"

Mendoza found himself smiling along with Jasper's quick little laugh. "I don't know what your job is there, buddy, but if there's anything you can do to get the word out, believe me when I say that the entire City of New York needs us to get that water."

"Jasper, I'll help. I don't even work here, my wife does. I just came with her from St. Luke's-Roosevelt to make sure she got here okay. Tell me more about what you need and I promise I'll do my utmost to make it happen."

Jasper described the situation in more detail and how their best bet was probably tanker trucks that could be filled with cold water and driven to the nuclear plant. Mendoza flashed on the silver truck sitting in the road he and Jana had walked by on the way over here. He had some connections with the police and fire departments—they had to have some trucks that were still functioning. *I've got to help with this!*

He gripped the microphone. "Okay, Jasper, you got it. I don't know exactly how I'm gonna pull this off yet, but I am going to do my damnedest. You hold tight, okay?"

"The state of New York thanks you," Jasper said. "Once you get within range you can use a regular walkie—channel eighteen—if you have one. Please hurry!"

"Copy that. Over and out."

Mendoza eyeballed the radio table. He spotted what he was looking for on the far end—a handheld radio sitting in a charging stand. He grabbed it and half-ran, half-limped from the radio shack, turning into the hallway in the direction he'd last seen Jana going. No way could he just leave her here without telling her where he was going, not after all they'd been through today. He ran down the long hallway, skidding to a halt when he came to an intersection, looking around, and then sprinting off again like a track racer.

He heard her before he saw her, laughing that cute little laugh of hers, somehow managing to find something humorous even in this dire situation. That was his Jana. He'd found her, she was okay, and she knew that he was all right. But now his city needed him. It was his turn to act. He just had to make sure Jana would stay safe while he was out.

She spotted him running toward her and froze in midsentence. He reached her and a group of MDs she'd been talking to, including Jackson. Quickly, he summarized the situation at the nuclear plant. Upon hearing the news, one of the doctors muttered something under his breath and pinched the bridge of his nose as if warding off a headache.

"I'll be okay, Frank. If you want to go, then go."

"I don't want you to leave this hospital," Mendoza said. "Is there a way you can help your hospital without leaving here until I get back?"

Jana looked at Dr. Jackson, who nodded. He said, "We were just discussing that. Jana's going to coordinate one of our EMT teams to take an ambulance to St. Luke's-Roosevelt. She'll oversee the loading of supplies and personnel, and send the ambulance on its way while she stays here." He looked at both Jana and Mendoza to see if this was agreeable.

"I'll be back as soon as I can. I've got to make some calls and I'm going back to that tanker truck we saw. Leave the shortwave radio in the communications room on the same station. That's the channel they're using from Indian Point."

With that he leaned in and kissed his wife.

"Be careful," she said.

Mendoza ran toward the elevator.

46

"Hold on, let me think about this," Sam said. Jasper watched the reactor technician furrow his brow in concentration while he gawked at a complex water flow schematic on a computer monitor. They were back inside the reactor building's cubicle workstation, where they had retreated after making the radio call. Sam had already made a couple of physical adjustments to pipe valves and flow regulators on the work floor. Now he was checking the schematic to be as certain as possible that if and when they did receive new water, it would be routed properly in order to save the spent fuel pool.

The ongoing din of systems alarms had long since given Jasper a headache, and they both knew that there was no margin for error. If the man from the hospital—Frank Mendoza (he had to remember his name)—was able to deliver on his end, Jasper could think of nothing more disappointing than having that water not be able to do the job.

And the truth was that he felt helpless at this point. He could see now that these reactor workers whom he'd always assumed were some kind of technical and scientific gods were in fact just people—well-trained people, but people nonetheless, doing a job with ups and downs like anyone else. They weren't perfect. They made mistakes and they didn't know everything. And right now Sam was being perfectly honest with him. He had jerry-rigged a solution for how to deliver the water to where it was most needed, but at this point it was still all theoretical. He'd never actually had to do anything like that before, so there was no guarantee it would actually work.

And that was his reality, Jasper thought, watching the flow lines on Sam's schematic change color in response to his keyboard input. Everyone else had either fled in fear or been killed, and so the fate of millions of people all came down to what Sam and Jasper—and hopefully Frank Mendoza—were able to do, right here, right now.

"I think this'll work," Sam declared in a flat voice.

Jasper bit back a sarcastic remark about *thinking* it would work. Sam was it. He had to believe in him. The City of New York had to believe in him. It occurred to Jasper that he didn't even know Sam's last name. He'd seen the guy for years, every now and then, walking into work or leaving for the day. Not much more than *Hi, how ya doin',* or *Almost Friday!* That kind of thing. Yet now they needed to work together on the highest level possible.

"Anything else we can do, Sam, to prepare?"

"Let me run one more sim." He tapped some keys and traced his finger ahead of the water flow simulation on screen, a moving blue line on screen depicting where the water would move with the current control settings. He gave a shrug.

"All we need is the water," he said, turning away from the monitor to look at Jasper, who eyed the handheld radio on the desk in front of him.

"I can't use this thing through the suit. But we need to be on a regular walkie channel, eighteen, I told Frank Mendoza."

"I can patch us onto eighteen," Sam said, moving to a

different computer setup. "But it'll be an open channel where anyone can hear us."

"At this point I want people to hear us."

Sam made some adjustments on the computer's radio application and then turned to Jasper. "Can you hear me?"

"Yes."

"Good. We're on channel eighteen. Inside the reactor building we can only hear each other. There's no way it'll transmit through the lead walls. But outside of here, it should work for a couple miles."

"Good, so we'll hear Mendoza if he calls us from the gate." Then Jasper asked, "So you're sure that the fill point will be reachable to a truck coming in here?"

Sam threw up his hands. "If it hasn't been damaged in the quake to the point that the fitting was compromised, then it should work. Last I saw it was okay. It leads to the same place as the river intake eventually goes to. It'll just be lower volume, but we can direct one hundred percent of it to the spent fuel pool, bypassing the reactor core and the whole Reactor Number One complex."

"How do you think Reactor One is doing, anyway?" Sam had just reminded Jasper that there were two functional reactors at Indian Point, and they had only been dealing with one of them. Could a drama similar to theirs be playing out within the other containment building, a few yards away outside? The thought made him nauseous.

But Sam shook his head definitively. "It's no problem. I saw it earlier after the last big aftershock. Didn't sustain much damage, and besides, the big thing is that it was shut down a week ago in preparation for the NRC visit, and its spent fuel pool was emptied out, the rods transferred to concrete casings and taken off-site for disposal."

Jasper nodded and said, "That's some consolation, at least.

What kind of damage do you think the guy who killed Jeffries could be doing up there, assuming he can't get down here?"

Sam glanced at his simulation for a moment before answering. "Impossible for me to say for sure, but I don't think they can do too much. Most of that stuff up there is for monitoring what goes on down here, not for control. The main thing I'd worry about is that they don't find a way in here. We already know they figured out how to swim in through the intake. Hopefully, whoever's up there doesn't try that, also."

Jasper looked up at the containment ceiling far above. "We should get out and patrol the floor. Watch for any signs that they did find a way to screw things up. Don't want to miss a radio call, either."

Sam stood. "Okay. I set my program such that we'll hear an alarm if the optimal settings change too much."

"Great, another alarm, just what we need."

Sam laughed a little. "Yeah, well in this case it would be a good thing if we want to be in two places at once. Let's go."

They made their way out of the cubicle area and back through the doorway Jasper had cleared earlier with the forklift. The dimly lit work floor looked the same as it had when they'd last left it.

Jasper pointed to the radio transmitter behind his faceplate. "Now that we're clear of the reactor containment, let me try my guys one more time." Jasper had been disappointed that he was unable to raise any of his employees on the walkie-talkie earlier when he'd wanted to tell them to get water. He tried again now, hoping that they were scanning the walkie channels and would hear him.

But no reply came.

He hoped that they'd left the perimeter gate open when they'd left so that the trucks (if they came) could get in. If not, like he and his workers had discussed on occasion over the years, it would be no big deal for a large truck to just ram through it, if it came to that. If something happened to this radio link, though, he didn't see how this was going to work. They had to be able to communicate in order to direct them to the pipe fitting area.

"They took off, huh?" Sam asked.

"Looks like it. Can't say as I blame them."

"Too bad, we could use their help now, though."

"We'll just have to work it, out, Sam. And then maybe after we get through this, I'll have a good justification to give my guys a raise."

Sam laughed. "The techs could use a raise, too. The ones who are left, anyway," he added dourly.

And that was when they felt it. At first Jasper thought he was getting dizzy; he was unsteady on his feet. But then he watched Sam nearly fall, too, and he knew.

"Aftershock!"

47

Lauren Dykstra awoke from a confused, groggy sleep during which she had dreamed the ground was rolling and shifting and dancing and twirling beneath her, and thought she'd been struck blind. Her eyes were open. She was sure of it. And yet she could not see. She wanted to wave a hand in front of her face as a vision test but both of her arms were solidly pinned. She was positive that earlier she could move one at least a little bit, but somehow it seemed like the bookcase she was trapped beneath had shifted while she was out, smothering her even worse than before. She could move her head somewhat, though, and when she tilted it, the shade of black lightened just a bit.

It's nighttime, silly, that's all. Chill out! With all the lights destroyed, the only light would be what filters through the wrecked library from the moon and stars.

Still, even her inner voice—the one that was usually right about things, like the time it told her the guy she liked in her junior year was going to ask some other girl to the prom, and that time when she decided not to study the obscure bonus material for the AP chemistry test because everybody said it wasn't going to be on there . . . That voice had an annoying habit of being right, and right now it was telling her that something was very, very wrong with her.

I'm dying, aren't I? she asked her inner voice. She didn't like to call the voice God. That's not really what it was to her. It was more like a guiding light that, when it chose to appear, was usually correct.

Though not always. She remembered the time when she was contemplating watching one of the tenth anniversary of 9/11 tribute specials on television, and the voice was telling her that if she watched it, she'd be able to recall a new memory of her mother. When you lose your mother at age five, every memory becomes vastly precious because five-year-olds don't have a large capacity for long-term memory and there wasn't a lot to choose from to begin with. If you lost your mother at age thirty-nine, on the other hand, while naturally it was a tragic event, you still had your entire childhood with her to look back on, not to mention all the adult years after that. Gone at five, it was like trying to hold on to a beloved phantom.

But every now and then, as she grew older, a new memory would hit her like a flash of lightning, at the most random times—waiting for the bus, taking a shower, walking down the stairs. . . . She'd recall some interaction or scene with her mother in the most striking detail—picture her so vividly that she knew in her heart of hearts she was remembering something real; maybe she'd be offering her milk and cookies in the middle of the night after she'd awoken from a bad dream, or telling her that she didn't have to go to school that day if she didn't want to, let's stay home and play dolls. . . .

When she got one of these flashbacks, she always stopped whatever she was doing, no matter how awkward that might be for the situation at hand, and replayed it over and over until she was sure she wouldn't forget it, until she had burned the images into her neurons.

So when the day before the tenth anniversary of 9/11 her special voice told her that if she watched one of the tribute specials on TV—something her father had sharply warned her against (You don't need to relive it again, Lauren)—she'd pick up a new memory of her mother.

So against the advice of her dad and family friends, even her own friends, she'd sat through the entire three-hour production, crying in places, even learning a few new facts about the tragedy. But by the time some stupid sitcom was on after the tribute, she still hadn't dredged up any new memories.

The voice had been wrong. It was not infallible. She'd been crushed to learn that then—it weighed on her heavily, knowing that not only did she not receive another memory but also that her inner voice was not perfect.

But now . . . Lauren managed a thin smile in the darkness. Now she couldn't be happier that she knew the voice could be wrong.

Because it was telling her she was going to die.

48

A metal dish of some kind banged into the floor next to them. Sam pointed toward the center of the massive room. "Let's take cover. There's a control booth over there," he said, pointing again. Jasper saw a squat, metal enclosure about a hundred feet away. They ran for it, more objects crashing around them. An aluminum metal bar glanced off Jasper's right forearm as he ran, and he stopped to see if his radiation suit had ripped.

Still in one piece!

He wasn't sure why he'd stopped. He hadn't been looking over Sam's shoulder to read his dosimeter or anything like that, but that was because his suit had been intact. He was doing what he reasonably could to prevent radiation sickness. A tear in the suit would change that. Of course, those two terrorists they'd fought hadn't been wearing radiation suits and they didn't instantly drop dead, that was for sure, but they were hell bent on killing themselves, anyway.

"Around this side," Sam said, disappearing around the metal shack.

Jasper followed his path. If anything, by the time he reached the open door the seismic activity had intensified. At one point he simply could not hold himself up and was flung to the floor. He felt a lull in the movement and jumped to his feet and ran. Inside the control booth, the very walls of the structure were in motion. It reminded Jasper of being inside the back of a small moving truck while it rolled down the highway. Thankfully, the workstation stools were bolted down. He sat on one and gripped the edge of the control station. Sam did the same. They could hear unknown debris raining down on the metal roof.

Not again, was all Jasper could think, while Sam stared out the shack doorway.

Then, just as suddenly as it began, it stopped.

Both men remained hunched on their work stools, clutching the edge of a machinery control console.

"I think that's it," Sam ventured.

As if to mock him, the ground vibrated once more—a quick but powerful jolt that almost knocked Jasper from his seat—and then all was still once more.

"I'll try not to jinx us anymore," Sam said.

"I think this last one lasted even longer than the original quake," Jasper said. Sam nodded in agreement. "Seemed like it could have been just as strong if not stronger, too," he said.

Slowly, Jasper released his grip on the workstation. He held his hands out for balance, testing the stability of the floor. He carefully rose to his feet. Sam remained sitting and turned to look at the controls in front of him. Jasper followed his gaze. Many of the lights that were on when they entered were now dark, Jasper noticed.

He shook his head. "How much more of this can the plant take?" he wondered aloud.

"Not much," Sam said, frowning while he toggled a switch back and forth. "In fact, I think we should go and recheck the work we just did on the water system, just to make sure it's all still functional."

Jasper sighed. Just when it seemed like they might have gotten a leg up on the situation . . .

"I'm curious as to what the spent fuel pool looks like now, too," he added. Then he picked up his dosimeter and stared at it. Jasper watched as he shook the thing and then looked at it again.

"What is it?" he asked.

"Reading higher now."

Jasper looked at the arm of his suit again, where the rod had hit, inspecting it even more carefully.

"How much higher?"

Sam let the dosimeter rest again at the end of its lanyard. "We'll be okay. Looks like that was it for the rumbling. Let's check out the damage."

They cautiously stepped out of the control shack and surveyed their surroundings. Jasper's heart sank as he surveyed the most recent wave of damage. Fresh scraps of metal and clusters of concrete lay everywhere. A clear liquid dropped in a stream from high above that wasn't there before. Jasper's initial reaction was to hope that it was only water and not some kind of acid or industrial solvent, but then he hoped it wasn't water because that could mean the elaborate plumbing system they'd just organized had been damaged.

This place is falling apart!

"This place is falling apart," Sam said. It spooked Jasper that he echoed his sentiment so exactly through the headset in his ear, but then again, he thought, looking around, there weren't many other ways to say it.

"Yeah, let's just hope we can keep it together long enough to cool that SFP. Speaking of, what are we closer to, the fuel pool or the cooling stations?"

"Cooling stations. We'll go in backwards order, visiting the primary cooling loop last."

They threaded their way across the ransacked energy facility. Jasper had the dead terrorist's pistol at the ready. What if this new damage had opened up a passage down into the fuel handling or reactor buildings? He missed Peterson. Twenty minutes later, they reached the station they'd visited second on their first go-around.

Sam went to work examining the control settings while Jasper kept watch. It seemed like there were a lot of streams of liquid pouring down from the ceiling in different places—some were sparse little trickles while others were damn near mini-waterfalls. He was about to ask the tech how it was going when he turned around and said, "We're okay here. Made a couple of minor tweaks but, honestly, they might have been necessitated even without the aftershock. Or, if that *was* the bigger quake, then technically I think they'll call the first one a foreshock," he lectured.

"Who *cares* what the hell they call it? Let's get over to the other station with the loop."

Sam looked up at him sharply, not saying anything.

"I'm sorry, didn't mean for that to come out so harsh," Jasper apologized. And he didn't. But hey, he was only human. He'd been drawn into this by degrees, and now he felt like he was in *way* over his head. Yet if he was to survive, and by extension if the entire City of New York was to survive, then he and Sam would need to maintain a solid working relationship. *Don't piss him off. He's only human, too. Last thing we need right now is to be fighting each other.*

"Apology accepted. I get a little long-winded sometimes. Believe me, you're not the first person to let me know. Okay, primary loop—this way!"

Sam set off toward the wall walkway. When they reached it, they were dismayed to see that it now hung down to the floor at a crazy angle in most places. They skirted its span along the floor instead. Ten minutes later, they arrived at the primary cooling loop arrangement on the work floor. Sam took a look at the equipment and cursed softly. He removed a pair of pliers and a wrench from a tool belt worn around his suit and did some work on one of the pipe fittings.

"All good now," he said, reholstering the tools. He led the way up to the control station, where they had to climb up the separated walkway. He played his light over the switchgear panels and made several adjustments, then stepped back as if to admire his work. Jasper heard him take a deep breath.

"What do you think?" Jasper asked.

"Pressure dropped a little more than I'd normally be comfortable with, but under the circumstances, it'll just have to do. Let's check the fuel pool."

Jasper nodded and they jumped from the walkway back to the floor, where they traversed the expanse toward the distant containment wall. Thirty minutes of careful navigating later and Jasper recognized the rod handling machine he'd manipulated under Jeffries's direction. They entered the walkway that led to the fuel pool deck and then Jasper was staring down at that turquoise water again.

And there in the middle of it was Alex White's body, floating peacefully in the midst of the chaos. Jasper almost envied him. His journey had come to an end. He no longer had to deal with this mess.

The pool itself didn't look any different to Jasper, and for that he was grateful. On the way over he'd been scared that they'd arrive only to see bare rods already smoldering.

"Who was that?" Sam asked, acknowledging that whoever it was must certainly be dead.

"Alex White."

"Damn." He said nothing more and Jasper didn't want to press him for details on how well he did or didn't know him. There'd be plenty of time for that later if they made it out of this.

The two let a moment of silence pass. Then Sam said, "Okay, I need to check something over here." He led Jasper off to the left where a computer monitor glowed behind a glass console. Sam tended to it while Jasper looked up toward the broken catwalk. He thought maybe he was looking in the wrong place until he realized that it was simply not there anymore. It had fallen from its remaining end . . . *into the pool*? That sure as hell wouldn't be good.

But then he spotted it, dangling precariously from some infrastructure about halfway down from the floor it used to be attached to and the pool surface. Well, at least the terrorists weren't getting across that way, that was for sure. No ladder was going to bridge that gap.

"All right, amazingly the pool is still holding water, which was my main *new* concern. We don't want it leaking out into the river or the ground, thereby lowering the level even faster. But the water temperature is still critical. This is gonna boil off any minute now."

Jasper jumped at the sound of a new voice over their communications channel.

"Calling Jasper Howard, calling Jasper Howard. This is Frank Mendoza, do you copy?"

49

Jasper watched Sam turn away from the instrument console at the sound of Frank Mendoza's voice. He nodded. *Go ahead.*

"Yes, Frank! I hear you. You must be close! Do you have water?"

"Copy, that, Jasper. Yes, I'm in a convoy of sorts. We've got six water trucks. About 50,000 gallons altogether."

Jasper looked over at Sam. *Is that enough?* Sam gave him a thumbs-up.

"Fantastic, Frank. You are the man! Where are you now?"

"I'm at the plant entrance gate. It's closed and locked. I don't see anybody."

Sam turned back to making his console adjustments while Jasper spoke to Mendoza.

"I'm sorry, but I don't think there's anyone up there to open it, and we're stuck down here. I'll need you to just take one of the trucks and ram on through. That gate will fold."

A pause ensued and for a moment Jasper was worried that he was going to say he didn't want to drive the truck through the gate. Then his com channel opened up once more with the sound of idling engines in the background.

"Will do, Jasper. Always wanted to try that. Give me a minute . . ."

While he waited for Mendoza to back up and drive through the gate, Jasper looked up and across the fuel pool to where they'd walked out on the broken catwalk. It unnerved him that a murderer with a gun was most likely wandering around up there somewhere. In fact, Jasper noted, if they were to walk out to the edge of where the catwalk used to be, they'd be able to see them down here on the SFP operations deck. And then a second worry nagged at his consciousness.

Should he ask Sam if the radiation exposure levels are safe enough for Mendoza and his drivers to even come onto the plant property? They'd been compromised after all, and Sam admitted that after the last aftershock the levels were higher. But to ask Sam meant that Mendoza could also hear, now that they were on the shared channel. He could not afford to scare him off now. But this man had gone way out of his way to help them. He simply could not in good conscience put him in possible danger without at least making him aware of the risks.

He walked over to Sam and pointed to his dosimeter. He hoped Sam would catch his meaning, but he merely held the instrument up for Jasper to see. Jasper shook his head and pointed up and away toward the outside. Sam followed his gaze and appeared to catch his meaning. He waggled a hand held out flat. *Iffy*.

That was it. Jasper had to warn Mendoza. He would not be able to live with himself if he did not.

"Listen, Frank, can you hear me?"

He heard the roar of revving trucks when Frank came back over the airwave. "Affirmative. I just broke through the gate. My boys are rolling through now."

"Okay, great. But listen there's something I need to tell you."

"Go ahead."

He looked at Sam to see if he would protest, but he only nodded. It was the right thing to do.

"There is a risk of radioactive contamination of you coming onto the property here."

Then Sam cut in, recognizing that his authority was needed. "It's not very high, but is higher than normal. My name is Sam Wilkson, by the way, Mr. Mendoza. I'm a reactor technician working with Jasper down here in the fuel handling building of Reactor Number Two to get the cooling system ready for your water."

There was a slight pause as Mendoza digested this. Then he said, "But it's not like we'd instantly get sick, right?"

Sam jumped right in. "No, nothing like that. I'm not a medical doctor, okay, but let's just say that the very long-term consequences may be unknown. And even down here where we are right now, it's not all that bad, although we are wearing hazmat suits. Up there at the water fitting, it'll probably be like you're getting the same amount of radiation as if you went and had about ten dental X-rays done in a row. But we'd feel it'd be disingenuous not to inform you that the radiation levels are higher than normal, that's all."

"I—we—appreciate that. But there's no one else you have who can do this, right? Your crew is dead or gone?"

"That's correct," Sam said.

"Yes," Jasper agreed.

"And if we do nothing, then you could have this radioactive fire Jasper was telling me about earlier, right, and then the whole city, including me, would be screwed."

"Right again," Sam said, adding, "and we need to get working on that."

"I'll let my guys know. Just give me one minute," Mendoza told them.

Both Jasper and Sam stared down at the fuel pool, the

surface of which was definitely bubbling now. They hoped they could spare that minute. He had absolutely no idea what they would do should Mendoza and his impromptu posse decide that they were going to leave. *I guess they could at least leave the water trucks. . . .*

Then Mendoza was back on the radio. "Everybody's okay with it. Ten X-rays to save the city? Bring it on. So where do we go?"

Sam issued driving instructions while Jasper kept lookout.

"On our way," Mendoza said. They heard him honk his truck's horn.

"When you get there," Sam said, "it's going to be one truck at a time. Connect the fitting of one truck, let me know it's ready, and I'll initiate the pumping process. When that truck's drained, disconnect it, move it out of the way, and bring the next one in line up to repeat the process. Clear?"

"You bet." Before long Mendoza was describing buildings to use as landmarks and Sam was directing him to the water pump fitting.

"Place is like a ghost town," Mendoza noted.

Haunted by terrorists, Jasper thought. He alternated his gaze from the former catwalk level above and the rapidly boiling water below, where Alex White's body floated around in circles.

Jasper wondered if they should also tell Mendoza about the terrorists, but the pump fitting area was far enough from the reactor building entrance that the gunmen probably entered that he didn't think it was a concern. And it would seem ridiculous to have to say now, after the radiation threat, "Oh, yeah, and by the way, be on the lookout for armed terrorists." *Do you want this water or not? Don't scare them off.*

He decided to tell them about the terror threat as soon as the trucks' water had been pumped. Remind them at that point not to go wandering around . . .

"I've got my tanker connected." Mendoza came through over the radio. "Now what?"

Sam answered him. "Be sure it's tight, because otherwise once I start the pump it could fly off and deck you in the face, not to mention we'd lose the water."

"Hold on." A few seconds elapsed and then Mendoza said, "It's on there tight."

"Okay. Then here we go. Stand by and I'll keep you posted."

Sam bent to the control station, flipping switches, consulting LCD readouts, turning dials. Then he stood straight, took one look down at the fuel pool, and punched a red button.

Jasper could neither see nor hear anything special happening. Sam stared at his instrument console intently. Jasper hoped that the most recent temblor didn't cause too much damage to their cooling system. *He mentioned before that the pressure was lower than he'd like. . . .*

"Yeah, I hear it pumping," Mendoza said.

"Wish the flow rate could be faster," Sam said. "If you're around 8,000 gallons, it's going to take about"—he squinted at a computer monitor—"ten minutes. Times six for all of the trucks."

"I'll let my drivers know and make sure they're all lined up good so we can move up smoothly."

Three trucks had emptied their payloads when Mendoza's voice crackled over the radio channel. It was higher pitched than normal.

"Jasper, Sam! What the hell's going on? We're getting shot at out here!"

50

Jasper's heart felt like it was trying to drop into his stomach. *I should have warned them about the terrorists!* He had no idea why they were outside. Did the aftershock scare them out? Were they seeking new ways into the containment structures?

Sam picked what was probably a convenient moment to adjust some controls on the pumping station, leaving Jasper to reply to Mendoza. He'd gotten him into this mess, after all, so he had to get him out. He squeezed the pistol he still carried in his right hand and wished there was a way outside.

"Frank, we're being attacked by terrorists. Are any of you armed?"

When Mendoza came back on the air, Jasper was alarmed to hear the sounds of gunfire, some of it extremely loud.

"Jesus. I was hoping they were overzealous security for the plant. I've got a Glock pistol," Mendoza said, "but I'm almost out of ammo thanks to a bunch of dogs in Central Park. Don't ask. I think one of our convoy drivers has a handgun, also. But what do these guys want?"

"Good question, but I think they want to cause damage to the plant, create a meltdown. Whatever the worst is that they can inflict. They shot and killed three of our employees in here earlier today."

"They're not wearing protective suits," Mendoza noted.

"Allah is their hazmat suit, I'm afraid," Jasper said.

Then he heard another volley of gunfire erupt.

"Can you get truck number four connected?" Sam asked. "Pool's just starting to stabilize. Hate to stop now."

They heard Mendoza shout "Cover me!" and then more firearms discharging, followed by, "He's hit! One down! The other guy's taking cover. Bill! Move into position."

Sam wordlessly nodded his approval. Jasper remained silent also, not wanting to distract Mendoza in the middle of a gun battle.

"Truck four's hooking up now," Mendoza said. "We've got one armed man with the truck at the pumping station, and another—that's me—watching the other guy run away, in case he decides to fake us out and come back this way."

"Which way is he running?" Jasper asked.

"Toward the river and north."

Jasper swallowed. That was toward the Reactor Number 2 containment building, where they were now.

"He's probably heading back to the reactor building complex they accessed earlier."

"Truck four connected!" Mendoza announced. "Never thought I'd be part of an armed water delivery service, but here I am."

"Just be careful," Jasper warned. He didn't want to see any more dying.

"Pump's activated," Sam said.

"Go, I'll cover you!" they heard Mendoza yell.

"What now?" Jasper asked.

"Going for the dead guy's weapon," Mendoza said matter-of-factly. To Jasper, it seemed like he was awfully calm in light of having driven completely unexpectedly into an armed terror skirmish.

"What did you say your job was, again?"

"I didn't. But I'm FBI. Not on duty at the moment, but some would say we're never off duty."

That explains it, Jasper thought. "Wow. Can you call for backup?" he asked.

Mendoza chortled. "This convoy *is* my backup, Jasper. Only they're not my fellow agents, but we've got somebody from NYFD—in a fire truck, by the way, because they hold some water—a couple of long-haul truckers, a mechanic who volunteered to drive a tanker that he fixed quick enough to get on the road with us. The FBI is preoccupied at the moment with preventing looting and riots and rounding up escaped criminals. You haven't been outside in a while, so you don't understand how bad it is in the city."

Jasper silently agreed with that statement. He'd been in a nuclear bubble all day.

"It's *bad*, Jasper—dire. The very, very last thing New York needs at this point is some nuclear meltdown on top of all that's already gone on."

"Fourth truck is pumped out, but it only had 3,000 gallons," Sam informed them.

"Affirmative, that one was only half full when we found it and no way to fill it on such short notice so we brought it along anyway," Mendoza said. "But Big Five, we call it, is up next. Get ready to pump it up!"

"Copy that," Sam replied, ever vigilant on the control panel in front of him.

"We've got the dead terrorist's weapon," Mendoza reported. "Mother! Semi-automatic. I think the other one just has a pistol. Glad we got this one first. Big knife on him, too."

As perilous as the radiation dangers here inside the containment facility were, Jasper was grateful that this same building also afforded him protection from the animals outside. Animal, he corrected himself. He was pretty sure there was only one left. And if he was to get out of this building, sooner or later he'd have to face him. Unless Mendoza and his merry band of water tankers got to him first. *Thank God for Mendoza*, was all he could think.

Jasper glanced down into the pool. It didn't look much different to him. Still fizzing and bubbling. Mr. White (*call me Alex!*) still adrift on his nuclear sea.

Sam collected the water from Big Five and Mendoza's team cued up the final truck.

"Water level's nice and high now. I no longer feel like I'm about to stare down onto bare fuel rods. Temperature dropped, too!" Sam rejoiced.

"Yeah, buddy! One more coming up," Mendoza said.

They transferred the water from the remaining tanker without incident while Sam monitored the spent fuel pool water temperature. "Still warmer than optimal, but there's enough water in there now that we're no longer in danger of it boiling off. Doesn't look like we have any cracks in the pool either, even after that last shock. Great job, people!"

"I can't thank you enough, Frank. You and all your guys. Make sure you tell them thanks from us, too, okay?" Jasper added.

"Hey," Mendoza said, "you can tell 'em yourself over a round of brews and pizza when things get back to normal. We'll get 'em to make us a 'radioactive special' with a lotta hot sauce and some green glowing beers. Sound good?"

"Now you're speaking my language. Sam, is there anything else we need to get done in here?"

Sam looked up from his controls. "Nothing critical, no. We should quit while we're ahead."

Jasper eyed the level high above them that led to the stairway they'd taken down with Jeffries.

"Great. So all we have to do now is figure out how to get the hell out of here."

51

Frank Mendoza watched as his water crew gave each other pats on the back and high-fives. He was feeling pretty good about things, himself, too. Saving the nuclear plant from a radiation disaster? He couldn't wait to tell Jana. But right now, it seemed like the problems just kept coming from this place. Jasper and Sam were still trapped inside the containment area, and the surviving terrorist was roving around loose somewhere, no doubt mad as all hell at the death of his associates.

He brought his handheld radio to his mouth. "Let's see what we can do about getting you and Sam out, Jasper. So you said you needed a ladder to get across something and it fell out of position?"

Jasper filled him in on the details of their catwalk crossing, the collapsed exit doors, and the details of taking the stairs down past Jeffries's control room to the containment area doors. Mendoza picked his brain for information about other possible exits, but it always led back to the missing ladder over the spent fuel pool.

"One of our water trucks is a fire company engine. It's got a pretty big ladder on it, but I'm not sure if it's attached to the truck or what. Let me go talk to Pete—the NYFD man driving it—and we'll see what we can do. Stand by."

Mendoza knew that there was a gigantic crane atop the fire truck for tall building access, but he was pretty sure it was fixed, and even if it wasn't, it was far too heavy and cumbersome to get inside a building. He strode up to Pete, who was dramatically rehashing the details of his water pump action, and waved the radio, indicating he needed to inform Jasper and Sam about something.

"What's up?" Pete asked.

Mendoza pointed to the fire truck. "We need a very long but portable ladder. Have anything like that?"

Pete answered him without even looking at the truck. "We've got the fifty-foot, but normally it's got a trained crew of six or eight guys to handle it."

"The two nuclear employees who've been communicating with me are trapped inside. Say they need a ladder to get across a space where a catwalk fell. Got to get it down some steps. Might be tricky, but can we try it?"

"You bet." He put two fingers in his mouth and gave a shrill round-up whistle. "Let's go, boys! It's volunteer firefighter day! Ladder detail."

Mendoza raised Jasper on the radio again and got him to give precise directions down to the containment overlook area once he was inside the building. He decided it would be beneficial to scout out the route ahead of the ladder crew, to root out any surprises. Including ones with guns. He trotted back to Pete, who already had a huddle going to instruct the men on how to carry and use the ladder. He informed him of the plan, saying he'd go on ahead alone and then in a few minutes come back up to guide them down and assist if necessary.

Then Mendoza was running across the open yard space of the nuclear property toward the containment building for Reactor Number 2. He called Jasper on the radio while he moved.

"Coming up on the entrance, I think. Brown door, got a sign over it . . ." Mendoza described what he saw.

"That's it," Jasper confirmed. "Not sure if it'll be open."

Mendoza saw that it was already ajar, wedged open by a small trash can. In the can was what appeared to be a bloody rag.

"I'm in," Mendoza said, slipping inside to the same hallway Jasper had passed through earlier that day. The alarm that had blared when Jasper passed through was now silent, however, imparting an eerie silence to the deserted nuclear facility. Jasper had seen documentaries on Chernobyl in the decades following the mega-disaster there, the Russian facilities abandoned exactly as they had been, entire towns on the way to being patiently reclaimed by nature. This vast empty complex reminded him of the beginnings of that.

Jasper directed him over the radio to Jeffries's office. "Two reasons I want you to go in there," he explained. "One, check on Jeffries, in case he's still alive. Two, see how many hazmat suits are in there and put one on. Have your guys put 'em on, too."

Mendoza flew down some stairs, but then had to stop himself on the landing before turning the corner. Never knew who could be waiting there. His Glock was at the ready, but he had precious few bullets left now, after his entire first clip had literally gone to the dogs, and a few more to the water pump skirmish. His ammo consumption concerned him enough that he paused to open his weapon.

Two rounds remaining!

Better than nothing. But he cursed himself for not taking the terrorist gun they'd recovered from his lifeless body. At least one of the ladder crew had it, but still, he should have asked for it since he was the point man on this crazy sortie.

He reached a door with a sign marked OPERATIONS ROOM

and Jasper told him that was it. Like the outer door, this one was also ajar. Glock held at the ready in a two-handed grip, Mendoza kicked it open.

He instinctively swept his pistol back and forth across the room, an innate motion bred into him from years of FBI field service. He stepped into the room.

There was only one man in here, and he was dead. Not only that, but Mendoza could see that his wasn't an easy death. He hadn't merely been shot, as Jasper had implied.

He'd been tortured.

Stephen Jeffries was trussed to his workstation swivel chair, bound with frayed electrical cords. His shirt had been removed and placed over his head. One of his ears lay nearby on the floor in a bloody smear. The thumb of his right hand was missing, and Mendoza quickly glanced around but didn't see it. He flashed on the possibility that perhaps it had been taken for the purpose of defeating biometric security devices—door locks with thumbprint scanners.

But that wasn't the worst of it. Mendoza could see that the shots which had incapacitated him would not have been fatal. Jeffries's body had been thoroughly mutilated, and even though he was a seasoned special agent who'd been exposed to all manner of human depravity and desperation in the face of illicit circumstances, he turned away from the bloody corpse and fell to his knees. He vomited onto the floor while holding his Glock out blindly in front of him in case someone should storm the room during this moment of vulnerability.

He was all too aware that, as a field agent, this was exactly the type of situation he'd been trained to avoid at all costs— alone and facing an armed and dangerous suspect. He did have backup of sorts, he told himself by way of consolation, but his group of ragtag convoy truckers was far from a highly trained special agent by his side and the full resources of the bureau on call.

But he was in it now, and it was sink or swim.

"Is he alive?" Jasper queried, the radio vibrating faintly in his hand with his transmission.

Mendoza struggled to his feet as he responded.

"No, he's not." He opted to leave out the details of Jeffries's grisly demise for now. It wouldn't do any good to scare the living crap out of them down there.

"Look over on the wall—how many suits are hanging on the rack there?"

Mendoza looked over and saw a whole row of blue vinyl hazmat suits. He quickly counted them. "Eight," he said, pleased. More than enough for himself and the whole ladder team.

"Great, go ahead and put one on, please," Jasper said. "It's pretty straightforward except for the headgear, but I'll talk you through—"

"Crap!" Mendoza said, enough disappointment creeping into that single syllable to let Jasper know that seriously bad news was forthcoming.

"What is it?"

"All of these suits have been slashed up. Completely ripped apart with a knife or something," Mendoza said, running a hand through the shredded rubber. He walked down the line, inspecting each one. All had been sabotaged.

The dead silence over the radio frequency said it all.

"There are no other suits I can get access to, are there?"

This time it was Sam's voice that answered. "Negative."

A long pause ensued.

"Talk to me, people. Believe me when I tell you that I don't fancy hanging out in here one second longer than I absolutely have to." He glanced over at Jeffries's disfigured body and then averted his gaze to the open doorway. He made sure he had a good grip on his Glock and the two bullets it could offer him.

"I'm looking at my dosimeter now," Sam began, "and while the background radiation levels have dropped significantly since the new water was introduced into the fuel pool system, they are still levels that normally would require a suit. Especially in this situation where much of the equipment and system controls have been compromised and could fail at any minute."

There was another beat as Mendoza digested this.

"That said," Sam continued, "those are OSHA and NRC type regs. The levels aren't dangerously high for a one-time exposure. In fact, if it were possible I'd gladly take my suit off and throw it over to you so that you could wear it, if you wanted, in order to effect our rescue."

"Can you do that?" Mendoza asked.

"No. Gap's way too wide."

Mendoza thought for another moment, acutely aware that every additional second he stood around was increasing the chance that an AK-47-toting fanatic would blaze in here and cut him down before he could even get one of his two rounds off. He took a deep breath.

"Look, I don't know what my guys are going to say— I think you two would be the first to admit that they've already gone way above and beyond, but I'll present the situation to them and let them make up their own minds."

"Hold on, there's one more thing you can do," Sam said. He told him about the potassium iodide pills Jasper had taken earlier.

"Where are they?"

"Should be in a drawer on the workstation, left side. Blister pack of brown capsules."

Mendoza went to the drawer, situated beneath an array of flashing LEDs, and removed the pills.

"Got 'em."

"Take two. However many are left, distribute them to your team. Anybody who comes down here."

Mendoza popped the pills from the pack and dry swallowed them. *Jana will be happy I took these.*

"Since I'm all the way down here already, maybe I should just run down and look at the space where we're going to need to work with the ladder. If there's corners it won't fit around, what's the point? Might have to go back outside the plant and find more help."

"Understood," Sam said. He gave him directions on how to get down to the containment overlook area where the catwalk had been.

Mendoza carefully looked left and right before exiting and jogged down the staircase. He took his time at each turn or landing, reaching the barrel of his gun around first and then charging ahead. He paused when he reached the oversized metal doors that led to the containment area proper.

Radiation, here I come. Sure you want to do this?

But the decades of service to the FBI wherein it was his job to rescue those in peril even at the potential expense to his own personal safety could not easily be overcome. It was just a few minutes; they said it wasn't really all that much, he told himself.

His resolve steeled, Mendoza kicked open the double doors and stared into the containment area.

He was not prepared for what he saw.

First of all, the space was so dim. He waited for his eyes to adjust. And what he could make out was less than comforting. Rivulets of liquid rained down from the ceiling in various places. Massive installations of machinery had been overturned or crushed. Huge chunks of concrete lay everywhere. Loose wires sparked deep inside the cavernous space.

Good God. I've got to get these guys out of here.

Seeing the destruction firsthand gave him a new appreciation for the patience and courage that those two plant employees must have to remain so calm in the face of such destruction. Then he realized that a lot of men would put on some level of airs that everything was okay, but it didn't mean they weren't scared shitless on the inside.

In addition to what he could see, his ears told him things weren't perfect either.

"Jasper, Sam, can you read me. Gonna be hard to hear with all these alarms."

"Oh, most of them have stopped by now. This isn't bad," Sam informed him.

Jesus.

"Okay. I'm walking out onto this large concrete area now. Anything I should watch out for?"

"Just watch your step. There's all kinds of debris everywhere."

Mendoza picked his way out to the edge of the platform. He could just make out some water that seemed incredibly bright blue to him. He recognized that it must be the spent fuel pool they had told him about.

He had nearly made it to the edge of the concrete landing and was taking in the distinctive sight of the SFP below when he saw something off to his right.

There!

A lone figure, standing by the edge of the platform.

He was looking over into the pool, and he had a grenade clutched in each hand.

PART SIX
Final Threat

52

Assistant U.S. Attorney Nick Dykstra was certain he was in the right place, and yet he couldn't see Columbia University anywhere around him. Could the subway signs have been deliberately tampered with? He supposed it wouldn't be impossible. He wouldn't put it past somebody like that psycho down there, Charles Leighton. *The guy I had to shoot.* But unbelievably, there was a street sign still standing. He directed the beam of his flashlight onto it: 116TH STREET.

This was it!

And then it hit him, like a sucker punch to the gut.

This was it!

Columbia University.

No . . . no . . . no!

All the way around him for 360 degrees the land was absolutely flattened. He couldn't make out a single building still standing. It was some of the worst damage he'd seen so far. He thought about the aftershock that had hit with sudden, uncompromising ferocity not long ago. Whatever buildings may have withstood the day's seismic events up to that point, they'd have been demolished for certain. Nick was only too glad to have barely emerged from the subway when it hit.

Lauren!

And then suddenly thinking her name was not enough. He tipped his head back and roared her name into the night.

"Lauren!"

But his voice merely rolled unanswered across the wasteland of destruction.

He sat on the ground, exhausted physically from his long journey across the ruined metropolis, and mentally from worrying about his daughter. Seeing the general place where she had been so thoroughly devastated . . . It was almost more than he could bear, but he knew that sitting around wasn't going to help anyone so he forced himself to his blistered feet. His pricy loafers may be perfect for the courtroom, but they sure as hell weren't made for the serious hiking he'd had to do today. Damned things were already falling apart, he noted, feeling how the sole of the right shoe had begun to separate.

Nick told himself that maybe the actual damage to the university wasn't as bad as it looked from this distance, once he actually got onto the campus. Surely there'd be some buildings still standing? Taking some care to orient himself amidst the sameness of the flattened area, he set off toward what he thought was the main campus.

The surroundings were dismal. Not only were all of the buildings he passed by leveled, but even the quaint little paved walkways that wound their way throughout the once parklike setting had been buckled and torn apart. This was the school where he'd wanted his daughter to study, so that she'd be close to him. And now look at it. He didn't see how it would be operational for a long, long time. Lauren, assuming she was okay (*How the hell could anyone have survived the likes of this?*) would have an easy out now for wanting to attend some faraway, out-of-state school.

But he'd already made his peace with that. No more dictating, cajoling, influencing, hinting, pushing, or demanding.

She was going wherever the hell she wanted to go and he would learn to deal with it.

As long as she had made it through this, he reminded himself. *Just let her be alive.* Please, *just let her be alive.* . . .

He continued on, twisting his way through snarls of uprooted trees intermingled with raw building materials. After a while he came to a large sign reading CAMPUS DIRECTORY which had been knocked to the ground. He walked over to it and turned his head at an awkward angle to match the random orientation of the sign on the ground. Found the YOU ARE HERE marker.

He raised his head to try to reconcile the chaos of what he saw with the stylized perfection of the map. He put his flashlight to good use, probing the inky blackness as far as it would penetrate. It took him a while, but based on the relative locations of the destroyed paths and the sign's former position, he was confident he'd properly oriented himself.

But now a new question pervaded his mind: where to look? He considered this. So far Nick had seen absolutely no signs of people, which terrified him. Unless . . . maybe they had evacuated the campus when the first quake struck? That was a prospect that filled him with hope, but also with dread, for if Lauren wasn't here, then he'd have to track her down somewhere else and hope that she was okay wherever she was.

If she was here somewhere, though, he reminded himself . . . He shook his head to wipe it of the horrendous possibilities it wanted to conjure up. He forced himself to focus on the facts. She was here for a campus tour. He looked down at the map again, but this time noting the names of the different buildings. The usual academic halls, labs, institutes and centers . . . there! Admissions. He wasn't sure but figured that the admissions department would run the campus tours for prospective students, so he might as well start there.

He made sure that he understood the route he would need

to take as well as possible, and then took off along what remained of a path that led in that direction. As he wound his way deeper into the beleaguered campus, he did begin to see some signs of surviving life: a small huddle of students crying together on an open lawn, a few lone stragglers wandering about in a daze, like zombies. He stuck to his plan of reaching admissions, not wanting to burn time to talk to people on the off chance that one might happen to be able to help him.

He found the admissions building easy enough because it was partially still standing with its sign still in place. If he was *very* lucky, Nick thought, Lauren would be in here. Maybe she breezed through the library and knew the place was for her and wanted to tell admissions right away? *If wishes had horses, and all that.* But then he thought about Lauren and her love of books and libraries, how she'd once spent seven hours in the New York City Public Library (*probably rubble now*) and had burst into tears when he came to take her home. Making that scenario seem more unlikely than ever.

He was preparing to climb the crumbled stone steps to the former building's entrance area when he heard a faint noise somewhere off to his left. High-pitched, sort of bubbly sounding.

Crying!

Someone was beneath a clump of uprooted shrubbery over on the left side of the building. Nick ran to the source of the noise. There, lying on the ground underneath the displaced foliage, lay a woman. Not college-aged, unless she was one of those nontraditional students Nick had heard about. But given her location, most likely an administrator. He parted some branches and stooped down low to make sure she could see him.

"Hello? Can you hear me?" Nick called out.

The snuffling stopped.

"Yes, yes! My goodness."

"Let me help you up." Nick reached out a hand. The woman looked at his face, as if judging his intentions, and then allowed him to grip her own arm and pull her from the bushes.

She had numerous small scratches about her face and neck. "What happened to you, are you okay?"

She wiped her eyes before answering. "Yes, I think so. Oh, my, I'm afraid I just fell asleep right here on the ground, how ridiculous. Thank you. I was . . . I was inside my building, what's left of it," she said, "when the shaking started. The windows shattered out and . . ." She carefully ran her fingers across her face. "How bad is it?"

Nick cupped his flashlight in his hand and shone it over her face. "Not too bad, really. Mostly surface scratches. Here, I see a couple of fragments that I can easily remove if you let me."

The woman held her face still while Nick extracted three small pieces of glass. He examined her neck and shoulders and removed one more piece. "I think you made out pretty well, all things considered," Nick said. "Tell me, what's your name?"

"Caroline Reignier, very pleased to meet you. I'm the director of admissions here at Columbia. Thank you so much for your assistance. You are a ray of sunshine."

"Don't mention it. Listen, it's a bit of a ray of sunshine for me that you're the admissions director, because I'm looking for my daughter, who unfortunately was here today for a campus tour. Just graduated high school."

"When the earthquake started, the tour would have been in the main library—Butler Library, it's called." She pointed off to their right. "About a five minute walk in that direction, under normal circumstances."

"Thank you very much, Caroline. My daughter's name is Lauren Dykstra. I'm her father, Nick Dykstra." He started to add more but could see from the look on Caroline's face that something about what he said had bothered or confused her.

"Wait, did you say Lauren Dykstra?" Nick's heart seemed to petrify. He thought that maybe she'd heard Lauren was one of the deceased and was about to break the news. But in fact what she told him chilled him even worse than that.

"Yes, Lauren Dykstra," he repeated. He stared at her intently. Although she'd been through some mild trauma and one heck of an experience overall, he judged her to have her faculties about her and to be a cognizant, reasoning human. She wasn't cracking up, spouting random nonsense.

"Well that's funny, because . . . unless I'm really losing my mind here, which is possible . . . but no, I'm quite certain of this. Another man already came by asking for Lauren Dykstra."

"What? When?"

"I don't know exactly. I don't wear a watch, but I haven't been asleep for that long. He wasn't anywhere near as helpful as you, by the way. He said he was her father, the Assistant U.S. Attorney Nick Dykstra. I recalled from her admissions application that's what his occupation was, so I believed him. But I'm positive he asked about her. And of course I remember Lauren, a terrifically bright young woman, asked some very intelligent questions before the tour started. Anyway—"

"Who was the man?" Nick demanded. It came out a little more pointed than he'd intended, but he couldn't help that.

"Well, I thought it was little strange because he was of Middle-Eastern descent, and Lauren, she's a Caucasian girl, but you know how it is these days—that doesn't really mean much, she could . . ."

But Nick was already off and running toward the library.

53

Butler . . . Butler . . .

Nick slowed his mad dash to a jog while he looked around for the library. Everywhere he glanced, he saw only mounds of rubble. He slowed to the point where he was only jogging in place, spinning in a circle while trying to determine in which direction he should go.

Alivi escaped the courthouse, made his way here and is going for Lauren! Do something! But don't do the wrong thing. No time to go running off in the wrong direction . . .

He eyed one heap of rubble that was much higher than the others and headed for that. As he approached, he passed the dead body of a young man who'd somehow been crushed beneath a large boulder fitted with a dedication plaque. *Gotta love that gift from the Class of '86, right, buddy*, Nick thought, as his light beam swept over the plaque.

He'd been exposed to so much death today that he guessed he was becoming desensitized to it. Here he was, cracking mental jokes over dead college students when less than twenty-four hours ago he'd never come across a corpse in his entire life. As a prosecutor he'd seen more than his fair share of crime scene photos, sure, but that was nowhere near the same thing. Not even in the same ballpark, he now understood.

But there was one body that should he come across it, he sure as hell wouldn't be trying out any experimental coping mechanisms, and that was Lauren's. He fingered the gun in his pocket and considered what he would do if he were to stumble across his daughter's dead, trauma-ridden body lying somewhere among this ruinous landscape, even without Alivi's intervention. He couldn't—didn't want to—guarantee that using one of his remaining bullets on himself might not be his preferred action. And if he were to find her in the hands of the jihadist . . . Well, then of course he would need his bullets in a different way.

But with Alivi on the scene, Nick knew that the chances of simply walking around, finding Lauren, and taking her home (if he still had one to go to) without incident were now approximately zero.

He kept going, hiking over a spread of bricks on the way to the massive rubble complex. He was petrified of what he might find there. Yet another possibility crept into his badgered consciousness: What if Alivi was lying in wait for *him* rather than Lauren? He might have chosen to come here because he knew it was only a matter of time before Nick showed up, rather than any real hope of finding Lauren. It was a possibility.

Keep telling yourself that, pal. He wants you, not Lauren. Yeah, put your head back in the sand.

No, Alivi was coming for Lauren—he could take that to the bank. That didn't mean he might not be hiding in a sniper's nest among all this rubble, though, waiting to shoot Nick in the kneecap so that he could take Lauren that much easier. As he ran, he allowed his thoughts to run with him, unbridled, dark, and out of control. Alivi would kill her—just take her life, if he was lucky. If he wasn't, he'd torture her or maybe even sell her into some Middle-Eastern sex slave ring. Whatever would bring the most pain and anguish to Nick, that's what Alivi would try to do. If he could, Alivi would do terrible things to Lauren and then kill Nick also.

No, if Lauren had survived the quakes, he had to find Alivi before Alivi found her. But was he already too late? It ate him alive that he had no way of knowing. His only option was to keep moving, cover more ground.

When he neared the wrecked edifice, he could tell that this building, while no doubt permanently destroyed, did still retain a limited amount of structural integrity. From where he stood, it appeared that the upper levels had collapsed completely, but the first, perhaps even second, he judged, looked like they might still be entered on foot. He could tell that before today it must have been an impressive piece of architectural work, too, with classical columns and balustrades and all that, but right now he didn't give a rat's ass what it used to be. What it was now was all that mattered: the possible location of his only child in the wake of the worst disaster in the history of New York.

He eased closer to what was left of the entrance, until at his feet lay a slab of marble with the name *Dante* chiseled into it. *Talk about circles of Hell. Alivi, you're on the bottom floor.* Glancing upward, Nick spotted more names on one of the toppled columns: Shakespeare, Milton, Voltaire. . . . This had to be the library. He was hyperalert for Alivi, scanning his uneven, 3-D surroundings intently, only using the light when absolutely necessary to avoid giving away his position, before committing to any significant forward motion.

And like a bolt of lightning burning his head, yet another daunting thought careened around inside of his skull. *What if Alivi isn't even alone? What if he has people with him? He'd already managed to find Lauren within hours of escaping, after all.* Nick knew that the terror leader's reach was nearly as long as the arm of the law.

He lifted a foot onto a large section of rubble and tested it for stability. Satisfied it would hold his weight, Nick climbed on top of it and had a look into the former university library. He was greeted with what looked to him like a never-ending field of ruin, a lethal hodgepodge of fallen load-bearing elements and randomly strewn chunks of wall, ceiling, and floor.

Jumping down from his perch, Nick trudged deeper into the mess, moving however he could—climbing, walking around, slithering under, whatever it took. He never knew for certain if the route he chose would lead him astray until he tried it.

But he did know one thing: He was now entering what was left of the building that Lauren Dykstra was last known to have visited.

54

If not for the moonlight Nick would have had no choice but to use his flashlight. As it was, he still needed it when negotiating particularly tight spots, but by cupping a hand over its lens he reduced the risk of being discovered by the lurking Alivi. But as he trooped through the postapocalyptic library, he began to suspect that one of the world's most sought-after terror radicals might not even be his largest worry.

Bodies lay everywhere.

He checked each one, both to confirm it wasn't Lauren and to see if any might still be among the living. He slid down the back of an overturned book stack into a ragged-edged pit filled with an incongruous assemblage of rare tomes, corpses, and random body parts. Never in his life had he even imagined that he would ever see anything as gruesome as this. To say that it was a "living nightmare" didn't begin to do justice to the sheer scope of the horror that confronted him. All of these lives . . .

He simply couldn't go on at that point, couldn't bring himself to take another step, and he sat amidst the annihilation in the dark. *How could anyone, especially my fragile little Lauren, have possibly made it through this?* She was sure to be among this bibliographic hall of horrors. He began to wish that Alivi would just find him and kill him. He didn't see how he would be able to go on after this. He didn't see how, even in daylight, he'd ever even find Lauren's body amidst this chaotic ruination. *Like 9/11 all over again . . . her body might never even be found . . . both of the females in my life . . .*

But Nick was not one to give up and there were two things that fueled his mind to will his body to rise to his feet and climb out of the pit of death.

Lauren. Until he saw her body, he would keep looking.

Alivi. Even if he found Lauren dead, he would track that bastard down and bring him to justice. That was his job, in spite of everything, and so he would do his best to complete it.

He shone his flashlight in a quick arc down in front of him, almost daring Alivi to come and get him. He still didn't hold out any real hope of finding Lauren alive. He found more un-moving bodies below. *How many people were in this library when it fell?* He knew that in the fall season, a new semester having just begun, it must have been packed. He checked the faces of the deceased he found and made his way toward a dangling but not completely fallen catwalk made of black wrought iron. Could this be a way to get to the second floor? Looking up there, he could see that, if he could get to it, there was some room to walk around up there. But it wasn't like he'd yet run out of bodies to check on this floor. And many of these must have fallen from the upper floors when the build-ing collapsed, Nick realized.

For the next hour he toiled among the ruins, painstakingly shining his light on each and every face he came across. And with each additional body came an increasing awareness that this structure collapse did not appear to be survivable. *None* of these people had survived. Not one.

A tear slicing down his face, Nick was working the far reaches of the rubble field when he heard something. He traveled closer to where he thought the source might be.

"Help!"

A voice! There it was again: "Help me."

Male voice, so it wasn't Lauren, but it was still a ray of hope that at least someone had survived this catastrophe, and so maybe Lauren had, too.

Nick started running to the source of the voice, but then halted, switching off his light.

Could this be a trap?

What if it was a ruse by Alivi, pretending to be a victim trapped in the rubble? When Nick went to him, he'd put a bullet in his head.

But he heard the voice again; it was so feeble, utterly desperate. He couldn't distinguish an accent from the single syllables so weakly vocalized, but while he couldn't be sure, it did sound like it might belong to a younger man than Alivi. He decided that sometimes you just had to take a chance, and this was one of those.

Still, Nick approached at an oblique angle so as not to take the most obvious route. When he was sure he was close enough, he aimed his flashlight into the dark recess from where the voice originated and switched it on.

He was instantly relieved to see the blood-streaked face of a young man—a college kid.

Nick moved the light so that he wasn't blinding him, sweeping the beam over his body to appraise his situation. He was lodged under a book stack, but also entwined in what looked like a section of metal railing. Spotting with his light, he saw thick, black blood oozing through the kid's jeans on one knee where it was wedged through the spacing in some spiraling metalwork.

"Hey there, young man. Stay calm, don't move. I'm going to try and help you."

Nick saw the man's eyes alight with an ephemeral hope that quickly transitioned to nervousness. "Thanks. Do you think . . . do you think I'm going to make it?"

"Look buddy, I'm not a doctor or even a paramedic, but from what I've seen so far, you're doing a whole hell of a lot better than most people today. Let's see what we can do here. . . ."

For the next few minutes Nick worked to free the man, cringing when he would cry out as Nick moved a piece of debris. Particularly difficult was the wrought iron entwined with his leg. If the piece of metal was any smaller he'd just as soon move him with it still entwined and seek specialists to cut it free. But it was too large to permit him to be extracted from the pit he was in, so he had to try to remove it. The poor kid screamed in agony, but Nick managed to slide his knee through the railing piece.

As soon as he did he switched off his light and took a look around. It was eerily quiet in the large, devastated space, and there was a good chance that Alivi could have heard the wails of agony. He would certainly be drawn to them like moths to the proverbial flame.

"What's wrong?" the kid asked.

Nick switched his light back on. He didn't see how he could break it to the kid that there was a terrorist running around loose in here somewhere, looking for him. He needed him to be calm.

"No problem, just hit the off button by mistake. Okay, I think we're ready to try and slide you out of there. You with me?"

"Yes."

"Good. I'm going to hook an arm under your shoulder and pull you out this way." He illuminated a path with the light. "I'm sorry, but it's probably going to hurt. There's nothing I can do about that, but just hang on and know that it'll be over in a few seconds."

"Okay. Thanks."

Nick positioned himself as best he could to be able to move the kid out. He'd heard that it was best not to move someone who had sustained a possible neck or back injury, but from the looks of the debris piled around him, he was in danger of being totally crushed, not to mention simply dying of thirst and shock and whatever else might be wrong with him. And if there was another aftershock . . .

So he pulled the kid from the wreckage, dragging him out and onto what looked like a flat piece of marble flooring that was tilted at an acceptable angle. He didn't scream much, either, which Nick was thankful for. He made sure he was lying in a stable position and then stood and went to his knee, directing his light on it.

"We're going to want to get you some medical attention for that leg, pal. Say, what's your name, anyway?"

"I'm Ray Knowles."

55

"Nice to meet you, Ray. I wish it could be under better circumstances. I guess you're a student here at Columbia? My name's Nick Dykstra, by the way."

"Yes, I'm a student. I was conducting a— Hey, did you say Dykstra?"

Nick had been scoping the wasted library for signs of Alivi, but at the mention of his name he turned his head sharply to look Ray in the eyes.

"Yes. I came here to look for my daughter, Lauren Dykstra, who was on a campus tour. She—"

Ray cut him off. "Wait! Did you say *Lauren Dykstra*?"

Nick crouched, wanting to be more at eye level with Ray for this communication.

"Yes. Lauren Dykstra. Seventeen years old." He described her physical appearance without the kind of details that could be construed as parental embellishments. *There is no girl more beautiful . . .*

"I was with her!"

"What? Say again?"

"I was with her when everything started falling apart. Lauren Dykstra. She was the prospective student that the director of admissions asked me to take on a tour of the library."

Nick knelt so that his head was level with Ray's.

"Ray, do know what happened to her?"

"We were only a few feet apart when—the earthquake, I guess it was—right?"

"Yes."

"Once it happened, I was trapped under that same stack, I guess," he said, pointing over at the massive bookcase Nick had just extracted him out from under. "And Lauren was trapped somewhere nearby, because at first we could talk to each other, but not see each other. She kept me real calm, just knowing she was there and hearing her talk. But then, a while later, there was a second earthquake."

"Right, maybe a couple of hours ago," Nick said.

"After that one, I remember being tossed around real bad, and then I fell into something, hard. I passed out and when I woke up I knew I wasn't in the same place anymore. I couldn't hear Lauren anymore." Ray tried to prop himself up on an elbow to look around. He got a look for a few seconds, but then the effort was too much and he winced with the pain as he settled back into his supine position.

"Take it easy, Ray. Don't move too much if you don't have to."

"I'm just trying to figure out where we are. What floor are we on?"

"First floor. I'm not even sure how many floors are left anymore. How many did there used to be?"

"Eight."

Jesus. "Looks like part of the second is still standing," Nick said, glancing up there, also scanning for Alivi.

"We were on the second floor!"

"You're positive?"

"Yes! Yes, we were in the stacks on the second floor and I

had just asked her who her favorite author was and that's when things got crazy."

"So you don't actually know what happened to her?"

Ray appeared to think about this for a few seconds before answering. "Well, not other than what I already told you. But if I fell down here," he said, looking around at the first floor, "then she may have fallen down here somewhere, too."

Nick was already probing the area immediately surrounding them with his flashlight.

"Were there a lot of other people besides you and Lauren when the quake hit?"

"No, not right by us. On the second floor, yeah, but we were the only two in the row of stacks we were in."

Nick couldn't help but reflect on the fact that his daughter had set foot on a college campus for all of an hour or so before she ended up alone with a guy. In a library. That was Lauren, all right. He forced himself to snap out of it. *Focus.*

"I'm not seeing anybody else around here. I should warn you that there are plenty of dead bodies back that way," Nick said, pointing, " but I checked them all and didn't see Lauren."

"She must be still up there, then," Ray said, looking up to the newly created overhang where the second floor had split in half.

Nick followed his gaze. He saw the hanging high stacks catwalk and traced its length to the floor, where it dangled maybe five feet above a smallish mountain of former construction materials. He turned back to Ray.

"Listen, Ray. I've got to go up there and look for her. Hang tight, I'll be back."

"Okay. I hope you find her and she's okay. She's a great girl."

Nick gave him a stare for a second and then stepped off the pile of junk he was standing on in the direction of the catwalk. When he didn't have to focus on what was immediately in front of him to avoid tripping, which wasn't often, he checked the far reaches of the former library for Alivi. Still no trace of him.

Maybe this was a positive sign? Nick mused. Maybe Caroline did in fact have a touch of delirium after passing out under the bushes? But she had sounded awfully convinced. And how could she have come up with "Middle-Eastern descent" on her own, at random? *No way. It's real.* Yet another seedling of hope stepped on by the boot of his own logic.

He reached the dangling structure and climbed the debris mountain so that he stood directly beneath it. He stretched out his arms and the bottom of the hanging walk was still a good two feet above his hands. He tried to talk himself out of what he knew he had to do next. *She could still be tucked away in some rubble pocket down here. . . . I could walk around some more and try to find an easier way up. . . .*

But he knew that every second was precious. This was a way up. He swung his arms in a couple of practice swings, flexed his legs, made sure his footing was as solid as could be atop the loose mound of stuff. He eyed the railings on either side of the catwalk. Then he jumped.

Nick grabbed on to both bars on either side and gripped hard, his legs swinging through the air. *Do not let go* was all that went through his mind. He did not need to fall back onto a sloppy pile of loose concrete, rebar, and broken marble slabs. He let go with his right hand for a split second in order to grip the railing a little higher up. Did the same with his left. He repeated the process several times until he was able to swing his feet up onto a step.

Yes! Now as long as this thing holds my weight . . .

Falling with the catwalk landing on top of him would be even worse than just dropping onto the debris pileup. The structure creaked and groaned as he advanced up its length, swinging mildly as he neared the rim of the second floor.

It made him nervous as hell, but there was nothing he could do other than to keep putting one hand above the other, and soon he was swinging a leg up onto a solid horizontal structure.

Nick was watching for Alivi as soon as his eyeballs cleared the level. As he rolled up onto the level he heard something clatter near him and saw an object fall off the edge back down to the first floor. Quickly he felt his pockets. *There's the flashlight. The gun!* His pistol had slipped from his pocket and was now back down from whence he'd started.

Shit!

He shined his light down on it to see it. It was there somewhere but probably slipped deep into a crack in the maelstrom of rubble and debris. He couldn't see it. Even if he could, he reasoned, Lauren was right up here, no more than a few yards away. The thought of going back down, finding the gun, then repeating the arduous process to get back up here, all while his daughter needed him so badly if she was still alive, was too much.

He turned back around to face into his new environment.

It looked to Nick like he was now in what used to be somewhere near the center of the roughly rectangular floor. To the left of him were a series of book stacks that had toppled like dominos. To the right lay some type of computer work area now in total disarray. The entire space was disorienting because it was open to the sky both above and looking straight across. In the middle of the former room lay what looked like a sea of loose books on the floor strewn about dozens of upended stack units.

Nick turned back around and shined his light down into the first floor. He spotted Ray lying on the marble slab and then quickly killed the light. If Ray was up here when he'd fallen, then he would have been over to the left more, into that group of nested stacks. And by extension, if what Ray said was correct and he was near Lauren when the quake hit, then Lauren should also be somewhere in those same stacks.

Nick walked as fast as he carefully could in that direction, a few feet from the edge of the remaining floor. His heart stopped when he stepped on a pale arm protruding from beneath a fallen stack. He spent three minutes lifting the massive unit enough to slide it off of the person. She was dead, but she was not Lauren. He was thankful for that, but at the same time the little statistics keeper in his head racked up another one for the Dead column, and lowered the odds just that much more for Lauren.

His intuition was on high alert when he spotted a wrought-iron railing that had been sheared off—same exact type as what Ray had been entwined with. He looked over the edge and searched with his light again, and there was Ray. Nick had found him directly under where he was now.

This is the area!

Then, in an odd moment of reflection that sometimes came to those facing stressful, life-and-death situations, Nick flashed on something unrelated to his immediate predicament. His friend Mendoza. He wondered how Frank was doing, if he had found Jana. Because for Nick, his moment was at hand. He was about to find out, one way or another, if this quake had taken everything from him. There was much agony in waiting to find out. He hoped that Frank already knew.

Turning back around, he stared at the procession of domino-stacked bookcases. The excitement that he was so near to Lauren overwhelmed any instinct for caution he may have harbored and he flipped his light on, running to the fallen book stacks that now concealed his daughter.

56

Mendoza watched as the lone figure on the edge of the overlook prepared to throw two hand grenades into the spent fuel pool. He looked up and started to fervently vocalize Arabic incantations.

Mendoza's handheld radio crackled with Sam's urgent voice. "This pool cannot handle any more stress! One concussion from an explosive and either the new plumbing configuration we just set up for the cooling water will be destroyed, or the pool itself will crack, or both!"

"I think I can line up a shot," Mendoza said, moving his head back and forth from behind his cover as he looked at the terrorist from either side of a steel support beam.

"No shot from down here," Jasper reported. "He's way too far away with all kinds of stuff in the way."

Mendoza's radio made a *beep* when the transmissions ended and apparently Alivi's man heard these, for he stopped his chanting and turned his head in Mendoza's direction, the incendiary devices still gripped tightly in his hands.

Mendoza saw the man's eyes go wide as he spotted him. He honestly didn't know if he could take him out from here.

Maybe. But it wasn't a sure shot, he knew that. He was reminded of the most tense moment of his FBI career thus far, nine years ago, when he had responded to a domestic hostage standoff in a Walmart parking lot after a man had transported his kid across state lines following a custody battle. He was holding one of those exotic looking but cheaply made "collector's" knives, with fake jewels embedded into the handle and a winged dragon wrapped around the hilt, to the throat of his young son, the ex-wife screaming hysterically nearby.

The negotiating took a turn for the worse when the guy declared that everything was unacceptable. "Un-fucking-acceptable," he'd shout after anything the FBI hostage negotiator said through his megaphone. *Take your time to think about what you need. There's no hurry here. . . . Un-fucking-acceptable!* When they saw blood start to trickle down the boy's neck, Mendoza had taken the shot that killed the man (*Un-fucking—*). Acceptable. And it was. He'd shot him exactly between the eyes from about this same distance, dropping him instantly so that he released the boy without harm. Every now and then he still had dreams where he saw that neat, red circle on the bridge of the guy's nose.

Mendoza took a deep breath as he relived the memory. But that had been using a high-powered rifle, in full daylight, with a lot of support personnel backing him up. Now all he had was his pistol with only two rounds in near darkness against a guy brandishing two grenades, either one of which he could decide to throw at Mendoza at any moment. He might have other weapons at his disposal, too. Worst of all, his hostage wasn't a boy, it was a nuclear facility on the brink of total destruction.

Now the terror monger was bellowing the word *Allah* a lot, becoming more agitated, moving more erratically, jumping from side to side, looking all around.

"*Don't* let him toss one of those grenades into the pool,"

Sam warned again. "Take him out. It's either him or the entire city of New York, including us."

That was all Mendoza needed to hear.

But apparently Alivi's disciple had come to a decision as well, for he turned toward Mendoza and issued one of the grenades with a surprisingly quick underhanded toss, reminiscent of the motion women's professional softball pitchers used. The result was a clattering explosive skip-hopping its way across the concrete floor at some scary foot-per-second rate right toward Mendoza. This thing was coming at him and coming at him fast, taking erratic bounces along the way.

He dove headlong to the right, away from the edge, making sure he covered his head with his arms as he landed. He couldn't see it, but the grenade exploded in mid-air not five feet from where Mendoza's head had been. He sure felt it though, a deafening burst of quick-released energy that made his eardrums feel like they had been damaged. But he knew the Quran-obsessed sicko had one grenade left to go, so Mendoza shot to his feet, feeling a trickle of warm blood ooze out of his left ear. He whirled around back toward the edge of the overlook.

"Frank, you okay?" Sam's voice was calling, but Mendoza blocked it out. The terror man's arm was wound up, more like a major league pitcher now, preparing to hurl his remaining grenade into the spent fuel pool below. Sam and Jasper were both shouting into the radio now, but Mendoza let the radio unit drop while he gave all of his attention to his Glock and its two precious rounds.

He lined up a shot to the jihadist's head in his sights, but didn't like how he had to keep correcting for the guy's motion and a little voice told him, *No!*

He adjusted his aim for a chest shot, held his breath . . .

. . . and squeezed the trigger.

The terrorist was jerked out of his smooth throwing motion as the slug impacted his sternum, and the grenade slipped from his hand, dropping to the floor and rolling a couple of feet away. From the way the man scrambled for it so madly, Mendoza guessed correctly that the pin had already been pulled. Alivi's man swept his hand at the grenade, no doubt intent on sweeping it over the edge into the spent fuel pool. He barely missed, already wriggling on the floor to try again, and Mendoza lined up another shot.

His last.

Don't miss this. If you only make one shot for the rest of your life, let this be it. Don't miss, don't miss . . .

Mendoza held his breath.

Lined up his shot. Head shot this time because of the way the guy was oriented toward him, prostrate on the floor.

He pulled the trigger.

57

Nick had to stifle his urge to call out Lauren's name. Alivi could be within earshot. He just wanted to find his daughter—alive—and carry her out of this hellhole to wherever they could be safe and together. He scrabbled over a pile of loose concrete and was about to jump over an overturned stack when he cautioned himself that Lauren could be beneath any one of these heavy objects. He didn't need to be adding his weight to them. So even though it took a bit more time, he worked his way around the stack without shifting it.

When he got to the other side of it, he traced along its long edge until it was high enough from the floor to stick his head under. He thrust his flashlight into the space and had a look. Just bare floor beneath this one, but there were many more to check in this area.

He did so, carefully positioning himself so that he could look beneath the stacks, but without moving them in case she (or anyone who by some miracle was still alive) was trapped beneath. After checking each stack, he would pause to monitor the area carefully for signs of Alivi. He wished a rescue crew would get here already, but knew that with the unprecedented degree of devastation the city had suffered that no cavalry would be forthcoming until after dawn at the earliest. Although he did hear the occasional emergency vehicle siren far off in the distance, he listened to far more of them on any given city night. This mega-disaster was so crippling that Nick knew the rescue agencies themselves were in trouble. The night air was downright quiet, which in itself was unsettling for any long-time New Yorker.

Some time passed—time filled with painstaking exertion—and frustration was beginning to set in. By now he'd checked all of the stacks nearest the edge by the snapped iron railing where Ray had fallen. In the area he'd identified as being the one where she would most likely be if Ray had been correct about the series of events, the only thing remaining to check was a jumble of stacks set a few yards back from the edge. He'd assumed she'd be close to the edge since Ray said they could hear each other and he had fallen off the edge, but then again, Nick thought, he always did manage to pick the longest line at the checkout counters.

But that's okay. Just let her be in this group of bookcases here.

He flipped his light on and quickly estimated there to be ten or twelve stacks crisscrossed atop one another, a few sliding off at a diagonal. Thousands of hardcover books also littered the floor, oozing out from the stacks like the guts of some well-read monster. He stalked around the pileup, studying it, trying to determine if any part of it was highly unstable and about to fall over. He looked under a couple of the units, but then the slowness of it got to him and he could take no more.

He began to call out his child's name. Softly, not yelling, so as not to alert Alivi, but with enough volume and projection that if she was awake and anywhere in this immediate area, she'd hear him.

"Lauren!"

He cycled around the mess of stacks, calling out her name. He had just resigned himself to the fact that he was going to have to start digging into every accessible crevice when he heard a response.

A response that ignited a homing response in him like none other could.

"Daddy!"

58

Nick heard it again.

"Daddy!"

"Lauren! I'm here, baby. I'm coming!"

Alivi be damned, there was no way in hell he could restrain himself from answering that voice. He turned on his flashlight and started moving toward the source of the cry.

She's alive! Lauren is alive! His spirits soared as he rolled over a small hill of books and looked up into an overhang created by a protruding stack.

"Hold tight, Lauren!"

No response came and he grew worried. How bad off was she? Had she already lapsed into unconsciousness, or even worse?

"Say something, Lauren?"

He still wasn't sure where exactly she was in the ungainly conglomeration of stacks.

"Here."

The brevity and weakness of her responses were not encouraging. He had to get to her now. But even the single word had given him some directional input to key in on.

Nick eyed the stack pile and guessed that she was near the bottom of it, maybe ten feet farther up. He went to that spot but found it to be impenetrable from all sides. He retraced his steps to the overhang he'd seen earlier and eyed the upper reaches of Stack Mountain.

Christ. He was going to have to climb again.

He didn't waste any time lamenting the circumstances, but set to work straight away. Although it appeared daunting, once he got started he saw that it was more like climbing stairs; much easier than the vertical catwalk ascent he'd had to get up here. At the top, he stooped under the overhang and took a better look at the opening.

It was pitch-dark in there without the flashlight. He shuddered to think of his Lauren down there all this time, wondering when—if—someone would come to get her; where her father was. He called down into the stack cave.

"Lauren, hold tight, I'm coming down for you."

Nick spent a few seconds eyeballing a downward route into the dark recesses, like a rock climber studying a difficult route before committing himself. Satisfied he'd located the easiest possible course, he swung a leg in and started down. The climb wasn't all that difficult but he was distracted by knowing he was in such close proximity to Lauren, and when a stack shifted under his weight he tumbled halfway down, knocking his head on the edge of a furniture piece as he hit bottom.

He felt warm blood sluicing down his cheek, but he didn't see stars or feel dizzy. He slowly got to a kneeling position and shined his torch around inside the artificial cavern. Looking behind him, he could see there were rough alcoves extending beyond his line of sight, as well as a longer, crooked passage leading off ahead.

"Lauren?"

"Here, Daddy!"

Nick whipped his head around toward the crooked passage.

That way!

He had to crawl to make progress, but he would go for miles on his hands and knees to reach Lauren if that's what it took. He experienced a moment of exasperation upon reaching a large enough opening into the cavern that he had somehow missed during his walk around from the outside. *Could have just crawled in right here without the climb. Whatever, I'm here now. . . .*

"Lauren!"

There she was! His little girl, the daughter of his dead wife, everything he had left that represented real meaning in this world. Lying curled in the fetal position—the same position in which he first laid eyes on her in that life-changing ultrasound seventeen years ago. *Lauren.*

He stood as high as the cramped space would allow and waded through books until he reached her.

"Baby, it's me, Daddy. I'm right here."

He knelt and softly put a hand on her arm while playing his light across her body, assessing her condition. Some blood, soaking through her clothes in multiple places, but he couldn't identify any major wounds and nothing seemed to still be flowing. He was grateful that the angle of her neck seemed natural. The side of her face he could see had some dried blood streaks on it but no deep lacerations. He examined her head, looking for skull fractures, not seeing anything obvious.

She might have just made it through this. . . . Nick was about to allow himself a faint ray of hope when he saw the object.

His heart stopped. What was that?

Not three inches from her head lay a roundish metal object.

Is that a . . . He brought the flashlight's beam to bear on the thing and recoiled in abject horror.

. . . grenade? Oh, Jesus.

Alivi!

He told himself to stay calm. Maybe it wasn't real. It could be some novelty gag gift for a costume party. Halloween wasn't that far away, right? College kids did wacky stuff all the time. . . . *There you go again, ostrich man. Bury your head in the sand.*

Maybe Lauren knew what it was. But if she didn't, then he did not want to frighten her in such a weakened condition. He'd heard that paramedics were trained never to let a victim hear them say things like, "This guy's in really bad shape," or, "I don't think we're going to be able to get her out of this one. She's in a real pickle, yessireebob. . . ." But he needed to know if this thing was real.

"Lauren. Darling. Can you hear me?"

"Yes."

Do you know anything about a grenade? Is that a grenade next to your pretty head?

He just couldn't think of a good way to ask without spooking her, but then, faster than a New York minute, it all became a moot point.

He saw the grenade wobble ever so slightly and then discerned a glint of light from an almost invisible monofilament fishing line. Nick sucked in his breath sharply as he realized the line was tied to a pin on one end of the explosive device, and that the mini-bomb was nested in a circle of books such that it would stay in place while the pin was pulled by the line. The circle of heavier books was arranged much too carefully to have been the result of random placement during a series of earthquakes.

And then suddenly he heard the sound of a single person clapping.

59

"Congratulations, counselor. You have found your daughter. I knew that if you had survived our little gift from Allah that you would come to her. And to me."

Nick followed the sound of the male voice to the left, through the stack cave passage he had missed. There, about thirty feet away in the shadows, was terror mastermind Feroz Saeed Alivi. He sat calmly inside an individual study cubby designed to ensconce a single person for private work, a life-long student of terror cramming for the ultimate final exam.

"What do you want, Alivi?"

The jihad leader stared at him across the gulf, not only one of space but also of experiences, of philosophy.

"I would like to hear you say that the United States District Court for the Southern District of New York, and by extension the leaders and people of the United States of America, were wrong for persecuting me."

Nick almost laughed in spite of the situation. "You're looking for an *apology*?"

"'Apology' is perhaps too simple a word, but that will do to start."

Nick's initial reaction was to tell the man to shove it, but of course he was holding the strings, here, literally, tied to a grenade next to his daughter's head.

Nick parroted the statement in a dry, rapid monotone devoid of emotion: "The United States District Court for the Southern District of New York, and by extension the leaders and people of the United States of America, were wrong for persecuting you."

"You must say it by stating your name and position at the beginning of your statement, and by using my full name, as well. Try again."

Nick was quickly losing patience but forced himself to comply for Lauren's sake. *Here we go again. Take two:* "I, Assistant U.S. Attorney Nick Dykstra, maintain that the United States District Court for the Southern District of New York, and by extension the leaders and people of the United States of America, were wrong for persecuting Feroz Saeed Alivi." It surprised him how vile it felt to utter those words, even knowing it was to save his daughter.

"Thank you, counselor. Now we will do it again, but this time I will be making a video recording as you speak."

Alivi produced the smartphone he'd taken from the entrapped woman at the courthouse and pointed its lens at Nick while he emerged from the cubby to walk closer toward him. Nick noticed he had an automatic rifle slung over one shoulder, a pistol in a holster on his waist, and a large knife on the other side of his waist in a sheath. Alivi shined a flashlight at Nick and asked him to lift his shirt.

If I still had my gun I'd have already tried to shoot you with it, he thought. But he merely complied. Now was not the time to anger this unpredictable man.

"Turn around."

Nick slowly spun in a circle so Alivi could see that he did not harbor a concealed weapon.

"Pockets inside out."

Nick revealed his empty pockets.

"Very well. Let us continue with our production, shall we?"

Nick said nothing. Alivi continued to shine his flashlight on

Nick while aiming the smartphone's camera lens with his other. "And this time, counselor, you will say it convincingly. Do you understand? The more sarcasm I detect, the more I pull on this little string." Alivi gently lifted the monofilament that was tied to the belt loop of the dead U.S. marshal's pants he wore.

"Understood. Let's do it."

Nick wanted to get the sham of a production over with, but he knew all too well that Alivi did not intend to let him live.

"Alivi."

"What is it?"

"Before we begin, I want to make you an offer."

"Tell me. What can you offer me?"

"I'll make your statement, with conviction, and then I'll let you kill me. But in return, my daughter lives. She's not part of any of this."

Alivi smiled his crocodile grin. "Why, counselor, did I not explain that in return for your public service announcement, both you and your lovely daughter will be free to go?"

Nick only returned his stare.

"Are we ready, then?" Alivi prompted.

Nick hadn't yet figured out what he was going to do, what he could do, when the video was over and the moment came when Alivi would either shoot him, or pull the pin on that grenade. He'd probably pull the pin first. . . .

The thought was too gut-wrenching and he momentarily lost his composure, doubling over and dry-heaving.

"Counselor? You aren't too ill to continue, are you?"

Nick stood up. "No. I'm ready."

"Then let's begin. You know your lines?"

Obviously, Alivi was under no illusion that Nick believed any of the horseshit he was making him say.

"Yes."

"Then let's begin in three . . . two . . . one . . . Allah willing."

Nick ran through the statement again, this time with a bogus enthusiasm that he did his best not to make sound too disingenuous. He thought his acting was on the mark, how-ever, because not only did Alivi clap for him when he was done, but again he was taken aback at how disgusting it felt to say the words with such fervor, in spite of the fact it was to save Lauren's life. Or at least prolong it. He couldn't yet see how the "saving" part was going to come into play.

"Can I go now?"

"No, counselor. I would like for you to wait with me."

"Wait with you for what?"

"For the dawn." He glanced down at the smartphone, rather than up at the sky. "It won't be long now."

Nick suppressed a shiver. This was starting to feel like an execution in the making. *The prisoners will be hung at sunup.* Would he do it in front of Lauren—make her watch?

"What happens at dawn?"

Alivi laughed, a bright, clipped barking sound that reminded Nick of a small dog.

"Why, the sun comes up, of course, infidel! Did you not realize this?"

If pressed, Nick could have summoned no words sufficient to express how badly he wanted to kill this man. But he seemed to crave some sort of discourse—he could have killed him already if he so desired—so rather than shut himself off completely, thereby angering his captor and jeopardizing Lauren, he engaged him in conversation.

"You do realize that when I was prosecuting you, I was just doing my job, right? I'm not prosecuting you for your religious beliefs or because of what country you're from or because you wear weird shit on your head and don't allow your women to drive. I'm not prosecuting you for the fact that you come from a nation whose leaders were blessed with the most spectacular natural endowment this planet has ever seen—I'm talking about oil—that made them obscenely wealthy, giving rise to the perversions of lifestyle you've grown accustomed to. I'm prosecuting you for what you *did*. For the mass killing of innocent Americans. The same way I would prosecute anyone who was accused of the same federal crime, be they from Iraq or Egypt or England or America or Japan or planet Jupiter. And if the court couldn't get me to do that job, they would get some other attorney to do it, and they'd be lining up down the block for the opportunity. So you shouldn't be targeting me."

Nick felt like he had just delivered the opening statement in defense of his life—and that of his daughter's. His role with respect to Alivi had done a total 180. He didn't know whether it was good or bad that Alivi had concentrated on capturing his speech on video. What would he do with it? Nick didn't really care, as long as Lauren would be okay.

"You are a part of the system of oppression, infidel."

"Why do you call me infidel?"

"All Americans are infidels. Without faith. Ones who do not strive in the path of God."

"That's preposterous. That would be like me saying all people from your country are terrorists. But they're not. There are plenty of good, moral people born and raised in the Middle East who do not feel the need to kill for their religious convictions. Islam is mostly practiced by peaceful people who seek only to better understand their world and their place in it. You are the exception."

"Only the few are blessed by Allah with the power to enlighten."

Nick wanted to shout how that was hogwash, that somewhere along the rough and tumble course of his life Alivi had been brainwashed. Nick had seen the videos of young children being indoctrinated by Al Qaeda "schools," and would have bet a year's salary (before this earthquake when money might still have meant something to him) that Alivi had been one of those students. He certainly helped to produce them nowadays. But he had to temper his hatred, and even his desire to truly make Alivi understand, for angering the deranged fanatic was not an option. He shifted tack.

"You never answered my original question—what happens at dawn?"

"At dawn the rescue crews will begin to search. I will be calling them, as well as the media." He waved his phone before continuing. "When they find us, I will demand a television interview—live on the scene, as they say in America—during which you will repeat the statement you just made, in addition to others that we will rehearse between now and then."

"So you're going to let everyone see that you're holding me and my daughter hostage with a grenade?" The thought of his daughter being blown to pieces on national television . . . he couldn't even process it.

"I'm going to let them know of a much worse fate than that," Alivi said smugly. "You see, the seat of your infidel power—Manhattan—is about to be rendered permanently unlivable."

"Hasn't that already happened?" Nick said, waving an arm (but not too violently lest it be mistaken for a combative move) at the earthquake's results.

Alivi barked his weird canine laugh again. "No, no, no, infidel! This is only the beginning. What I am talking about has to do with the most unnatural source of energy—the splitting of atoms—used to power the Western Way."

"The nuclear plant?"

Alivi nodded slowly. "Any moment now it will experience a catastrophic meltdown of the highest order."

Nick didn't know whether he was bluffing, but he did know that even without the threat of terrorist intervention, the earthquakes alone were bad enough news for the nearby nuclear plant.

"And you think the oil from the Mideast is so natural? The refining process doesn't look so natural to me. The shipping process doesn't look natural."

"It is Allah's bounty to reward His people for an obedient life. . . ."

And so the conversation went, a circular waste of time as far as Nick was concerned. But it did serve one purpose. Every minute that elapsed was another minute Lauren was still alive.

As he watched the sky begin to lighten in the east, he began to question how many more of those minutes he and Lauren had left.

60

For a split second Mendoza thought that he had missed the shot with his final round. The terrorist was still in motion toward the grenade that he had dropped after being nailed by Mendoza's first triggered round. But it was the look of horror on the man's face, not any outward indication that he had been shot, that told Mendoza he had found his mark. There was no blood spatter. No scream of surprised anguish, no dramatic death throes. Only an unforgettable expression on the wayward soldier's face—a look that said he'd been pushed by Mendoza's second bullet just out of reach of the live grenade, and one that would haunt Mendoza's darkest thoughts for a long time to come.

The fallen terrorist tried one more sweep with his fingers to push that grenade away from him and over the edge of the spent fuel pool, where no doubt it would cause enough damage to shatter what little structural integrity it still retained following the day's seismic events.

But as Mendoza watched, breath held, he saw the tip of the Islamic extremist's fingers miss the grenade's knobby surface by scant millimeters. Then, with his arms locked in an awkward position, legs interlocked, the man could do nothing more than close his eyes as the explosive detonated inches in front of his flabbergasted face.

A projectile spray of blood and gore was airborne instantly.

Mendoza watched in disbelief as the hellish precipitation rained down over the spent fuel pool, a pinkish mist falling like snowflakes, the heavier chunks of flesh and bone plummeting into the water like hail.

Out of the overabundance of caution that his job called for, Mendoza carefully observed the blasted terrorist for a full minute before moving to him to confirm what he already knew. Mendoza turned away from the gruesome, incomplete cadaver in disgust. Sheets of blood ran over the concrete edge and into the pool, making it look from below like a fancy indoor waterfall with red mood lighting.

Then he heard his dropped radio erupt with excited chatter on the other side of the concrete expanse. He ran back to it and picked it up.

". . . no damage, showing no damage to the fuel pool so far!"

Mendoza broke into his transmission. "He's dead. There won't be any more damage."

He was pretty sure he could hear them down there on the operations deck even without the radio, hollering and whooping it up, right through their suits.

Jasper squinted into the early morning light as he walked out of the power plant. He couldn't believe that he'd been in there for almost a full twenty-four hours. Sam was right behind him, while Mendoza and his convoy team brought up the rear.

They had successfully used the fire ladder to get Jasper and Sam out of the plant, and on Sam's recommendation, they left it behind as potentially contaminated equipment, which was fine with them. After what they had all been through, no one felt like lifting a finger at this point, much less a fifty-foot ladder.

Once the group had reached the parked water tankers, Mendoza and the firefighter began transmitting radio status reports: disaster averted at Indian Point! Security should be maintained. Reinforcements needed. More nuclear technicians and operators needed to assess next steps for the plant.

A National guardsman replied that they were now operational enough to send a unit to the nuclear plant.

With that piece of business done, it hit home for the group that they had done it. Their efforts had saved Indian Point—and the entire surrounding region including New York City—from a horrendous, irreversible catastrophe. The men bear-hugged one another while giving rounds of congratulations.

In the midst of this, Sam walked up to Jasper. The two of them still wore their full hazmat suits. Sam undid the fastenings on his headgear and slowly pulled it over his scalp, letting it drop to the ground. Jasper did the same, and the two men stared at one another unencumbered by the headgear for the first time since their ordeal began.

Jasper was surprised to see that Sam's wavy brown hair—now matted with layers of sweat—was much longer than he remembered it. His brown eyes were bloodshot; his skin a shade paler than usual. Without his radiation suit's mask he seemed to Jasper less of the nuclear wunderkind he had depended on for his life in there, and much more like a man—a very mortal man who had just done his very best and come out lucky on the other side.

Sam smiled wryly as he appraised Jasper in a similar way. The two had gotten through yet another workday.

"Almost Friday," Jasper said.

Sam laughed as they heard sirens from the National Guard grow louder in the distance.

Frank Mendoza also turned toward the sound of the approaching cavalry. For him it represented some closure, although unknowns still remained. He wondered if Jana's hospital had received the supplies she'd worked so hard to get to them. And he thought about Nick Dykstra. Somehow the celebratory mood was dampened for him without yet knowing his fate.

Had he found his daughter yet, and if so, was she okay?

61

As the sound of sirens neared the ruins of Butler library, Nick became even more convinced that Alivi did not intend to let him or his daughter live. Moreover, it didn't even appear as though he planned on living himself. Though he was well armed for an individual, he couldn't hope to stand against the responding law enforcement that would appear with the new day, eager to demonstrate to New Yorkers that they were down but not out. If that's who was on the way, Nick thought. They could just be ambulance and fire. Still, there was no doubt that Alivi could be escaping right now instead of sitting here within range of advancing sirens.

And his next move only cemented Nick's concerns.

Alivi put the smartphone on speaker and a representative answered, "World News Network, how may I route your call?" Nick thought that Alivi was going to identify himself and was sure the network would laugh in his face, not believing it was him. But the terrorist instigator had not grown his organization into one of the most feared extremist movements on the planet by not knowing how to manipulate the media. He was able to lessen the Middle-Eastern accent from his voice and pose as a bystander (Brian Watson, even gave a return phone number, never mind that it belonged to an earth-quake victim) reporting that he saw the escaped Alivi in Butler Library on the Columbia University campus—with hostages. He said that the terrorist is asking for live micro-phones and cameras in order to make some kind of statement.

He's staging his own spectacular death finale, Live on Infidel TV *with your host, Feroz Saeed Alivi!*

Nick didn't know what, but he had to do something. Once Alivi had an audience, he'd make Nick parrot his lines and then probably blow them all up live on camera.

He appraised his chances of a frontal assault. His foe was well armed and could easily fell Nick with the assortment of weapons at his disposal, but he allowed himself to be fre-quently distracted with the smartphone—making media calls (a sign that things were ever so slowly improving, Nick thought—outgoing cell calls were again possible), trying out camera angles, even snapping pictures of himself and then adjusting his looks as best he could, searching for the care-fully cultivated image that would best enable him to dissem-inate his twisted message of hate.

But of course there was still the damned grenade. If it wasn't for that, he might consider bum-rushing Alivi from here, catching him by surprise. He pictured him looking up from his ill-gotten iPhone in surprise, struggling to pull his pistol as it snagged in his belt. . . .

But Nick knew that was fantasy. Reality was a monofila-ment line tied to Alivi's belt loop, which meant he only had to fall backwards and . . . *welcome to the boom-boom room.* Nick caught a glimpse of the line a couple of feet off to his right as it passed him on its way into the stack cave, on its way to Lauren's head, where it would blow away every thought she'd ever had of him only to provide lunch break fodder for a world audience hungry for sensational news.

He heard the first of the vehicular sirens driving up to the edge of the Butler rubble field. It would take them time to locate their exact position and make their way up here, but not much. Not with Alivi coordinating things on the damned phone.

And then they heard a voice. But not one of a rescuer or media person.

"Mr. Dykstra? Are you up there?"

That voice belonged to Ray Knowles, whom Nick flash-processed in his mind as having gotten scared he'd been gone so long and shouted up to ask where he was. Something inside Nick's brain told him, this was it, this is your gift, don't let it go to waste.

Everything seemed to dissolve into slow motion. . . . Alivi turning his head to the right to look for the source of the voice; simultaneously drawing his pistol in what was clearly a smooth, practiced movement. . . . Instinctively firing his weapon toward the phantom threat, a threat he could not know was no such thing.

Nick saw the fishing line sparkle once in his flashlight beam and he lunged for it.

Do not pull it the wrong way!

His two hands converged around the monofilament and he yanked on it *toward* him and Lauren, so that it ripped away from Alivi's belt loop, the proverbial big one that got away. Nick's body tensed and clenched so tightly for a moment while he waited to see if he had done the wrong thing—if the grenade would somehow explode anyway—that for a second he thought he was having a heart attack. But when nothing happened—no explosion came—Nick mentally rejoiced and his muscles loosened.

He sprang back up from the floor to track his captor's whereabouts. Alivi had fired off a few pistol rounds down into the first level without aiming at anything in particular, but as soon as he realized the grenade line had been severed, he whirled and went for Nick with his arsenal. He popped off one-handed pistol rounds while removing the automatic rifle slung over his shoulder and moving it into a ready position.

Nick knew that to try to go for Lauren now would be suicidal. He had to somehow take out Alivi first, or it was just a matter of minutes before he and Lauren were on the receiving end of Alivi's AK-47.

Nick ducked behind the nearest fallen stack. *Sorry, Alivi, turns out I couldn't make that guest spot on your show after all. Rain check?*

Nick really cursed himself for dropping his gun now. *How am I going to take this guy out?* He slipped on something smooth and picked up a large hardcover book. Deciding it might help, he shoved it into his pants so that it covered his lower back. Cheap body armor. Then he picked up another and did the same for the front. It limited his motion somewhat, but he thought the extra protection was worth it.

Alivi was letting his guns do the talking for him, releasing quick bursts of controlled automatic weapons fire followed by the occasional pistol shot. Nick recognized that he couldn't hold this position for long. He ran around to the far side of Stack Mountain.

Alivi had found that low side passage into the cave, so maybe he hadn't discovered the high road? As he began to climb, Nick sure hoped not. He scaled the stacks much faster this time, knowing that if Alivi were to walk around while he was in mid-ascent, his back turned, he wouldn't stand a chance.

"I was looking forward to our broadcast, counselor. I said that you and your daughter would be released unharmed once we concluded. What are you afraid of?"

Nick had paused to take in his adversary's words. He noted that they came from the left. When he resumed his upward scramble, he put a bit too much force into his lead-off step and the stack moved, throwing him off balance.

He fell, bouncing off the corners of stacks as he went, until the scattering of books on the floor broke his fall. Nick was up on his feet in a split second, blood dripping from a couple of different places, turning to the left to see if Alivi had already rounded the corner.

Not yet.

He threw himself back into the stack climb, truly worried he wouldn't make it to the top before Alivi turned the corner and sprayed him down with his AK. *Don't fall, don't fall, don't fall . . .*

He reached the most difficult section of the ascent at around the halfway mark. Had to get a leg up on a slight overhang and pull himself over.

Don't fall.

But he executed the maneuver in one fluid motion and was on his way skyward, clawing his way back to the top of the stack mountain. He had just reached the opening at the top and was preparing to drop through when he heard Alivi's heavy footfalls, running.

"Infidel!"

Nick heard the clatter of automatic weapons fire and he dove headfirst without consideration for his landing into the irregular aperture at the top of the stack mount. He was chased by weapons fire on the way in, and when he hit the ground, landing hard on an elbow, flakes of wood were still raining down on him.

His second trip here, he knew the way and rolled to his feet and off to his right.

Lauren!

He reached her and found she was still lying in the same position, unmoving, the grenade still next to her head.

Was she alive?

But then he saw the shallow rise and fall of her chest and concentrated once more on their attacker, no doubt now heading for the way he knew how to get inside the stack cave.

It's time for Escape from Stack Mountain, *honey.*

He heard something else, too, in the distance. Voices. More sirens. People were coming—he wasn't sure if they were cops or fire or a media team—but at least somebody was coming. He was under no illusion, though, that the presence of others would dissuade Alivi from committing the murders he'd come here with every intention to carry out.

He looked quickly about the confines of the enclosed space. What could he defend himself with against Alivi? The books he'd wedged into his pants bothered him now, and he removed them, letting them drop to the floor.

What's that?

He picked one back up and took a closer look at it. A close grouping of three bullet holes sat in the upper left corner, where it had been positioned over his lower back. Nick picked the books back up again and shoved them back into place in his pants. As he bent down to pick up the second book, his eyes alighted on the grenade, still nested within its circle of books, its tether to Alivi now broken.

Nick reached out and carefully plucked up the palm-sized explosive by his daughter's head. Quickly, he examined the pin mechanism while he heard Alivi running around the outside of his inner sanctum. *Just pull on that ring, where the leftover string's already tied . . .*

Quickly!

He needed to get into position fast. If he allowed Alivi to get inside here with him, they would be slaughtered like the proverbial fish in a barrel. Nick scuttled over to the low side passage and hunkered down to one side of it. He heard no more trash talk from Alivi but he could hear him running this way.

Nick considered his options. He could wait at the far end of the passage, so that as soon as Alivi reached it he'd tackle him with the grenade in hand, blowing them both into oblivion, but saving Lauren. . . . That outcome would be acceptable to Nick, but all Alivi had to do to foil it was to spit some fire from his automatic into the tunnel before he actually stepped inside. And even if he succeeded, that still left Lauren lying in here unaccompanied. What if no one found her for hours more; she could die of thirst, hungry and alone. . . .

Nick had always aimed for the best possible outcome—in his court cases, in his life, and here, too, he decided, there would be no exception.

He heard the terrorist's footsteps slow as he approached the tunnel. Nick had a plan, but he prayed for just a little background noise to make it work. He hefted the grenade in his right hand and prepared for a bowling-style shot. He lined up the path he would try to get it to take down the passageway to reach Alivi at the other end when he stuck his Allah-loving nose inside.

Baby needs a new pair of shoes. . . .

But then he flashed on actually buying Lauren's first pair of shoes, marveling at how tiny they were, and he almost lost it. . . .

Then a clamor of activity brought him back, reminding him at the same time that it was exactly what he needed. He heard new voices—several of them—calling up here. They were still on the first level by the sound of it, and no doubt would find plenty of distractions down there, including a very distraught Ray Knowles.

They would not get up here in time to help him, but in a way they already had. He did not want Alivi to hear the grenade rolling towards him. Nick took the most careful aim of any type of physical shot he'd ever attempted in his life.

Feroz Saeed Alivi stuck the barrel of his AK-47 into the stack tunnel just before the hand grenade rolled to the opening. Nick shrank back into the stack cave and covered his ears. For one heart-stopping moment, it seemed like the grenade wasn't going to detonate.

Game over, Dykstra, it's a dud. Or possibly even a fake that he used to control you with.

He had begun to think about how he would have to try to grab Alivi's gun when he started to enter the cave, and how overwhelmingly likely it was that he would lose that kind of hand-to-hand combat with the hardened terror fighter . . .

. . . when the grenade exploded.

62

Nick double-checked that Lauren's seat belt was securely fastened, even though it had been snapped into place by one of the flight crew medics. One seat behind them in the helicopter was Ray Knowles, who, like Lauren, had also been given immediate first aid before being prepped for flight to a hospital in New Jersey. Nick put an arm around his daughter as they prepared for liftoff. He looked out the window at what remained of Butler Library, now crawling with emergency personnel searching the rubble for survivors in the midday light.

One person they wouldn't be helping was Feroz Saeed Alivi. The terror leader had been killed instantly by his own grenade after Nick's well-placed toss.

Nick had already done a couple of media interviews about his showdown with the terror fugitive, but the media fire had been dampened by the competing story up at Indian Point, where the nail-biting tale of a handful of plant workers and everyday New Yorkers who had saved the city was only now coming to light. Nick had already seen Mendoza being interviewed in the wake of the tense series of events, all smiles and thumbs-ups, and it had brought a huge grin to his own face.

There was one thing Nick had hid from the media, though, and as the helicopter lifted off, he removed it from his pocket. Alivi's appropriated cell phone. Nick fully intended to return it to whomever it belonged to, or, if that person was no longer alive, to their family. But there was something that didn't belong there. Something no one but him needed to see.

Nick found the movie file Alivi had taken of him reciting his propaganda. He couldn't help but watch it now, couldn't help but see how scared he looked, even though at the time he'd thought his acting job was worthy of an Oscar. In the background was the pile of book stacks that Lauren had been trapped beneath for so long.

He looked at her now as their craft banked sharply toward the Hudson. She was almost asleep but he wanted her to see this. He tapped her shoulder and pointed out the window. They looked down on Columbia, only a few of its buildings still standing.

"I understand completely if you want to go to Stanford, now, honey."

Lauren slowly looked away from the heart-wrenching view growing smaller beneath their window. She stared into his eyes and shook her beautiful, bandage-wrapped head.

"No. I've made up my mind. I'm going to Columbia, Dad. I've already spoken to Caroline Reignier about it when she visited me in the medical tent. They've already got possibilities for a temporary campus picked out—in New York—while the rebuilding goes on. This school is going to be reborn better than ever, and I'm going to be reborn right along with it. No more running away. My place is here, with you, with Ray—he's still going, too—we talked about it." She paused in her declarations to gaze down at what remained of the celebrated skyline while they buzzed over Manhattan. "And with the city."

Nick told her that was more than fine with him, and he watched her settle into a comfortable sleep.

He turned his attention back to the view of Manhattan. They were flying by One World Trade Center now, miraculously still standing proud, the spectacular monument of rebirth from the episode that had taken Lauren's mother from them—9/11. Lauren was right. The city would be reborn, stronger than ever, and they right along with it.

As Nick looked over at the majestic freedom tower—eye level with the very same airspace where his wife had perished all those years ago—he picked up the smartphone again, Alivi's video of him still on the screen.

They had rebuilt their life since 9/11, after all; they would rebuild from this as well.

Recognizing that his journey was different from that of his daughter's, Nick rethought the phrase in his head. *He* would rebuild from this, too.

Thankfully, Feroz Saeed Alivi would not get that chance, unless there really was a heaven with endless virgins waiting for him. Assistant U.S. Attorney Nick Dykstra hit the smartphone's delete button and looked down at the tiny screen.

The button's text read "Confirm Deletion?", but to Nick's mind it might as well have read, "Move On With Your Life?"

As One WTC faded from view, Nick clicked "OK," and promptly fell asleep in his seat alongside his daughter.